RESOLUTION OF STARS

The sequel to 'Doom of Stars'

By

Martyn Rhys Vaughan

Print ISBN 978-0-9574894-4-8

Published by
Llyfrau Cambria Books, Wales, United Kingdom.
Cambria Books is a division of
Cambria Publishing.
Discover our other books at: www.cambriabooks.co.uk

REVIEWS

Other books by Martyn Rhys Vaughan

Devouring Darkness

'Chilling, poignant, haunting, and thoroughly gripping.
Darkness, intrigue, and ambiguity mark Vaughan's deeply immersive latest, a collection of science-fiction stories...Vaughan's storytelling is immersive as he digs deeper into a complex world and multi-faceted characters, offering life-and-death maneuvering, deadly conspiracies, and looming catastrophe via swiftly unravelling plots. This is a stunner.'

The Prairies Book Review

'These stories are sinister and dark. Martyn's imagination is amazing. The world he has created in these short stories is much appreciated...Go ahead with this book without thinking twice.'

Kia's Reviews, Goodreads

Quantum Exile

'A mind bending mix of physics and environmentalism. Vaughan tells an exciting story, and manages to weave important aspects of quantum theory into it. He also has an important message about what we are doing to damage the world's environment, in the bleak picture he paints of a planet which has gone past the tipping points and is sliding towards cataclysm. All in all, thoroughly recommended.'

P. Brown, Amazon Reviewer

Doom of Stars

'Fabulously written end-of-the-world tale of survival, with brilliant female characters leading the story. If you enjoy SciFi with real feeling science, great female characters, and the end of the world, definitely give this a read. You won't be disappointed.'

Chelsea Hauth, Reedsy

'This book has a twist because not only is it post-apocalyptic, but it is on the verge of the complete cataclysmic end of the human race...Entering the dystopian future the author paints, you have to admire the skill in which he immediately draws the reader into the narrative...There are many different settings in the book, and the author describes them with vivid and vibrant explanations...As the narrative progresses, then it becomes more imaginative and inventive and an absolute joy to read.'

John Derek, Net Galley

Hideous Night

'Reading this brilliant novel was just like riding a very scary roller-coaster! I found myself hanging on with an enjoyable sense of dread throughout the many thrilling plot twists and turns, as I the reader was propelled along with each new page to what seemed like an unavoidably hideous climax.'

Wayne Edwards, Author, Amazon Reviewer

The Cave of Shadows

'Martyn Rhys Vaughan's book is shot through with big ideas and big questions and in that sense it's a bold and brave undertaking. The book picks up pace throughout and is never less than entertaining, but the fact that the speculation is set squarely within the realms of possibility means that the book, which at first seems like science fiction melding with fantasy, might actually be a guidebook, a guidebook to chaotic times ahead.'

Jon Gower, Nation Cymru

This book is dedicated to all the creative writers who work their magic in my home city of Newport.

Cover designed and created by Terry C. Evans (www.terry-evans.com).
The cover is a photo-montage made up using multiple images supplied by www.123rf.com from contributors including Eric Isselee, Mizina, Pakhnyushchyy, Photografia, Bwf211, Melynyk58 and Kimberrywood and the base image of the tunnel is from www.dreamstime.com by Maren Winter.

Doom is coming upon you, dweller in the land; the time is coming, the day is near, with confusion and the crash of thunder.

Ezekiel 7:6

Do not go gentle into that good night.
Rage, rage against the dying of the light.

Dylan Thomas

...when the moon was overhead,
Came two lovers lately wed;
'I am half sick of shadows,' said
*   The Lady of Shallot.*

Alfred, Lord Tennyson

for who would lose,
though full of pain, this intellectual being,
those thoughts that wander through eternity,
to perish rather, swallowed up and lost
in the wide womb of uncreated Night,
devoid of sense and motion?

John Milton, Paradise Lost,
Book II

CONTENTS

DOOM AND THE DESTROYER

The Destroyer was visible to anyone with the courage to look at it.

It filled most of the sky, blocking out the entire Universe beyond. It stretched from the horizon up to the zenith and beyond, giving the impression of being a titanic concavity.

Its swirling cloud belts looked like ribbons of varicoloured paints, which had been swirled into a cosmic sea and then stirred by the finger of a god. They curled over and around one another, forming a kaleidoscopic medley of mind-bending complexity. There were uncountable curling streams of vivid luminescence; some twisting around each other; some breaking into finer and finer tributaries; some fading away; some combining into mighty flows whose giddy fluctuations were obvious to the unaided human eye.

But there was no unaided human eye to stare in trembling awe at the Destroyer. Indeed, there were not many human eyes in existence; unaided or not.

Maya shuddered as she looked at the representation of the Destroyer on the monitor screen. In a deep, still somewhat disinterested, stratum of her mind, it occurred to her the vast panorama was eerily reminiscent of the paintings of Turner's last years. There was the same misty numinous quality to the scene, the same sense of something tremendous hidden by veils of intricate cloudscapes.

However, the image was clearly not a painting as it shuddered and flickered in its frame while dazzling white flashes periodically dazzled her as they shot across the screen.

Professor DeGroot was beside her.

'Switch it off, Maya,' he said, in the voice of a man whose courage trembled on the point of collapsing, 'we're too deep in the magnetosphere now. Relativistic electrons are scouring the surface. Their energies must be in the high tens of mega electron-volts by now, and the bombardment will only get worse. Why stare at the damn thing—we know what it looks like! We've been watching it approach for years, haven't we!'

She nodded, glad someone had made the decision for her, and a slim finger sent the screen into blackness.

It was never to show an image again.

She turned from the silent monitor and looked at her fellow scientists.

They were mainly sitting, as the seismic shocks were now so intense and frequent that standing took constant concentration. She and DeGroot had been two of those brave souls, but she gladly moved to the nearest vacant chair. A powerful quake hit at that instant and momentarily the entire room and its occupants became an indecipherable blurred image of meaningless shapes.

Cries of anger and surprise came from the group but not too much fear: they were beyond the most obvious manifestations of fear now. The quakes and the rising heat were familiar now; invisible tormentors to which they had become accustomed.

Her image of the room stabilised, and she could discern their features again.

A small burst of pride rose in her thoughts as she regarded them: McQuade, Duquesne, Takemoto, Hilbert.

Their faces, man and woman, were drawn, exhausted, lacking the slightest show of joy, of contentment. They were facing the greatest threat in the history of humanity, but they had accepted their fate—whatever that should be.

Veronica McQuade looked across at DeGroot, tightly holding her chair arms to keep herself from tumbling to the floor.

Maya smiled sadly as she stared at the woman.

McQuade was a brilliant scientist and it was she who had found a way of stabilising the time crystal, and yet it meant nothing: she was as insignificant and helpless as the humblest rodent before the might of the Destroyer.

2

And now she asked the question which everyone else had wanted to ask but somehow had been unable to arrange their lips into the necessary shapes.

'How long?'

DeGroot lowered himself slowly onto a chair.

He looks like an old man! Maya thought, but was instantly ashamed of herself.

That was unfair. The horror of their situation had aged them all. She did not know what face she now presented to the world. The days of caring for appearance were long since gone. All the things that had seemed important—fashion, cosmetics, hairstyle—all dead and buried.

Like most of the human race.

Except for the "buried" part.

'I've had no more communications from Cheyenne Mountain,' he said in a dry monotone. He was looking at his hands rather than McQuade. 'The decision will be mine. And mine alone.'

'And?'

'One hour's time. We may as well make it a round number.'

There was a sudden susurration in the room, a dry whispering from people who had known it was coming but had not known the time. Now they did, and there would be no more wondering.

Maya found she needed to ask for reassurance; to have an older, wiser adult tell her things would be fine. But when she finally spoke, she said, 'What are our chances?'

DeGroot did not look at her.

'The time crystal will stabilise the quantum computations. Its periodicity is good for several millennia. We have Veronica to thank for that.'

'I know all about the time crystal. That's not what I asked.'

Now DeGroot did look at her.

'I can tell you what our chances are if we don't do it—zero. Nothing. The surface will soon be fused into glowing slag; *irradiated* glowing slag. We must assume we are the last representatives of humanity on the surface, the very last. I've had no contact with the base in Australia for two days.'

There was a communal intake of breath at that revelation: he hadn't told them until then. Grimly, he continued, 'We all know about the lightsail project for saving a remnant of our species. I must tell you, I strongly believe that not one of those craft will survive that vast journey.'

'What about the Burrowers?' McQuade said, 'they have a chance, don't they?'

DeGroot's mouth thinned into a tight line. 'Perhaps. A very slim one. It all depends on how the mantle rocks react to the gravitational strains. There's no telling what they will do to the thermal profile. I wouldn't like to make an estimate of the probability of survival of those idiots. There is one sure hope for rebuilding after the passage, and that is the Space Arks out in the asteroid belt. My brother is a man of action; of incredible resourcefulness. He won't fail us. All the arks contain the genotypes of all our most important plants and animals in DNA form, adjusted for the arctic conditions we expect to obtain on the transplanted Earth.'

But Maya wanted yet more reassurance, more hope. 'That's very good to hear, Professor, but what about us? To be reconstituted like dried soup. It's impossible! It's never been done before!'

'Obviously not with people. But the science is clear, and animal experiments have had a forty percent success rate. And there is no compulsion if you don't want to participate.'

Maya's head dropped. She and her colleagues were being asked to make decisions of greater weight than anyone had ever been asked before. How could the human brain contemplate what lay ahead and stay sane!

She lifted her head.

'Forgive me, Professor, I know we've been through this hundreds of times. I knew what I was signing up for. It's—it's just now it's so close. So damned close!'

To her surprise, he crossed to her over the shuddering floor and put a hand on her shoulder.

To her greater surprise, she burst into tears.

'It's the same for all of us, Maya. There will be a sleep. A dreamless sleep. But when the computer decides the environment is safe, we will awake.'

'*If* the computer itself stays sane in the ages to come.'

'The time crystal will keep it sane. Its patterns will repeat over and over in an unchanging sequence. It will not fail.'

'We hope.'

She looked up into his lined, exhausted face and saw an expression she had not seen it produce before.

He smiled.

'Yes, Maya, we hope. That something can be salvaged from this cataclysm. A catastrophe we all are innocent of causing.' He reached for her arm and pulled it, very gently. 'Let's go.'

Takemoto stood and faced them.

'I'm sorry, I can't do it. I won't do it.'

No attempt was made to dissuade him; he had made his decision and there was no time left to argue.

All the other occupants of the room rose as one and walked to the recording room; there the hour of preparation passed—all too quickly.

There they lay on the couches, and the transparent sides rose around them, confining them within strange chrysalises. Some looked alarmed at their confinement, and Hilbert tried to escape, before realising the futility of such actions, and subsided with his eyes tightly closed.

The headsets gently attached themselves to the craniums and zettabytes of data were transcribed and transferred to imperishable, indestructible media.

When the transfer was complete, an invisible gas killed them humanely, painlessly, and so swiftly they had no awareness of their passing. Thus, they were spared the terrors ravaging the surface.

The bodies were then instantly cremated.

The great machines swung into long-planned action, programmed to deny the Destroyer the destruction of the last hopes of a species on the edge of extermination.

The recording room immediately began to descend into the shaft which had opened up beneath it. But just before the descent had picked up speed, one particularly energetic charged particle ploughed a path through the sheltering stone and scored a direct hit on the time crystal. Thousands of such particles had previously passed to the sides of the recording room or had spent their energies many metres above it. This one, however, lay on the extreme positive tail of the energy distribution and it was neither deflected nor absorbed in the intervening layers.

Down the recording room swept, kilometre after kilometre; down, down into the crust of the planet, until it was below the shudderings and splinterings of the tormented rock. Below it and, ever increasingly above it, was the escape shaft, long planned for this exact moment. Made from reinforced, incorruptible fluorocarbon polymers, it would bend and twist under the seismic stresses, but would not break, could not break, and when the Destroyer's fury had finally passed, it would slowly bend back into its original shape.

The room finished its seemingly endless plunge and settled gently into the void that had long been prepared for it.

Then, far above, mighty cubic kilometres of ferroconcrete were blasted into place, sealing the room from the hell that was gathering its horrors above it. Ferroconcrete that would retain its durability, its strength, for three short centuries, but then begin to disintegrate into sand.

The quantum computer, now stabilised by McQuade's time crystal, began its vigil.

A long vigil.

Above the now quiescent recording room, the Destroyer wreaked its worst.

Oceans evaporated like drops of water on a red-hot griddle.

Mountains were flung down as if they were pitiful mounds of dust, and their ashes tossed into darkening skies.

The entire planet shook like helpless prey in the jaws of a terrible saurian.

But after years of relentless destruction, the Destroyer passed on its appointed way.

And still the computer waited, as age was piled high upon age.

THE PEOPLE AND THE WORLD

One

Karn looked down at the greyish mass of fungus as it slowly bubbled and swirled in the great tank. The cloying fungoid smell hung in the air of the cavern like the smell of a wet dog.

Or at least, it could have been described in those terms if there had been such things as dogs, but there were no such fabulous creatures in the World, and in any case none of the People were aware of the smell of fungus. It was so omnipresent in the air that the People had long since lost the ability to detect it. To them, the hot moist air was sweet and wholesome.

The tanks had once had mechanical stirrers, but these had ceased working long before Karn, or even his grandfather, had been born, and so it was one of his duties to stir by hand the glutinous mass of mycelia that bubbled and belched below him as he stood on the platform above. Sometimes he wondered how long a man would live if he fell into the mass of churning semi-liquid. But no-one had yet done that, so the answer remained purely theoretical.

He had tried to take his mind off the boredom by seeking out particularly large bubbles and seeing if he could make them pop with his long stirring-pole. But they were infrequent, and he soon tired of such a repetitive form of entertainment. He looked around to see if Grath was near enough to be watching him, but as he was not, Karn lowered his pole and leaned back against the railing.

He yawned as he looked around, making sure Grath was not behind him.

He saw what he had seen during every Wake-Period, namely the enormous cavern which stretched so far into the distance that air itself blurred out its furthest reaches into impenetrable obscurity. In the immediate vicinity stood the circular tanks that held the yeast, interspersed with rectangular ones that held the algae. Those tanks were different, as their sides could be seen through as if they were not there at all. Of course, those walls were real, as children soon discovered when they tried to walk through them. No, they were actually there, but made of some peculiar substance that let light pass through it. Nobody knew what it was or where it came from. It had always been there. Except there were one or two tanks where the material had split and cracked. Those tanks now stood empty and lifeless.

As a younger man, before family responsibilities had tied him down, Karn had travelled far in the World, but eventually, he had seen there was little profit in travel: one part of the World was very much like another. There were always the same types of townships, made of the same hard, grey-coloured material; the same tanks, mostly full of the bubbling, belching fungi, plus the occasional algae tank; and above all the same mighty grey walls of impenetrable rock.

Those walls were mighty indeed, and totally unclimbable because they had a tremendous concave curvature to them so they met high above the inhabitants, forming the grey sky. So high was the sky that diaphanous masses of vapour, which some people called "clouds", could be seen drifting gently along, going from one part of the World to another.

And when Karn arrived at another village, it would, of course, have a Sun, indistinguishable from the familiar Sun of his childhood. It would look exactly the same: a long rectangular shape giving off a mild yellow-white shine. And like his own Sun, it would periodically dim to a faint reddish glow. Karn had heard of one village where their Sun had actually gone out, and the wretched inhabitants now had to rely on the light spilling over from nearby habitations, but he had never gone that far.

The only difference he had noticed in his youthful travels was the further he went from his own domain, the odder was the speech of the inhabitants. Sometimes it was just a peculiar

9

intonation; a slightly different vowel sound. But he had even come across totally unknown words for everyday objects—once or twice.

But such novelties did not amount to a sufficient inducement for long journeys, and so he had given them up. There was easily enough to keep him in his own area: the work on the food tanks, his friendship with his childhood friend, Yarl, and—of course—his ownership of Thylassa. Coupled with the occasional times when he managed to avoid Grath's searching eyes and did not stir the vats quite as vigorously as he should have been doing, what more could a man want?

He came to full alertness with a start, realising the memories of his odysseys into the far reaches of the World had lulled him into an abstracted reverie.

And who should be standing next to him, but Grath—bullet-headed, bull-necked Grath, the man with muscles straining at the thin fabric of his tunic; muscles he wasn't afraid to use on workers who did not meet his exacting standards. The tunic was a badge of his authority; ordinary workers were not allowed such luxuries. However, that was not a problem for Karn; like the vast majority of the People, he wore only a small loincloth, which was more than enough in the World's omnipresent heat. Although Karn was impressed by Grath's physique, the converse was most definitely not reciprocated. Grath saw a man no longer blessed with the energy of youth, just an average man of average height, his watery blue eyes set in an average face, which in turn was topped by a thin layer of rust-coloured hair—his only memorable feature.

'Daydreaming again, Karn?' he said, his slitted eyes betraying the pleasure he was feeling at catching out his wily subordinate.

'No,' Karn said, immediately rotating the pole with theatrically extravagant energy, 'I was just moving the pole from one hand to the other. My right hand is getting a bit raw.'

Grath laughed ominously. 'Hah! Your hands are as soft as a Woman's sexhole.' Pushing past Karn, he peered at the glutinous mass in the tank. 'I can see the solids have separated and gone to the bottom.' He straightened and turned back to Karn, a wicked grin twisting his mouth. 'You know what this means, boy?'

'No,' Karn said, unconvincingly trying to sound unconcerned.

'I'm cutting your rations for three days. How do you like that, you work-shy waste of fungus?'

'Three days!' Karn yelled, not caring he was showing a dangerous amount of insubordination, 'that's not fair!'

Grath moved closer until his brawny chest was almost touching Karn's slim one.

'Would you like to come down to the ground and talk it out with me, boy? With your fists, I mean.'

Karn looked down at the floor.

'No.'

'No *what*, Karn? Louder, boy!'

Reluctantly, Karn raised his head.

'No, Supervisor Grath.'

Grath jerked his head in the direction of Karn's home. 'That's alright then. Off you go, boy. And take *one* packet of fungus. I'll know if you've cheated.'

Silently, Karn descended the steps to the ground, and walking over to the food rack, lifted one parcel of food from the shelf.

The parcels were not all exactly the same size, of course, having been packed by hand and, with a quick glance back to the platform to check if he was being observed, he selected a pack slightly larger than the others.

Fortunately, Grath had his back to him and was busily giving Karn's shift-replacement his orders.

Karn began the trudge back to his hut, silently cursing himself for having allowed Grath to catch him daydreaming. He had thought he was cleverer than that, but apparently he wasn't. And now the family's food had been cut to almost nothing.

He marched into the hut and Thylassa, who had been sewing, instantly knew she was in for a bad time.

'What's the matter, Karn, My Master?' she said, instinctively and unconsciously drawing back into the shadows.

Karn threw the bag at her.

'Grath's cut the weekly food! You'll have to go without for a day or so.'

She lowered her head. 'Yes, My Master.'

Karn felt a slight pang of guilt at giving the entire cut to Thylassa, but it passed briefly.

Any man would have done the same. He was not being harsh.

Even so, he felt a small need to soften the blow slightly. Walking to her, he picked up the bag, which was now lying in her lap, and placed it on the food shelf.

'Two days will soon pass, Thylassa. You won't die.'

Thylassa lifted her head and gave a weak smile. 'Quite so, My Master. I do not want to leave you in any way. I need you.'

Karn frowned as he sat on the simple wickerwork chair Thylassa had made a year or so back.

Didn't want to leave?

What kind of talk was that?

No Woman left her man, except through death—natural or otherwise.

He shrugged. It wasn't his job to try to interpret the thoughts of females.

In fact, it wasn't anyone's job.

He looked at her as she resumed her sewing.

The light in the hut was dim, of course, as it always was, but he could see a thin, but pleasant-looking, Woman, with a sweet, oval face framed by a sweep of auburn hair. *Mainly auburn*, he corrected himself; he had spotted a few white hairs recently.

He had almost grown fond of her, but had kept those thoughts to himself.

He didn't want to get into any more trouble.

Later the same day, they had their routine, simple meal. Thylassa had outdone herself by adding some unusual flavours to the fungus strips and had even added some dried algae flakes.

Despite himself, Karn was impressed: he had no idea how she did it. For a brief moment, he considered giving her one of his food strips but decided against it, which was just as well as Yarl chose that moment to call in and would have been revolted by any sign of effeminate behaviour by his friend.

'Still eating?' he said, stretching his long legs out on the couch, 'I would have thought you'd be ready for the Ceremony by now.'

Karn rapidly swallowed the last strip and threw an accusatory glance at Thylassa. He rose and crossed to the sand clock. It was a simple affair: a cone which slowly dribbled sand into a container. When the cone was empty, it was her job to fill it, and after she had done that she needed to move a pebble from one hole in the Time-Log to the next, until she reached the last hole.

When that hole was reached it would be almost the end of the Wake-Period, and the Sleep-Period would be near. In The World of The People, the Sun never moved or changed its illumination until the Sleep-Period. Without the sand clocks, the inhabitants had no way of registering the stages of the Wake-Period. It was Thylassa's responsibility.

And she had forgotten to refill the cone.

Karn's face darkened and, returning to his partner, he dealt her a stinging slap across the face.

'You have shamed me in front of Yarl!' he shouted, 'Shamed me! Is this my reward for taking you and your barren womb into my house? Well, is it!'

She fell to her knees before him and lifted a tear-stained face.

'No, My Master! I have failed you! Thylassa asks for forgiveness!'

Karn lifted his hand to deliver another blow but was surprised to feel Yarl's hand grasping his wrist.

'Come on, Karn,' the latter said, 'If we don't go now, we'll miss the Punishment.'

13

Karn gave his partner another flinty stare and muttered, 'Later, Thylassa, later.'

Yarl tugged at his shoulder.

'Come on, man. There's no time for this—we're late already.'

Reluctantly, Karn followed his friend out of the gloom of the hut into the steady, constant light of the Sun. Yarl pointed beyond the circle of huts.

'It's in the usual place. Get a move on, man!'

The two men hurried towards the small ravine, which lay beyond the last few huts. Karn's annoyance increased when he saw that the Punishment had already begun.

And thanks to Thylassa, he'd missed the beginning recitation!

The Supreme Leader of the village, resplendent in his brown, long-sleeved tunic, had reached the closing part of his speech.

'And it was due to the evil of Woman that Men were thrust out of Paradise and driven into the World. In Paradise, we had wanted for nothing. We had merely to stretch out a hand and birds would drop fruit into our expectant palms.'

Karn felt a thrill as he listened to the age-old words. The language did not make much sense, but that was to be expected from a speech so mystic, so sacred. No-one knew what "fruit" or "birds" were but they sounded like good things to have. From words earlier in the chant—which he had missed!—it sounded like "fruit" was a type of fungus; but an especially sweet and desirable fungus. As for "birds"?—well, that was more difficult. From the fact they fetched and carried things, they could have been a type of Woman, but a much better type, free from the ancestral sin which stained the present ones.

Yarl elbowed him gently. Karn gave a sheepish grin: he'd been daydreaming again. He really must stop that.

The ceremony was approaching its climax.

The Leader had a powerful, sonorous voice, apt for his exalted status, and was using it to full effect. All the Men looked down into the ravine at the huddled group of Women who were standing there, pathetically hugging each other in their distress.

'And now, you Women, what do you have to say? How do you wish to show your shame and guilt for what your ancestors did to we Men?'

A collection of faint, wavering cries rose from the bottom of the ravine.

'We repent! We accept our shame, our guilt! We are the ones who disobeyed the gods and drove Men from Paradise! We accept the guilt! We are the guilty ones!'

Some of the Women were so overcome with emotion at the utterance of the sacred words that they had collapsed to their knees, their arms wrapped around the legs of the ones still standing. Tears were rolling down their faces. This was as it should be, of course: any Woman not showing sufficient repentance would be singled out for further punishment.

The Leader's chin sank slowly onto his throat. He too was deeply moved by the august nature of his actions.

Then he raised his face, and turning to the waiting Men, said, 'They have accepted their guilt. Let the Punishment begin.'

There was a small cry of satisfaction from the crowd, and immediately they began to rain down small stones and lumps of dry, bone-hard fungus on the cowering Women. It was a splendid opportunity for the Men to show their throwing skills and Karn was among the first to score a direct hit, catching one old Woman on the bridge of her nose with an expertly thrown pebble. Only the old or barren were selected for the Punishment, of course, it would have been stupidity of the worst kind to put a good-looking one in the ravine for this special Ceremony of Atonement, of Expiation. But Karn wished it could be held more often; to his dismayed surprise, he had missed his targets twice with his last throws.

He needed more practice.

All too soon, it was over, and the Leader ordered the excited Men to desist.

15

'Enough! We have made them confess their evil actions to the gods enough for today. Their sins are unforgiveable, of course, and in due time we will once again invoke this majestic Ceremony of Expiation. But we have pleased the gods, and they will reward us with a generous bounty of fungus in the Wake-Periods to come. Leave these wicked ones to their thoughts so they may meditate upon their sins.'

As they walked away, Karn said to Yarl, 'It's always over too soon. If I was Leader, I'd really show those Women.'

Yarl did not answer at once and walked on with a downcast expression.

Then he stopped and, looking Karn full in the face, said, 'Karn, do you think it's all true?'

Two

Karn was so taken aback by Yarl's unexpected question that he stopped and spent a few seconds staring at the other.

'What do you mean—true?' he said. He tried to expand on the question but was so shocked that all he could do was repeat: 'What do you mean?'

Yarl indicated they should sit, and when Karn was beside him, he continued: 'What I mean to say is—how do we know we were driven out of Paradise?'

'How do we know?' Karn echoed, and a smile came to his lips. What a stupid question!

'Why,' he began, 'it's…'

He came to an unexpected stop. 'What I mean is…'

'Yes?' Yarl inquired, the innocence dripping from his voice.

'Well, it's what everybody says,' Karn finally managed to enunciate, 'it's what the Leaders have told us. It's what everybody believes.' He felt a hot flush of anger begin to sting his cheeks. 'What are you saying—that everyone's a liar!'

'No, no, I don't mean that. But if we were driven out, how did we get here? Why can't we simply turn around and go back? Where is Paradise?'

Karn frowned as he looked at his hands. This kind of questioning was infuriating! Yarl always thought he was the clever one, and this wasn't the first time he had tied his friends up in knots.

'It must be a long way away,' he finally said, grating out each word slowly as a warning.

'Hmm. You're a well-travelled man, Karn. You've seen much more of the World than I have. Did you meet anyone who knew where Paradise is?'

Karn removed his gaze from his friend and looked straight down the centre of the gigantic cylinder which comprised the World. Looked as far as eye could reach, to where the thickness

17

of the air itself blurred and smudged the details of the far distance.

'No. Which means it's a long way away.'

'It must be. And why were we kicked out?'

'We had nothing to do with it. It was the Women. They angered the gods and brought down the Destroyer upon us. That's why we have the Ceremony of Expiation, so the gods don't get angry with us again and drive us out of the World. There's nothing but darkness outside the World. Everybody knows that!'

Yarl was silent for a while, and then: 'The gods. Where are they?'

That was too much. Karn leapt to his feet and glared at his companion.

'That's enough! You've gone too far, Yarl! Not believing in the gods is the final sin! If they decide to punish you, they're not taking me with you!' He looked up to the vaguely discernible roof of the World. A faint streamer of vapour hung at some unknowable distance above, slowly drifting towards the Sun. (For some reason Karn had always thought the gods would be above him, rather than to the sides or below.)

'I believe!' he cried, and then turned to Yarl, who was now standing beside him. 'And you stop this kind of talk! You think you're so clever! But tell me something'—he grabbed the nearest arm of his companion and made it point at the Sun, 'did you make that! Do you know how to make a Sun? If it wasn't the gods—who!'

Yarl looked shamefaced. 'I'm sorry Karn. I like to play with words and see where they lead me. You're right—I do think I'm clever, but maybe there's such a thing as being too clever. The World is'—he looked around with a vague expression—'just the World. We should be grateful to the gods for giving us such a wonderful place to live, so warm and comforting. Always enough to eat. And although Women are evil, there are compensations to having to live with them.'

Karn looked delighted at the reminder. 'Yes, there are, aren't there!'

Both men laughed at that and it seemed as if their little disagreement had never happened.

But then Yarl seemed to remember something, and his thin face grew contemplative again.

'There's just one thing I don't understand.'

Karn pulled a face. 'Alright, what terrible thing have you thought of now?'

For answer Yarl pointed a bony finger at one of the distant tanks.

'If the gods love us, why have so many algae tanks stopped working?'

**

It was not far to Yarl's hut, but there was something of a strained silence between the two Men. Karn did not like these weird thoughts intruding on everyday life. His friend's ridiculous comments had brought him crashing down from the delicious high that he had been enjoying since arriving at the Ceremony of Expiation, and he told Yarl just that.

Yarl had nodded gloomily, accepting the blame for spoiling the day.

Finally, Karn stopped outside the entrance to Yarl's hut and clasped the other on a shoulder.

'I know what's wrong with you; why you keep coming up with these crazy ideas.'

Yarl looked wary. 'Oh, and why is that? I didn't know you had become a Leader.'

Karn began to grin, and a knowing look spread across his thin features. 'You've lost your Woman, haven't you?'

Yarl nodded slowly, reluctantly. 'Yes. She developed these sores all over her. She wouldn't let me near her towards the end. I was angry, I can tell you!'

Karn gently patted his friend's shoulder. 'That was tough for you, not being able to use your Woman. Perhaps you were just too considerate. Personally, I'd have taken what's due to me, there and then!'

Yarl nodded wistfully. 'Yes, I guess I am too easy with them. It's a weakness with me.'

'Well, forget it now. I won't mention it to anyone.'

Yarl gave a grateful smile. 'Thanks, Karn. You're a good friend.'

Karn left Yarl to enter his hut, to spend another Wake-Period on his own. As he walked back to his own, Karn shook his head as thoughts crowded into his usually placid mind.

It was not good for a man to be without a Woman. That was undoubtedly the reason why Yarl had said those terrible things. No one who was at peace with himself would ever have allowed those words to escape his lips. For a second Karn wondered if he was not complicit in Yarl's sins by not reporting him. The enormity of the thought stopped him in mid-stride while horrible visions of him being accused by the Leaders played themselves out in his mind. But he balled his hands into fists and shook his head.

No, he would not report Yarl; those words could only be due to the stress he was under by not having a Woman to slake his needs. The problem would pass soon enough.

He continued the short walk back to his dwelling, but as if to torment him, another unpleasant realisation struck him.

There were substantially fewer Women than Men in the World, due to the former's greater mortality. It wasn't simply his own community either: he had observed the same skewed ratio between the sexes during his travels. It was obviously the natural order of things, but it did generate friction between the Haves and the Have-Nots. It was the leading cause of male-on-male violence in the World. He grinned as another thought struck him: the other, of course, was insubordination between worker and supervisor—like him and Grath!

His dialogue with himself ended at the door to his hut. He couldn't solve everyone's problems and Yarl would have to solve his particular dilemma by himself. He had his own Woman, and no one would be taking her from him—not even Grath!

Thylassa welcomed him effusively as he walked in, clinging and pressing kisses upon him in a rather obvious attempt to distract him from his earlier threat of punishment.

Of course he hadn't forgotten, but after the punishment was complete, he sat by himself and allowed his mind to go over recent events, yet again.

He could not shake off the nagging doubt that something was not right with his affairs.

Although he was in the other room, he could still hear her muffled sobs, so he shut the door and, sitting down, resumed his musings.

At last, the gnawing worry rose to the surface and he sat back with a faint grunt as he finally saw it for what it was.

He was worried about him and Thylassa.

Several times over the most recent Wake-Periods she had not done things she should have done and, even worse, had done things she should not have done. And he could remember that there had been a few times when, instead of properly punishing her, he had merely warned her she must behave better in the future.

He gnawed a knuckle as the worry crystallised further. Was he becoming effeminate? It was a sacred duty to remind Women of their crime of getting Men thrown out of Paradise—the holiest duty there was, in fact. If the gods saw that the Women's crime was going unpunished there was no telling what they would do. All the People had the same deep, predatory fear: that the gods would turn off the Suns, plunging Men into the darkness which prowled hungrily beyond the walls of the World. Nothing could be worse than that! If they saw Men had forgotten or, worse still, *forgiven* that epochal crime, then punishment would surely follow, just as Wake-Period followed Sleep-Period. Then in the horrors that followed, the culprits would be hunted down by the flickering light of flambeaux, and dreadful things would be done in the howling blackness.

Karn shuddered. His own thoughts had terrified him.

During the Sleep-Period as he and Thylassa lay naked on the bed, glistening with unseen sweat in the humid heat of the World, she, with the intuition of the Woman, knew something was wrong and pressed her slim body harder against his back. He could feel her naked breasts mashing against him and heard her softly ask him what was wrong. But he gave no answer. How could he tell his Woman he feared he was becoming effeminate? And so he remained silent on the bed, his unseeing eyes staring into the darkness.

***

The next Wake-Period he was back above the fungus tank, morosely stirring the greyish glop while his mind ran over the same problem that had disturbed his sleep not long before.

He could not shake off the fear, but also could not share that fear with any of his fellow Men. Once he had uttered the dread word, a hundred tongues would pick it up and broadcast it throughout the village. He would go straight to the bottom of the social heap and probably stay there.

He lifted his gaze from the clinging yeast brew and looked around, realising yet again Grath would have cause to threaten him for his lack of attention. His lips thinned as he scanned the nearby territory, trying to spot Grath's hulking form lurking behind one of the other vats, gloatingly watching his lack of attention, biding his time until Karn's dereliction of duty was undeniable, and then pouncing!

But he could not see any part of his irascible supervisor's body, and so he let his gaze wander beyond the area of the food tanks until it was looking down the central axis of the stupendous cylinder that comprised the World. It looked exactly the same as it had on every other Wake-Period: the mass of food tanks gradually thinned out, and a few huts appeared, then more and more until he was looking down at the entirety of his own village. And beyond the old familiar huts, there was a gap filled with stubby, pallid vegetation, then another area of food tanks, and beyond that another village, and so on in monotonous repetition until the thickness of the intervening air blurred everything into a haze which stained the Sun-Light into a bluish veil.

He understood most of what he had seen in the World; after all, there weren't many sights to understand. He had discovered that fact during his youthful travels: beyond every settlement was another; one that looked remarkably similar to the one he had just quitted.

Sometimes he felt a strange, inchoate feeling stirring in the basement of his mind; a wish that something would change, that there would be a Wake-Period which was not an almost exact replica of the previous one. He could not bring that feeling up into the light and examine it; it always slipped through his mental fingers.

There were a few, almost pitifully few, things he did not understand in the World. Perhaps the chief amongst those things was the purpose of the semi-cylindrical structures which occasionally broke the monotony of the curving walls of the World.

He had gone up to one several times on his travels. Each one was the same: an outward bulge in the wall's substance, but one that did not follow the curvature of the wall of which it rested against but reared up straight until it disappeared into the wall at a great height. Sometimes he had thought they were some kind of tube or tunnel. But that couldn't possibly be right; if they were a tunnel, they would be leading to somewhere which was not in the World. Karn was no logician, but he realised the statement was self-contradictory.

The concept of something outside the World contained its own refutation because, by definition, the World *was* everything that *was*. And yet…there was a rectangular outline right at the bottom of each structure, looking for all the World like a door!

He had allowed his mind to slip into a loop of conjecture and counter-conjecture and so did not hear Grath's heavy footfall on the platform as that individual bore down on him.

But there was no possibility of not noticing the large, powerful hand which closed on one of his shoulders and shook him violently.

He looked up to find Grath's heavy features just above him and felt his fungus-laden breath sweep over him.

'Dreaming again, Karn?' his deep voice rasped, 'Once too often, I think.'

Karn extricated himself from the other's grasp and instinctively moved the stirring-pole between them.

'No, no, Supervisor Grath,' he said, forcing himself to meet the other's stare, eye to eye. 'I felt there was a solid mass just below the surface and was thinking of what it could be and how to move it.'

'The only solid mass in there is going to be you in a few moments, you weak-wristed excuse for a Man!'

Karn backed away; he knew he was in real trouble this time. But Grath was not to be deprived of his prey and once again advanced on his retreating subordinate.

For a few seconds, they presented an almost comic display as one figure walked backwards while staring at another who was bearing down on him.

However, the comedy was short-lived as Grath caught up with his retreating worker and this time grabbed both of his shoulders.

'Now,' Grath began...

And stopped.

The platform shuddered slightly, and there came a sound from far away; a sound like that which might be made by a gigantic carnivore that had at last found its prey.

Karn finally saw something he had not seen before.

There was a rapid succession of shadow and illumination on his captor's face. Grath must have been seeing the same on

Karn's face, because the words died in his throat and his hands fell limply from Karn's shoulders.

And Karn saw another thing he had never seen before—fear—fear on Grath's face.

Having lost all interest in each other, the two Men turned and looked upwards to find the cause of the strange fluctuations in the light.

And what they saw sent a cold rapier of terror into their hearts.

It was the Sun.

It was flickering!

Three

The terror in the sky drove all thoughts of petty squabbles from the two men. They had seen what should not have been possible, and the fear made both men's legs buckle as they gazed upon the dreadful apparition of their Sun becoming insane.

Each looked at the other, saw their own fear mirrored in the other's eyes, and then parted.

Karn rapidly made his way towards his hut, pushing others out of his way, somehow feeling that returning to familiar surroundings would calm the shuddering turmoil of his thoughts, but he was halfway there when the Sun abruptly gave one blast of excess brilliance and then resumed its steady, soft illumination. All around him, the screams and shouts of the terrified villagers abruptly stopped, and he heard a great communal sigh of relief take their place.

Thylassa met him at the door of their hut and flung her arms around him.

He looked down into a terrified, tear-stained face.

'My Lord, did you hear it? That terrible sound? And the Sun... the Sun!'

She could not complete her sentence, and Karn could not help her.

He pushed her aside and sat down, head in his hands.

"My Lord...' she began.

'Be quiet!' he snapped, 'I don't know what it was, so stop your stupid bleating!'

She sat in a corner of the room, folded her hands in her lap and looked at the floor.

Karn ignored her.

Something was terribly wrong. His desire for a change from a routine life had been realised, and the result was terror! What could he do? Was there a way of escaping?

He shook his head at the absurdity of his thoughts and tried to still the boiling turmoil of his fears.

This event was not unknown—he remembered there had been a village which had lost its Sun. The people there had survived, although they had depended on light seeping in from the villages nearest to them. But ordinary life had not been long maintained in the tenebrous twilight that now hung over that stricken settlement and its inhabitants had been inexorably reduced into miserable penury.

Now the same might happen to his own beautiful township. Would its gently bubbling fungus tanks soon be abandoned, its bustling huts silent?

It was horrible, unthinkable!

But what if all the Suns went out? Surely if one could fail, then it was not impossible they all could. And then darkness, nothing but darkness, full of maddened, screaming people! Was there any way he could escape from the World if he needed to?

He wrestled with the idea for a long time before abandoning the ridiculous train of thought. Although he was well travelled, there was no sign that there was anything other than the World and its multitudinous villages, one after the other. In fact, so great was the similarity he had begun to think that if he travelled far enough, he would come back to his village—but from the opposite direction! Before he had abandoned his odyssey of exploration, he had met an old man in the last hamlet he had visited, who had made precisely that claim.

Karn had laughed in his face, but now he was not so sure.

It didn't matter—if, as everyone else believed, the World went on forever, or if it was some kind of weird, bent shape, he was still in it, and in it he would stay.

Thylassa was still sitting silently in her corner when he heard a commotion outside and rushed out to see what was happening.

'What's going on?' he asked a Man who was rushing past.

'The Leaders are holding a village meeting,' the Man replied, 'about the Sun.'

Karn immediately followed him to the village meeting place—an empty area at the township's exact centre.

There, standing on the Proclamation Dais, was The Supreme Leader, flanked by his deputies. All three faces were grim, showing the immense strain they were under. Their appearance sent a chill through Karn: obviously things really were bad. The nearer deputy motioned impatiently to the gathering crowd, indicating they should hurry up and form an orderly arrangement.

But even though people were still arriving, The Supreme Leader began to speak and his words were as grim as his face: 'People of the village, today we have been sent a warning, a terrible, terrible warning.' He glanced up briefly at the distant grey curve of the roof of the World. 'The gods are displeased with us, perhaps even angry. And you all know why!' Suddenly his features became a mask of rage, florid features suffused with blood, and eyes bulging in a crimson face. 'You have neglected your sacred duties! You have allowed the foul taint of effeminacy to spread through your veins! Do you think the gods are fools! They have seen you choosing not to chastise your Women, seen you drop the hand of justice rather than strike at the root of evil in these foul creatures. Have you forgotten our teaching? Of how they caused us to be driven from Paradise? Shame on you, you things that dare to call yourselves Men!'

Many Men in the assembled throng lowered their heads; obviously The Supreme Leader's words had struck home. But he hadn't finished. He walked to the very edge of the dais and slowly scanned the crowd below him.

'Let me make myself clear: we will only receive one warning. One warning and then darkness! And if the darkness comes, you all know there can be only one way to expiate those who control us—we must sacrifice one of those accursed creatures who have brought this doom upon us.'

There was a confused murmur from the crowd, and Karn could see some of them turning to look at each other. Obviously, The Supreme Leader's words were a little strong for some of them. And that had not gone unnoticed by their apoplectic chief.

'I see you doubt me! Even in the depths of your sin, you still doubt me! Let me tell you this, you unworthy creatures. Yes, unworthy! The gods have given you this World, this beautiful World, even though you deserved nothing but the Darkness. If you anger them again, I personally will choose one of your Women for the sacrifice!'

Once again, there was a buzzing, a mixture of sounds which Karn would have likened to angry bees if he had known of bees, if anything like bees had still existed in the World of Men.

The Supreme Leader had reached the end of his patience.

'Go now, you wretches! Out of my sight. But remember my warning: if the gods are angry again, I will take one of your Women and give her to them.' His voice rose to a scream. 'Do not dare to defy me, staring with your weeping, effeminate eyes! Go, get out of my sight!'

The crowd broke up slowly. Some of the braver ones cast quick glances at The Supreme Leader as they dispersed, but not many.

And Karn was not one of them.

Yarl joined him on his trudge back to his hut. For some time the two men did not speak, then finally Yarl said, 'Things are pretty bad, aren't they?'

Karn grimaced. 'Yes, they are. You're lucky, you know.'

Yarl looked puzzled. 'I am? How so?'

'You haven't got a Woman to boss you around, so no one can accuse you of effeminacy.'

'I hadn't thought of it that way,' Yarl said, 'you make it sound as if I should be grateful for being alone.'

'And so you should!' Karn snapped, 'I've seen the way Thylassa looks at me sometimes when I'm punishing her. As if she wanted to punish me back!'

Yarl was shocked. 'That's bad, that's really bad. I mean, after getting us kicked out of Paradise.'

'I thought you didn't believe in Paradise.'

Yarl stopped walking and grabbed his friend's arm. 'You mustn't say that! I was just letting my ideas run free, if you know

29

what I mean. If the Leaders heard I'd said I didn't believe in Paradise...'

He left the dreadful statement unfinished. Silence fell again.

Then as Karn's hut came into view, Karn said, 'I think I'd rather be alone for a while, for the rest of this Wake-Period, so no game tonight.'

'What, no dice play? Some friend you are!'

Karn looked at his companion long and hard. 'Yarl, I need time to think. Everything's spinning around in my head. We've nearly lost the Sun, for gods' sake!'

Yarl accepted the inevitable. 'Alright, I'll see you again in the next Wake-Period. I hope you're in a better mood by then.'

Karn watched him go, and abstractedly rubbed his hairless chin. It was wrong to be upset with Yarl: he hadn't made the Sun flicker.

He walked into his hut. Thylassa was waiting for him and leapt up from where she had been sitting in the shadows.

'Welcome, My Lord, welcome! Did the Leaders put the Sun back to its rightful way?'

He growled, 'Yes, of course they did. Now be quiet!'

'But, My Lord, it was so frightening! When everything went dark, I wanted to...'

He crossed to her, arm raised.

'I told you to be quiet!'

She looked up at him, pliant, obedient, subservient and yet still managing to express love for him in her soft gaze.

He drew his arm back to deliver a stinging blow across those gentle features.

And found he could not!

The desire, the need to assert his authority, to remind Thylassa of her inherited sin for the terrible thing the Women of the past had done—it had gone, crumbled like dry, malformed fungus between the fingers.

A look of horror transformed his face into a weird mask, causing Thylassa to cry out, 'My Lord, what is it!'

He pushed her away, rushed into the other room, and flung himself on the bed, the blood roaring in his head.

It had finally happened!

He was no longer a proper man!

How long would it be before the Leaders found out!

***

Karn awoke with a start, realising he had been asleep during the Wake-Period and had wasted valuable time. He left the bedroom at once and found Thylassa dutifully at her sewing.

She flinched slightly at his sudden eruption from the other room but relaxed when she saw his hands were not balled into fists.

'Does my Lord desire anything?' she enquired but he did not answer. Instead, he walked out of the hut and looked up at the colossal curve of the sheltering sky.

How far away was it?

He knew it was a foolish question because there was no way of answering it. Climbing to any height on the walls of the World was impossible, due to their curvature.

He gave a brief smile of quiet satisfaction because he had not misjudged the time, despite the failure of Thylassa in properly maintaining the sand clock.

He looked at the Sun and found he had no need to squint. Although the Wake-Period effulgence was not blinding, it was still too bright to be looked at for any length of time, but now the Sun was definitely dimming.

But it was the comforting, slow fading he had seen many times before and meant that whatever paroxysm had seized the village's luminary, it was not going to be repeated. His smile became broader as he watched the great rectangle of the Sun very slowly fade through yellow-white radiance, through a warm, buttery yellow, into a comforting orange glow. He would have been reminded of the dying light of a cooling cinder if he had ever seen such a thing.

But there was no fire in the World because there was no need for fire. The World was always warm; indeed, sometimes it was more than warm.

Now the bustling noise of the village was fading along with the light. There were no lengthening shadows because the Sun was not in motion, remaining in its appointed place directly above the township. Gradually, very gradually, everything became dim, grey and indistinct.

But things were as they should be.

The Sun never went out completely, of course, because that would mean total darkness, which was the ultimate horror the People feared the most. The settlements either side of Karn's own had their Sleep-Period at the same time, so no light came from them, but the Sun always gave out a small amount of reddish light so people could move around if they needed to; if there was some emergency—but there never was.

Gradually Karn felt his doubts, his fears of effeminacy, fade away as if gentle fingers were sweeping fungus dust from his hair. The Sun's stumble had reminded him of what really mattered in life and that was the strength and resolution of a Man.

Refreshed, reassured, Karn returned to his dwelling.

He felt so invigorated, he wondered if he could find some fault with Thylassa's sewing so he could punish her, but he found he could not summon up the necessary anger. He was too relaxed, too satisfied that the World had returned to its old certainties for violence to have any appeal. Feeling strong and revivified, all worries of effeminacy dispelled, he had sex with Thylassa in the Sleep-Period and was so content that he did not notice an unusual reluctance on her part.

And then they slept.

Four

Karn faced the new Wake-Period with renewed optimism. The light from the Sun seemed more kindly, more tender than he remembered it. However, he was not conscious of any heat beaming down on his shoulders as he began his walk to the yeast vats. The Sun gave out very little heat; which was just as well, for the average temperature of the World hovered on the brink of being uncomfortable. No-one believed the old Men when they said the World had been even hotter when they had been children. Old Men were useless, but nothing was done to relieve the People of the burden their continued existence caused. They were still Men, after all.

Old Women were a different matter, of course.

None of these thoughts troubled Karn as he made his way through the rows of vats to the one which was his own responsibility.

But his heart sank when, looking up the ladder that led to the encircling platform, he saw Grath staring down at him. So he pushed his pleasant daydreams away and called up his reserves of determination to face whatever Grath had in store for him as he began his slow ascent.

But he received another pleasant surprise, for Grath too was now filled with the new flood of optimism that had swept over the village since the return of the Sun and, slapping Karn on his thin shoulders, he grinned and said, 'Good to see you back. Let's forget about what happened in the last Wake-Period, eh?'

Karn returned the grin but being somewhat unsure of how to make friendly banter with his supervisor, he gave a quick nod of agreement and, picking up his pole, began to stir the glutinous mass that bubbled and hissed below them. Grath smiled tolerantly and left him to it.

Karn felt distinctly relieved after the departure of his usually truculent boss, and as he stirred the resistant semi-liquid he allowed his mind to slip back into comfortable daydreams.

His lips jerked into a smile as he allowed visions of his blessed life to drift through his consciousness: Thylassa was a good-looking woman who did enough things wrong to allow him to punish her with an adequate frequency. Her failure to deliver an heir was starting to annoy him, but there would be time enough in which to replace her. And he had a good friend in Yarl, even if the latter's attempts to show how clever he was were increasingly annoying.

But most of all Karn had a good job, one which made full use of his talents and sharp mind.

Not many of his fellow Men had the strength to stir the fungus as long and as quickly as he could. Let them try! The Men of the village regarded him as quite well-built—not in Grath's league, of course, but Grath was a giant among the People, which is how he had ended up as supervisor.

The Wake-Period passed peacefully. Karn had long since learned how to get his stirrings into a rhythm which produced the maximum movement of the fungus for the least output of effort, and he had a pleasant time conjuring up images of the unattached Women of the village and ranking them in order of desirability so he could begin the process of choosing a replacement for Thylassa.

His head jerked up as a loud, powerful voice broke into his reverie.

'Hey, Karn!'

He looked down: it was Grath. What did the Man want now, for gods' sake? He was slightly alarmed to see him bound up the ladder and, pushing past him, gaze down into the pulsating mycelia.

His heart rate accelerated momentarily as he stared at Grath's corded back and, not for the first time, he entertained the delicious idea of propelling his boss down into that mass.

But when Grath turned back to face him, he was grinning again, revealing large tombstone teeth.

'Well done, Karn. I think this batch will be ready to draw off later this Period. You're almost at the end of your shift. Take the rest of the Period off.'

Karn stared speechlessly at the other, feeling his mouth open wider than was really appropriate when in the company of another Man. This feeling of bonhomie had undoubtedly taken hold in the community!

Fearing that the mercurial Grath might just be toying with him, he quickly said, 'Thanks boss!' and thrust the stirring-pole in Grath's hands. Then, not giving him a chance to change his mind, Karn almost leapt down the ladder and was off, soon to be lost among the maze of yeast vats.

His mind raced as it ran through the possibilities that now opened up with all this free time that had been expectantly bestowed upon him.

However, as the opportunities for entertainment in the village were a little limited, he had still not thought of anything to fill the time when he arrived at his door.

Wanting to surprise Thylassa, he gave no shout to reveal his presence as he pushed into the main room of the dimly lit hut. Strangely, there was no sign of his partner, but there were odd groaning noises emanating from the bedroom; the groaning and grunting of two distinct voices; one of which was definitely Thylassa's.

A sickening suspicion hit him like a punch to the belly, and he pulled the bead curtain to one side and saw what he had thought he would see but did not want to see.

Yarl was on top of Thylassa and was obviously in the process of penetrating her.

His sweaty face, contorted by his arousal, turned momentarily in Karn's direction. For a few moments, his lust-blurred eyes did not register Karn's presence, but then as the realisation burst into his befogged brain, those same eyes opened wide in horror and he leapt off the Woman. Thylassa turned to Karn a second later, saw who it was, and screamed.

Karn stood utterly immobile, unable to speak, hardly able to breathe.

Yarl hurried to pull on his loincloth, not without some difficulty.

'Karn,' he stammered, 'I, I...'

'Get out,' Karn said, slowly, evenly, coldly 'Just get out.'

Yarl nodded dumbly but had to pass close to Karn to make his escape, so closely they rubbed sweaty flesh in the passing.

Karn made no motion, did not turn to watch the Man who had been his friend extricate himself and rush out of the hut.

Thylassa was now sitting on the bed, looking up at him imploringly, her slim arms raised in supplication.'

'My Lord,' she said in a faint whimper. 'I have failed you. Punish me, do what you like to me. I am yours to do with as you will.' Her tear-glistening lashes dipped. 'Like the other Women before me, I have erred.'

He did not move, did not change the angle of his gaze.

Without apparent emotion, he simply said, 'Why?'

She slid off the bed and walked unsteadily to him.

'My Lord, I know I am unworthy, like all Women. But you have punished me so much that sometimes I cannot remember what I did to deserve it. I know I must have angered you with my laziness and foolishness but sometimes I just cannot remember.' She broke down, hot tears snaking down her cheeks, mixing with the shining sweat. Her voice rose to a bitter scream. 'I cannot remember!'

He hit her then. Hard, but just once.

She collapsed and lay sobbing at his feet.

He pulled her up, but she did not look at him. He pulled her chin up, forcing her to see him.

'Get out,' he hissed, 'get out. You are no longer my partner. Don't waste time trying to collect your things. Just go. If you hesitate for a single moment, I will kill you.'

Her lips opened briefly as if she were about to make one last plea but seeing the merciless glare in his eyes, she gave a quick nod and left.

He thought about watching her go, but in the end, he just stood there until there was no chance of seeing her departure.

***

All Karn's fears came sweeping back after Thylassa's ejection.

Although the Woman was naturally the guilty party when this kind of thing happened, there was always an undercurrent of mockery among the People when they learned of such an embarrassing event. Most times nothing was actually said, individuals would walk around grinning and there would be smirking conversations about the reason for the transgression. And that reason was always the same: the stigma of effeminacy.

The Man had been too easy-going, too gentle; too ready to overlook mistakes or impertinence.

Karn thought he had shaken off those fears, but now they came roaring back as he sat alone in the hut. He began to feel angry with himself; he had genuinely liked Thylassa, for she was a strikingly good-looking woman, and he had, in his innocence, thought that being forgiving with her had been part of the reciprocal affection they had felt. But quite obviously, he had gone too far with his undemanding ways, and Thylassa had resented it.

(Although there had been those times recently when she had looked unhappy when she was being punished.)

He shook his head: it was that kind of thinking which had gotten him where he was now.

Time passed as he sat there, staring down at his interlinked hands, slowly wringing them in his misery.

And Yarl—that Man had been his only genuine friend in the village, and he had enjoyed their walks and conversations. But admittedly, Yarl had said some very dangerous things recently; things about the gods that could have caused real danger for him, and—by extension—for Karn as well.

But it was all over now. He was alone. There was a stain on his character that could never be expunged.

He slowly raised himself off the chair, surprised at how stiff he was: he realised he had been sitting for a very long time. But a look of determination had chased the despair from his features. He now knew what to do—he would leave the village and find another. Unlike the vast majority of his fellow Men, he was not afraid of the new. His earlier travels had shown him there were several settlements with a shortage of Men; all conveniently far from his current location. They would welcome someone like him with his well-honed skills with the fungus tanks. And with so few competitors, there would be little difficulty in gaining a new Woman. In fact, he'd have the pick of the crop!

As that conclusion burst into his brain, a broad grin swiftly curved his lips.

Why, this whole thing could work out to his advantage!

There was only one thing to do now and that was to go out among the People; show them he accepted no responsibility for Thylassa's desertion. And if any of them tried to mock him, well, he was quite a well-built man—they would regret it.

As it turned out, several villagers did try to mock him, and, as Karn had predicted, they did regret it. But as he stood there, gently sucking his sore knuckles, a youth came up to him and signalled that he had important news.

'What do you want?' Karn snapped; his blood was up, and he was in no mood to deal with trifling distractions.

But this was no trifling distraction.

'The Supreme Leader wants to see you,' was the terse message.

Karn felt as if his insides had suddenly liquefied. A command from The Supreme Leader was something that could not be ignored. And had to be obeyed immediately.

And so it was that in a remarkably short time later, Karn found himself on his knees in the approved fashion; abasing himself before the all-powerful head of the community. When allowed to raise his head, he found himself being regarded by a

38

pair of watery blue eyes, glaring down at him from under bushy white eyebrows.

'Karn,' a deep, resonant voice said, 'Karn, you have much to answer. Much to tell me. Is this not so?'

Each word seemed to crash upon Karn like a physical blow. He lowered his head again. His neck felt like it was supporting a huge stone. This was the first time he had been this close to the great Man, and most definitely the first time he had been directly addressed by him.

'What do you wish to know, Supreme Leader?'

The Leader leaned back in his chair, its dried fungus construction creaking somewhat as the forces upon it altered.

'There are rumours about you,' the sonorous voice continued, 'rumours which I am beginning to believe.'

'Rumours, Supreme Leader?'

'Yes. Whispers have reached me that you are not entirely happy with our way of life here. That you care too much about the Women.' Without warning, the Leader leaned forward, his face suddenly transformed into a mask of terror, 'that you may be—effeminate!'

Despite his determination not to flinch, Karn rocked back on his heels, his own features distorted into an abject display of cringing fear. A plea for pity, for mercy, hung unspoken on trembling lips.

But the Leader did not recognise the emotion, or, if he did, decided it was beneath his dignity to acknowledge it. So instead, he continued his dread interrogation.

'Do you have anything to say, boy?'

Karn winced internally. By dropping his name and substituting the term "boy" the Leader was indicating he was in danger of losing his status as a true villager. In his youth, Karn had seen it happen. Someone he had known had been stripped of the privileges of *Man* and left without employment and thus the means to support himself. Karn still remembered the horror of seeing him grow more and more skeletal as the Wake-Periods had passed by. Eventually the "Man" had staggered off into the

39

land between the settlements, leaving his bones to be discovered by playing children sometime later. Karn would do anything to avoid that fate! But all the Leader had to do was utter the words of relegation and it would all be over. There was no appeal against the sacred words, nor could they be called back.

Once uttered, the course of events was ineluctable.

He waited for the words to be spoken and his fate sealed.

But the Leader did not utter the sacred words; instead he placed a heavy hand on Karn's shoulder and said, almost gently, 'I will not remove your status, boy—on this occasion at least. You are too good a worker on the fungus vats to be dismissed quite so lightly. But the entire village knows of your shame, of how your Woman deserted you. If I am seen as weak, the people will begin to murmur against my high office, and that I will not tolerate. I have thought about your fate many times since I heard of your offence and, very reluctantly I must say, I have decided to give you one last chance.

'You must find yourself a new Woman and this time you must treat her properly, administering the proper frequency and severity of punishments. Have I made myself clear? Look at me, boy!'

Karn lifted his head and saw The Supreme Leader's face above him; a face stern, hard, deeply lined with marks carved by the weight of the responsibilities of his high office. In that moment, Karn almost did not care what his fate would be—he loved the Leader with all the emotion he could deliver.

'Yes, Supreme Leader,' he finally stuttered, 'yes you have.'

A smile added more creases to the care-worn face of his Supreme Leader, and he placed a hand on Karn's other shoulder.

'Good. I do not want to lose you. You may go now—Karn.'

Karn's heart leapt within him.

Karn! The danger had passed!

As he stood in the Sun-Light outside The Supreme Leader's hut, he felt his life had begun again, almost as if he had been born into a different World. He no longer hated Yarl or Thylassa; they

40

had been simply instruments to make him realise what truly mattered in life.

He knew what he had to do. To prove himself worthy of The Supreme Leader's mercy, he had to have another Woman. As all the desirable ones were already taken, he would have to fight another Man for her. So be it. That would be another proof he was not effeminate.

Filled with fresh energy, fired by a new purpose, he strode away from the Leader's hut into the heart of the village.

Five

Karn moved swiftly through the village, the blood pounding through his body with new urgency. He was still feeling a little dizzy from his interrogation by The Supreme Leader, and he understood only too well that what he did in the next few Wake-Periods would determine the direction of the rest of his life. If the rest of his life was long enough to have a direction, of course.

He needed time to think, time to plan. There was a drinks-bar at the intersection of tracks linking storage warehouses and he strode in, trying to give the impression of a Man who knew what he wanted and would brook no opposition to him getting it. Every Man was entitled to a number of drinks each Wake-Period and he knew he had two drinks left. So did the barkeep who saw him come in.

'You're early, Karn,' was the laconic comment, 'have you lost your job?'

'No, I've been having a talk with The Supreme Leader,' was the equally laconic reply.

The barkeep raised an eyebrow at that most remarkable statement but received only a steady stare from Karn in return, so eventually he shrugged and said, 'Usual?'

A few moments later Karn was sat at a table made from dried fungus stalks and staring down at a beaker which held a thin, faintly green liquid, a liquid which was definitely not his usual. He had blown his remaining two-drink allowance on an algal beverage. These were much-coveted premium drinks now that many of the algae-breeding tanks had failed, but he didn't care. All his priorities had been drastically reset.

The drink had only a small amount of alcohol in its composition due to the lack of readily fermentable materials in the World but the People had a low tolerance of that substance for the same reason. And so, Karn began to feel its effects shortly after he had tipped the last of the insipid greenish fluid into his mouth. His feeling of strength, of power, of grandeur, already increasing after his encounter with The Supreme Leader, were suddenly boosted. He felt like he could take the World in his hands and tear it up so he could build a better one! He pushed the beaker away with such force that it fell off the other side of the table.

He didn't care—despite the cry of protest from the barkeep.

He strode out of the bar, the Sun-Light streaming down upon him in a gentle benediction.

He was on the hunt, a hunt for a suitable Woman. She had to be as good-looking as Thylassa, of course, but this time she would need to be fertile. He had lived with a barren Woman for too long; there was a distinct air of failure, of inadequacy, associated with a Man who had not fathered a child, even though it was —as was always the case—the fault of the Woman.

He passed several examples of his quarry on his quest through the narrow tracks of the village but every time, they were with a Man. And the Men appeared to notice something different about Karn because each time they felt his intense stare they interposed themselves between him and their Woman. Reluctantly, he concluded that violence would be needed.

Well, he was ready for that. His hands instinctively balled into fists as he reached that dire conclusion.

And then he came to a crossroads where met two of the largest tracks that the township held.

And there, just in the act of crossing from one track to the other, were Thylassa and Yarl!

His blood, stimulated by the unaccustomed presence of alcohol, seemed to boil in his arteries. His face contorted into a snarl of rage, and he leapt towards them, fists raised.

Yarl saw him coming and, pushing Thylassa behind him, raised his own fists. Then, confronted by the reality of violence, the realisation the intended victim might actually fight back, Karn stopped a short distance from the pair.

'You walk around together,' he said, slowly, measuredly, 'not caring about the shame you have brought upon me.' A terrible idea struck him then. 'Was it you that reported me to The Supreme Leader?'

Yarl shook his head with magnanimous pity. 'No need. Everyone knows about you—about your effeminacy.'

Karn moved closer, standing full-on to his ex-friend, now his adversary. He planted his feet as firmly as he could into the dry dust, seemingly trying to embed himself in the ground.

As he did, something a little strange happened.

For an instant, just for an almost undetectable instant, there was a kind of shiver, a sort of trembling, that ran up his legs, causing his knees to buckle, ever so slightly.

He looked down. Was this fear? What had happened to his resolution, his determined will? Was he afraid of Yarl?

What nonsense—he was twice the Man Yarl was!

Their respective stares met and locked. Yarl showed no sign of having experienced the same mystery as Karn had. Instead, he waited, apparently calmly, for Karn to advance.

Realising that this was the supreme moment in his new life, Karn moved even closer, and his right arm drew back to deliver the first blow.

And the World went mad.

Without further warning, the ground shook and shuddered like the surface of a drum at the moment of crescendo. Everything became a horrific blur of quivering madness in which nothing could be recognised. There were sounds of destruction all around as buildings shivered and shattered into flying fragments.

And then came the real noise. As before, it was as if a titanic carnivore was loose, but this time standing directly above the village, pawing the ground with immense talons and roaring with bestial fury. It was a sound beyond human endurance, a great tsunami of thunderous power that smashed every inhabitant to their knees or tossed them to the ground like rag dolls.

Karn was thrown facedown and found his eyes and nose stuffed with stinging dust as he lay there with hands clamped over his ears in a completely vain attempt to shut out the terrible roaring. The screams of the inhabitants, even Yarl and Thylassa, were utterly inaudible, drowned out by the flood of insurgent noise. He finally managed to roll over, to lie helplessly supine on the shuddering ground. He felt that at any moment it would throw him into the sky and crush him against the roof of the World.

So this was it—this was the end of his wonderful plans, his new life!

But the great carnivore was not done with him yet.

As he lay there, staring at the Sun, it gave one tremulous flicker.

And then went out.

Darkness took the village and its stricken People.

***

Karn didn't know how long he had been wandering without purpose, automatically pushing howling Men and gibbering Women out of his way. He was moving in a completely random walk, for there was nowhere to go.

The village was not in total blackness; was not sunk in the sanity-destroying absence of a single photon. No mind could dwell in such a horror and survive. The village to the "north" of Karn's was similarly blacked out, but the one to the "south" was still illuminated and a faint overspill of weak yellowish light allowed shapes to be recognised in the dark. Karn also realised his eyes were adjusting and he was becoming more proficient at distinguishing one black shape from another.

Some of the People had congregated at the southern boundary of their community and were trying to gather enough courage to attempt to cross the gulf between their township and the still-illuminated one, but most were so afraid of the unknown they were still milling around in a vicious loop of indecision. Karn, of course, had made that epic journey many years earlier and so he was unafraid of repeating the feat, but he did not join

45

the jabbering crowd. Somehow he knew that escaping to another village would be only a temporary respite; that the darkness would follow him there too.

So he walked on, completely unknowing whether he had walked that way before, of whether he was crossing and re-crossing paths he had trodden earlier. He had no conception of what to do next, indeed of whether there could be anything to do next.

Perhaps this was the end of the World, and he should just lie down and accept it.

Finally, weariness took him, and he stopped and rested against a huge shard of what had once been someone's home. His whirling mind wondered where he was, whether he had known the occupant of this hut; if he had talked with the Man and looked covetously at the Woman. He shook his head: what did it matter now? All those things that had seemed important—all gone into the dark.

It was then he heard a faint voice coming from a great distance. In actuality, the distance was not great, but the howling and moaning and weeping of the villagers threatened to drown the voice out.

He recognised that sonorous voice—it was The Supreme Leader! He had not lost his mind with fear but was trying to drag the survivors back into a semblance of order, of civilisation!

Hurriedly, Karn straightened himself and ran toward that welcome voice, that infinitely reassuring voice, not caring in the gloom with whom he collided.

By the time he reached the author of the voice, Karn's night vision was fully operational and, though he could not distinguish features at his distance from the throng around the Leader, he could see they were Men, just like himself.

He pushed his way through the crowd, all civilised niceties forgotten, and positioned himself in the front row so he could hear the Leader's voice and learn how he would lead the People out of this nightmare.

The Supreme Leader was standing on a pile of the broken remnants of a dwelling and was in full declamatory mode.

'I warned you!' he shouted. His voice held no fear, no indecision, just anger, righteous anger with his wretched subjects, 'I warned you this would happen, and you ignored me! No, worse than that—you defied me! I told you what would be the result of your sinful weakness, your lack of Manhood! Now look around at what you have brought on yourselves, of how your sloth and effeminacy have destroyed our entire way of life, turned our beautiful village into heaps of trash. What future do we have now? I'll tell you—from henceforth we will live on the sufferance of those outside of our habitation, strangers we know nothing about and who in turn know nothing of our ways, our customs, our very culture! This is what you have done!'

There was a low moaning from the crowd as they accepted the verdict upon themselves; a moaning of those who had lost all their pride, their arrogance, and knew themselves to be unworthy.

Karn was about to ask something when a dark shape to his left asked it for him.

'What can we do, Supreme Leader?'

The Leader did not look in the direction of the anonymous questioner, but spoke to the entire group.

'We will do what I told you we would have to do if we continued to displease the gods: we will sacrifice one of those despicable creatures that had us driven out of Paradise.' His voice rose to a great roar as if a mere human could command the thunder. 'Find me a barren woman, and bring her before me!'

Immediately some dark figures left the crowd and sped off in different directions, obedient to the Leader's demands, desperate to do anything that might bring about the return of normality. Karn was not among them. Somehow there was a doubt growing, perhaps festering, in his mind. Ever since Yarl had voiced those heretical thoughts, not long before, he had felt himself being tugged in different directions. When he had

47

cowered before The Supreme Leader he had for the first time gotten a close-up view of that august individual.

And he had seen a Man; a Man made from the same material as himself, but in a somewhat more well-worn state. At the time, the Leader's powerful voice had cowed him; made him ready to abase himself, to squirm like a chastised Woman. But why was the Leader so sure of himself and his solution? As he stood there in the noisome semi-darkness, Karn wondered if the Leader's analysis had any weight. Were things so lax now, that the gods had been forced to intervene? Karn was not old, but he could look on many Wake-Periods which had come and gone. Were Women being treated so much more leniently now than in his younger days?

Had the canker of effeminacy spread so widely, as sometimes a blight did upon the fungus broth, blackening and shrivelling it?

Reluctantly, he conceded there was no evidence of an epidemic of effeminacy among the People. He wanted the Leader to be right; he wanted him to have the power to bring back the Sun, but somehow he seemed to be losing the necessary faith.

Irresolute, he stood there as the throng thinned around him until, with one last mental effort, he decided to throw off his doubts. He would bring a barren Woman before The Supreme Leader. She would be executed as was just and proper, and the Sun would return.

Already in his mind, he could see the joyful rejoicing of the People as the warm, buttery Sun-Light shone down upon them once more; a People who had seen the error of their ways and never again would anger the gods so much that this dreadful punishment would be brought upon them again.

He smiled grimly in the eerie twilight and, resolute once again, turned, ready to begin the hunt for the sacrificial Woman.

But others were there before him. A great shout had gone up and the remaining crowd members eagerly parted as two Men brought in a struggling figure and threw it before the Leader.

From where Karn stood, he could hear female wailing coming from the crumpled shape. The requisite Woman had been captured! The crowd was beginning to reform now the hunt had been successful, and so Karn had to push his way between the excited Men to get a closer look at developments.

The Supreme Leader spoke. 'Well done, my fellow Men. Now we will have the necessary expiation and the gods will smile once more and our life-giving Sun will shine once again in the sky of the village.' He removed his stern gaze from the shivering, sobbing creature below him and looked around. 'Where is my mighty Man, my beloved executioner?'

A large Man on the other side of the Leader broke free from the crowd and approached him.

'I am here, Supreme Leader.'

Karn started at that voice for he knew it well; only too well.

It was Grath.

The Leader looked down at him for a while, and it seemed as if a powerful current of love was passing between the two Men.

'Do you have the instrument of execution on you, my Son?' the Leader said softly. Gently.

'Yes, Supreme Leader. When I saw the Sun had been taken from us I knew you would call upon me, so I made one in readiness.'

Grath held something up between his hands. It was difficult to be certain in the tenebrous half-light, but Karn thought it was a rope made from twisted fungus strands. Strangulation: the approved method of execution.

Karn had never seen anybody killed before and, his heart hammering with excitement, he roughly forced himself through the lines of observers so there was no-one between him and the ghastly tableau.

The Supreme Leader stepped down from the pile of debris; very gingerly, as the components rocked alarmingly as he changed position. He stood before the Woman, who now lay hunched on the ground, her arms stretched out imploringly.

'Do you have anything to say, Woman?' The Supreme Leader said, and his voice was like iron.

The Woman spoke, weakly, desperately, tearfully.

'I beg for your forgiveness, Supreme Leader. I have done nothing wrong. It was not I who made the Sun go away. I have done nothing to anger the gods!'

'No,' the Leader replied, 'not in your own actions, but you have corrupted your Man into soft weakness and that is why they are angry.'

The sacrificial Woman said something else in a jerking, gasping voice but Karn was no longer listening.

It felt as if his stirring-pole had been thrust deep into his belly. His knees buckled and he had to hold onto the Man next to him to prevent himself from collapsing.

Once again he recognised a voice.

It was Thylassa!

Whatever Thylassa had said, The Supreme Leader had ignored it. Instead he waved to Grath and simply said, in a quiet, calm voice, 'Do it.'

A great wail came from Thylassa and she jumped to her feet, looking wildly around to see if there was a gap in the crowd she could escape through.

But there was none, and, even as she was desperately searching, Grath came up behind her and slipped the fungus rope around her neck. Her face was turned towards Karn and he could see her eyes suddenly open impossibly wide under the shock of finality. Her mouth opened to let out a terrible cry, a vocalisation of despair in the form of one word: 'No!' But there were to be no more words as Grath rapidly began to twist the rope, using a stick entwined in it. Thylassa slumped as the rope tightened and Karn could hear desperate rasping noises coming from her, could see her small hands pawing at the rope—to no avail.

Karn stood gazing in horror, and he began to shake and tremble. He wanted to run towards her, push Grath aside, and save her.

But he couldn't move.

Soon the horror ended. Grath released the tension, and Thylassa slumped bonelessly to the ground. The Supreme Leader grunted in satisfaction and stood over her. He looked approvingly at Grath. 'You did well, my son. Our village owes you an enormous debt. I'm sure the rest of the Men will agree with me your fungus ration should be increased, and, in all probability, you will receive some algae as well.'

The crowd dispersed, first one by one, and then en masse.

Soon only those who had been allocated the task of disposing of Thylassa's body and Grath were left. Karn stared at him long and hard. Many thoughts came and went, like bubbles in boiling water.

Grath caught Karn's stare and returned it.

In the gloom, Karn could see a flash of yellowish teeth as the other Man grinned.

And then Karn knew what he had to do.

He had to kill Grath.

Six

Karn was never sure why that command had suddenly erupted in his mind. But he was instantly gripped by a cold, hard determination to do the thing; to remove Grath from the World.

Did Grath deserve such a fate? He had tossed the question back and forth for a while. Was Grath an evil man? The Supreme Leader genuinely believed the People needed a sacrifice to restore the Sun, and he had issued a command that such a sacrifice be made. Surely, Grath was simply the instrument which the Leader had employed to bring about the salvation of the People?

But then Karn remembered the faint sight of Grath's lips revealing the yellow teeth below, lips curved in an insouciant grin, a carefree lack of concern that he had just ended a life.

No, it was worse than that—Grath had *enjoyed* ending Thylassa's life!

There was no more arguing with himself: the vow was made; the determination established—Grath would die and Karn would do it.

He had left the site of the execution and walked in as straight a line as possible through the remains of the village, back to where his home had been.

When he got there, it was obvious nothing of the ramshackle structure had survived, just torn remnants piled crazily upon other remnants. He sat upon a large shard which was reasonably horizontal and thought, long and hard. How long would The Supreme Leader be able to maintain his control over the People if the Sun did not return, and, if control was lost, what would replace it?

Karn stood and looked directly upward. He could see a black rectangle against the slightly lighter black which comprised the sky. He could make out where the glorious Sun had been, but there was not the faintest illumination seeping from that dark rectangle. Like Thylassa, it was dead. Somehow, Karn knew that to be true. No matter if The Supreme Leader slaughtered everyone in the village it would not return. Then the epiphany hit him in what was almost a physical blow; a realisation so awful, so dreadful, he staggered under the mental impact.

First the old Men saying the environment was getting colder, then the algae tanks failing one by one, now the Sun going out: the pattern was suddenly obvious—*the World was dying!*

The conclusion was so mind-murderingly horrific that he cried out in his despair. Everything was dying, Thylassa had simply been the harbinger of that coming doom.

He knew then for certain the Sun would not return, the darkness having claimed them, it would never let them go.

And so it proved; periods of time that in the beneficent past would have been termed Wake- and Sleep-Periods passed but the Sun did not flare back into life. The People began to mill around aimlessly with eyes seeing nothing but the encircling darkness. The Supreme Leader had ordered his dwelling must be rebuilt, but having had that done, he retreated into it and was not seen again. Instead, he sent his deputies to try to calm the People. One thing they made clear to the bewildered multitude was that they now faced starvation; they must attend to the yeast tanks and try to coax them back to life. Karn was one of those selected to ensure the People's food supply did not fail.

He soon discovered there was a distinct pattern to the destruction, as if the terror had struck in concentric bands. Many of the vats closest to one edge of the village had been totally destroyed, their contents motionless and desiccated upon the ground. But in the direction of the neighbouring village that still had its Sun, some were merely holed and leaking dying fungus down their sides. And a few of the vats nearest to that fortunate community were basically unharmed and could be saved, including the one which had been Karn's own responsibility. During his early days above the vats, he had noticed that darkness did not appear to affect the yeast; unlike the algae which, like the People, slumbered during the Sleep-Periods. So there was hope there would be food to eat in the blackness. And so it was not long before one of the Deputies sought Karn out and delivered a staccato series of commands that he get back to work for the sake of the People. Karn obeyed without hesitation, as it felt that he was being offered some small shred of normality in a World that, quite literally, had gone mad.

And so on several occasions, he stood on the platform stirring the revivified fungus, clinging onto a few pieces of flotsam from his old life. He could hardly see the broth beneath him, but he could hear it murmuring to itself, listen to its soft popping as bubbles of carbon dioxide finally finished their long climb to the surface, hear the familiar sucking noises as he moved his stirring-pole through the glutinous mass.

But all the time, there was one thought, and one thought only, echoing and re-echoing in his mind: *How do I kill Grath?*

After his Work-periods he joined the restless throng of bewildered People as they milled around, looking for comfort and finding none, looking for answers and finding none, looking for rationality itself—and finding none.

Sometimes he joined them at the "southern" edge of the village, looking out through the threatening darkness to where the yellow light of the neighbouring dwellings was just visible. He smiled bitterly as he listened to them as they endlessly debated whether they should try to cross the ebony gulf to that strange place. What would they find there? Would the inhabitants welcome them or kill them? Were they like themselves or some kind of strange creature that could talk but was not truly of the People?

Karn came to realise just how different he had been from the rest of the inhabitants of his home when he had undertaken his epic journey. No wonder Thylassa had never really felt happy in his company. But he did not try to encourage the fearful survivors to cross the Sunless gap between the villages, for after all what was the point? If he were right, then the darkness would follow them there in its own good time. In the end, with overflowing pity, he left them there; unable to advance, unable to retreat.

Soon he was standing there in the fetid twilight, once again stirring the resistant fungal brew. He felt, rather than heard, a heavy footfall behind him. Knowing, without turning, who was there, he turned and found his assumption true. Grath stood there, heavy, bulky, strong, arrogant.

'Working hard, Karn?' he said, displaying once again the row of yellow teeth that Karn had seen some time earlier, behind the body of his dying partner.

Karn looked hard at him, harder than he had ever done before, measuring the Man, gauging the strength of the muscles that sloped on the arms, the power of the thighs.

But it was no good, the light was too dim; Grath was just a darker shape against the greater dark. Whatever Karn did, he would have to do blindly, trusting his rage would give him strength.

He had stared at the other for too long, and Grath had realised that he was being studied.

'What's the matter,' the latter said, 'have you forgotten what I look like in all this darkness?'

'No,' Karn said, 'I remember very well what you look like.'

Grath moved closer, so Karn was forced to look up. 'Is there something troubling you, my friend?'

Karn found he could not reply; that the words of accusation would not form on his lips, but it seemed Grath had guessed his thoughts.

'What, are you sorry I dispatched the Woman?' Grath was now so close the stench of his sweat was filling Karn's nostrils. 'What are you, some kind of Woman-lover? Is that it?'

The opportunity had arrived, Karn thought. *Now, strike, strike hard! Kill him!*

But he could not.

'You know,' Grath continued languidly, 'The Supreme Leader has very firm views about Woman-lovers. I believe he's already had words with you. Am I right?'

Karn's mouth was dry, almost painfully so. 'A few,' he finally said.

Grath's large hand came down heavily on Karn's shoulder. 'You know, boy, she had it coming. Don't you get it? They *all* have it coming. We wouldn't be in this mess if it weren't for them—what, did you miss that lesson at school!'

'Why her?'

'She was barren. There's one thing we keep them for—the only thing. And she couldn't do it. So she was no loss.' Then suddenly, he grasped both of the other Man's shoulders and pulled him hard against his chest. 'Was she?'

Kill him! Kill him now! Thundered Karn's thoughts.

But he could not.

Grath did not give Karn long to answer. Tiring of the short silence, he abruptly straightened his arms and sent him crashing into the barrier above the fungus. It shuddered and bent but did not break. He walked away, casting one mocking glance behind him.

'I'm watching you, Karn. There's something not right about you.'

Karn slumped against the barrier, disgusted with his irresolution, his weakness.

Why was he so concerned with Thylassa's death, a Woman who had left him for his supposed friend?

But he straightened himself and looked up at the black concavity of the sky. Memories of happy times with her flooded back to him. Perhaps he had driven her away. Perhaps—and his mind reeled under the thought—it had not been effeminacy that had caused her to desert him. Perhaps there had been a justifiable reason for the looks she had increasingly given him when she was under punishment.

And there was something else.

'If it was necessary to kill her,' he whispered to himself, 'where is the Sun?'

***

56

Periods of time which in the old days would have been termed Wake-periods and Sleep-periods passed, but still the Sun did not burst into effulgent splendour above the joyous faces of the villagers. Still, the darkness held them in a pitiless grasp, unconcerned by their despair, their tears.

Karn made several visits to the southern boundary of the township. To his mild surprise, a few of the individuals encamped there had found the courage to attempt to cross the dark wilderness that lay between them and the comforting glow of the distant habitation, no longer paralysed by the debate of whether it was the welcoming domain of new People, or of hungry monsters.

But society was disintegrating, of that, he was sure. Some of the People had begun to talk openly about The Supreme Leader, unafraid to call his knowledge, his competence, his very authority into question. Still the Leader remained entrenched in his rebuilt hut, giving his diktats via the Deputies. And a rumour began to spread among the dispirited villagers—the sacrifice of Thylassa had not been enough. There would have to be another offering to the gods, who were still quite obviously displeased with the disobedient Men.

And one Woman had not been enough. The next time, two Women would be given up to the wrathful deities.

It was Karn who pointed out the flaw in the Leader's supposed plan: there were not two barren Women in the village. Surely, fertile Women could not be offered up. That was against all the People's values!

There was much murmuring at his words, much shaking of heads. Karn realised he was gradually being thrust into the role of an opponent to The Supreme Leader.

A role not guaranteed to produce a long lifespan.

And so he withdrew from the increasingly desperate People, leaving them to reach their own conclusions, and spent more time above his food vat, even when there was no need for him to be there.

But he found no peace there; sometimes he wished he had not made his vow to kill Grath for he could see clearly now how difficult a task that would be. His opponent was obviously stronger than him and would not let go of life easily.

Also, he was now alone; he had no partner, no friend. He had glimpsed Yarl in the dark streets once or twice, but the two Men had avoided each other. Loath though he was to admit it, he understood Yarl too must have been distressed by Thylassa's execution. But he did not know for sure, because they had not looked each other in the eye since just before the fateful seismic shock. And so he continued to stand on the platform above the fungus, stirring the gurgling brew without conscious effort.

When he had descended from his work, he could be found sitting on the remains of his hut, morosely chewing on a wad of dried fungus, hardly looking at the increasingly dispirited crowd shuffling past him. He knew more and more desperate individuals had overcome their terror and set out into the darkness towards the enigmatic yellow glow in the distance.

Unlike them, he knew they would face no monsters when and if they arrived; he knew the inhabitants would be almost the same as the People. He was aware from his travels that villages became more and more unlike his own the further one travelled, but the "southern" one was sufficiently close so that any differences would not be too great.

However, he also remembered the wariness of the natives when a stranger had appeared among them, the coldness, the suspicion of someone who had undertaken this weird journey.

And that had been just one unexpected visitor—what would their reaction be if a horde of maddened strangers suddenly descended on them?

Karn was sure the villagers' fears would be found to be justified—no monsters, but other Men who did not want hungry alien mouths destroying their way of life.

Eventually, there would be violence.

In the humid gloom, he sighed deeply, sadly.

Violence—was it the inevitable attendant of all living things?

So much violence, so little peace.

And, ironically, he was hoping to add to that violence.

As time passed, the Wake-periods and Sleep-periods no longer distinguishable, he became more and more depressed by the hopelessness of his situation. A feeling of self-disgust began to seep into his every thought. He now realised he had set himself a task he could not achieve. But, having made the vow, there was no escape. There were only two ways for the dilemma to be resolved: either Grath must die—or he would. Unaware of the theatricality of his actions, for there were no dramas in the village, he stood and shook his fist at the indifferent sky.

'Him or me,' he said, 'him or me!'

And so it was, not long after the renewal of his vow, that he felt a heavy footfall behind him as he mechanically stirred the fungus. And he felt a familiar, heavy hand descend on a shoulder.

And hear a familiar, mocking voice address him.

'Wakey-wakey, boy! Daydreaming on the job, again? You want to be careful, Karn. If you fell in, we wouldn't be able to tell which bit was you and which was the fungus!'

Grath obviously thought his witticism was hilarious, for he threw back his head and bellowed his laughter.

And it was then, with his gaze fixed on the dark sky, that Karn hit him. He drove the dripping end of the stirring-pole deep into Grath's belly and as the other doubled up, sent his head rocking back with an uppercut with every iota of his strength behind it.

But that strength was not enough. Grath indeed crashed against the barrier with blood tricking from a burst lower lip, but he was far from incapacitated. Instead, the main effect of Karn's onslaught was a look of total, utter amazement on his features, a look that was very swiftly replaced by one of fury.

'I knew there was something wrong about you, boy!' he roared, 'for what you just did, you die, and The Supreme Leader will thank me!'

Karn knew his life depended on maintaining the initiative and, without waiting for Grath to recover, he charged the bigger

Man, pinning him against the barrier and raining blows upon him. But even as he crashed onto Grath, he knew his attack would be futile. In the instant of collision, he felt the hardness of the other's body, the firmness of the muscle, the coiled strength.

Moments later, Grath seized him and, whirling him around, wrapped thick arms around his neck and pulled them back, cutting off Karn's air supply without apparent effort.

The darkness before Karn grew darker, shot through with dancing red sparks. His lungs seemed on fire as the pressure on his larynx increased. He could hear Grath chuckling.

Him or me was his only thought, *him or me.*

Then suddenly, magically, the pressure was instantly released. He fell on the platform, gasping and choking.

What had happened?

He rolled onto his back and could see another had joined them—Yarl!

Yarl was indeed there, and was smashing blows into Grath's face, his own face contorted with hatred. But, if anything, Yarl was even less well-equipped to defeat Grath than Karn. Soon he received a return blow from Grath which sent him sprawling on the deck.

Grath stood over him, fists clenched. 'What has gotten into you boys?' he laughed, 'Who do you think you are!'

The laughter was cut off as Karn swung the stirring-pole onto his head with such violence the bottom third snapped off and went flying into the darkness. And this time, Grath did stagger and fell back onto the railing.

And then Karn saw the answer.

'Yarl!' he yelled, 'help me!'

But Yarl had seen it too. Together they rushed at the dazed Grath and each grasped a leg and with a combined effort lifted him up so only his wildly thrashing legs were still on his attackers' side of the railing.

Grath realised what his fate would be and struggled desperately, trying to kick his assailants. But it was too late: he was already too far over.

He screamed as with one last mighty effort Yarl and Karn sent him tumbling over the railing, down, down into the mumbling fungus.

The splash was so large that drops of fungus gloop showered down on the two Men, who stood watching a dark shape thrashing around in the viscous liquid.

It did not take long for Grath to be sucked under. Even a strong swimmer would not have been able to make much headway through the clinging broth, and even if such a swimmer could have reached them, the walls of the vat were smooth and steep.

And there was no such thing as swimming in the village.

Karn looked in amazement at his panting saviour, his mind reeling under the realisation of the terrible thing they had done, as he gasped out his thanks.

Man must not kill Man.

'I didn't do it for you,' Yarl said, between gulps of air.

'That doesn't matter!' Karn said, 'you saved my life and I thank you. But we can't stay here now! We've killed a Man!'

Yarl shrugged. 'We're finished, I know that. But he paid for killing Thylassa. That's all I care about.'

Karn shook him. 'No! We can't let The Supreme Leader avenge him! We've got to get out!'

Yarl turned a dark face to Karn, a slightly darker shape in the darkness.

'Where can we go? There's nowhere to go.'

'No!' Karn said, almost shouting, 'the village is not all the World. I've seen beyond it, and there are other places!'

'Other villages. The Supreme Leader will find us.'

'No, no!' Karn pleaded, 'there are other things!'

And as he said that, an old image came to him.

Something he had seen on his travels.

In the walls of the World.

The outline of a great door.

Seven

Karn's mind was churning in a way that seemed oddly familiar to him; it was like the surface of the fungus broth under a particularly violent stirring. But Yarl seemed less affected by the enormity of what they had just done and motioned to him to hurry as they plunged into the clammy dimness. Finally, they reached Yarl's hut, which had withstood the shaking of the ground distinctly better than Karn's had. Yarl motioned to him to wait and disappeared inside, emerging a short time later with a satchel slung over a shoulder.

'These should last for a while,' he said, revealing the contents to his companion. Karn saw the inevitable strips of dried fungus but also precious algae cakes and a gourd, which presumably held water. Karn had the feeling Yarl had been hoarding food in defiance of the unspoken rule that all Men should help one another.

'I don't want to be with you,' Yarl said to him, 'but we're in this together, now. You're the much-travelled Man. So where do we go?'

'I have an idea,' Karn said, 'but we're wasting time standing here, talking. We must have made enough noise to alert the whole place, so let's go!'

He saw Yarl give a reluctant nod, and together they headed for the "southern" border of their shattered community.

As soon as they were beyond the last hut, Karn saw Yarl stiffen and begin to look around with short, jerking movements. Karn understood what was happening to his erstwhile friend and current companion.

'It's alright,' he said, giving him a pat on the upper arm, 'it's only an area without huts. It's exactly the same land, just without buildings on. Do you understand?'

'Yes, I think so,' Yarl said, in a voice hardly above a whisper, 'but it feels—wrong, somehow. There's too much space; not enough People.'

Karn was suddenly annoyed. 'Well, you'd better get used to it. This is the way it'll be from now on. Or do you want to go back? I mean, go back and be executed by The Supreme Leader?'

Despite the gloom, Karn could see Yarl's face twist with annoyance.

'No, I'll be alright. If someone like you can do it, I'm sure I can!'

Karn said nothing. Although, like most Men, he was given to over-estimating his uniqueness, he was reasonably sure he had been the only inhabitant in living memory to venture out to see what there was to discover in the vast, untrodden World. But occasionally, even he wondered how he had managed to do it.

Slowly, very slowly, the last of the familiar huts was swallowed up in the encircling obscurity. Ahead was the faint yellow glow of the next outpost of human habitation.

Karn became conscious his companion was beginning to shiver, despite the cloying warmth of the endless night.

'You've been there,' Yarl said, 'the things that live there: what are they like? Are they able to speak? What do they eat?' He stopped, suddenly, and turned to Karn. 'Why am I following you? You're mad! There's no escape for us! Those things will kill us as sure as The Supreme Leader!' He turned, facing in the direction from which they had come.

Karn knew this was the moment in which he would either keep or lose the Man who had saved him. He seized the other and forced Yarl to look directly at him.

'Yarl,' he said, in as soft and reassuring a voice as he could manage under the circumstances, 'I'm going to say this for the last time: I've been there; they are People. They're not exactly the same as us—their speech is a little different, but we can understand it. They won't kill us. They won't eat us. Now, if you're a Man, start acting like one! I'm going on, with or without you! Do you understand!'

Yarl cast a few more desperate glances in the direction of his home, but then he looked again at Karn and gave a short nod.

'Yes, I believe you, Karn. I hate you for what you did to Thylassa but I accept you're telling the truth. I'll carry on and I won't behave like a Woman again.'

Karn gave a relieved smile, and the two Men resumed their journey. However, Karn wasn't sure his reassurances had been strictly correct: he was indeed certain the two of them would not end up on the dinner table—but was he sure they wouldn't be killed? His visit had happened in the days when the World had been normal, before it had descended into insanity. Even then, the inhabitants had regarded him with suspicion as a stranger, an outsider, someone who was doing something which—if not exactly forbidden—was definitely highly unusual.

If a few of his own People had already managed to cross to the next settlement, it was more than likely its inhabitants would discover their desire to be hospitable had totally faded.

'Yarl,' he began, 'I don't think we should be trying to get to the next town. I...'

Yarl stared at him. 'What, we just wander around until we run out of food? Is that your idea?'

'No. Look, I think all the Suns are going out, one by one. So even if we are accepted into the next place, eventually the Sun will go out there as well.'

The two Men stood, face to face in the humid twilight. Yarl's face was contorted by something that looked very much like hatred.

'What is wrong with you? That's not possible! You persuaded me to leave my home and now you're going to leave me out here?'

'I told you exactly what I think is true—nothing more, nothing less. I'm not going to leave you because I'd like to be friends again.'

'Friends!' Yarl spat the words and then literally did spit on the ground between them. 'I helped you with Grath because I needed you in order to kill him, not because I wanted to save you. That was just an accident.'

64

There was a silence between them, and then Karn said, 'Alright. You're hurting because you thought you'd found Thylassa and then had her taken from you. And you think she left me not because I hadn't punished her enough but because I'd punished her too much! Is that it?'

'That's it.'

Another silence, then:

'Very well, against my better judgement, we'll go to the next town, Yarl, and together we'll see what they think of us.'

Yarl stared back at his companion and then, surprisingly, a broad grin creased his features as he slapped the other on the shoulder.

'That's settled then. And, Karn…'

'Yes?' Karn said, balling his fists and withdrawing slightly.

But Yarl's grin got bigger, and he said, 'And if they do eat us, you'll never hear the end of it!'

Karn stared at him in puzzled amazement, and then he too grinned.

Together they set off into the clammy-fingered gloom.

***

'We're close now,' Karn said, as they crested a slight slope covered in coarse, stubby vegetation.

Ahead of them was a wide expanse of warm, welcoming light, giving each nearby bush a long tapering shadow, which pointed towards them in shapes disconcertingly resembling teeth.

And further into the light were rectangular shapes, crowding together into what was unmistakeably a settlement.

'Are they huts?' Yarl asked uncertainly, 'they don't look like ours.'

'Each town has its own style of buildings. They are huts— just not ours.'

'There should be only one type of hut,' Yarl muttered, 'it's not right.'

65

'Well, let's hope we get to see the inside of one. Come on.'

They resumed their weary march, sweat dripping from their faces for neither Man was accustomed to so much exercise.

They had not gone far when a shadow among the shadows moved and revealed itself to be a Man.

A Man from their village.

He rushed to Karn and Yarl and flung himself at their feet.

'Are you of the People?' he cried, looking up at them, the whites of his eyes the only distinguishable feature in a dark face.

'We are. What do you want?' said Karn.

The Man shuffled close and grasped his ankles.

'They won't let me in,' was the muffled reply, 'and they killed two of the People. Killed them with sharp sticks! Terrible, horrible—so much blood!'

Karn gave Yarl a sharp look, which Yarl ignored.

'How many of you were there?' he demanded.

'Three. I escaped.'

'Well, there's three of us now,' Yarl said, 'and we two are not used to strangers telling us what we can and can't do.'

'Yarl...' Karn began, but the other helped the Man to his feet. He threw Karn a quick glance.

'Well, are you with us? Grath's not there, so you should be alright.'

Karn decided not to reply, and the three began to walk towards the light.

The light grew stronger as they walked on, as welcome as the return of a loved one's touch. Karn and Yarl smiled broadly as the sweet light gradually grew stronger, revealing each other's features, features almost forgotten, features glistening with sweat.

Yarl was in an expansive mood as the end of their journey approached. He glanced at Karn.

'So that's what you look like! I almost wish it was dark again!'

The newcomer was not smiling, however, and was glancing left and right, with a hunted look on his sharp features.

Then the three stopped abruptly.

66

Bushes not far in front of them parted, and Men emerged.

Men dressed differently, outlandishly, bizarrely. Men with hair parted in foreign ways. Men with patterns inscribed on their foreheads. Men with teeth filed to points.

Men with long sticks in their hands; sticks with ends carved into wickedly sharp points.

'Stay there!' one of them shouted, 'take another step and we will kill you.'

At least that's what Karn heard; Yarl only caught two words out of every three.

But he got the message.

'We want to join you,' Yarl called across the intervening scrub, 'let us in, we mean you no harm.'

The largest man in the opposing group yelled back. 'But we mean you harm! We do not want foreigners invading our town, people like you who killed their own Sun! Do you think you can come here and kill our Sun?'

'We didn't kill...' Yarl began, but stopped—Karn was tugging his arm.

'Can't you see they mean business?' he whispered, 'if we stay here they will kill us. Haven't you noticed they've got weapons and we haven't?'

Yarl whirled to face him. 'So what do we do? You dragged me out here and we're no better off than if we'd stayed in the village!'

Karn stared at him, speaking rapidly and quietly.

'I said moving to another town wouldn't work, but you wouldn't believe me. We have to find another way.'

The other group stood motionless, watching in mystified puzzlement three creatures that looked like Men neither retreating nor advancing but arguing together, apparently oblivious of their danger.

'What are you offering, Karn? I don't see any way out. We can't attack these creatures. We just have to throw ourselves on their mercy and hope they will accept us.'

67

At that, their new companion began to moan, muttering, 'No, no, no mercy, no mercy. They killed my friends. No mercy!'

Karn and Yarl both ignored him and carried on their argument while the defenders of the new settlement stared on in growing impatience, raising and then lowering their spears while they waited for the order to attack; an order which could surely not be delayed for much longer.

'On my travels,' Karn said in increasing desperation, 'I saw something strange. In the Walls of the World I saw a door. A way out!'

'Out of what?' Yarl sneered, 'out of the World? That's just silly baby-talk. There is only the World!'

'Yarl, I remember you talking about the gods. You said, "Where is Paradise"? Yarl, what if Paradise is behind that door? What if the gods are behind that door?'

Yarl cast a quick glance at the defending group to see if they were advancing. They were not, so he returned to Karn. 'And this door, I suppose it's like the door to The Supreme Leader's house, you have a key, do you?'

'No, of course not! But we may be able to find a way to open it. Yarl, think, think Man, we could get back to Paradise!'

'Paradise, Paradise,' Yarl repeated, sharing his gaze between Karn and the still bemused townsfolk, 'you expect me to risk my life on a story for children?'

'I'm offering you a chance!' Karn said, the desperation thickening his voice, 'which is more than those Men are! In a few moments they'll decide to kill us, can't you see that?'

Yarl was staring at the ground, his head twisting back and forth in his anguish. 'Children's stories. Stories for children!'

But the townsfolk had waited long enough. If the strangers weren't advancing on their settlement, they weren't leaving either. One of the group stepped forward, drew an arm back and a needle-sharp missile flashed towards the intruders. It landed between the legs of Karn's new companion, who stared in horror at the savage object which had very nearly emasculated him.

Then without a further word, he ran off, back into the sweltering night, which swallowed him as would a hungry black beast.

Karn tugged at Yarl and the two retreated from the unwelcoming villagers, who broke into a deafening cacophony of hoots and yells of derision as they saw their unwanted visitors depart, stamping on the ground with the spear-butts. Soon the noise had faded into nothingness and Karn and Yarl were back in the dark No-Man's Land between the townships.

Karn knew Yarl was glaring at him and, deciding they were far enough distant from the spear-men, turned to confront him.

'Well?' Yarl demanded, 'that didn't work out too well. First you persuade me to leave the village and then you nearly get me killed! What kind of Leader are you?'

'The only one you've got. You've obviously forgotten I warned you we wouldn't be welcome. Now we try my real plan.'

Yarl sat wearily on a tussock of grass-like plants: none of them was used to this much movement at their age. After a moment, Karn joined him. Together they stared into the gloom.

Yarl spoke first.

'You know you're mad, don't you, Karn? Thylassa never liked you, you must have known that. Thinking you were something special, just because you wandered off when you were young, claiming to have seen this, claiming to have seen that.'

'I saw a door. In fact, several doors.'

'You saw something that *looked* like a door, that's all.'

Karn was seized with a great weariness. What was the point? They weren't going to get out of this; the grim No-Man's Land would hold their bones.

But he tried again.

'Look, Yarl, you've always been open to new ideas, let's just try this one.'

Silence.

'You wanted to know where Paradise is. You wondered about the gods, about where they were.'

Silence.

69

'I think you were trying to say you didn't believe there are any gods. But that can't be true.'

Yarl lifted his head.

'You're right, that was what I was trying to say but I didn't know if you would report me. But why do you think there are gods?'

Karn's words ran into themselves in his excitement.

'Think, Man. Did you build the World, did you climb up and put the Sun together? No Man could have done that! Where does fungus come from? There's none in the land between the towns. Call them gods, call them anything you like, but someone, *something*, was here before us and put us here and gave us the means to live. We didn't create ourselves. There used to be devices which stirred the fungus. In all my travels I never met anyone who said they had made one. The walls of the algae tanks that we can see through. What is it? Who made it?'

'And you think they're behind your—*doors*?'

'I do. There must be something beyond this World, it doesn't explain itself. And if we were put here, then there would be a way in and out of this World. And there, we may find the beings who are behind it all, who put us here.'

'And who put *them* there?'

'That doesn't matter; one problem at a time.'

Silence.

Then Karn said, 'You have a choice, Yarl. I am going to find one of those doors, I know they repeat at regular intervals along the Walls of the World. I don't need you but I'd like to have you with me.'

'Why?'

Karn stood and forced Yarl to his feet.

'Because you are my last link with a life that's gone forever. Because Thylassa was something special to the pair of us. Because you used to be my friend.'

Yarl looked up into black nothingness, then back to Karn.

'Alright. I realise there's no hope for us in any of the towns. You're almost certainly deranged but if there's even the smallest chance you've got a way out, I'll take it.'

The two Men shook hands and resumed their walk, Karn leading, heading for the Walls of the World.

Eight

Even though he had not seen one for a long time, Karn remembered that the door-shapes repeated at regular intervals along the Wall. The distance between them was not great, although he smiled grimly when he recalled he had been a significantly younger Man when he had first discovered them. They might repeat on the other Wall, of course, but he had never crossed the great plane of World to find out.

Yarl, he knew, was a reluctant companion and he did not know for how much longer he would be able to rely on him to follow his plans. He would need some kind of success before too long.

They struck out in a right-angled direction to their original route. The settlements of the World were all strung out like beads on a string along the central axis of the great cylinder which comprised all they knew. It was not a complete cylinder, of course; its lower region was cut off by the horizontal surface on which all the dramas of the People were played out.

And was it, in fact, a tremendous torus? Karn had never considered that possibility since it had been mentioned by the old Man many Wake-periods ago: he certainly had no intention of attempting a vast circumnavigation to find out if it were true.

In the moist semi-darkness, everything looked the same: a monotonous plain, dotted with clumps of insipid vegetation. Ahead was only genuine darkness, as the feeble light from the still illuminated townships was absorbed by the thickness of the air; sucked into invisibility and then destroyed.

'How much further?' Yarl finally said. Karn could tell from his ragged breathing he was finding the trek hard-going.

'Not far,' Karn lied. In actuality, he had no idea how far the first door-shape would be. He could estimate the distance to the Wall itself but not to how far they were from their target. They might strike lucky, or reach the Wall exactly midway between the shapes.

Yarl returned to silence and then tripped over a tussock. Karn tried to help him up but stopped as the other struggled up, ignoring his proffered hand. Karn could almost feel the anger radiating off Yarl. He wondered if he should offer some words of encouragement, but decided against it.

They walked on. As they did so, the blackness ahead of them lightened to grey, while the greyness behind them darkened to black.

Karn wished he could think of something to say, some words which would lighten their mood, remove the choking fingers of despair from their throats. But he could not.

It was then he saw it.

Before them a great curved shape slowly materialised from the obscurity, a tremendous surface that slowly bent over until it became the sky and, continuing with its curvature, continued downwards, transmuting back into a Wall, but this time on the other side of the central plain.

'What did I tell you! Karn cried, standing in front of his weary companion.

'You've found the Wall,' Yarl said, 'any fool could do that. Where's your door?'

'We're not close enough yet. We'll see it soon.'

And so it proved. It was difficult to see much on the colossal grey surface due to their distance from the nearest illuminated village and for a while Karn was worried he might be imagining things. But before much longer they were standing within touching distance of the Wall and, even in the pitiful illumination, both Men could see lines in a great buttress that rose straight from the ground, ignoring the curvature until it disappeared into the Wall itself.

'What did I tell you?'

Yarl said nothing but, pushing past his companion, walked up to the buttress. He ran an index finger along the nearest line of the door-shape.

'I can't feel any depth,' he finally said, 'how do we get in?'

Karn felt a cold shock run up his spine. He had been so fixated on finding the door that he had never considered it might not be possible to open it. He joined Yarl in front of it.

'We—ah—we...'

Yarl turned to him.

'You don't know, do you?'

Karn tried to force his fingernails into what should have been the gap between the door and the buttress but his desperate fingers could find no depth into which they could insert themselves.

'Here, let me try.' Yarl reached into his satchel and drew out a small knife made from carefully shaped dry fungus. He put the point against the line of the door and pushed. The knife did not move. He flexed the blade back and forth as he continued to push.

The tip broke off and flew off into the gloom.

Karn slumped to the ground, defeated. His plan had come to nothing.

He realised now that it had been hopeless. Why had he just assumed they could walk up to a door and just open it? He couldn't even do that with The Supreme Leader's dwelling.

Then he realised Yarl was standing over him.

'Get up, you fool. Now.'

For a moment the two Men just looked at each other, then Yarl said, 'This is the end. I am going to lie down and allow my bones to sink into the ground. You gave me false hope, which I was almost as big a fool as you to believe. But one more thing...'

'And that is?'

Yarl was still holding the remains of his knife.

'To do what Thylassa wanted to do. Kill you.'

And with that, he launched himself at the other, bringing the knife up in a deadly arc destined to land under Karn's ribcage.

Karn slapped the arm away at the last moment and landed a blow on Yarl's chin which sent him tumbling backwards. He jumped on Yarl and the two Men rolled back and forth on the sparse vegetation, Yarl trying to bring the knife up, Karn trying to pin the weapon arm to the ground.

Karn knew he had to tire his opponent while avoiding the knife; Yarl was the weaker of the two and eventually Karn's greater strength would prevail.

The fight continued for some time, both Men gasping and grunting in their unaccustomed exertions. Karn felt Yarl's arm lose its resistance and knew he had won. He pulled the knife from his hand and tossed it a short distance away.

It might come in useful later.

He pinioned both Yarl's arms to his sides, and looked down on his opponent, his friend.

'Stop this!' he commanded, 'I don't want to kill you, Yarl. We are Men and Men do not harm Men! Aren't the gods angry enough?'

Yarl turned his head so he was no longer looking at Karn.

'There are no gods,' he whispered, 'there is just nothing. Nothing.'

Deciding the fight had gone out of Yarl, Karn rose unsteadily, his breath coming in great ragged gulps. Even so, he found the knife and tucked it away carefully in the folds of his loincloth.

'I'll make you a deal,' he said finally, 'we'll find one more door and if we can't open that, we'll part forever. You will find somewhere to lie down and die and I will find another place to lie down and there I'll die. Then the gods will come for me, but not you.'

'Very funny,' came a weak voice from the encircling greyness.

Yarl staggered to his feet.

'Can I have my knife back?'

'What do you think?'

Yarl looked around, looking at nothing in particular for there was nothing to see.

'One more door?' he said.

75

'One more. Then we go our separate ways and lie down and die.'

'With a bargain like that...' He paused, and for a moment the old Yarl with his sense of humour was back, 'how can I turn it down?'

And so there they stood, transfixed by the enormity of the structure that only superhuman, perhaps supernatural, beings could possibly have fashioned. Where were those beings now, why had they forsaken the People?

Yarl turned away.

'Let's go.'

***

Karn knew the end was near now. There was little of the water and food that Yarl's foresight had provided. Soon it would be time to rest, to lay down and die.

Yarl's strength had almost failed and he was now trudging along some distance behind Karn.

'I'm going to stop soon,' came his weak voice, almost like a thin breeze rustling the tussocks.

Karn did not reply. He had reached the same decision.

For some reason, he whispered, 'Just a little further.'

At that moment he tripped and collapsed, face down.

Don't get up, just lie down. This is it, he thought.

Yet he did return to his feet.

And then, not too far away, was the next door.

And it was open.

'Look, Yarl!' he cried, 'the door!'

Yarl joined him.

'Why is it open? What's different?'

Karn looked around, seeing he had fallen because the land was torn and buckled as if it had been beaten repeatedly with a giant's hammer.

'The land must have shaken here at some time, like it did back in the village. And that burst the door open.'

Slowly they approached the open door until they were standing directly in front of it.

They stood like nervous children, staring at the great open space the door revealed. The door was tremendous, reaching high above them. It had been torn from its upper hinge and hung drunkenly, threatening to tear itself free at any moment. Behind it a great black space leered at them, like an open mouth.

Unconsciously, the two Men held hands, overwhelmed by the towering scale of what they were seeing, shaken by the manifest work of the gods.

Eventually, Karn said, 'Well, this is what we came for. We must go in.'

But Yarl held back.

'Karn, we don't know what's in there. Maybe we're not meant to see these kinds of things. It means we'd be leaving the World! Think of it, Karn—leaving the World! Men can't do that!'

Karn pointed at the darkness beyond the door and then the darkness behind them.

'Yarl, the World is leaving us. It's dying. If the gods are there and they made us, then they should want to help us. Perhaps we can persuade them to make a new World, a better World. Well?'

Yarl did not reply. His features were twitching and flexing, showing the strain he was under.

'I'm going,' Karn said, and then he grinned 'I have a few things to say to the gods.'

Yarl stared at him and then also smiled. He fell in behind Karn and together they walked up to the massive entrance. The nearer they approached the more awesome and forbidding the aperture seemed. Karn began to wonder if his idea had been such a good one after all. By his side, Yarl muttered, 'Karn, I don't like this. I don't like it at all.'

They stood at the very lip of the entrance; the door itself hung above them at such an angle that they were now underneath it. Beyond the threshold, darkness loomed, an impenetrable cloak of nothingness, refusing to reveal even the smallest detail of what was hidden therein.

Karn glanced at Yarl, who stood at his side. Yarl's eyes were wide open and his breath was coming in sharp staccato bursts. He turned an imploring gaze upon his travelling companion.

'Karn, I...' he began.

Karn knew if they did not go in now, they never would and, as prophesied, their bones would whiten among the sparse grass-like vegetation of the great plain of the World.

And so, drawing upon reserves of resolution that he had not known he possessed, he said, 'Let's go.'

They entered, leaving the World behind them, leaving behind the vats of fungus, the broken algae tanks, the huts, the rituals, the ceremonies, the townsfolk—both those friendly and those hostile.

It was a transition as sharp as birth—or perhaps death.

Inside, the first thing they noticed was the cold. Even a short distance inside, the air was completely different: it was, to their mostly naked skins, unpleasantly cold, and cold was something the People were not familiar with. And that cold air held new sensations other than temperature. It had a tang to it which assaulted their nostrils. They did not recognise the odour, although other humans would have termed it *metallic*. The People had seen metal, of course, as the devices which once had kept the fungal broth well mixed had contained metal. But they had no recourse to metal, they did not know from whence it had come, knew no way of working it, and so had no use for it. Plant material and dried fungus had been their only useful materials from which to forge their tools and dwellings. This weird smell was metal—but they did not know it.

Another odour which they did not recognise was more difficult to categorise. Indeed, in most of the languages of humanity there was no one word which specified it exactly. The best explanation that could be attempted, is some population other than the People would have said the air smelled *old*. And this air smelled very old indeed.

On the other side of the door, the feeble light from the World was totally extinguished. It was as if a great cloak of ancient blackness had been thrown over them, even though they were still only a short distance from the entrance.

'Karn,' Yarl said in a tremulous whisper, as if he was afraid something might be listening, 'we can't go on. We can't move if we can't see. Let's go back, go back and die.'

But Karn had seen something. He lifted an unseen arm and pointed with an unseen finger.

'Look. There is a light.'

Yarl was not sure which direction was being indicated but by slowly turning his head he eventually saw what his companion had seen: in one direction there was a very faint glow, a light of the same colour as living algae; what others would have termed "green."

'That's where we're going,' Karn said in a voice so firm he surprised himself, 'if there are gods here, that's where we'll find them.'

Yarl gave an unseen nod and said, 'At least we'll be able to see something before we die.'

They set off towards the mysterious light. Many times they walked into obstacles strewn randomly over the ground—or rather *floor*, because the surface was too regular and smooth to be simply soil.

Slowly, slowly their surroundings began to take shape around them as the greenish light continued to intensify. They discovered they were in a tremendous corridor with a ceiling so high above them that its light hardly reached them. As before in their expedition, they had no word for what they were seeing because there were no structures of even remotely comparable dimensions in their experience. The only enclosed spaces they knew of were the interiors of their huts. As the light steadily grew stronger, they saw Cyclopean walls on either side, strengthened with great buttresses like the ribs of an enormous cetacean. But many and often, there were tremendous rents in those walls, gaping wounds in the metal beyond which rugged, grey rock could be glimpsed. And all over the floor were torn and twisted strips and shards of metal; metal that had been warped and rent, and then flung around as if they were thistledown.

They walked on; their eyes staring, their gaze stupefied. They saw without comprehending; without a framework of reference they were almost as lost as a new-born.

'Karn,' Yarl finally said, 'this is all wrong. It doesn't look like the World. This can't be where the gods live; if they're anything like us.'

Karn had already reached that conclusion. Also he was bone-tired.

'I need to sit,' he said and walked to where the wall had been particularly badly ripped and where a great bulge of stone protruded. He was exhausted, hungry, desperate for water and—frightened. He wasn't sure what he had expected to find but this empty metal mausoleum was most certainly not it. In his hopeful fantasies, he had seen friendly Man-like beings welcoming him, succouring him, solving all his problems.

Not terrible corridors, echoing to the faint sounds of his and Yarl's footsteps.

He leaned forward and put his head in his hands, on the verge of collapse.

It was then something cold hit on his back.

He whirled around to face this new peril but there was no visible threat.

Then realisation hit him. He touched the spot on his back where the cold thing had hit and then looked at his fingers. They glistened in the green light.

Water.

He called to Yarl and together they saw a faint sheen moving on the rock surface. Gingerly, Karn touched it and slowly transferred the liquid to his lips.

It was water. It had an unpleasant, bitter taste but it was water. Life-giving water.

'Just as well,' Yarl grunted, 'I didn't want to tell you, but I finished the last of what was in the gourd a while back.'

'I knew it was almost gone. But this means we can go on.'

'Go on where? I don't see any gods, or anything to eat for that matter.'

'The light, Yarl, the light. People don't make light: only Suns do. There is a Sun in here and where there's a Sun there'll be People. Or gods.'

'Let's hope they're friendlier than the last People we met,' was the terse reply but soon they were moving again, drawn to the source of the green light like strange moths to a strange flame. Now they could see the light was coming from regularly spaced strips in the roof, looking like miniature Suns, but with a different quality of light. Many were black and dead, but the further they went the fewer there were of the dead ones.

And then they discovered another wonder. Where the walls were badly torn, sometimes the fallen rubble and had been worn down into a fine scree. And in some, there were unusual objects; they had a thin, basically cylindrical, base, on the top of which were flat appendages, dark red-black in colour.

'Plants,' Karn said, 'by the gods, plants. Things are growing here!'

Yarl had more practical things on his mind. He tore off a leaf from the nearest plant and, very slowly, nibbled the tip. Then he took a bigger bite. And then he ate the whole leaf.

'Careful,' Karn warned, 'we don't know what it could do to us.'

But Yarl grinned.

'I tell you something: it tastes almost as good as algae. If it's going to kill us, then at least we'll die smiling.'

Karn needed no further encouragement and together they reduced the strange plant to shreds. They even tried the root but that was far too bitter. After waiting a short while to see if their meal would try to make a bolt for freedom, Karn was moved to further speculate on their surroundings. He pointed at a softly shining rectangle directly above them.

'That must be a Sun but why is it so small? And why so many? And why such a strange colour, not like the Suns of the World at all?'

Yarl was resting his legs by lying flat on his back. His eyes were closed.

'Am I a god now, that I can answer all these questions? We've got food and water so it'll take us a bit longer to die than I was expecting. After you die, I'm sure they'll give you all the answers you need.'

Having failed to stir Yarl's curiosity, Karn lapsed into silence. He was becoming accustomed to the temperature so he too stretched out on the floor.

Yarl was already asleep and it was not long before Karn joined him.

Nine

He did not know how long he had been lost in sleep, and he woke up gradually, without fear, feeling strangely rested. For a short time, he stared uncomprehendingly at his new surroundings, but he soon remembered.

He stood and looked around. In the direction they had come, the corridor was illuminated only in patches by the small Suns, but where they had not yet trodden, the Suns were more plentiful and the way was brightly lit.

He gently nudged Yarl with a foot and, after a few moments of muttering, his companion's eyes opened, and he rolled into a crouching position.

'Oh, so it wasn't a dream then? We really are here?'

'We are. And we're going on.'

'Still hoping to meet the gods, then?'

'No, not hoping—expecting. No one from the People built this. Look, they've provided food for us and water. That can't be a coincidence. They must expect us to carry on until we finally meet them.'

Yarl was fully upright.

'If you say so. Let's get on with it.'

They walked on. The dead Suns became fewer and fewer until all the Suns were lit, and the corridor had become so bright it was easy to avoid the obstacles on the floor. Those, however, did not seem to be getting fewer and there were still twisted hunks of metal to walk around along with huge holes in the walls with scree at their feet in which plants were growing. Most were the food plants they had already encountered but occasionally there was a new, taller plant. They tried it, but it was distinctly more bitter than the familiar one.

The corridor appeared to be perfectly straight and headed in a direction perpendicular to the Wall of the World. So wherever they were going, they were leaving the World farther and farther behind.

And then they came across something new.

In one side of the corridor was a deep recess, and there was a peculiar object in it. They approached.

As was customary for them now, they had no words to describe it. It was like a very large box, so big that ten men could have sat inside it. And in the side facing them, and along its side, were panels which revealed the box's interior. At first, Karn thought the panels were empty but as he walked closer, he could see they were not.

He stood in front of the large panel in the corridor side of the box and said, 'Yarl, look at this.' He tapped the centre of the panel and there was a faint clicking noise.

'It's the same material that we have in the algae tanks. It is there, but you can see through it!' Excitement burst into his features. 'Yarl—this is the proof! We didn't make those algae tanks with this strange material in them. So this thing—whatever it is—has to be the work of the gods!'

Yarl walked alongside, frowning.

'Well, when you meet them ask them what it's for. I can't see any use. What are these, for instance?'

He was resting a foot on a metal plate that was under the main box. Each plate joined onto another, and that to another, forming a continuous ribbon of metal. At the front, the ribbon curved downwards and then continued under the box in the opposite direction so that the entire thing was a single band of conjoined plates.

Karn was annoyed.

'You're not showing the right attitude, my friend. Stop asking me to explain these things; they're the gods—not me!'

Yarl was unabashed.

'You seem too easily impressed. A metal box with parts you can see through. A box that does nothing.'

'Nothing to us, perhaps. But once again, if you would only open your eyes, you'd realise it isn't anything the People could have made!'

Yarl was at the far end of the object now. He pointed at something.

'Well, I'll be interested to know what this does.'

Karn joined him. A great finger of rock had fallen and had pierced the top of the box. Some force had shattered the transparent substance in the nearby panels into the shapes of savage teeth.

'It seems the gods don't take much care of their creations,' Yarl remarked dryly, 'perhaps that's why they haven't taken too much care of the People.'

Karn was furious, but no words of refutation came to his lips.

They spent a little while longer with the object, but no idea of its function came to Karn. Yarl had noticed something else, however.

'Are you sure we're going in the right direction?' he asked, pointing upwards.

Karn followed his pointing finger and saw that directly above the object the roof was pierced by a huge shaft, rising directly upwards. It rose so high it seemed to be about to narrow into a single point, but, once again, a fall of rock had closed it.

He had no suggestion to offer, and so they resumed their journey in silence, as Karn struggled to think of explanations for what they were seeing and failed to do so.

The trek continued. They drank the water that dribbled down the rock face; they ate the plants (especially a new fleshy one that was tastier than the original); they slept; they woke; they walked on.

They found another of the huge boxes, in roughly the same condition as the first and, as before, with a ruined shaft above it.

A nagging doubt began to nibble at the foundation of Karn's certainty. It felt like they had been walking forever, and were doomed to walk on, forever.

The walk had been silent for a long time. There was nothing new to say, nothing to do but put one foot in front of the other.

And then it ended.

Ahead of them, completely closing the corridor, was a shining wall of metal; a brilliant bluish metal that appeared to have cut into their path, an intruding metallic mass that had sealed off the remainder of the corridor.

'What is this?' Yarl whispered.

They walked up to it and stared. It was a completely different substance to what they had seen earlier. It was so shining and lustrous that for the first time in their lives they saw their reflections. So novel was the sight that it took them a while to realise they were looking at themselves.

'Well,' Yarl said, 'this is the end. We can't go any further. This really is the end. Just a wall. No gods. No salvation. Nothing.'

'It must be here for a reason,' Karn said in growing desperation. He was walking back and forth in front of the gleaming cliff. 'This can't be all there is. This can't be the end.'

Then he noticed something. At a height just beyond his reach was a rectangular protrusion and, on it in bas-relief, was the shape of a human hand.

He jumped up, trying to reach it but could not.

He whirled round to face Yarl.

'Help me up,' he said in a voice dry and crackling with tension. 'I must reach it.'

Yarl nodded silently. His face was grave as he, too, had reached the conclusion they had reached a turning point. He bent over and Karn struggled onto his back. Straightening, he saw the mysterious panel slightly below him. The embossed shape seemed to call him, and he placed a trembling hand upon it.

Instantly there was the screeching noise of metal moving, metal moving for the first occasion in a very long time, if ever. In his shock, Yarl tried to stand, sending Karn tumbling to the floor.

Before them, a large, softly illuminated room had opened up, its sides the same lustrous metal as the outside.

It was just a room. And it was empty.

'I'm going in,' Karn whispered.

Yarl clutched his arm.

'You can't—there's no way out. We'll be trapped!'

'I trust the gods!' was the snapped reply. And with that, he stepped into the room.

Yarl remained outside, twisting his head from side to side in an agony of indecision.

Then he, too, stepped into the room.

Instantly, his fears were realised as the door closed behind them, leaving them alone in a featureless metal box.

In growing horror, Karn rushed around the room, pressing random areas of the walls.

Nothing happened.

Eventually, despair took him and he joined Yarl, who was sitting helplessly in the centre of the floor. He turned a tormented face to his companion.

'I'm sorry, Yarl. I'm sorry I've led you to this.'

But Yarl just shrugged. 'It doesn't matter. I never expected to live. I hope we suffocate, though; starvation is not a good death.'

But then there was a whirring noise and the wall opposite the entrance slid back, revealing a much larger room behind it.

And standing in the gap was a woman, a woman with short black hair and—completely naked.

But one such as neither of them had ever imagined.

She was taller than either of them, and possessed of much more voluptuous flesh than they had ever dreamed.

Yarl was the first to respond. Deprived of female company for so long, he jumped to his feet and instinctively rushed at her, hands open wide to clutch the female delights so openly displayed.

The strange woman picked him up like a child and threw him against a wall.

MAYA AND THE DARKNESS

One

There was no period of nothingness for Maya, no conception of unconsciousness, no wandering in dark labyrinths of un-being.

She had lain in the container and had felt a puff of gas on her face, and then she had opened her eyes to find herself in a different part of the room. There had been no detectable delay between the faint puff of gas and her current state. As her eyelids parted, she saw two transparent curved surfaces moving up and away from her as if she had been ensconced in a kind of plastic flower bud, whose petals had begun to open to greet the sun.

However, there was one difference: when she had lain upon the couch she had been wearing her regulation fatigues; now, she was naked. As she peered down her body to check whether her toes were functional, she noticed there was the sheen of a thin coating of some liquid on her torso, but it was rapidly evaporating.

Having wriggled her toes, drawn her knees up and down and placed thumbs to fingers in rapid succession, she decided there was no reason to lie there any longer, and so she swung her feet off the couch which had been supporting her, and slowly raised herself to her full height. She then raised her arms up as high as she could and stood, momentarily, on tip-toe.

Then she smiled.

She felt fine.

Looking around, she recognised she was in the part of the recording room which had been designated as the re-establishment suite, (although it had also borne a more informal, more hopeful nickname among some of the scientists).

She walked around, finding five more couches like her own, all with their transparent covers wide open. Two were unoccupied but three had figures upon them. She stood looking down on them, one by one. The faces were both familiar and dear to her. She saw the motionless features of McQuade, Hilbert and Duquesne. Lovingly, she touched each of those faces, stroked their cheeks; one, McQuade, she kissed. But there was no response. The eyelids did not flutter; the fingers did not twitch; hands did not reach up to her to joyfully clasp her own.

'My friends,' she whispered, 'to have done so much, to be so brave. And yet you didn't make it.'

She felt the need to weep but could not. It had always been known success could not be guaranteed, but to see failure here in the motionless forms of her friends and colleagues was heart-wrenching. But then she remembered two containers had been empty. One should have held Takemoto, but the atoms which had comprised him were scattered across the long centuries. But the other unoccupied couch; that meant—She was not the only survivor!

She walked around the entirety of the re-establishment suite, but there was no-one else there. Then she noticed the door to the main part of the recording room was ajar.

He must be in there!

And so he was. As naked as she, DeGroot was hunched over a monitor and punching buttons with what seemed to Maya to be a great deal of annoyance. He was unaware of her approach and so gave a start when she gently touched his shoulder.

He turned and produced an expansive smile on seeing her.

'Maya! You made it! Thank God—I thought I was the only one!' Then he took in her nakedness and said, rather hurriedly, 'Don't you think it's time you put some clothes on?'

Unconsciously, she folded her arms to cover her breasts and said, 'Professor, we've only just arrived. Most of the machines haven't come back online yet. They'll weave us some suitable clothing soon enough.'

DeGroot nodded and turned back to the monitor. Maya definitely preferred that view to the full-frontal one she had just endured, even though she was now presented with a wrinkled back, dotted with black senile moles.

'That's just it,' DeGroot was muttering to the keyboard, 'quite a few of the machines aren't coming back on. It looks like we over-estimated their resilience." He suddenly looked up at the ceiling, although without seeing it. 'Unless...'

Maya finished the thought for him.

'Unless we've woken at a different time to what we were expecting.' She paused. 'Could some external stimulus have woken us?'

He (unfortunately) turned to face her again.

'Yes, that could well be right. But waking up early wouldn't explain the failure of the equipment. Check the monitoring bank, I'm pretty sure that's working.'

Maya instantly fell into her established mode of obeying the professor without demurring. After all, he had been the main driving force behind the whole project.

Experienced fingers flew over the controls and she was gratified to see the machine respond—though remarkably slowly. However, both the external and internal cameras were not functioning and so she was forced manually to interpret the numerals which appeared on a display.

'Professor,' she said slowly, hesitantly, 'it looks like two animals have gotten into the holding room.'

He crossed to her.

'Yes, some variety of mammalian creatures, by the look of it. That's good. Shows there's still life out there. Go get them, Maya.'

'What if they're aggressive?'

'You'll be able to handle them now. Collect them, Maya, we need to see what life is out there. I think we'll be pleasantly surprised.'

Somewhat reluctantly, she walked to the interior door of the holding room and pressed the button that controlled it.

There was the grinding noise of metal being forced into reluctant motion, and then she was standing at the entrance, looking in.

Her eyes failed for a moment to interpret what she was seeing. There were two creatures huddled in the middle of the floor in what looked like abject misery. Their heads turned as they heard the door open and after a moment in which all three stared at each other in stupefaction, the smaller of the creatures leapt to its feet and launched itself at her. Instinctively, she caught it in mid-flight and tossed it against the nearest wall.

It bounced back to the floor but did not seem to be injured as it quickly scrambled back to its companion in the centre of the room.

She continued to stare at the things, but slowly she realised what she was seeing, especially after they rose to their feet.

She could now see they were some type of human, although a distinctly unimpressive type.

Their skins were snow-white with prominent blue veins clearly visible underneath. Apart from a thin reddish fuzz on their scalps, they were completely hairless, and with the barest minimum of musculature. Their legs were so thin it was hard to see how they could stand, and yet both boasted large pot-bellies. Apart from badly-woven loincloths, they were as naked as she.

The overall impression was of drawings of matchstick men made by a not particularly talented child.

'What in God's name...' she whispered to herself as she approached them to get a more detailed view. But on her approach, both scuttled into a corner where they sat hugging each other and covering their eyes, as if they found the light too bright. Maya was immediately reminded of frightened children but, Good God, no children ever looked like this pair! She immediately repented of her act of violence against the smaller one. Obviously, it had acted instinctively on seeing a naked female. *I should have dealt with it more gently*, she reproached herself.

She held out a hand and said, 'Look, I'm sorry to have hurt you. I was taken by surprise but I won't hurt you again, I promise.' They lifted their heads to stare silently at her with large, wary eyes. She knelt before them and looked deeply into those eyes but, no, they were not albinos.

'Can you talk?' she said, while pointing to her mouth.

The larger one appeared to understand and made some liquid sounds, pointing to his own mouth as he had seen her do. She cocked her head whilst listening and made motions that the creature should speak again. It did, but she shook her head and rose to her feet .

If it was a language, it was not one with which she was familiar.

And she was now familiar with a great many languages.

She became aware DeGroot was standing just behind her.

'What are these?' he said, 'some kind of ape?'

She turned. 'No, they're a type of human, I'm reasonably sure.'

'Human? So what's happened to them?'

She turned back to look at the pair, and suddenly her mind filled with pity for them.

'It's obvious they come from a very impoverished environment. Their physical appearance is reminiscent of kwashiorkor.'

'Oedematous malnutrition,' DeGroot agreed, 'remind me of the cause.'

'It's straightforward; they have not been receiving enough protein and key vitamins. Yet they are not children, despite their stature. The one reacted sexually when he saw me, which suggests they have managed to reach breeding age—though God knows how. They also seem bothered by the light, which implies their natural environment is less-illuminated than standard.'

'So what are we going to do with them? They're of no use to us.'

She turned back to him, her mouth open in dismayed anger.

'Do with them? Professor, they're people; people who've obviously had a very tough time in whatever place they come from.'

'Not our problem, we have enough real issues to deal with. Return them to their natural environment and let them get on with their lives. And we'll get on with ours.'

She half-turned to begin the eviction, and then she stopped. For the first time in her relationship with DeGroot, she did not want to instantly obey.

In fact, she didn't want to obey at all.

'No, I won't do that.'

'I beg your pardon?'

She tried to smile, to soften her insubordination.

'Professor, let them be my special responsibility. I'll do everything else you ask me but,' and the smile vanished, 'I won't kick them out. Professor, they're *people!*'

He stared back at her and for a few seconds it looked as if he was going to react badly. But then: 'Alright, on your own head be it. You'll have to do all the work the ones who didn't come through would have been doing, and look after these wretches as well. You're sure that's what you want to do?'

'Yes.'

He shrugged.

'So be it.'

As he began to turn to return to his console, she said, 'Professor, is the biogenerator online? Because if it is, I'm going to give them a meal. By the look of them, the best meal they've ever had.'

'It is. Oh, and Maya...'

'Yes?'

'The biogenerator's not the only thing online. Get some clothes on.'

***

Maya handed her two charges the bowls of soup and watched them stare down at it in bewilderment. They looked at the spoons she had supplied and then back at her with what looked very much like pleading in their eyes. She took one of the spoons, dipped it in the soup, brought it close to her lips, then returned its contents to the bowl, pointed at the bowl and then at the two watching individuals. The larger individual finally understood and, hesitantly, brought the spoonful to his lips. She nodded and smiled and made "Go On!" gestures. To her relief, he swallowed some, and she was rewarded by a big smile—which unfortunately revealed yellow, misshapen teeth. The other, seeing his companion had suffered no ill-effects, began attacking his own meal with sudden energy,

Maya sat back on her heels watching them enjoy what must be new sensations. She had no concerns being this close to them as she was now clad in a new one-piece outfit. It is true that her curves were in no way disguised, but she had already proved she was much stronger than either of them; or, as she knew with a calm certainty, the two of them together.

Now she had time to study them more closely she was sure that they were mature males of their species: she was still not quite sure whether or not they qualified as *homo sapiens*. They had a language, that was also certain, because they had been chattering to each other when she had come into their quarters. She had moved them to a new secure room (by the simple expedient of picking them up and carrying them) which had washing and lavatorial facilities. They had used the latter but were terrified of the shower and had retreated to the far corner when she had demonstrated it. That was not particularly important; they had no strong smell, except for a strange mushroom-like odour.

They finished the soup, wiping up the last remnants with protein-rich rolls. The look of hair-trigger alertness had faded; they had evidently decided they would not be harmed. She smiled and retrieved the bowls, leaving them to their own devices behind an impenetrable door.

DeGroot was still studying the various displays on his console; mercifully, he was now dressed in a one-piece suit, similar to hers, and which found only a few bony angles to display.

'How are you getting on with the chimps?' he said, not looking over his shoulder as she approached.

94

'They are *not* chimps,' she said with some heat, 'I think they're a subspecies of us, but one that has been trapped in a very impoverished environment for a very long time. If I'm right, they must be hovering on the edge of extinction.'

'Very poetic. I don't care what you do with them as long as your real work doesn't suffer. What about communication—have you activated your language module?'

Maya cursed inwardly; she had completely forgotten about that.

Two

Maya forgot about her new guests for a while; she had fed them and any further study of them could wait. Although her thoughts kept returning to the odd pair, she soon had other duties to distract her.

It was very strange standing there in the recording room, looking down on the couch where she had lain a long time ago. *(How long?)*

She moved from corner to corner, looking at the various items of furniture and equipment, thinking to herself *I sat there* or *I looked at that monitor when it was showing the Destroyer.* The room was much as she remembered it for, from her point of view, it had only been a few hours since she lain down on the couch and watched the transparent covers fold themselves lovingly over her.

And then instantly after they had closed above her, she had realised she had passed through the transition. She had seen the covers close, and then in a flash they were wide open again, and she had descended from the couch. There had been no sense of passage, no journey, no periods of peaceful or troubled sleep.

Nothing.

And the room was just as it had been when she had lain down. She was in a different part of it, but that was all. Nothing had changed position or fallen over. There were no holes or tears in the fabric of the great cube in which the recording room sat. There was a very thin layer of grey dust over the surfaces, dust which made a black streak on a finger if touched, but very little. The air in the room had been withdrawn during their wait and only replaced as they awoke. Air was necessary for the efficient operation of some of the equipment, but it was air that was antiseptically clean, free of dust motes, free of bacteria, free of viruses.

Nothing could be allowed to grow or mutate during the waiting time before the world settled into a calm, safe orbit.

Three hundred years, that should do it. But that was long enough for something dangerous to develop and grow, and wait for them to awake.

But that had been foreseen and accounted for. The recording room was as sterile as the interior of an autoclave. Or, it had been until the arrival of those strange humanoid creatures.

Sometime after she had finished her circumnavigation of the recording room, she sat like an awed acolyte before DeGroot, admiring his austere profile as he sat before the master computer.

'Do you think there's any hope for our colleagues, professor?' she asked, 'is it possible there's simply a delay in the activation?'

DeGroot turned to her, half his face illuminated by the soft light from the computer.

'I doubt it, Maya. If the systems are working as planned, then we should all have been conscious at the same time. I'm afraid it's just you and me. Does that worry you?— after all we're not exactly cut out to be a new Adam and Eve.'

She gave a thin smile.

'No, of course not. We could never re-enact that old tale. But be straight with me, please. What do you expect to find when we emerge onto the surface?'

He turned the chair so he was fully facing her.

'Destruction of course. Terrible, terrible damage. The course of many rivers will have altered, in places seas will cover what was once dry land. But elsewhere new land will have arisen, new mountains will take the place of the old. You see this Earth of ours is very resilient. Ever since the Gaia Hypothesis was first formulated, we've realised just how tough the old girl really is. Look at what she's been through before: the Great Dying at the end of the Permian, the Cretaceous-Palaeogene event. It has taken centuries to recover but she always did; always will.'

'But people, fragile creatures of flesh and blood, will there be any?'

'I'm sure there will be. Although the Venusian cloud cities were destroyed, humanity would not have lost its spacefaring abilities. They would have hidden out in remote places until Jupiter settled into its new orbit, closer to the sun than Mercury—if that's still around. And slowly they will have repopulated the land.'

'But what will that land be like, now we're so far out, so distant from the sun?'

He smiled gently, as if he were dealing with a student who had made a common and elementary error.

'Maya, although we're now as distant from the sun as Mars was, we won't be a new Mars, a desolate, radiation-blasted desert. We still have our thick atmosphere, our magnetic shield. The ice caps will be much bigger, of course, but the equatorial regions will be a lot like Norway was in our day. We won't notice the slightly weaker sunlight, and just think of the cold fresh air on your face; the skiing, the snowboarding.' He leaned back for a moment and clapped his hands. When he leaned back to Maya, she could see he was now displaying a much broader smile. 'Maya, I can't wait!'

She smiled back, carried along by his enthusiasm, his confidence. But there were still some things of which she was not quite sure.

'And what will our role be, professor, when we emerge among them? After all, there will be so much we did not see or experience; all the suffering we were spared. What can we offer them?'

'Our knowledge; the accumulated wisdom of the human race. I'm sure much will have been lost in those centuries of chaos we missed. But we have it here, in imperishable digital form so we can give it back to those survivors. We can undo at least part of the harm Baldwin caused.'

Maya smiled happily: DeGroot had put most of her doubts to rest.

'So when will we return to the surface?'

'Soon, very soon. I just have to work out exactly how much time has passed. I must calculate our new orbital parameters and find out what the average surface temperature is.'

98

'Just one thing: will the conduit still be intact?' A new fear suddenly gripped her with talons of steel. 'What if we're trapped down here!'

He shook his head.

'Maya, Maya, always the worrier. That was foreseen as well; everything has been foreseen. The ferroconcrete was designed so it would lose its cohesion after three hundred years. And surely you haven't forgotten we have autonomous rock-boring machinery down here? In the worst possible case, we could simply drill our way to the surface; after all we're only a few kilometres down.' He leaned forward and gave her hand a fatherly pat. 'Now, instead of getting worked up over nothing, go and check the conduit yourself.'

***

Maya stood at the entrance to the transfer tube, which DeGroot always referred to as the "conduit."

The shaft was constructed from an imperishable, near-indestructible, tube of a reinforced fluorocarbon polymer that, like a willow before a hurricane, would bend and twist under the seismic shocks but would not break or tear. It would regain its original shape and continue to provide an escape route nearly up to the surface; an escape route which would endure for millennia.

The designers—of whom DeGroot was by far the most senior and able—had chosen the site for the recording room's descent well. Situated in the centre of an ancient craton, it would be least affected by the tectonic stresses and strains which the close passage would certainly inflict upon Earth's crust.

It was through this tube, on a platform buoyed by supernally strong magnetic fields, that the inhabitants of the recording room would return to the surface of their wounded planet. Drills and explosives would make short work of the thin layer of crumbling artificial rock which sealed the far end of the conduit and then, finally, they would step out into the sunshine, like cicadas emerging from their subterranean world.

And if that way should be impenetrably blocked? Why, DeGroot had thought of that too, and the heavy drilling machine would bore its way to the surface.

One way or another—they were going back.

She was standing before the bank of instruments that controlled the ascent platform. DeGroot had given her the job of testing it so their triumphant return would suffer no delay.

A transparent sliding door was between her and the platform and she could see it quite clearly through the material: a simple flat surface with six bucket seats arranged in front of its own control panel. She felt a flutter of excitement as she imagined herself rising up and up, reversing the fateful descent that had happened so long ago. *(How long?)*

She pressed the control button which would activate the instrument bank so she could initiate a system diagnostic. To her surprise and irritation, nothing happened, except a brief glow from one of the indicators. Then it went dark, and the control panel was as it was when she had first seen it.

She looked down upon the unresponsive instrument panel and shook her head.

This was a new experience: the machines of her century never failed to respond and were quite capable of detecting errors within their workings and correcting them without humans ever realising anything had happened.

She tried again. As before, one of the indicator lights glowed dully for a few seconds and then went dark. Now realising the device was not going to activate, she found herself in the unusual position of having to strip it down. She removed the outer casing and studied the mass of circuits inside. There were no breaks in any of them and there were no signs of damage that her probe could detect. She rocked back on her heels, baffled.

She did not like the idea of having to tell DeGroot she couldn't test the ascent system because the controls weren't working and she couldn't find why they weren't working. What would he think of her?

Then she had an idea. At first, she felt like dismissing it because it was such an unlikely possibility, but having failed to find any break in the complex wiring, she decided it was either that or having to admit defeat to DeGroot.

She held the tip of her probe against the liquid helium reservoir.

And her eyebrows rose as the probe came back with an impossible reading.

The reservoir was empty. There was not one atom of helium in it.

She had no alternative than to report to DeGroot because only he had access to the main helium reservoir—and he needed some convincing.

'The tank is empty? That's impossible; the tanks are completely secure against any external force; they have to be given the volatility of the helium. And you say there was no puncture?'

'None that my probe could detect.'

'Then where is the helium?'

Maya felt she was making a fool of herself; that she had overlooked a more likely, a more obvious explanation. 'I don't know,' she finally said.

Silence fell and Maya felt herself wilting under DeGroot's stern gaze. Then she said something, without knowing why she was saying it, so crazy was the implication.

'Perhaps the atoms diffused through the container walls.'

She winced as DeGroot brought the palm of a hand down on his desk, with such violence that it made the surface shudder.

'What! Are you insane? What kind of a scientist are you, Maya? Don't you know how long that would take?'

She looked at her hands.

'A long time, professor.'

'Precisely. Well, we can't waste time looking for supernatural ghostly helium atoms that can pass through walls in the blink of an eye. I'll get you some more of the stuff, otherwise we'll never get out of this place!'

He went to another corner of the room and spent quite some time there. When he finally returned with a vial of the quantum liquid, he looked troubled.

'What is it, professor?' she said, alarmed at his expression.

He did not look directly at her.

'The main tank. Over half of the helium is missing.'

***

DeGroot could find no explanation for the missing helium and so Maya returned to her testing of the ascent system. Although he had tried to hide it, Maya could tell he was shaken by the mystery of the missing helium. She knew her leader to be a man who dealt in certainties, not probabilities. He liked seven places of decimals in the results of his calculations. And he had always obtained them.

But not this time.

She had plugged the helium canister into the system and, once again, activated the console. This time the displays flashed into lambent pastel colours and obediently ran the diagnostic she had ordered. She had studied it and, once again, felt that prickling sensation that all was not well. The whole thing was taking far too long; it was as if a metaphorical glue had been poured into the innards. To someone used to lightning-fast conclusions from her AI systems, this was like the crawling of a sick gastropod.

'Computer,' she rapped, 'explain your processing speed, it is far below normal tolerances.'

'Processing speed is at maximum for the ambient conditions,' the computer replied.

'That explanation is not adequate. Calculate your current speed as a percent of optimum.'

The computer took some time to respond, which in itself was unusual.

'Current speed is thirty-eight percent of optimum.'

'Explain that fraction.'

'It is optimal for the ambient conditions.'

She could get no further.

Turning to the operation of the ascent platform, it responded to the superconducting magnetic flux as well as it should, although only after an odd delay, yet again inexplicable.

She shut down the power and frowned.

She had the feeling something was watching her, gloating in her confusion, smirking at her inability to see the obvious.

Although it had taken much, much longer than it should have done, she considered the test complete and returned to the main part of the recording room.

Her footsteps felt oddly heavy to her; she felt a creeping loneliness invading her mind. For the first time, she felt a sense of claustrophobia as the realisation of her situation became clearer to her.

She was in a metal box, kilometres beneath the ravaged surface of Earth.

What lay above and, much more importantly, would she ever see it, ever walk beneath the shrunken sun?

For a second she almost staggered, and had to support herself by leaning against a workbench.

DeGroot was quick to reassure her.

'It's a natural feeling, Maya. I feel a little bit confined myself and I'm not usually like that at all. But soon all this will be behind us.' He tried, and failed, to give an avuncular smile.

And then suddenly, in mid smile, he fell silent.

Three

Maya's eyes widened as she noticed DeGroot had gone completely still, and was motionless in an odd, rigid posture.

'Kees,' she said, forgetting his honorific in her surprise, 'what's wrong!'

He did not answer so she rushed to his side, grasping his elbow in an attempt to break him out of his frozen state. 'Kees, speak to me!'

To her relief, he began to move, turning slowly to face her, but his face was oddly blank. He passed a hand over his forehead.

'I...I feel so strange. I...' He stared at her. 'The time crystal, I'm not sure...the equations, so complex, some solutions are indeterminate. I...'. His voice was oddly high pitched.

She stared back.

'The time crystal? Kees, that was Veronica's responsibility. She solved the equations, remember? They controlled the temporal dimension of the computer. Kees, do you remember?'

Before her concerned gaze, DeGroot shook his head several times and then straightened himself.

'Well, Maya, have you determined the quality of the external atmosphere yet? I'm concerned about the humidity.' His look slowly morphed into a glare. 'Well, have you? I asked you over an hour ago?'

She took a step back. 'Are you all right, Kees? You were speaking in an odd fashion for a moment.'

He frowned. '*Kees?* We're still in a work relationship, Maya. I prefer to keep things formal until we're certain what the situation is.'

'You were talking about the time crystal. About the equations.'

'The time crystal? That was McQuade's job. As far as I was concerned, it was working fine. So why are you mentioning the crystal?'

'You mentioned it. As if you were still working on it.'

He passed a hand over his forehead again. 'Nonsense. I don't know that much about it. But,' and he sat down heavily, 'I do have a terrible headache.' He leaned back, closing his eyes. 'A really bad one.'

She was more than alarmed now. As far as she knew, she and DeGroot were the only human beings in an unknown world. Any sign of illness might have catastrophic consequences.

Then DeGroot opened his eyes and smiled.

'Sorry to scare you, Maya. It's just the strain of being in such an unnatural environment. I'm alright now.'

She smiled back, but a terrible thought kept bouncing off the walls of her mind.

No, professor, you're not.

***

The professor did not show any other symptoms, and Maya's fears receded. In any case, she was caught up in the work the others would have been doing, if they had survived the transition.

And, of course, she had her two house guests to study.

She quickly decided it would be more profitable to learn their language than to attempt to teach her own. They did not seem to grasp the idea that there could be more than one language. She had done the classic routine of pointing at her torso and saying her name. After many looks of bemusement, she had finally learned the slightly larger one was "Karn" and the other was "Yarl", but their understanding of her language began and ended with saying her name. However, they were now looking distinctly healthier than when she had first seen them; their bodies had filled out, except for their bellies, which had shrunk and flattened somewhat. Their skins had lost that pasty, brittle look, and the once prominent veins were now just vague blue lines. As they had grown stronger, they began to look more of what they were—human beings, but ones who had been struggling to survive on the edge of extinction.

105

She treated them like animals she was training, however. If they were cooperative, they got food rewards, but if they sullenly withdrew into themselves and refused to help, they got nothing.

And it worked. With her language skills now fully functional, she very rapidly made progress in understanding them and where they come from. Slowly, haltingly, with many back-and-forth misunderstandings and partial understandings, she learned about them and the strange environment.

From time to time, she reported back to DeGroot.

'I think I can determine the source of their speech. The language is analytic, so syntax is supremely important for meaning. Also, there are no gender terms for inanimate objects. I'm now reasonably certain that their language's roots lie in a western dialect of English, but with a significant proportion of their vocabulary being loan-words from Mandarin.'

DeGroot pursed his lips. 'That would clinch it. You were right, they are an evolved form of our species.'

'Yes. One that had adapted to an extremely resource-poor environment. They clearly have been living on the very edge of existence in a world which could only just sustain them.'

'It certainly looks that way. But they couldn't possibly have started out like that; they must have degenerated from a more positive existence.'

'I think "degenerate" is a pejorative term, professor. We don't know what has happened to Earth since the Destroyer passed. It may well be that some catastrophe devastated the original conditions of these people. Professor, I think we have discovered a colony of the Burrowers!'

DeGroot sat down near the softly glowing displays of his console.

'Burrowers? Yes—that would explain much. But, Maya, there was not supposed to be a Burrower colony anywhere near us.'

'I think perhaps it was a private enterprise, funded by the remnants of the great combines that existed just before the passage. It wouldn't have been in the government records because it wasn't funded or built by government.'

'And when we sealed ourselves off from the surface we came down right on top of them!'

'Not right on top. From what the bigger one—Karn—has told me we came down in a service tunnel; although of course, they don't know it to be a service tunnel. There are machines in it which were designed to allow people to return to the surface, but they're all ruined.' Maya's face suddenly changed to an expression which DeGroot could not put a name to. It was a weird combination of amusement and pity. 'And there's something else. Professor, they think we're gods!'

Now DeGroot had an unusual expression of his own; his was also a mixture, but of amusement and sadness.

'If only we were, Maya, if only we were.'

***

Slowly, Maya learned much about Karn and Yarl and from whence they had come.

She learned they called themselves "The People", and believed they were the only thinking beings in the Universe. She learned of the claustrophobic environment they termed "the World" and its regularly spaced settlements, whose inhabitants were like the People, but not exactly like them. She learned of how these other inhabitants were normally indifferent to the other Men they shared the World with, but how dissension and even violence had come upon them lately.

She learned in horror about the Suns and how they were going out.

And she learned of an even greater horror—they knew of some great catastrophe in the distant past which had destroyed their original state of bliss.

And that those who had done the act of destruction were Women.

Who must be regularly punished for their sin.

107

She now understood why Karn and Yarl had sometimes refused to cooperate with her.

They were simply not used to being controlled by someone so obviously female.

Time passed.

DeGroot seemed reluctant to accept the readings Maya was giving him and constantly handed them back, demanding that she check again.

Maya moved Karn and Yarl together to proper quarters with bunks, chairs and—horror—a shower. Eventually. Karn agreed to go in, and she chuckled as she watched his expression change from apprehension to delight, as he became used to the feel of warm, soapy water. After Yarl had plucked up enough courage also to face the unknown, she burned their stinking loincloths and provided them with the same type of grey, one-piece suit as she and DeGroot were wearing, tailored to their meagre dimensions.

Time passed.

She was now fluent in their language and she spent some time amusing herself in tracing its development from the languages of her own time—however long ago that was.

But now she faced a problem which could not have arisen before—how could she explain the true nature of reality to them, now they had been plucked from their so-called World?

She began slowly, starting with basic astronomy. She explained the Universe consisted mainly of empty space—a challenging concept to explain to beings who had lived out their existence in a confined, constrained, subterranean world. The idea that normal life was spent on the outside of large lumps of matter was an enormous mental leap for them. It was only the obvious awe in which they held her that allowed them to eventually accept the absurd idea. She agonised how she could break it to them that she was not in fact a god, but for the moment, it was to her advantage they held that view: it meant that they were readier to believe in the crazy ideas she kept piling on them.

108

Time passed.

Then came the day when she was ready to take the penultimate step of explaining how they had gotten trapped in the human warren from which they had so recently, accidentally, escaped.

'So you understand you've been living inside the large ball we call Earth and, more importantly, that is not the normal way human beings live?'

'Yes,' Karn said, 'why should a god lie to us?'

Maya winced inwardly at such devotion—but it was not time for the ultimate step of revealing her lack of divinity.

She continued: 'But there are other balls floating in space, some smaller than Earth, others much, much bigger. And all kept to their safe paths through space until there came a time when something happened to disturb that safe set-up.'

Karn and Yarl's eyes went wide with anticipation.

It's like telling a bedtime story to young children! She thought, *but this is no bed-time story.*

'There came a woman, a woman scientist. You understand what "scientist" means?'

They nodded.

'Her name was Baldwin, and she had one of the greatest intellects the human race has ever produced, almost superhuman. She proved the Riemann Hypothesis on her nineteenth birthday.' (No reaction.) 'With the help of another woman called Adekola, she found a way of producing a short-cut to the far distances of space. But although she was nearly superhuman in intelligence, she was all too human in her desires and she took a terrible risk in producing that short-cut to the stars. It was something we call a "wormhole" but you don't need to understand what it was. But what happened next was terrible beyond belief, beyond all imagining, the worst disaster that has ever happened to us humans. She broke up the orderly arrangement of the other floating balls—remember I called them "planets"? And the biggest of them all, one called "Jupiter", was sent flying towards our planet—our Earth. And as it swung near, it threatened to kill everything on the surface.

'And your ancestors—and many others, we believe—tried to hide by burrowing deep into the ground, away from the rays and heat which Jupiter was producing.'

'And eventually, these "Burrowers" became the People,' Karn said.

Maya clapped her hands in joy.

'Yes, yes, Karn! Well done! That is what happened. But you have been down here for a long time' (*How long?* flashed a thought from Maya's subconscious) 'and the machines your ancestors set up have gradually been breaking down, making your lives more and more difficult. Tell me, do you have any legends about things that looked like men, but were made of metal?'

Yarl spoke this time. 'No, there had only ever been the People.'

Maya nodded. At the time of the cataclysm, robots had not been very reliable; that was how Baldwin had expected to gain her riches—by making a breakthrough in their design. It was not likely any robots in the World would have lasted long.

But Karn was speaking again, and his words were chilling to Maya.

'But Maya, this means our legends are true—we were in Paradise and it was a woman that had us thrown out. That's why we punish the women, why they *have* to be punished.'

Maya realised it was supremely important to convince them of this explanation, otherwise she could never trust them, never accept them back into the tribe of humanity.

'That is only part of the story: Baldwin did all those things and, yes, it would have been so much better if she had not lived, but we are here because of another woman, the one I mentioned earlier—Adekola.

'There came a time after Baldwin had done the terrible thing, when Adekola had fifteen seconds to save us, fifteen short seconds and then it would have been too late, we would all have

110

been destroyed. She took action, and we were saved; not in the way it would have been without Baldwin, but still life, the chance to undo the great disaster we have suffered. And her reward was to be tossed into a black hole by Baldwin and killed.'

Maya realised she was not telling the story too well; there were so many concepts which were key to the drama, which she could not give to Karn and Yarl: black holes, wormholes, negative matter—a whole technical vocabulary which was needed properly to explain those epic events that had occurred a still unknown number of years ago .

For a moment, she forgot about Karn and Yarl, and felt she was there in Plato Base at that supreme moment of human existence when the continuation of humanity hung by a strand of disintegrating spider silk, when the actions of one woman had held off total annihilation.

Could she, Maya, have acted in time?

She shuddered at the thought of such awesome responsibility, surely appropriate only to a true god?

Later that day, she recounted her discussions with their guests to DeGroot. He nodded when she finished her tale.

'That gives us the latest possible date for this group going underground. They must have gone in just before Cloud City One broadcast the truth about Baldwin and Adekola. And that in turn must mean they were the very first of the Burrowers.' He shook his head. 'They must have been a group of extremely wealthy people and their families who decided to act before things got too bad. Maybe they acted without being fully prepared.

'And look at what they have become. Barely human.'

'No,' Maya said, 'truly human. Just very unfortunate.'

DeGroot did not reply and returned to his instruments, trying (unbeknownst to Maya) to force them to give him the answers he wanted, rather than the ones they were actually giving.

Maya stood, watching him for a while, as his arthritic fingers slowly passed back and forth over the keys.

What was he looking for? What was it that was eluding him? 'Professor,' she finally said, 'what is troubling you?'

'Nothing. Everything is working out the way I expected.'

She crossed to him.

'You're not telling me something. Are you concerned something has gone wrong? That we are not where you expected us to be?'

He was silent.

'Are you concerned that your hopes, your plans for us, are not going to be fulfilled? That we are all that is left of our species? You know, there are always the lightsail ships to preserve humanity.'

He snorted. 'The lightsail ships! Would you really want to be aboard one of those floating coffins? Dying alone after a frenzy of cannibalism out in the black emptiness beyond the Bow Shock? There are many ways to die, but that is one of the worst.'

She fell silent; DeGroot had encapsulated her own view in a few pithy words. She felt suddenly enervated, drained of all hope. Something was wrong and it was gnawing at the base of her conscious mind. Perhaps it would be better to have been one of the innocent inhabitants of the World.

She wished she could sleep—but she could not.

***

Time passed. DeGroot became more withdrawn with each passing day. It seemed he was searching for something, something that would give him some kind of reassurance, some kind of resolution; but if so, his search appeared to be in vain.

Karn and Yarl were becoming restless, too. They had been engrossed in helping Maya learn their language, but now that had been mostly achieved they were no longer content merely to eat and sleep inside a metal box, albeit a spacious one.

Maya too, was troubled. Nothing was happening—surely they were not destined to spend eternity inside the recording room? That was not what DeGroot had promised.

And then came an event which chilled her to her innermost core.

Each individual had their own private room within the greater space of the recording room, an area they could retire to, to rest or sleep. Maya was stretched out in her room when the door suddenly opened without her permission, and the professor entered.

She sat up immediately, thinking that something alarming must have happened.

The professor drew up a chair to Maya's bed and reached out a hand to her.

'Yes, professor, what is it?' she said, fear clouding her mind.

DeGroot looked from side to side, as if searching for listeners.

'It's DeGroot,' he said conspiratorially, 'there's something wrong.'

'DeGroot?' she echoed, 'but…'

'I've always had my doubts,' the professor continued, apparently unaware of Maya's confusion.

'Doubts?'

DeGroot moved closer.

'Yes, his analysis of the orbital trajectories; I always thought he had made too many oversimplified assumptions.'

Maya had the feeling she was trapped in some kind of surreal playlet, but she nodded.

'Go on.'

'The equations describing the perturbations caused by the close passage of Jupiter generally produced chaotic results. There were only a few deterministic outcomes, namely collision, ejection or displacement. Of the three, displacement was always the one with the lowest probability, whatever clever mathematical tricks we used to tweak the parameters.'

'I didn't know that,' Maya said. Although she didn't understand why DeGroot was talking about himself in the third person, the import of his words so far seemed to be hinting at a worrying situation.

113

'No,' the other replied, 'he always hid that. But as you know, his view was that after Jupiter destroyed Mars on the way in, Earth would be tossed outwards to adopt a stable orbit which crossed Mars' old one.'

'Yes, of course, which is why we did what we did. Earth would enter a glacial state but life would be possible upon it, especially as the sun is slowly brightening. The human race would be put under great stress but it would adapt. Life would continue.'

'I pointed out to him, years beforehand, he had made an arbitrary assumption which gave the orbital injection outcome the highest probability but he didn't listen. And then I was side-tracked onto stabilising the time crystal and I left him to it.'

Despite the gathering threat slowly emerging from the other's words, Maya felt another, completely different, stab of fear.

'But professor, that was Veronica's work, not yours. Why...'

DeGroot looked puzzled.

'What are you talking about? I'd just said it was my job. Why are you quoting my words back at me?'

Maya fell silent, momentarily. There were two issues here, and she only had the resources to deal with one at a time. The situation with DeGroot's confused state would have to wait.

'Alright...Veronica. What do you think has happened?'

DeGroot reached out and, to Maya's alarm, grasped her wrist.

'We can discount the collision outcome as we're still here. But the displacement outcome is really only a special case of the other main probability.'

Maya finally saw what the other had been building up to.

'Ejection. You think we are not in a stable Mars-type orbit.'

'Exactly. And I think DeGroot has been fighting against accepting that. I think the problem is he doesn't know where we are or how long it's taken us to get here—wherever and whenever that is.'

Maya felt a sick wave of terror wash over her. Everything they had done had been predicated on the belief that DeGroot had correctly predicted the outcome of the passage of the Destroyer. They had undertaken their terrible journey based on the faith that they were being led by a great man who had seen a possible future for humanity.

But if that faith had been misplaced…

She rocked back against the wall as the full implications of his words sunk in. No, that couldn't be so; DeGroot couldn't have altered the parameters to give him the answer he wanted. He was a great scientist!

There must be a way of finding out exactly what had happened. She leaned forward again.

And stopped.

DeGroot was holding his head, which he was twisting from side to side. Then he stopped and looked directly at her.

'Maya. What are you doing in my room?'

'This is my room, professor.'

'It is?' He looked around. 'You're right—it is.' He gave a twisted, unnatural smile. 'I'm sorry, my dear, but I've no idea why I came in. Can you enlighten me?'

'You just came in to ask me how Karn and Yarl are adjusting.'

'I did? And how are the little devils doing?'

'They're fine, professor, just fine.'

After DeGroot had left, Maya sat on the edge of the bed, her mind racing.

Something was wrong with DeGroot; that was now certain. But how dangerous was his condition; did it put their entire existence in jeopardy? Not for the first time, she cursed the brilliant and beautiful scientist who had brought this terrible disaster down on them all.

She tried to push those thoughts away: it was time for her visit to Karn and Yarl.

When she found them, they were engrossed in looking at the screen of their personal computer. Undetected, she stood behind them and shared their viewing of the displayed images.

Immediately, she felt a tug on her emotions: the scene was of ineffable beauty. It had to be a video of the Rockies, in Alaska or Canada. There were snow-capped mountains, reaching up to pierce a cerulean sky. Great pine trees clung to their rugged sides, but at this distance entire forests looked just like patches of blue-green moss. A bridal-veil waterfall was descending from the lip of the nearest mighty bluff; its tumbling waters torn into wisps and streamers of spray before they could touch the ground.

A tremendous sadness swept over her. No doubt those mountains still existed, but the forests would have been blasted into radioactive charcoal by the close encounter with Jupiter. The elk, the bears, the caribou—all gone, gone as if they had never been.

And humans—had they in truth survived that deadly passage or had they simply delayed their inevitable demise? DeGroot and her, the People, the doomed refugees on the lightsail craft: she could not avoid the growing suspicion that it had all been for nothing. That humanity had not escaped the doom of stars.

She felt she should be in tears—but she was not.

Yarl had realised she was behind him and he turned, smiling. 'Hello, Maya. What have you got for us today?'

She smiled back, but she knew there was little she could offer them. Their time together had been spent in her learning their language, but beyond that it looked as if there was no more the two groups could do together. There could be very little understanding between people like DeGroot and Karn: one was a man who had wrestled with abstruse mathematical dilemmas, and the other an innocent who had believed that a panel on the roof of a cave had been a sun.

But she continued to smile, and said, 'What do you think of these pictures?'

'They're very pretty,' Yarl said, 'but I don't really understand them.'

Maya nodded, sadly. Her two charges were unable to truly appreciate what they were seeing. For a start, they could not grasp the scale; there were no mountains or mighty forests in the World; no tumbling waterfalls. They were seeing only two-dimensional pictures of unknown objects; they could not mentally convert those images into a representation of physical objects; objects of dimensions the World could not have contained.

There were no lofty mountains or shining waterfalls in their stunted minds.

So much has been lost, she thought, *so much of what made life more than just existence!*

Once again she felt she should be weeping: but did not.

She realised she was now at a loss what to do with her unexpected house-guests. She had tried telling them a little of human history just before the Cataclysm, but they had no points of reference and her attempts had simply bored them; something they made no attempt to disguise.

And as for any attempt to teach them simple mathematics and science: that failed even more miserably. Their lives had been severely practical and abstractions were of no interest to them.

Unfortunately, one eminently practical subject was beginning to make itself obvious. Although lacking the most basic education, they were not unintelligent. And despite their lack of knowledge, they were not children. They had long since realised she was not a divinity, and had begun to show that they found her female proximity arousing. They had taken to "accidentally" brushing up against her during their lessons.

Reluctantly, Maya came to the conclusion that she would have to eject them from the recording room—but to where? In their own world, they were wanted for murder. She was certain there must be other Burrower colonies but had no idea where the nearest one could be.

117

And in any case their World, and every other similar colony, was dying. To return them to the World or another colony would be a death sentence.

But even as she thought that, another possibility revealed itself.

What about us, we refugees from the Destroyer? Are we also under sentence of death?

For the second time?

Four

Maya was convinced that DeGroot was hiding something from her—and maybe from himself. Many days had now passed since they had woken from their transition and yet there was no sign that they were ready to move out of the recording room. DeGroot continued to stare at his console; continued to mutter over his printouts; continued to avoid saying anything about his future plans.

Maya tried a direct approach.

'Professor, what is your estimate of how long it will take us to settle into a stable Mars-like orbit?—after the encounter with Jupiter, I mean.'

'The same as when you last asked me that—about three centuries.'

'And how long has it been since the encounter?'

'I'm still working on that.'

Maya knew that could not possibly be true; a man of DeGroot's mathematical ability should have worked that out long ago.

'What about readings from the surface instruments?'

'All destroyed. There are no readings.'

Maya mused to herself; that comment might be true; after all it was the violence being wreaked on the surface by the close passage that had forced them and the Burrowers underground. It was quite possible that all of the instruments had been swept away.

But there were many simple ways of calculating the passage of time.

He must know!

She decided she would no longer trust him and would find out for herself.

She took to hovering near him when he logged onto his systems.

119

Several times she had been able to glimpse parts of his password before she had been forced to pretend she was just passing by. It was a random series of numerals and letters, containing no pattern which would allow the next symbol to be deduced. She would have to learn it all.

Against DeGroot's express commands, she allowed Karn and Yarl into the computer area on a few occasions and, while DeGroot was yelling and expostulating, tried an experiment or two with her best guess at the password, always without success.

Later she would attempt to explain to her students what they had seen her do; that there were machines that could do more than stir fungus. They could not understand that—how could they?—but they did believe her.

But Karn and Yarl were increasingly unhappy, Karn in particular.

Although they no longer believed they were in the abode of the gods, they had expected they would be spending their time in more interesting ways. But Maya was more and preoccupied with her own problems and spent less and less time with them. They began to toy with the idea of breaking out and finding another World, unaware Maya had reached the same conclusion about their future.

And then one day something happened which brought everything to an unexpected crisis; a crisis which made Maya question the very foundations of her sanity.

She had written the section of the password she had managed to gather on a scrap of paper, which she normally kept under her bed. But now she was staring at the missing end part of that vital code, trying to magic the missing portion into existence by the sheer force of her will.

Once again, her door opened without her permission and she looked up guiltily, while pushing the scrap of paper down the side of the bed.

She had expected to see DeGroot, or even an escaped Karn or Yarl.

But in the doorway stood the naked figure of Veronica McQuade.

Maya was struck dumb. She was familiar with the ancient cliché of not being able to believe one's eyes but now for the first time she was experiencing it.

Eventually she stuttered, 'Veronica! I, I…'

McQuade walked into the room and Maya retreated before the creature, further onto the bed.

'Where is Duquesne?' the apparition said, 'I gave him some calculations to check.'

Maya could only stare, unable to utter a coherent sentence, or even a recognisable word.

The McQuade-thing came nearer.

'It's a simple question,' she/it said, 'If you don't know that, perhaps you can tell me where I can find Maya.'

Maya's mouth was hanging open but somehow she forced herself to look McQuade in the eye and say, 'Veronica. I'm Maya. You're talking to her.'

McQuade made no sign of having registered the reply and, without saying another word, turned and left, leaving Maya stunned into immobility on the bed.

After a minute or two, she heard raised voices from outside: DeGroot, the McQuade-thing and a man's voice.

She walked to her doorway as if in a dream and peered out.

McQuade was there, talking to DeGroot and there was another figure standing nearby—a naked Hilbert. She couldn't quite catch the complete conversation but apparently McQuade and Hilbert were looking for Duquesne, but if he was not available Maya would suffice. DeGroot on the other hand, did not seem in the least perturbed by the apparent resurrection of his colleagues and was peevishly complaining he had work to do, apparently having forgotten that Maya's room was a few metres away.

Maya retreated back into her room and sat heavily on the bed, head in hands.

The room seemed to whirl around her in an ever accelerating kaleidoscope of images dredged from the depths of insanity. Was she mad? Was an overloaded brain generating its own unreal reality?

She had looked down on the motionless bodies of Duquesne and Hilbert. She had kissed the still form of McQuade. There had been no movement, no reactions. As far as she knew, those bodies had continued to lie on the couches while she and DeGroot had gone about their business, while she had met Yarl and Karn and had begun their fitful education.

And yet here they were, looking for her but not seeing her.

Madness. It was the only answer.

Madness.

But she fought her despair and pushed it back down into her subconscious. Something had happened but there would be a physical, real-world explanation. There would be a chain of cause-and-effect which terminated in this weird tableau.

All she had to do was find it.

She closed the bedroom door behind her and crossed to the still arguing trio.

'Still looking for Maya?' she enquired of Hilbert.

'No,' he said in a slightly puzzled tone, 'I'm looking for Duquesne.'

She had no answer to that, and just stood, looking at the newcomers.

They were just as she had remembered them in the last hour before they had all lain down to die, except now their features were relaxed, apparently under no great strain.

It was DeGroot who broke the impasse.

'I'm glad you have finally joined me,' he said, 'but I would prefer it if you were properly clothed. You know how to work the weaving machine: get some clothes on.'

***

122

A short while later, the now clothed newcomers were being briefed by DeGroot; that is, if you could call it a briefing: he gave them no more information about the date than he had Maya.

She slipped away and walked the short distance to the re-establishment suite.

There she saw the same couches as before, but now all vacated.

Except one.

The naked form of Duquesne was still lying on his, his arms neatly folded on his chest, his eyes closed.

She gazed down on him, more than half expecting those eyes suddenly to open and two strong arms to reach up and hold her, in loving recognition. But they did not. She lifted an arm; it was somewhat stiff but only what she had expected. She let go, and the arm slowly subsided back to Duquesne's side.

'Are you there, Alain?' she breathed. 'Are you there?'

There was no reply.

She returned to the central part of the recording room and positioned herself some distance away from the group, which was still in earnest discussion about something. She heard the word "asthenosphere" but not the context in which it was uttered. McQuade realised she was standing behind and turned an unsmiling face upon Maya.

'Ah, Duquesne,' she said, 'have you found Duquesne yet?'

Maya fought to keep her emotions under control as she felt the whirlpool of madness begin to suck her closer to its centre.

'No, I haven't. But I'll keep looking.'

'Good, we need him. There's something damn peculiar about these temperature profiles.'

With that, she turned back to Hilbert, who was looking over DeGroot's shoulder.

'Can you show me what's concerning you, Kees?' Maya heard him say.

Then she realised DeGroot was swivelling his chair to face the master computer—and he hadn't yet activated it. In turn, that meant he would type in the vital password!

But apparently, DeGroot was as cagey with his new companions as he had been with Maya.

'Could you please stand back while I call up the machine,' he said to them, and dutifully they moved back.

But he had forgotten about Maya. As the two newcomers backed away, she darted rapidly between them and DeGroot, who now had his back turned to the rest of the room.

And as she swept past, she saw the last characters: 'aW!3n>''.

She stored the missing part of the password in her basal memory and backed away before anyone could comment on her odd behaviour. She returned to her room, retrieved the piece of paper with the beginning of the password on it, mentally added the additional part to it, added the complete password to permanent memory, and tore the paper into pieces as small as she could manage. During her next visit to Karn and Yarl, she would flush them down their lavatory.

Now she was ready to probe deeper and discover exactly what DeGroot was hiding.

All she needed now was the opportunity.

***

Maya soon found DeGroot was no longer interested in keeping her up to date with developments (assuming, she thought grimly, that there were any). Instead, there were endless meetings of the new group of three, from which she appeared to be excluded. She kept a lookout for a restored Duquesne, but he did not put in an appearance.

Slowly, a plan began to develop in her mind of how to force the issue and pierce this fog of inaction that had surrounded her since her awakening.

After disposing of the torn pieces of paper (much to Karn and Yarl's puzzlement) she realised there were certain comments they had made about their earlier life she had not followed up.

'You say the World is slowly getting colder,' she said to them both, although Yarl was staring at a monitor screen.

'Yes, at least that's what the old men said.' Karn looked puzzled. 'But this place is much colder than the World.'

Maya did not respond to his comment but said, mainly to herself, 'Getting colder; that implies a steep thermal gradient.'

'Thermal gradient?' Karn asked (Yarl was still looking at pretty pictures of the Lost Earth).

Maya ruffled his hair as if she were talking to a child. Karn disliked the implication, but he enjoyed the closeness.

'Yes, it's very simple. It means that somewhere, somewhere in contact with the World, there is a place which is colder, very much colder.'

'How could that be? This place is much too cold for us. There couldn't be anything colder.'

'How indeed.' She was standing, looking down at Karn, an adult man not much bigger than an adolescent child. But she noted with approval that he no longer looked like something hovering on the edge of death, that his skin was now fully opaque and starting to look as if it covered the beginnings of muscles. 'How indeed.'

She realised Karn was staring at her, as if trying to say something, but had not yet found the courage.

'Yes?' she said, gently.

'Maya,' he said, with some hesitation, 'we know now you are not a god, but what exactly are you?'

'In what way?'

Karn pointed around the room, indicating the many glowing monitor screens.

'No-one in the village could have made these; how is it you can?'

'I told you before. People, ordinary people, people just like you,' (*Well, maybe not exactly like you*) 'they made them. People could do lots of wonderful things before the catastrophe happened.'

'You mean before the Baldwin woman did that awful thing. What happened to her—was she strangled like Thylassa?'

Maya straightened up, lifting her gaze from Karn.

She remembered those terrible days when the basic foundations of reality had been shaken; when they realised that doom had been unleashed upon them all.

'No,' she said after a long pause, 'she was not executed. She died when a planetoid—that's another one of those floating ball-things I told you about—fell on a village called Greater New York. Nothing was ever found of her—or anybody else in that village, I'm sad to say.'

She thought briefly about Baldwin; they had never met, separated by centuries, but she had seen the other's image on the screens often enough, in historical documentaries about the events that had led to the displacement of Jupiter.

And now she saw her again: aloof, imperturbable, glacially brilliant, and more beautiful than the human eye could accept. What would have happened to her had she lived? Would she have accepted her guilt, repented of her world-destroying sin?

Maya thought on for a few moments and then decided: *No, she would not.*

If only I could have been there! She thought, *you would not have found me as easy to dominate as you did poor Adekola!*

She dragged her mind back to her patiently waiting students. She was about to ruffle Karn's hair again, but the lowering of his brow warned her not to.

'I think I will soon have something for you to do, something exciting,' she said, taking a step back from the annoyed Karn.

Yarl turned from the display of a beautiful Pacific atoll and said, 'About time. We're going mad just sitting here. We're men, not ornaments.'

He joined his companion, and both looked up at her like eager puppies, expecting some immediate orders.

She found she was experiencing something she had not felt for a long time. (*How long?*)

126

A feeling of affection, but also responsibility. Although adult men, both Karn and Yarl were so utterly unequipped to understand what was happening to the World, and what had happened to the world. She was about to use them as human tools to solve the enigma in which she was living. And what then? It did not seem likely that life could continue in the recording room for much longer now it had become the abode of madness.

But what lay beyond?

She did not know, but feared it would not be to their, and her, liking.

***

Maya felt a growing impatience; a crisis was approaching— she was sure of that, and it would arrive if she took action or not. But at least she would have some control if she took the lead in producing the crisis. And yet, it would be so easy to pretend all was well, to wait for DeGroot to reach an actual conclusion, to detail some course of action, instead of this endless Kafkaesque drift.

Maya thought back to those dreadful days of the close passage of the Destroyer. The course of action they had taken— had it been a genuinely rational choice, to hope infinitesimal odds would fall in their favour? Would it not have been simpler to accept that there are situations where there is no escape, where a calm acceptance of inevitability would have been better than this gigantic leap into the unknown—invoking death in a ludicrous attempt to escape death?

She was jerked out of her reverie by a timid knock on the door.

Strange, most people just walked in.

She opened the door to her visitor, only to discover it was Hilbert.

'Please, come in, Bernard,' she said mechanically, musing that the mental afflictions her colleagues were experiencing had not entirely removed manners. She indicated the chair while sitting back on her bed.

'What can I do for you, Bernard?'

Hilbert shook his head and appeared to be in some distress.

'Why do you keep calling me "Bernard"?'

Here we go again, Maya thought.

'Isn't that your name?'

Hilbert's head motions became more frantic, more desperate.

'No, no, I mean—it's all muddled. I know I'm Cornelius DeGroot but I keep getting these sudden flashes of light, making me dizzy. And when things stabilise, for some reason I think I'm Bernard Hilbert. I mean—be honest, do I look like Bernard Hilbert?'

'No, no, of course not,' Maya soothed, 'nothing like him.'

Hilbert nodded in recognition of that reassurance, and went on: 'I've got so much to do! The thermal gradient—it's all wrong! The time crystal, I've seen the readings and they're meaningless! How can I guide the team if I keep having these crazy episodes?'

Maya shook her head.

'That's a problem. But why have you come to see me; how can I help?'

Hilbert shocked her by jumping up and sitting next to her on the bed. Then to her further alarm, he reached over and clutched her hands, squeezing them slightly too tightly.

'Veronica, you seem so calm, so in control. Tell me, have you been having these episodes? It's not just me, is it?'

Maya was no longer as disturbed as she had been by these strange switches of identity; she had come almost to expect them. Slowly, she extricated her hands.

'Yes, I've been having them—Kees. They come and go, but they're getting fewer now. So I just sit down and wait for them to go away. And then I'm fine—completely fine.'

Hilbert smiled broadly.

'I knew it! It's obviously just a side effect of the transition. Really, I should have expected it.' He gave a strained laugh. 'I mean, it's not like moving a flower from one part of the garden to another, is it?'

'No, you're right there, Ber—Kees. It most definitely is not like that.'

He gave her nearest hand a friendly pat.

'You've put my mind at rest. You don't mind if I come and see you when I get these attacks, do you? I mean, until they go away. You've made me feel so much better!'

No, not in the least, because I don't intend to be here when you call!

She forced herself to smile.

'Whenever you feel like it, Kees, I...'

She stopped. Hilbert was looking around the room as if he were seeing it for the first time. He turned his head slowly, and his eyes narrowed on seeing Maya.

'Maya, I...I was looking for Veronica. Is this her room?'

Maya guessed who it was who was now speaking.

'No, Bernard. It's mine—Maya.'

He stood up suddenly, as if pulled by invisible strings.

'I'm well aware of who you are, Maya. And I'll remind you that I prefer to be addressed as "Dr Hilbert".'

And with that, he was gone, leaving the door open.

She shut it and sat on the bed again.

It was now beyond doubt there was something seriously wrong with her colleagues.

So serious that she could expect no help from them in extricating herself from the recording room.

How far would this aberration take them? Would they lose all contact with reality, perhaps become violent?

But as she sat there, the room seemed to become colder and darker as she reviewed the situation.

One colleague had not been able to face the transition, so long ago even his bones were now dust.

There was one colleague who had not recovered from the procedure, and was still lying cold and still on his couch.

Three who had successfully transitioned but were showing indisputable signs of mental deterioration.

And then there was her. Someone who believed she did not have any mental deterioration.

But how likely was it she would remain untouched; how likely was it she was not carrying some flaw which would gradually eat away at her until there was nothing left?

What was the point of running if she already had some condition from which she could never escape?

And, instantly, she felt alone.

Completely, utterly alone.

***

Karn and Yarl stared up at her. For the first time in a long while, she saw animation in those faces, a kind of sparkle in the eyes.

'So you know what to do? You must lead them away from the computer with the big screen. You must not go near it yourselves.'

'Yes, Maya.'

'Yes, Maya.'

Just like kids in infant school! She thought.

There was no point in delaying. For some time she had been telling them not to eat all their dry food but to build up a store, as much as they could carry in their backpacks. Similarly for water.

'Will we be going far?' Yarl had asked.

She could only manage a weak smile, one that barely curved her lips .

'I don't know. But probably, yes.'

And now, the moment of crisis had come. She pointed to an image of an hourglass that she had generated on one of the screens. Digital sand was falling silently from one lobe to the other.

'When the top is empty—come out!'

They nodded their understanding, broad smiles of anticipation lighting up their faces.

Now there was no time to waste. She left their living quarters and rushed to the principal part of the recording room, where the others had already gathered, mumbling and muttering their meaningless comments. As she approached them, she could not shake the feeling that they were no longer real, that they were simply people-sized marionettes, jerked this way and the other by an unseen puppet master.

'Crystallisation of the upper mantle,' McQuade was saying.

Hilbert was shaking his head.

'No, no evidence for that, not enough time for significant crystallisation to have occurred.'

She stopped a few metres away.

'Do you want to know what I think?' she enquired.

They turned blank eyes upon her.

'And just what do you think, Veronica?' McQuade said in a dull, grey, inflectionless voice.

This was the moment—no turning back.

'I think none of you is real. I think something has happened that has turned you into puppets. You're just paper cut-outs. Clockwork dolls.'

'Yes, an interesting theory, Duquesne,' Hilbert said, totally unmoved by the bizarre accusation that had just been levelled against him, 'but what has that to do with McQuade's crystallisation theory?'

Maya was a little shaken by the lack of response, the absence of anger, of outrage, but she continued with her plan.

She moved away from the precious main computer, so jealously guarded by DeGroot.

'Nothing. Not a fucking thing. But how about this?'

Now some distance from the group, she switched off one of the peripheral machines, holding up the power connector as if it were some kind of hunting trophy.

They stared blankly at her.

'Not impressed? How about this?'

She sent the machine crashing to the floor. A shower of blue sparks shot up from its shattered frame.

Now they were moving toward her, still with faces not displaying any emotion.

And then chaos broke out.

Karn and Yarl erupted into the room, yelling and screaming like banshees, tossing chairs and tables over in a frenzied whirl of motion. They descended on the group, tugging at their clothes, kicking their legs, punching stomachs with what strength they had, and then rushing off.

Finally, the group showed some emotion and began, jerkily, to follow them, leaving DeGroot's computer unguarded. Maya did not know how long she would have to solve this conundrum. She leapt from the shadows where she had been hiding and sat before the computer.

It was in sleep mode and, with trembling fingers, she activated it and typed in DeGroot's very long, very complex password.

Of course, she had remembered it perfectly.

She was confronted with a complex set of nested files and, for a moment, a surge of despair shook her.

How could she find what she wanted—how would she have time to find her answers amongst these multiply nested documents?

But then she calmed herself. She was not dealing with some primitive twenty-first-century kindergarten toy.

If she asked the right questions, she would get her answer. 'Computer,' she said, in as firm a voice as possible, trying to ignore the crashing and yelling sounds of the mayhem in the far corners, 'how long has it been since the close encounter with Jupiter?'

A pleasant female voice emanated from the machine: it was like having a friendly young woman sitting next to her. And it, at least, knew who she was.

'Please rephrase your question, Maya, in unambiguous terms. What other object was involved in the close encounter?'

She cursed inwardly. Every second was vital; Karn and Yarl could not hold out long against the three scientists. She tried again.

'How long has it been since the close encounter between Jupiter and the planet Earth?'

There was no delay whatsoever, but when she heard the reply, Maya sat still and rigid for some seconds, her head spinning, the answer echoing and reverberating in her mind.

The friendly young woman sitting next to her had given her the answer—but not one she had expected in the least.

'One hundred and seventy-five thousand, four hundred and seventy-two Solar years.'

She fell back against the back of the chair, a hand clutching at her hair.

No, no, not possible! Three hundred years, that was the expected time for orbital stabilisation!

'Check answer,' she croaked.

'The data retrieval was performed correctly,' the cheerful woman said, 'and the answer is correct. Would you like the figure extended to decimal years or decimal days? Would you like the figure converted to lunar years?'

'No, that will not be necessary.' She stared at the screen for quite a while and then added: 'Thank you.'

She rose from the chair, just as the computer was saying, 'You're welcome.'

And looked around. Whereas before she had seen the room as the cradle of a new birth, she now realised it was not a cradle but a tomb.

She must get out.

But Yarl and Karn—what about them, those poor innocents, trapped in a web of forces beyond their understanding? She had no duty of care to them, no responsibility for their well-being, but in that instant she knew she could not leave them.

And she would not leave them.

Five

The commotion in the far reaches of the recording room ended, to be replaced by an ominous silence. Maya leapt up from DeGroot's chair and moved away from the master computer. She did not know why she felt so afraid to be caught using it— but she did. Her entire perception of her situation had changed: whereas before it had been one of impatient expectation, now it was an awareness of an as yet unknown danger, an invisible threat she felt growing stronger with each instant. The recording room, which before had been simply an antechamber to a glorious adventure, was now a tiny box, holding her trapped with lunatics as companions.

Her ex-colleagues appeared, dragging Yarl and Karn behind them. Both men looked dazed and bore red marks, which would assuredly develop into multicoloured bruises.

DeGroot was in the lead and tossed Karn to the floor in front of him. Karn looked up at Maya imploringly, and she felt a stab of guilt at what she had asked them to do. DeGroot, in turn, was glaring at her.

'This has gone far enough,' he said, and there was ice in his words, 'I cannot tolerate the presence of these creatures here, interfering with serious scientific study any longer. They have to be gotten rid of.'

Maya continued to move away from the master computer.

'But you can't send them back to the World! That would be a death sentence!'

McQuade was holding Yarl, and she threw him like a bag of rags so he landed on top of Karn.

'I'm not going to send them back to their so-called World,' DeGroot said, 'I want them killed.'

'Killed!' Maya gasped as if she had been struck in a physical assault. 'You can't mean that!'

'Oh, but I do. My studies are at a critical point now, and I can't allow anything to distract me. If I just throw them out, they might find a way of getting back in. No, they must die.'

Maya strode forward and helped Karn and Yarl to their feet. Instinctively, she pushed them behind her. She stared at DeGroot.

'I don't know who or what you are, but I am certain of one thing: you are not Cornelius DeGroot. He was a gentle, kind man who would never order death for any living creature. I don't recognise you. You are not DeGroot!'

DeGroot stepped forward again, so he was in front of Hilbert and McQuade, emphasising his authority.

'And I don't know who you are. The Maya I knew would never allow childish affection for grotesque subhumans to impede scientific research. You have been no help to me since the transition. In fact, you have hindered my studies. As a punishment, I want you to kill these creatures, and you have one hour to do it.'

Maya felt Karn tugging at her clothing. She turned to them, seeing the concern on their bruised faces. They could not understand DeGroot's words, but somehow they had picked up his tone and knew he was referring to them and that it was not good.

'Don't worry,' she said in the language of the World, 'it will be alright.'

But DeGroot had moved to the master computer and had activated the screen. His grey eyes flickered as he read something on it. He stared at Maya.

'You've been using my computer. Do you think I want a simpleton like you nosing around in there like a pig grubbing for filth?' Suddenly he lunged at her and she felt a heavy blow on the side of her face. She fell backwards, and only the quick reflexes of Yarl and Karn stopped her from hitting the floor.

'You are no longer part of my team,' DeGroot continued, 'Now show me the dead bodies of your little friends within one hour or I will show these true scientists behind me your motionless body. Now go!'

She hurried with Karn and Yarl back to their room.

A great calmness had now infused her. The crisis had come and, in a way, she was glad of it. Now there would be no more creeping uncertainty, no more wondering if everything was alright.

Now she knew it was not.

She addressed the worried pair.

'We have to leave and do it now! Have you packed the food and water, as I told you?'

They nodded and retrieved the two backpacks.

'But you are bigger than we are,' Karn said dubiously, 'you'll need more food; will there be enough for the three of us?'

'Don't worry about me, just think of yourselves. You're in great danger, which is why we have to get out.'

She did not tell them that DeGroot had appointed her as executioner.

'But where will we go?' Yarl asked, 'we thought the World was all there is and then we found this place. We thought you were gods but if you are, you're mad gods.'

'You're partly right,' she said, with an unconvincing smile, 'gods we are not—but we may well be mad.'

'But to get out,' Karn said, 'to where? Are there places apart from the World and here?'

She hesitated. Anything she said would be supposition, a guess. She had no actual idea what was left of Planet Earth.

'Yes, I know there are,' she lied, 'and we are going there. Get your backpacks and follow me. We must run as fast as we can and not stop for anything. Don't get separated from me, whatever you do, or you are lost. If anyone tries to stop you, fight, fight as hard as you can!'

She opened the door of their room and peered out cautiously. There was no one directly in view.

She turned back to them.

'It's not far, but run as fast as you can—I will be!'

Their reddened faces were set hard and firm. They no longer showed obvious fear. She smiled at them.

'Now!'

They hurtled out of their living quarters, Maya in the lead. Hilbert was just crossing the room in front of her, to talk to DeGroot who, as usual, was sitting before the master computer. Maya crashed into him and sent him spinning to the floor. DeGroot began to rise from the chair. McQuade appeared from nowhere, reaching for Karn and Yarl. They kicked her legs from under her and ran on, the sterile air of the recording room seeming to burn their lungs.

She glanced behind her. The Men of the World were still there.

'Not far!' she yelled, but she had also seen that DeGroot, Hilbert and McQuade had recovered from their shock and were not far behind.

She rounded a corner and there was the transfer station. She did not know where it would send them; perhaps to death. But to stay meant death in any case.

Hilbert was upon them. She whirled, tore a computer from its mounting, and smashed it on his head. He collapsed, momentarily blocking the way for DeGroot and McQuade.

She shepherded Karn and Yarl onto the transfer platform, following close behind. Her fingers scrabbled at the control keys. Had she tested the device properly? Would it work?

It responded, and the transparent door slid shut, cutting them off from DeGroot and McQuade, who rained impotent blows upon it.

She stared at the rank of glowing controls for a few moments and tried to recall the various operational modes.

She succeeded.

The transfer platform jerked, shuddered, and then gradually, grudgingly, agonisingly slowly, it began to ascend, up through the tube to whatever unknown territory awaited them.

Maya glanced at Karn and Yarl. For a moment, she could not understand why they were looking so nervous; then she

137

realised that they had never been in a moving vehicle before, even one which was moving not much faster than walking pace. But when she had been looking down at McQuade and DeGroot hammering on the door, it had seemed that she would never lose sight of them, so agonisingly slowly was the capsule moving. And yet it must have felt so unnaturally fast to her companions! She smiled a little at their innocence.

She knew now why it was moving so slowly: it had never been intended that it should remain silent for a hundred and seventy-five thousand years; it was little short of miraculous it was moving at all. Only the vacuum in which it had slumbered had saved it from terminal decay, but even in such conditions the most perfectly designed machines would very slowly deteriorate.

An unpleasant thought struck her: if it should break down now, how would they get out? Fortunately, Karn took her mind off that possibility by asking, 'How long before we get there?'

The question reminded her so much of the ancient trope of impatient children wondering when they would reach their holiday destination; she burst out laughing, much to Karn and Yarl's puzzlement.

'Have I said the wrong thing?' Karn asked, his brow furrowing as he tried to think what could be wrong with his question.

'No, nothing,' she said, the laughter dying more quickly than she would have liked, 'I just don't know the answer. The surface isn't too far away, but we're moving very slowly.'

'We are?' Karn said, 'it seemed very fast to me when they were banging on the door.'

The transparent walls of the capsule gave a full 360^0 view, and they were all looking out in different directions at the encircling wall of the tube. However, the wall had no mark or blemish on it to reveal their speed, so she wondered for a moment if DeGroot could have interfered with the mechanism, and they were now stationary.

No, she would have felt the jolt as inertia tried to keep her moving if they had stopped. Instead, they were still on their way, travelling towards an unknown terminus.

And almost instantly, as that thought was completed, there came a jolt, and the platform stopped. There was the ominous noise of the motor straining as it strove to push the platform up but something was stopping any further ascent. She killed the power to prevent it from burning itself out and now, seriously concerned, tried to find the reason for the halt. The roof of the capsule was opaque but by standing on the sloping control console she was able to reach it. Before Karn and Yarl's astounded eyes, she drove a fist into the junction of the roof and wall and caused the roof partially to rip free. A spar of stone was revealed, crossing the tube from side to side. She peeled more of the roof away so she could grasp it and pulled it down into the capsule, causing the entire structure to shudder as it hit the floor. She looked up into the tube and saw nothing but darkness. Perhaps it was just a stray fall of stone rather than a general collapse.

'One way to find out,' she said to herself and the platform resumed its ascent, but now even more slowly under the increased load. She stared at the stone, seeing a rod of grey rock, tapering to a sharp point and looking unnervingly like the fang of an awesome predator. She said nothing to her companions, but she knew that if one mass of stone could be dislodged, so could another. And another. A great many things can happen in a hundred and seventy-five thousand years. She said nothing.

However, despite their lack of experience, Karn and Yarl were not childlike. They too looked at the mass of stone with troubled eyes. The ascent tube suddenly felt a great deal more confining than it had only minutes earlier. No one spoke; they just sat and listened to the humming noise of the motor, waiting for it to cough and splutter and finally give out.

But it did not, and the ascent continued smoothly.

Then Karn broke the silence.

'You never explained what changed, why we had to get out of that place so quickly. Why your people suddenly turned against us.'

Maya stared at him for a while. He was obviously no fool and was learning fast. There was no point in keeping things from the two of them, or underestimating them.

(Apart from one thing, which she was not sure whether or not to reveal.)

'You remember I told you about how our world nearly collided with the much bigger Jupiter.'

They nodded.

'Everyone on Earth could see it approaching, and they all knew that there would be much destruction; much death. People tried different ways to escape the terrible event. Some people tried to travel a long, long distance away from Earth in special transport machines called lightsail craft, but they all died. Some, like your ancestors, burrowed deep into the crust so that they would be as far away as possible from the terrible events on the surface. We had a different way.'

'And what was that?'

Maya hesitated for a long time. She knew this point would be reached eventually. What should she do?

She decided to dodge the issue—the time was not right.

'We too hid, deep underground, but not like your Burrower ancestors. We slept, and we were due to wake up after a certain time.'

She stopped again. How to explain the passage of tremendous amounts of time to these men? In the World, there was no concept of weeks, of months, of seasons, of years. There was only Wake-Period, followed by Sleep-Period, followed by Wake-Period, and so on and on.

Until the time when it all stopped, of course, but that was a different issue.

She began again.

'Imagine many, many Periods, as many as you can think of. Think of your grandfather living and passing, your father living and passing; you see after a big, big number of those Periods we were due to wake up and return to the surface. But something went wrong: the number of Periods that had passed was very much bigger than we had planned for, and because of that, things which should have worked, didn't.'

She stopped and stared at them again, trying to see if they had lost interest, but their eyes were still bright and focused on her.

But it was so hard explaining all this in such baby-terms!

She continued.

'And because things had gone wrong because the time was so much longer than it should have been, my friends were changed. They weren't themselves. They had become confused and also cruel. Karn and Yarl, they wanted to kill you.'

That caught their attention; she saw them stiffen.

'So we owe you our lives, Maya,' Yarl said softly.

She shrugged.

'It is hard for us to say these things,' Karn said, 'all our lives we were told women were terrible creatures who had caused all us men to suffer when we were thrown out of Paradise. We were taught to despise you and to punish you at every opportunity.' He gave a lopsided grin. 'It is difficult to find there is a woman we can't punish!'

She laughed.

'No—I wouldn't advise it!'

Just then, the platform hit something with the sound of buckling metal and stopped instantly.

Six

Maya leapt to the controls and switched the motor off before it tore itself to pieces. Ignoring the men's questions, she looked up through the gap she had earlier torn in the roof. This time it was not darkness that filled her vision but the dull grey of a mass of stone; a mass which this time entirely blocked the conduit. Bracing herself on the sloping bank of controls, she pushed up with all her not inconsiderable strength. The great slab of stone showed not the slightest motion: their ascent had come to an end.

She dropped back to the floor, her mind numb with shock. This was serious. Karn and Yarl knew it too and looked at each other, despair returning to their eyes.

'What are we going to do, Maya?' Yarl finally managed to say, though his mouth had become so dry he could hardly articulate.

She waved him into silence: she had to think! But it seemed there were only two alternatives: she could stay there and watch Karn and Yarl starve to death, or they could return to the recording room. Perhaps they could surprise its occupants and seize the drilling equipment and resume their journey that way.

Unfortunately, there were two problems with that solution: firstly, she did not know where the drilling equipment was, and secondly, she did not know how to operate it, even if she could find it. Was this the end then, after one hundred and seventy-five thousand years, just to end like this? It was tragic and bathetic at the same time.

Then Karn said, 'Maya, what is this?'

She turned. He was pointing at the wall of the tube and, at the bottom of the canopy, she could see a black rectangle against the grey of the fluorocarbon material.

Maya looked closer: no, it was not *against* the wall; it was *in* the wall. She was looking at the top of an opening, an opening

142

which they had nearly passed. She quickly measured the dimensions of the remaining gap.

Maybe Yarl could squeeze through it; maybe not. But Karn would have great difficulty, and she definitely could not. And so, to escape there was only one thing to do, and that—quickly!

'Stand back!' she ordered her bemused companions. She drove her rigid fingers into and through the join between the transparent wall and the floor, curled those fingers around the outside and, with a great ripping noise, peeled the canopy away so she could reach the wall of the tube. Maya leaned forward, turned on her back, and placed her palms on the underside of the opening, her arms bent back as far as they could go. Then slowly, firmly, forcibly, she straightened those arms like powerful pistons. Once again, there was the noise of materials resisting the force, a grinding, groaning cry of recalcitrant disobedience.

And the capsule slowly moved downwards, revealing more and more of the dark entrance. With her head twisted to the limits of the movements of her joints, she watched each millimetre of featureless blackness as it came into view, made her calculations, and then jumped erect. She pointed at the entrance and, as she did so, she felt the capsule quiver and shudder beneath her.

'In there! Now!' Maya commanded. Karn and Yarl had felt that ominous shudder, too, and knew what it meant. Yarl was first in and turned to help Karn.

'Go back! Get further in!' she yelled as she felt the capsule break out of its hesitancy and begin a downward plunge of death. She leapt.

She leapt, and the capsule started to fall. Its top edge hit her retreating feet as she wormed her way into the entrance and almost pulled her back out as it passed, but she braced her arms against the sides of the opening and did not join in the descent.

Maya wriggled her way around and looked down into the shaft, but the capsule was long gone. It was descending much faster than it had ascended and would burst into the recording room like a bomb.

She hoped there would be no one near it when it hit.

The entrance, or tunnel as it had now become, was only one person wide and less than one person high, but it was widening. Eventually, they were able to stand together as a group. Maya became aware that Karn was studying her with a penetrating gaze of suspicion.

'Yes?' she said, after accepting his stare for a minute or two.

'Are all women outside the World like you?' he said.

She smiled. 'No, not all.' Her returning gaze warned him not to pursue the topic, and so he turned and looked along into the mystery of the tunnel.

'Do you know where we are?'

'Not in the slightest. From here on I'm as lost as you are.'

Yarl made a grunting noise; it was obviously not what he had wanted to hear.

She caught his mood.

'Yarl, I know you're disappointed I'm not a god but we may find a way out of this if we work together.'

'But where are we going? Sometimes I think we'd be better off going back to the World. After all, we'd have you to protect us.'

She shook her head.

'Yarl. Your world is dying—remember? There's no going back.'

Then she approached him and, holding his shoulders, looked down at him.

'I'm not here as your protector, your defender. I'm not your mother. I want you to live your own lives as free men without depending on me. As for where—I don't know as yet. But I will find out, I swear. Who knows what this planet of ours is like now? It's been so long since the disaster that the inhabitants may have made the surface into a garden. A place of beauty, completely unlike your narrow, stultifying world.' She turned slightly so she could see Karn as well. 'But the three of us—we'll find out.'

144

The men remained still and silent. She could hardly see their features in the gloom. But then, slowly, they smiled. She smiled back, immediately.

'Come on then.'

They resumed their journey into the tunnel.

They had not gone far when Maya stopped abruptly. Karn and Yarl walked on for a few minutes until they realised they were alone, and hurried back.

Maya had stopped because a thought that was not her own had come into her mind. It was faint, as if coming from a great distance, or through a mass of a resistant substance. It was a whisper as if a breeze could speak, a breeze in the depths of winter, blowing fitfully in darkness over ice-bound streams, under bitter stars.

We are here.

She remained motionless, still as a statue, uncertain if that thought had been hers or not. She waited.

Then: *We are here. We search. We are here.*

She reached out, trying to send a vital question.

Who are you? she wanted to send, but she did not know how.

And the intruding thought did not recur.

Karn and Yarl rejoined her, obviously concerned at her immobility.

'Are you alright, Maya?' Karn said, reaching for a hand that lay limply at her side.

She shook her head and tried to smile.

'I'm OK. I just felt a little strange, that's all.'

There was no point in telling them she had received a strange message in her head; they had enough new developments to deal with as it was. But they looked unconvinced. Maya realised, with some concern, just how much they had come to depend on her.

Time would tell.

'Let's go,' she said, and pointed into the gloom ahead and so they walked on, but all the time Maya thought to herself: *Who are you? What do you want from me?*

After many hours of weary walking, Karn stopped, and said, 'We're not getting anywhere. I need to eat.'

They sat. All around was a tenebrous gloom. There was a source of light, but it was far ahead of them, looking like a single eye, but one which glowed a sickly yellow. There was a faint breeze coming from that direction as well, a breeze so slow and lethargic that it hardly disturbed a hair on their heads. But it had an unpleasant odour, one almost as faint as the light, but it spoke of unpleasant things, of decay, of corruption.

Maya had noticed that smell, but her companions showed no awareness of it. She suspected that the sense of smell was another human ability that had atrophied in humanity's long incarceration in the World.

She put it from her mind as she watched Karn and Yarl open their backpacks and select their food items. Although the variety of items on offer was pitifully meagre, it was still more exciting than their normal fare and, with a ghost of amusement playing on her lips, she watched them devour the simple foodstuffs.

Karn glanced up at her, brushing crumbs from his lips.

'Not eating?' he asked.

'No; I'll wait for you to finish.'

And finish they did, and after a gulp of the tepid water, they rested their backs against the curved wall of the tunnel. Through drooping eyelids, Karn watched Maya take some items from a backpack and move off into the encircling dimness. Almost immediately, he was asleep.

An unknown time later, his eyes fluttered open, and he saw Maya bent over the same backpack, her back toward him. Her hands were inside it.

Karn felt a stab of indignation. Maya was taking more than her fair share! He tried to rise, but the strain of the past few hours was too much. His eyes closed again while he thought: *I'll have to speak to her later.*

But when he was fully awake, he decided against it. After all, she had saved their lives on more than one occasion. If she wanted a little extra, surely she was the one person in the group who was entitled to it! He felt a little ashamed he had even considered confronting her.

Maya noticed Karn studying her as he rose to his feet, but she said nothing, and neither did he. Yarl had slept through it all and saw nothing pass between the other two. He said, sleepily, 'Time to be moving on, I see. I wonder where we're going.'

At that, Karn looked directly at Maya.

'You say the surface might be a garden. If we're going to see that garden, shouldn't we be going up, not farther into this world?'

'Indeed we should, but unless you can burrow through rock with your bare hands, we'll have to keep going until we find a way up to the surface.'

'And if we don't?'

'Sooner or later, we will. All the people down here originally lived on the surface. So if it's possible to come down, it must be possible to go up.'

Karn was obviously in an argumentative mood.

'So we wander around until we find it.'

Unusually for Maya, she felt herself becoming annoyed with her fellow traveller. And then she stopped herself. Perhaps Karn had a right to be sceptical. After all, she had no real idea of how to reach the surface, ever since the conduit had proved to be impassable.

But the memory of that strange, intrusive thought came back to her. *We search.* Was it possible someone was looking for her? Or maybe there was a more ominous explanation: perhaps the mental deterioration she had witnessed in the recording room was beginning to claim her. She returned her attention to Karn, pushing speculation into her subconscious.

'There must be shafts that lead to the surface. Maybe we'll spend twenty years looking for one. But the alternative is to lie down here and die. Tell me, Karn, is that what you want?'

When faced with such a blunt expression of their choices, Karn backed down. He gave a conciliatory smile.

'You're right. Let's get moving.'

147

She returned the smile to show the crisis had passed, and they resumed their trek down the tunnel.

She let them lead the way, partly to make sure that she was not outpacing them and leaving them behind.

She looked over their russet heads towards the light. Its yellow colouration was not the pleasing yellow of a flower, or the sun as it begins its descent to the horizon. It was a jaundiced, sallow luminance, giving the impression of some sickness of the liver. Karn and Yarl did not seem to be affected by it; indeed, as they approached the source, their walking became brisker, their faces showing anticipation.

There is something familiar to them in what they're seeing, she thought, *as if they are returning to something within their experience.*

And then the tunnel opened out to many times its previous width and Maya realised she was standing on a great lip of rock overlooking a scene completely outside her experience.

Before her, she saw a colossal cylinder; a tube of truly epic proportions. On lifting her eyes, she could see the semi-circular profile of the roof of the cylinder, a roof so high above her that thin, wispy clouds were hanging underneath its grey, pitted surface. And in that roof were rectangular objects which were emitting the vomit-coloured light, one behind the other, separated by a wide gap, and then another and another, so that eventually they merged into a thin line of insipid yellow that melted away into the blue haze of the far distance.

She realised her companions were literally jumping up and down with joy.

'The World!' Yarl was yelling, 'we're back at the World!'

An apron of rubble and talus allowed the trio to descend from the lip of the tunnel onto the floor of the cylinder. Maya looked around, realising she was seeing a Burrower colony for the first time. She looked from side to side at the beaming faces of her companions as they flanked her, obviously straining to run off and explore.

'I thought you didn't want to return to your world,' she said.

'After what I've seen of your world, I've changed my mind,' Karn replied happily, 'all those machines, and stories about big ball-things floating in space. This, I understand!'

'And being wanted for murder?'

'I doubt The Supreme Leader is still in power. Lots of the People didn't like his way of doing things!'

She decided there was no point in trying to hold them back and let them run off into the little group of huts towards which they had been walking. A wave of disappointment swept over her. After all they'd been through, after she had risked everything to save them from the insanity in the recording room, it had all been for nothing. She might just as well have let DeGroot kick them out when he had first ordered her to do it. In her search for answers, it looked like she would be doing it alone. And she also realised how much she had enjoyed their company, the simple pleasure of speaking to humans who, though entirely unsophisticated, were rational adults.

There was a large shard of a wood-like substance nearby, and she sat on it while watching them disappear into the cluster of huts, chattering like children. But as she looked around at the silent buildings and the empty streets of beaten earth, she soon realised what it was they had discovered. She wondered how long it would be before her companions came back to her.

It was not long, and she could see the downcast expressions for quite some time before they were near her.

'No one home?' she said, immediately regretting her flippant tone.

'No, the place is empty.' Karn looked at her sharply. 'You knew?'

'It wasn't difficult. When you enter a new village, you're not usually greeted with absolute silence. And there's something else, isn't there? Like where we are.'

It hadn't seemed possible for Karn's expression to get any more disheartened, but somehow it did.

'This isn't the World.'

Despite herself, Maya felt the need to display her irritation at having been abandoned quite so easily.

'Yes, the fact that your so-called sun has come back to life might have been a giveaway.'

Karn and Yarl squatted on their haunches; Yarl stared at the ground, but Karn was still defiant.

'Well, so it isn't our World, but it's one very much like it. We could fit in here easily.'

'What and go back to fungus stirring?'

'And what's wrong with that? It's honest work.'

'Haven't you learned anything from me?'

'Yes, things we don't want to know,' Yarl said, finally lifting his head, 'machines that show pictures of things we can't understand, stories about big balls hitting small balls, weird people trying to kill us. Nothing makes sense!'

Maya thought for a few moments. She wasn't entirely sure things made sense either. She had been rocked to the core by the message from DeGroot's master computer, and was still unsure whether she had absorbed all its implications. But in a crazy, dangerous world, she decided she needed companions more than she needed points-scoring.

She smiled.

'So, what do you want to do now?'

Karn and Yarl stood and looked up at her.

'We're not giving up, that's for certain. We're not abandoning hope just because the first village we meet doesn't have any People in it. We'll walk to the next one, and the one after that until we meet someone.'

'It's a long way. Shouldn't you rest first?'

'No need,' Karn said, and then added, in a meaningful tone, 'it's not like we're going to run out of food, is it, Maya?'

She stared at him blankly for a moment and then shrugged.

'Let's go.'

As they left the silent township behind them, Karn recalled their desperate flight in the darkness from his home village, and the reception he had gotten from the next one. Was it any more likely he would be welcome in this one, a settlement which wasn't even in the World?

Maya strode on, finding it a little difficult to match her pace to the short steps of her companions. The walk was no effort to her, but from time to time she had to stop so that they could catch their breath.

'How is it you can just walk and walk?' Karn demanded, between gulps of air, 'We can't keep up. Is it all the food you've been eating?'

She shook her head.

'No, it's not that.'

Silence fell, and they walked on, with increasingly frequent stops, until they were at the outskirts of the next village.

'Careful,' Yarl warned, 'new men don't always like strangers.'

'I'll bear that in mind,' Maya replied, 'I'm sure my natural charm will win them over.'

However, it soon became apparent that there would be no need for charm, natural or otherwise. This village appeared to be as deserted as the last. With growing disappointment, Karn and Yarl led the way.

And then stopped.

Lying on the ground between two huts was a human skeleton, its yellow-white bones completely picked clean, its eyeless sockets staring up at them as if in supplication.

'That's strange,' Yarl said, 'why wasn't he recycled into the fungus vats?'

Karn shook his head and walked on.

It wasn't long before they encountered the next skeleton.

And after that, two more.

And then three more.

The entire village was a sepulchre.

Maya looked at the two men. It was obvious they were deeply shaken as they stood there, almost completely surrounded by human remains, some complete skeletons, some pitiful mounds of disarticulated bones. Karn turned a stricken face to her.

151

'What has happened here? I've never seen anything like it. This isn't the proper way. When we pass, we give our substance to the vats so the next generation will not go hungry. This isn't right!'

Yarl pointed at the sun. It was shining steadily, casting its bilious light over the open graveyard.

'And there's nothing wrong with their Sun. So why did they die?'

Maya had a feeling she knew and said, 'Show me one of your food vats.'

The village layout was almost identical to their hometown, and the three of them were soon standing by a tank which had clearly once held the life-giving yeast-like fungus. It had a great rent in its side and the broth had spilled out and solidified on the ground as a dull tarry mass; a long time ago.

She motioned them back and scooped up a handful of the black substance. She brought it dangerously close to her eyes and then flung it away.

'I thought so,' she said, 'mycelia.'

'What?' 'What?'

'It's a different kind of fungus to your food-type. A disease, a parasitic organism that fed on the broth and killed it.' She pointed to the fleshless bones, which lay scattered in all directions. 'These people starved to death.'

Involuntarily, Yarl clutched at Karn for support.

Hunger. The one thing that had always terrified the People. The threat of famine: the great horror that haunted their dreams. Why else would they return the goodness of their flesh to the vats if not to stave off that invisible monster?

'Starved to death.' Karn looked at the dry piles of random bones and shivered. 'Please, no.'

Against his will, he had visions of the last days of this cemetery-town: the desperation; the wailing; the hopeless ceremonies to appease the indifferent gods; the lingering end of the last survivor, dying alone in a roofless charnel-house.

Maya said nothing for a while, as there was nothing she could say which would lift the despair from her companions. She looked around and examined a few more of the huts but soon returned to the others: it was the same everywhere.

Eventually, she felt she could speak without causing more misery.

'I don't think it's just this village; I think this entire colony is dead. All of it.'

Karn almost spat his reply.

'How can you know that? Are you a god, after all? There must be some people in this World—somewhere!'

She shook her head.

'No. I have listened carefully. I hear nothing. There is no noise coming from the villages ahead of us, farther into the colony. Nothing.'

'So, what can we do? I was hoping they would take us in, feed us, women…'

'No,' Maya said, and gently raised his chin so Karn's eyes locked with hers, 'No food, no women. We have to move on.'

'But where? Everything is dead, everything.'

'We must find a way to the surface. People must have found their way back there in all this time since the Jupiter-passage. It may not be a garden, but it must be better than this.'

Defeated, the two men nodded.

'Alright, Maya. We will trust you. We will follow you.'

'Good. But as we walk on, you must be careful; you must be alert.'

'Why?'

'Some of these bones have been moved a long way from where they had fallen. Some of them have been gnawed on. And not with human teeth.'

Seven

They walked on in silence; Karn and Yarl were too shocked to speak, and Maya had no more she wanted to say on the subject. However, she could not escape a gathering feeling that all of humanity's attempts to escape the doom of stars had been in vain. It looked like she was the only sane survivor from the recording room, but she had no guarantee she was immune; it might simply be that the mind rot was taking longer in her than it had in the others. She now knew of two Burrower colonies: one was dying, and the other was dead. That did not suggest any other would be in a good place.

They had visited another settlement after the second one. It had held fewer corpses than the previous one, but it was just as dead. After that confirmation of futility, they had given the villages a wide berth.

Eventually, she could not bear the silence any longer.

'You say there are doors in the wall of the cylinder—I mean, the world,' she added, seeing Karn's puzzlement at the word "cylinder."

'Yes, the one we went through led to a long tunnel. And then we found you.'

She quizzed him about the things he and Yarl had found in the recesses in the tunnel walls. Despite Karn's lack of a suitable vocabulary, she formed a meaningful image from his confused description. He was describing motorised vehicles, ones with caterpillar tracks. But any excitement at that realisation was very short-lived: the chance they would be in working order after one hundred and seventy-five thousand years was precisely zero. Most of the machines in the recording room which had been capable of reactivation after that colossal period, such as the computers, had been ones without moving parts.

But the existence of such vehicles at the bottom of shafts clearly showed the Burrowers had made plans to return to the

154

surface. But they had not done so. Instead, they had remained in their "Worlds", gradually losing all memories of their history.

Why had they remained in these confined cylinders for millennium after millennium, slowly degenerating into such barely-alive creatures as Karn and Yarl had been when she had discovered them?

She had looked at the walls of the cylinder through which they were trudging and calculated its curvature. There was little doubt the cylinder, in fact, was a vast torus, like the mythical World-Serpent biting its own tail. That being so, there was no point in continuing their journey. Their path led nowhere, except back to the first silent village, after a huge amount of wasted time.

The only hope was to find a door and hope that something beyond it would lead them away from this subterranean prison. Not only that, but the men had also said the passage they had discovered contained edible plants—and the supply in the backpacks would not last forever.

Karn explained the doors occurred at regular intervals all along the wall, so they could not be far from one.

Nor were they, and Maya was soon looking up at the outline of an extremely large door, set in the gently curving side of the great cylinder. She went right up to it and looked at where it joined the wall. It was very slightly open, and she could insert her fingers through the gap. She gave it an exploratory tug—and it did not move.

'We'll have to find another,' Yarl said, 'the one we got through was already open.'

'We're running out of time,' she said, 'and we need to get more food.'

'Yes, I can see why that would be important to you,' was Karn's half-muttered comment. She stared sharply at him, but he met her gaze steadily, unwaveringly. She shrugged and returned to examining the door.

'It must have a mechanism so it can be opened from both sides,' she said, mainly to herself. But then she gave a wry grimace: no doubt it did, and no doubt it had crumbled to dust sometime in the past millennia. She looked over her shoulder.

'Stand back,' she said in a tone which brooked no disobedience. Once her peripheral vision told her they had obeyed, she drove her fingers into the gap between the door and its surround. She braced herself; her arms bent into expectant power, ready for the task.

And then she pulled back on the door.

For a second or two, nothing happened, and then, very slowly, complainingly, it began to inch open. There was a grinding, snapping noise as it moved, and ahead of it, a miniature bow wave formed in the soil which had piled up around its base.

She pulled and pulled until a gap wide enough for all of them to pass through had been created, and then she turned to the astounded pair and said, 'What are you waiting for? Let's go!'

Words having failed them, they meekly followed.

Once inside, Karn and Yarl saw a depressingly familiar sight. The passageway was almost completely dark, except that there was a faint green luminance at the end of a tunnel of ebon night.

'What is the point of this?' Karn asked, 'we don't want to end up with your crazy friends again.'

'You said there were shafts leading upward,' she reminded him, 'you want to go up, don't you?'

They set off toward the green light.

**

'I can't walk anymore,' Yarl said as he slumped on a pile of small stones, 'we're not getting anywhere.'

They had walked a long way but had not found an alcove with one of the strange machines inside, unlike in their previous expedition. However, they had found plants very similar to those they had seen in the other place, and Maya had been busy harvesting them and putting them in the backpacks.

'You can rest now,' she said, rising from her knees, 'sleep if you want to.'

'We do.'

She pushed a backpack towards Yarl.

'Eat first.'

Maya watched them as they ate, and then, as their eyelids fluttered, she took a root from the pack and went off into the gloom.

But Karn was not completely asleep, and he stiffened into alertness when he saw her walk off. Through half-closed lids he waited for her to return. She did after a surprisingly short time, and he saw bend over the backpack and place a hand inside.

Instantly, he leapt to his feet and dashed over to Maya and grabbed her wrist.

'I've got you!' he hissed, 'you've been stealing food! We trusted you, we thought you were our friend and all the time, you've been cheating us!'

She turned to him and he stared into her face, seeing their no guilt, no embarrassment, no shame but only pity and sympathy. Vast, tolerant sympathy.

'No,' she said softly, 'you have caught me, Karn, but not in the way you thought.'

He snatched the bag from her and looked inside, ready to display his righteous anger.

His jaw dropped.

There was more food in the bag than there had been previously.

He dropped the backpack and ran a hand over his forehead.

'What, what? How is this possible?' He stared at her, his eyes wide. 'You've not been eating?'

'No,' she said softly, 'I've been collecting more roots. Or putting back the food you saw me take.'

'But—not eating? How is that possible? Why have you been hiding this from us?'

Maya smiled sadly, and for a moment he was aware of the incredible gulf between them, of the vast reserves of understanding that this woman-being possessed.

'Karn,' she said, 'you've had enough to deal with; things which your upbringing has not prepared you for. You've had so much to adjust to. You've found out what you thought was the world was just an underground prison. That there are other real worlds separated from this one by immense distances, that all human life was very nearly extinguished by the actions of one woman. That's enough for you. More revelations might drive you insane.'

'More revelations,' he whispered, 'how much more is there? And you're right—all of this is destroying me; I can't go on just walking, never getting anywhere.' He stopped and stared, long and hard, at her. 'And you, you're the biggest mystery of them all. I don't know much about women, especially ones outside of the World, but you—the power you display, the things you can do. No Woman or Man could do them.' He stopped and fear began to invade his expression. 'There is only one answer—you really are a god, aren't you?'

Once again that smile, with its tinge of pity.

'No, I'm not a god. If we manage to escape from this prison, I will tell you all about me. But for the moment—just trust me. I mean you no harm, and I will do my best to protect you.'

The sound of talking had roused Yarl, and he looked up from where he lay.

'Can't you let me sleep? What are you arguing about now?'

She crossed to him and ran a soothing hand over his brow.

'No arguing, Yarl. Everything is alright. Go back to sleep.'

***

'This tunnel is different from the last one,' Karn said, 'by now we'd passed three of those machines, and we haven't seen one.'

Maya frowned. This was not good. If they could not find one of those shafts they had described, then she saw no hope for them. The machines themselves would be of no use; they'd only be memories of what they once were, flimsy casts made from rust that would fall apart under the lightest touch.

They were standing directly under one of the roof lamps, bathed in its soft green light; a light which had the unfortunate effect of giving a ghoulish cast to the features of her companions.

She was trying to think of what her next move should be when there was a loud CLICK! from directly above her.

And the passageway was instantly plunged into total, utter blackness. Karn and Yarl gave cries of shock and alarm. She felt them reach for her in the darkness.

'What's happened!'

'I don't know,' she said, 'the way the light went out is strange. There was no warning I could detect. It was as if someone just switched it off.'

'Switched *them* off, you mean,' Karn replied, 'can you see any lights at all, Maya?'

She looked ahead.

Blackness.

She looked the way they had come.

Blackness.

'We have to go back,' Yarl said, 'we can't go on in complete darkness like this.'

'No, we can't start all over again. We must go on.'

'We can't,' Yarl shouted, 'how can we do that without being able to see anything?'

'I can see a little way.'

'How?'

They heard her sigh.

'There's something called infrared. I can detect a little of it.'

'How?'

'Does it matter? Just accept I'm telling the truth. If we go back, we will have achieved nothing. There should be light further down this tunnel. And a shaft to the surface.'

There was silence as well as darkness. The silence seemed to make the darkness even more impenetrable. Then Karn said,

'Alright, Maya. You asked me to trust you—and I will. Shut up, Yarl, we're going on!'

'Good,' she said, 'get in front of me and stay there. It's more important than ever we stay together.'

'What if there's a big hole ahead? A ravine or something.'

'I will detect it before you fall in, Yarl. Now come on, we'll never get out of this dark if we just stand here arguing.'

They moved off, but very slowly. *Apparently*, she thought, *they don't entirely trust me about detecting big holes.*

They walked on and on. But the light did not return. Even at the limit of her detection, Maya could not register a single photon of visible light.

'I've got to stop,' Yarl said suddenly, 'it feels like my feet are bleeding.'

Maya did not reply but they swiftly knew she had stopped walking and was standing completely still, some distance behind them.

Karn moved back slowly until he bumped into her.

'What's wrong?'

She did not reply, and he had the feeling she was turning her head from side to side.

He asked again, and she replied, very slowly, very carefully.

'I hear something.'

'Like what?'

'We're being stalked.'

'What! How can you know?'

'Stop asking me that! I know, right? Something is out there in the dark.'

'Then how can it find us?'

'It's using echolocation. I can just pick up the lowest frequency of its signals.'

'Is it dangerous?'

'What do you think? Something that lives in the darkness and uses echolocation to find other creatures. Do you think it just wants to say "Hello"?'

'What can we do?'

160

'I'm not sure. I have to think of a way so that we can see it. It probably doesn't like light.'

Karn fell silent. He had no experience of any dangerous creatures. There had been none in the World. In fact, apart from the People, there had been no creatures capable of movement. There had been the People, fungus and scraps of algae.

Nothing else.

Karn felt something brush against him and, in sudden fright, struck out at it.

It was Yarl.

'I heard what you said, and I'd like to know what we can do as well.'

But Maya was no longer responding to their questioning. She was thinking *Light! I must have light!*

Her infra-red vision was very restricted and could only make out basic shapes, and then only as images only just distinguishable from their background. It seemed to her that in the left-hand side of the wall ahead of them there was a darker patch, as if she was seeing into a greater distance at that point.

They'd finally found one of the recesses her companions had discovered in the other passageway.

'Hold my hands,' she said, 'I can see a recess ahead. That way, we'll be able to protect our backs.'

They obeyed, and she could feel that the hands of both men were trembling. Only a short while earlier, she'd been trying to protect them from disturbing new experiences, and now this! As quickly as she could, she moved toward the recess, half-pulling her companions behind her. She stopped, cursing her limited vision. Had something moved ahead of her then, a slightly lighter blob against a dark background, something betraying itself by its thermal radiation?

Karn was on Maya's left side as they approached the recess, a destination utterly invisible to him. Then he felt something brush against him and he knew it was not Yarl. He felt harsh, coarse, wiry hair press briefly against his arm and at the same time his feeble sense of smell picked up a revolting stench, as if

161

from a corpse that had not been disposed of soon enough in the yeast vats. Maya's superior senses had picked up the intruder's presence before him and she swung him around and threw him before her into the alcove. She whirled back to protect Yarl.

But she was too late.

She heard him scream in visceral terror, a scream suddenly cut off, replaced by the crunching sound of bone being bitten through.

There was a horrible silence, and the air was abruptly heavy with the smell of fresh blood.

She backed into the recess, bumping into Karn and driving him behind her, further back, away from the thing in the darkness. She could hear him whimpering, but ignored it.

'Light,' she murmured, 'light.' She scrabbled around on the ground. There was plant material, fronds and stems. It might be dry enough.

It might.

Something else was needed. A source of ignition. What could that be?

She saw something large and dark enter the recess. Her hand closed on a stone. She threw it, and knew her aim was true as she heard both the thud of the impact and the grunt of the creature.

From beyond the dark shape, she could hear crunching and gulping noises begin again, and then a sinister silence.

So there were two of them, whatever creatures were abroad in the darkness.

She reached for another stone to throw, and her hands felt there was a group of smaller stones. She felt their smooth surfaces. Quickly she took the roots and stems of the plant remains and twisted them together. Then she took two of the larger stones and smashed them together in a sidelong blow. There was a transient brilliant blue spark.

Again and again.

Faster, stronger.

A fat spark flew onto her makeshift brand, and the dry material caught. Triumphantly, she held it aloft so she could see the face of the enemy.

Rats.

Rats as big as she was, with scarlet eyes like glowing coals and long yellow fangs. One set of fangs was stained scarlet with Yarl's blood. They backed away slightly but stopped, just outside the circle of flickering light thrown by the brand. She knew it would not take long to burn down.

'Karn, come here! Now!' she thundered. She gave him the brand and told him to hold it high. His quivering grasp made the shadows dance evilly. She stared at the fearsome rodents.

'So it's you hiding in the shadows, is it?' she hissed, 'killing Yarl for your meat? Now I'm going to kill you.'

She advanced.

The rats did not retreat and looked up at her with vermillion eyes fixed on her throat. They readied for the spring.

And then they leapt as one. Maya's arms lashed out and sent one monster spinning into the darkness. But then the other was on her, its bloody fangs centimetres from her face. She felt its foetid breath wash over her in a putrescent wave as she stared into the hellish glow of its bulging eyes; eyes in which she could see her own miniature reflections.

She grasped its throat, letting its body dangle with its pink hind paws scraping the ground, and then her hands moved slowly inward, propelled by arms with the power of pistons. The animal thrashed madly, making gasping, gurgling noises as her hands moved inexorably closer to each other, the sinews and cartilage of its throat yielding before her thrust. She stared into the swelling eyes, watching the lifeforce ebb. But Maya was not finished. She flung it to the ground, placed a foot on its back, rammed her hands under the repellent head and pulled and twisted. There was a wet ripping noise, and the head came away in an eruption of blood and torn tissue. She whirled to face the other rat, which had returned to aid its fellow-creature. She stepped over its corpse and waved the head at the other monstrosity.

'Now it's your turn.'

Then behind her she heard Karn screech as the flambeau burned down to his hand and went out.

Darkness returned in a deadly black comber. In the terrible second before the light died, Maya had seen the rat begin its leap. In the instant of its arc of attack beginning, she calculated its position and brought up a fist in a pile-driving punch to where she believed the creature to be. The fist connected and, with a hiss of pain, the rat was knocked back out of the alcove.

'Run!' she screamed, 'run! Tell all of your nest that death has come among you! Go!'

No sooner had those words left her lips, when Maya heard a loud CLICK! directly above her and the passageway was filled with soft green light again. Looking down, she saw the rat's head almost between her feet and kicked it away.

She gazed up at the roof light and murmured, 'So you've been watching us, have you? But who are you, I wonder?'

Karn walked up to her, sucking his burnt hand. He stared at the two pieces of the rat corpse and said, 'What a horrible thing.' Then he remembered something. 'Yarl!' he cried, 'where's Yarl?'

She hugged him.

'He's gone, Karn. I'm so sorry. I said I'd protect you both, but I failed. I am so sorry.'

In the returned light, Karn could see a snaking ribbon of blood leading away into the distance.

'So that thing got him. What a horrible world this is. All the time we lived in the World, we never knew how lucky we were.'

Maya chose not to remind him of how darkness had driven him and Yarl from their world.

It was best to let him grieve in his own way.

But she had learned something. The disappearance and reappearance of the light before and after the rat attack could not have been a coincidence. It meant that there were other players, other agents, at large in this drama of theirs. Agents who had far more control over their environment than Karn and Yarl had ever possessed.

Perhaps they would know how to reach the surface!

But, then again, perhaps meeting those agents would not be for the best. What kind of people would have deliberately exposed them to such a horrific experience?

Just as she completed that thought, once again there came a faint whisper of an alien thought into her mind, one so feeble that for a moment she doubted it was there.

But it was.

We are here. We search.

She felt a kind of anger at the elusive nature of these messages. Summoning all her mental energies, she tried to respond.

Who are you? Where are you?

But the message had gone. There was only the background hiss of her own tumbled, troubled mind.

Putting that mystery away, she examined the recess in which the recent battle with the giant rodents had been played out. As Karn had said, a caterpillar-tracked machine was standing there, but a single cursory glance was enough to be certain it would never move again. She raised her head to examine the shaft which rose above the shattered machine.

She could see at once there was a great slab of stone blocking it.

Another hope dashed.

She beckoned Karn to join and for a moment was seized with a desire to hug and caress him, to put away all thoughts of subterranean captivity, of monsters that stalked their prey in the dark.

But she did not.

'We must move on,' was all she eventually said.

But despair had seized Karn.

'Why? We're not getting anywhere. Now the light's back, let's just sit here. It will be peaceful.'

'No. You don't really mean that. And even in the light, we're not safe.'

'How so? Those rats don't hunt in the light.'

'No, they don't. But the bones in the village. They'd been gnawed—but not by the rats. There must be more than one predator at loose in these tunnels.'

Eight

Karn wondered at Maya's composure. How could she make statements like that without fear showing in her voice or her features? As he walked beside her, he felt a strong emotion begin to stir within him. It was something like he had felt with Thylassa on occasion, but subtly different. Unlike the feeling of ownership he had known with his late wife, this was a deeper feeling. It was like he wanted somehow to discard part of his own identity and merge with hers.

He shook his head. He didn't understand it.

But Maya had her own thoughts, which she also didn't understand. There was intelligence at work in this tunnel, not just carnivorous monsters. But why did they simply say, "We are here" and "We search"; why not come out of the shadows and reveal themselves?

They passed another recess, containing the now standard wrecked machine and blocked shaft. Finally, they reached another area where the plants were growing and where water trickled down the walls of the passage. Karn said, 'I can't stop thinking about Yarl. I need to sit down for a while.'

She nodded.

'Of course.'

When they were sitting, she touched him gently and said, 'I am very sorry, Karn. I promised I'd protect Yarl, and I didn't. I let those foul monstrosities take him.'

Karn lay on his back and stared at the ground.

'He should have been my enemy, after what he did with Thylassa, but somehow he wasn't. She was happier with him than with me; I see that now. Some of the Women used to talk about something called "Love." I never understood; it just seemed like a way of avoiding punishment. Do you know anything about love, Maya?'

She also stared at the ground, twisting a piece of root between her fingers. She made no attempt to eat it.

'No, I don't.'

Karn made a decision: he rolled on his side and placed an arm across her chest, below her breasts.

'Could you and I have love, Maya? You're a Woman, but so different from those in the Village. Could you teach me to love?'

Gently, she removed his arm, and said, 'You mustn't say things like that, Karn. It's impossible for us to love.'

He returned to the sitting position and stared at nothing.

'I know why. I'm sure I look nothing like the Men of your People. I'm short and weak and ugly. You tell me you're not a god, but everything I've seen you do tells me that's exactly what you are.'

Maya's mind went into overdrive. She had shielded him from the truth in order not to overload a mind already groaning under the weight of new experiences, new revelations. But the lack of honesty was now driving a wedge between them.

She made the decision.

She turned to him, a soft, uncertain smile playing on her lips.

'No, it's none of those things, Karn.'

He looked unconvinced.

'Then what is it?'

'We cannot love because I am not exactly a woman, as you would understand it.'

'What?'

She reached for his hands and spoke with a new note of urgency in her voice.

'Please listen to me, Karn. It's a long complicated story, one you couldn't possibly have understood if I had said it earlier. Promise you'll listen and not interrupt.'

He looked wary, but finally said, 'Alright.'

She turned away from him and stared into uncountable infinity.

'It was the time of the doom of stars. Baldwin, in her impatience, had disturbed the equilibrium of the entire Solar system. Her actions had sent the massive planet Jupiter out of its orbit and careening into the inner system. Its close passage would sterilise our world, even if there was no actual collision.

'All of Earth's population could see it getting closer every year. Everyone wanted to live, to escape this terrible, undeserved fate. Some people attempted to escape the Solar system in things called lightsail ships, but the distances were too great and their efforts were in vain.

'Others tried to hide from the killing radiation by burrowing deep into the planetary crust.'

She forestalled his interruption.

'Yes, they are the people you are descended from. They must have intended their stay to be temporary, but for some reason they became trapped in their colonies and slowly deteriorated.'

(She briefly thought *But why did all the colonies become trapped?*)

'And then there were us. We were led by a man of great genius called Cornelius DeGroot. You met something that looked just like him: his thin grey hair, the moles on his back, his irritability. But it wasn't him—exactly.

'At the moment of Jupiter's closest passage past the planet Earth, a group of scientists killed themselves. They knew that their fragile bodies could not survive the inferno that was just beginning to rage. So immediately before their death, their mentalities were copied, uploaded into digital form and stored in order to be downloaded at a future date.

'When the appointed time came, when Earth had settled into a new stable orbit—albeit a much colder one than the original—the mentalities would be downloaded into mechanical bodies, receptacles which would be 3D-printed when needed, and they would be themselves again. The mechanisms they then inhabited would look exactly as they had done at the moment of their death, so they could adjust better to their new existence. And at least they would *think* they were the same individuals. They would emerge onto the wounded Earth's surface, bringing their knowledge with them, and aid the survivors in reconstruction.

'You like how I look, I can tell, and if I weren't wearing this tunic, you'd see that I, Maya, have nipples, a vagina. I look just like a woman.'

But Karn said, 'But you're not *that* Maya, the real one, you're just some kind of unnatural copy!'

Maya looked at him strangely. 'Am I really only that? Tell me: when you sleep, where does your consciousness go?'

Karn was confused. 'Go? It doesn't go anywhere. I'm still me, whether or not I'm asleep!'

Maya held him motionless in her stare, like an insect pinned to a label.

'But are you? When you are unconscious, everything that constitutes you is gone: your memories, your will, your volition, your plans for the future, your personality quirks, everything that makes you—you.

'When you wake, you are in some respects born again. The essence of you reinhabits your brain. But is it exactly, precisely, the same you? Could you tell? You slept—and you were not. You awoke—and you were *you* again. You slept for some hours, and then you returned. I have slept for tens of thousands of years and I have returned.'

'But you were a creature of flesh and blood! Now you are some kind of machine!'

She smiled. 'I forgive you, Karn. These concepts you are dealing with are very subtle, more so than a stirrer of fungus should be called upon to grapple with. I am me—what particular platform houses that complex of qualities that makes me human has no bearing on my identity. From the point of my self-awareness, it is totally irrelevant what compounds comprise which platform; whether they are proteins and nucleic acids or polymers and titanium, I repeat—for the last time—I am ME!'

'But why did you do it? Such an unnatural act—to be copied, to die, and then the copy to be pasted into a mechanism! How can you live like that? Surely better to accept natural death!'

'Some have said death is the price we pay for the privilege of being alive, but my colleagues and I did not accept that. Once there is consciousness, that consciousness wants only one thing: that it should continue. You talk of death—but what can the living know of it? What I do know is summed up by the answer to a simple question: *for who would lose, though full of pain, this intellectual being, those thoughts that wander through eternity?*'

'I don't understand those words. But how is what you did even possible?'

'The science of my day could copy a human mind and store it. It could download that mind into a mechanical brain and place that brain in a machine, so it could have freedom of movement. We could do that but we could not create a vessel of flesh and blood into which to download a mind. This machine that looks like a woman is the best we could do at the time.'

'And you are happy?'

She smiled, sadly, wistfully.

'Not entirely. We hoped that if we lived long enough in these structures, we would be able to solve the problem of creating a biological vessel into which to pour our minds. But it now seems certain that none of us will have that time. I am me, but you are right, Karn, there is something different, something lacking, things I truly miss now I am inside this metal box. I do not feel the ebb and flow of the hormones, I don't feel the blood rush to my cheeks with embarrassment, I would not hear the thud of my heart at the moment of orgasm.'

Karn shook his head as if this ceaseless barrage of abstract concepts was causing him actual pain. Then he looked up at her again.

'I knew there was something strange about your companions: when I kicked them—they felt too rigid, too heavy. But there are simpler questions to ask: you don't eat, so how can you live?'

'My energy comes from radionuclides from the Island of Stability region of the periodic table. I have the ability to top up my reserves with direct electrical input but I don't see any power points around here, unfortunately.'

At that, Karn gave up.

'The fact remains, the original Maya is dead. You remember being her—but you weren't, and you aren't.'

A silence fell. Maya wondered if she should have continued with her deception; so profound had been the shock that Karn had suffered. But he was still not satisfied.

'But something has gone wrong. Your friends went mad. You can't find the way back to the surface. I know you can't—you'd have found it by now instead of this pointless wandering. What happened?'

She nodded in a gesture of respect.

'Yes, Karn. You have learned much, and now you understand much. We slept—or waited to be copied back to an inert substrate, whichever way you want to look at it—for much, much longer than we should have done. So long that the machines which held our consciousness had begun to decay. The copying back appears to have been faulty and the mentalities have been mixed and badly downloaded, corrupted. The result seems to be a growing insanity.'

'But *you* are still feeling alright, aren't you?'

She hesitated.

'I'd like to think so, but it is improbable that just one mentality was downloaded perfectly and all the others weren't. I must be an outlier, a point a long way out on the distribution.'

'You think you will go the same way.'

'Yes. I keep running diagnostics on myself and so far they are clean. But there have been a few worrying events recently.'

'Such as?'

'I hear thoughts which aren't mine. Someone seems to be saying *We are here.*'

Karn ran that through his mind for a moment, and then said, 'So why did you "sleep" for such a long time?'

She stood.

'That is the big, big, question, my friend. If I knew that, I'd understand a lot more of why we're in this mess. The difference between the planned time and the actual time is enormous. I think it was only your arrival that awoke us, otherwise we'd still be existing as ones and zeros in a memory bank.'

Karn realised he had gone as far as his understanding could take him. Perhaps beyond.

'Alright. I will try to forget some of what you told me. You're still the Maya who saved my life on more than one occasion—I've lost count. And,' He held out his hand, 'I still feel something for you. I don't know what the word for it is.'

She smiled and accepted his hand.

'And I feel something for you, Karn. Whatever the word for it is.'

***

Not knowing what else to do, they walked on. The tunnel stretched endlessly before them and after them. Unchanging; one metre looking exactly the same as the next one and the previous one.

Then, without warning, Maya stopped, so suddenly Karn collided with her. He looked at her with growing concern as her gaze was fixed directly at nothing at all. He tugged at her, but she remained as rigid and unmoving as a rock.

Then she spoke.

'The time crystal. I'm not sure of the periodicities, how they may evolve, or perhaps decay is a better way of putting it. Three hundred years, is that a safe period? What is the theta function at that boundary?'

Karn screamed soundlessly. She had spoken of possible mental decay only a short time earlier, and now it was upon her! He beat upon her abdomen, trying to wake her from her confusion, but she continued to discuss possible indeterminate solutions to the theta function.

And then she stopped, looked down at his pummelling fists and said sternly, 'Karn, may I enquire as to why you are hitting me in the stomach?'

He collapsed against her, almost sobbing.

She spoke quietly, seriously.

'Karn, what happened? Was I saying strange things?'

He looked up at her with moist eyes and said, 'Yes. Things I didn't understand. You kept talking about "the Theta function".'

'Oh,' she said, and her voice was dull, flat, inflectionless. 'Was I? The theta function. The time crystal. McQuade.'

Now he did sob.

'I don't know what that means!'

She ruffled his hair and he did not complain.

'It's what I said might happen. It looks like I was right; I'm not immune. I wonder how long I've got.'

'Don't say that!' he screamed.

'Let's walk,' she said, 'we may as well rather than wait around for something unpleasant to happen.'

They walked.

'Is there nothing that can be done?' he said.

'No; well, perhaps, but not without advanced technology, which seems to be in short supply around here. I don't think a fungus stirrer will quite cut it.'

'The people on the surface!' Karn shouted excitedly, 'they will be able to help you! We must get there.'

'Yes,' she said, and her smile was wistful, 'we must. If only it were as easy as pressing a button.'

Then she stopped. Once again, she was motionless.

No, not again, not so soon! Karn thought.

'Talk to me,' he begged.

'No, it's not that. I thought I heard something.'

'What?'

But she waved him into silence, and cocked her head slightly.

'Yes, I did hear it.'

'What?'

'The sound of claws clicking against the ground. It must be the second predator I mentioned.' She looked down at him. 'Run!'

They ran and ran, until the air burned in Karn's lungs in stilettos of fire. His backpack fell to the floor but he did not attempt to retrieve it.

And then he could hear it too; the clatter of long claws and a sibilant hissing, a wet panting, a hungry susurration.

'There! Over there!' she cried and pointed off to one side.

Karn followed her finger and saw a small recess set in the wall.

'It's a dead-end!'

'It has electricity, I can detect it. I think I know what it is. It could take us to the surface!'

They ran into the alcove. Maya pushed him behind her. There was a bank of controls set in the wall and she studied them.

'It is an elevator! It must have been made by the people who control the lights. I'll force them to tell us the way to the surface if it's the last thing I do!'

Karn was pulling her arm.

'Maya...'

She looked up.

She looked out.

There was a movement behind an apron of rocky detritus.

And something came out from behind it.

She stared wide-eyed as it approached, its foul, feral lust hideously apparent.

Karn could not speak.

'No', she said, shaking her head from side to side in her maddened denial, 'no, you can't be real...'

Desperately, her finger jabbed a button.

A door closed, sealing them off from the slavering obscenity.

The elevator compartment shivered once.

And then flashed into rapid motion.

Downwards.

SUBTERRA AND THE THREE

One

The elevator reached ground level with a shuddering impact that Karn felt punch its way up his spinal column. Maya was flung against the door, which opened instantly under her weight. A wave of humid air, so hot it bordered on the painful, crashed over them.

Both occupants fell helplessly out of the elevator onto a soft surface, covered with short green plant life. Karn lay face-down in the vegetation for a few minutes, his mind still reeling with the crawling horror of seeing that repellent thing rushing towards him. All his voluntary muscles were trembling.

But slowly, he raised his face from the grass-like vegetation and looked up, more than half afraid of what he would see.

And what he did see was amazing. He had spent all his life in confined, enclosed spaces. He had gone from the World to the corridors beyond the World, then to the recording room; and each time he had felt comfortingly enclosed, surrounded by the reassurance of nearby walls and boundaries. Never had he been forced to face terrible open spaces; to stare into immensity.

And now he was.

The elevator terminus was at the side of a massive, near-vertical cliff, which rose up and up, until the very thickness of the air blurred its outlines. And in the other direction stretched a colossal cavern, whose far reaches were also lost in the blue obscurity of distance. The massive fluted and corrugated cliff next to where he was standing slowly curved over and became the roof of this new cavern, but unlike the roof of the World, it was so high he could see no detail upon it. To Karn, it was just a blue-grey sky—if he had known what constituted a sky. The cavern was brightly lit, but there were no Sun-strips in the roof: instead, there were many great panels along the cavern walls, blazing brilliantly with a slightly bluish light.

A gently sloping bank led down to the flat base of the cavern on which various buildings stretched out in a regular pattern into the dim distance. They looked hard, angular and metallic, much like he had supposed the exterior of the recording room would have looked like if he could have gotten outside it.

And figures were walking up the slope to meet them; figures shrunk by distance and yet even at that distance having a strange, not-quite-human look to them.

Then, aware Maya had risen to her feet, he turned and said, 'Do you know where we are?'

'No, but I can tell you this: we're even further from the surface than we were before.'

'If getting to the surface means meeting that monster again, then I'm happy to keep it this way.'

She looked troubled.

'Perhaps. We had no weapons, of course. It would have been a different story had we been armed. But I see we are not alone; perhaps these people can tell us more.'

She stared down at the three slowly approaching figures and her expression grew more troubled.

'Strange. They look like...could they be...'

She did not have to wonder for very much longer. The figures were now so close that Maya could easily see what they were.

Robots.

Karn too could see that they were not human and instinctively drew closer to Maya.

'What are they, Maya? They're not Men!'

'Machines, Karn. Just machines, no better than the elevator, or the computers you saw in the recording room. Just ones that can walk about by themselves.'

'I don't like them; machines should not look like Men.'

But the time for discussion was over. The three robots had now reached the top of the slope and had stopped in front of them, a few metres away. They were slightly taller than Maya and were of a standard humanoid build: two legs, a cylindrical torso,

177

two arms terminating in a variety of manipulative structures, and topped by a head which bore two optical sensors in a similar arrangement to the human face, and with a grill at the bottom of the head for speech. The optical sensors glowed a dull, faint red, the colour of dying embers.

Maya was unimpressed. Their structure was very basic. She had seen much more elegantly designed types shortly before the cataclysm. But one thing was abundantly clear: the very existence of such mechanisms showed whoever lived in this tremendous void were at a totally different level of sophistication than Karn's benighted People.

The nearest robot spoke. Its voice was very mechanical: uninflected and with pauses in the wrong places. Maya grew even less impressed.

'We see you are strangers. This is our world.'

Maya had the feeling that the robot was not even speaking autonomously but was merely relaying a message from somewhere else. Its language was not identical to Karn's but similar enough so she could rapidly adjust.

'Thank you; we are indeed strangers. What is this place?'

'This is the world of Subterra.'

She nodded. Apparently, some knowledge of the classics had been retained after one hundred and seventy-five thousand years. The name of this place was conventional enough and a little uninspired.

What do I do now, she thought, *should I say, "Take me to your Leader"?*

But she had no need to ponder for the nearest, apparently chief, robot then said, 'You will come with us now to be judged by the Council of Three.'

Maya stared at the mechanisms.

'Surely it is polite to request the pleasure of our company?'

The lead robot fell silent for at least a minute; obviously not accustomed to such a reply. Eventually, it repeated, 'You will come with us now to be judged by the Council of Three.'

Maya looked down at Karn, who was perspiring so freely his exposed flesh glistened in Subterra's harsh light, then back at the robots.

'Is it always so hot here?'

'You will come with us now to be judged by the Council of Three.'

Either the robot actually is doing the speaking, or the man at the other end has a very short script, Maya thought and then gave the silent Karn a little tap on the shoulder.

'Come on. Let's see what they have to offer.'

'I'd rather not stay here,' Karn muttered, 'I don't like these things.'

'Well, Predator #2 is still up there if you want to go back.'

'Let's go.'

As they began their descent towards the habitations, the lead robot led the way, but the other two silently moved behind Maya and Karn. Maya noted the slightly ominous rearrangement but decided to await developments.

She turned her attention to the buildings below as they came into clearer view. Immediately, she could see she was dealing with a completely different level of achievement to the tawdry villages of Worlds like Karn's. They were constructed of lustrous metal, rising to several stories, and were organised around a system of what looked like metalled roads. And by any definition, this was not a "village" or "settlement": this was a town, and an expertly constructed and orderly one.

Karn was impressed.

'This is a wonderful village,' he said, wiping the constant flow of sweat from his eyes, 'it looks like your recording room copied many times over. I hope they're not mad here, like they were in your place.'

'No, not mad perhaps,' Maya murmured in reply, 'but there are other alternatives.'

Karn did not understand her meaning and continued gazing at the Subterran town, having apparently forgotten about his metal companions.

179

On arrival in the town, they were escorted a little distance along a road until they arrived at a building which was nothing more than a great metal cube. There was a door in the side facing them, with a rectangular window above the door, but the place gave off an air of grim functionalism and forbidding indifference. It held the cheery welcome of a police cell.

'You go in,' the leading machine said and pressed a small button beside the door, which obediently opened.

Maya looked inside. There were nothing but two benches and some structures for sanitation.

'This doesn't look very welcoming,' she said, turning to the lead robot.

Two mechanical eyes stared down at her, machine eyes the colour of a fading fire.

'You were not invited to Subterra. You chose to come here. Therefore, there is no need to be mindful of you or to consider your comfort.'

Maya stared back at the talking machines, as a growing sense of alarm began to take hold of her.

Whatever the Subterrans were, they were most definitely not the helpless yokels that had populated Karn's World. She would have to be very careful over many things, not least about revealing what she really was and what she was capable of. As yet, there had been no overt hostility towards them, but she was now on alert. There was only one thing she wanted from the people behind these mechanical things and that was a way to escape these unending underground mazes and stand at last upon the Earth's sweet surface.

'So what happens now?' she finally asked.

'You go in. The Council of Three will decide when to call you, and they will study you to see if you are of use to Subterra.'

'And if we are not?'

'That is not within our capacity to answer.'

With that, the robots indicated Karn and Maya should enter the cube-building. Maya noticed Karn hesitating and she touched

180

his shoulder and said, 'It's alright. We'll go along with what they say until we know more about this place. I'll look after you.'

But even as she said that, she remembered how she had made a similar promise to Yarl.

They went in and sat on a bench, looking at the doorway.

The door shut, swiftly and silently. Karn glanced nervously at Maya.

'What if they don't come back? What if they just leave us here?'

She extended a hand to ruffle his hair but then thought better of it.

'Don't worry. I had a look at the walls as we came in. I can burst out of this room whenever I feel like it.'

That satisfied him, but there seemed no more to say, and so they just sat, looking at their hands or the floor as the empty hours crawled by. Once Karn tried the door, but, to the surprise of neither of them, it was locked.

Then suddenly, the door opened and Karn blinked a little under the influx of harsh Subterran light.

And carried on blinking.

Silhouetted against the light was the unmistakable shape of a woman.

A woman of Karn's race.

Much to Maya's amusement, Karn shot to his feet as the small woman approached, and held out both hands in greeting, as was the custom amongst the People. However, the woman ignored both the gesture and indeed Karn himself, and addressed Maya directly.

'The Council of Three have required me to talk to you and learn about where you come from and why you are here,' she said, in a curiously flat tone. It was not dissimilar to the voice of the robots.

'And are we to meet the Council of Three?' Maya asked in a similarly unemotional voice.

'It is probable that you will be brought before the Councillors. In the meantime, I am to ask you some questions and, depending on your answers, show you some of Subterra.'

'Do you have a name?'

The question seemed to confuse the woman. She remained motionless and silent for a few seconds, and then said, in a manner which suggested she had just received some kind of communication, 'You may call me "Arthrena".'

'Thank you, Arthrena. We are pleased to meet you. I am "Maya", and this is "Karn".'

A blank stare.

Karn was finally tired of being ignored.

'Arthrena, is there any food for us? We've been doing a lot of running, I lost my backpack and we're very hungry.'

Arthrena turned to Karn, behaving as if she had just noticed him.

'There will be food for you later. But I have to ask you questions.'

Now that she was facing him, Karn could finally get a good look at their interlocutor.

She was the same scrawny, weak-muscled type as the People. But unlike the People, her thin hair was black, streaked with abundant grey. She was wearing only a set of shorts and her small breasts lay flat on her chest. But there was something peculiar about that torso, in that it glistened, but not with sweat caused by Subterra's tremendous heat, but as if she was wearing a very thin, flexible, transparent covering.

And yet all the details of her skin—the large, open pores, the blue veins threading through the doughy flesh—all were clearly visible.

Arthrena rapidly grew tired of Karn gawping at her and turned back to Maya. It was not lost upon the latter that she was the main object of interest of the unseen Council of Three.

'You are the more important, Maya. I shall address my comments only to you, henceforth. I have been instructed to show certain aspects of Subterra.'

'We are going nowhere,' Maya said, 'until we have eaten.'

Again the slight delay, as if instructions were being awaited, then: 'Very well. A maton will bring you some food. After which I shall return.' And with that, the strange woman departed.

Karn watched her go.

'She looks like a Woman of the World, but she doesn't talk like one. And no Woman would ignore a Man like she did without being punished.'

'There's something about this place I don't like,' Maya said, half to herself, 'until we learn more, we must be on our guard.'

'I'm already on my guard. I don't like being ignored by a Woman.'

Remembering the status of females in the World, Maya couldn't resist a dig.

'You'll soon get used to it.'

And then instantly regretted it, when she saw Karn's expression become even more woe-begone. Fortunately, she was saved from more embarrassment as the door opened again. A robot came in carrying a basket of food items; it was evident that "maton" was the local name for "robot." But Maya decided to check.

'Are you a maton?'

'Yes.'

And that was the end of the conversation.

After the maton's departure, Maya examined the contents of the basket. It was mainly types of fruit; types she was not familiar with, although some could have been descendants of the varieties of her own time. Karn regarded them with obvious distrust: he was not used to fruit. But there were also strips of fungal protein, and those he attacked with vigour.

'I'm afraid you'll have to eat all of it,' she said.

Karn stopped chewing.

'All of it? These red and green things as well as this lovely fungus? Why?'

'I can't give anything away until I find out whether I can trust these people. I can't demand food and then leave it uneaten.

183

They mustn't know I'm not flesh and blood until and unless I decide to reveal that fact. So eat up!'

Karn took quite some time to consume all the food, finding the fruit too sharp in flavour to a palate used only to the blandest of the bland. Maya watched him reluctantly swallow the last piece of an apple-like object and gave him a brief round of applause.

'Well done! I'll make you into a gourmet in no time at all.'

'I wish you'd stop using words that don't mean anything,' he said, with annoyance plainly evident in his features. He gave a belch that was surprisingly loud for his size, and vigorously rubbed his belly to calm it. 'Those soft things were horrible. And they made my teeth tingle. In any case, what was the point of all this if we're being watched?'

'We're not.'

'How do you know?'

Maya was about to say *I just know,* but decided Karn was worthy of at least an attempt at an explanation.

'Spy equipment would use something called electromagnetic radiation, invisible waves in the air. I could detect them even at very low levels. And there aren't any. And there are no cameras that I can detect either.'

Karn sighed.

'*Invisible waves in the air.* And things used to be so simple.'

The dull minutes dragged by; Karn was used to enclosed spaces, and so he showed no signs of agitation, but Maya was very glad when the door finally opened and Arthrena returned.

'You are ready to talk now.'

The words were said without any inflection, but Maya assumed from her brief acquaintance with the woman that it had not been a question.

'Yes.'

'Where are you from?'

Maya had already decided that there was no point in dissembling.

'From the late Twenty-fourth century of the Common Era.'

Again the pause, as if instructions were being awaited. Then: 'We know of no such place.'

Maya shrugged.

'Your lack of knowledge has no bearing on the truth of my statement.'

Again the pause.

'Does the troglodyte also come from the late Twenty-fourth century of the Common Era?'

'If you are referring to my friend, I have already told you his name is "Karn." And no, he does not come from there.'

'Why are you here?'

'We came here by accident. We were escaping from a dangerous carnivore. We do not mean any harm to the people of Subterra. We only want one thing.'

'And that is?'

Karn suddenly noticed Maya had gone rigid and was no longer looking at Arthrena. He groaned inwardly. He knew what was coming.

Maya was staring at an invisible audience, and began to speak in a voice as unnatural as those of the matons.

'The concept of a "Time Crystal" was first articulated by the physicist Frank Wilczek in 2012. He envisaged a macroscopic object whose internal configuration would cyclically switch between stable internal states without an external stimulus. However…'

Maya stopped suddenly and glanced between Karn and Arthrena with growing alarm.

'I'm sorry—what was I saying? I, I…'

Karn looked at his hands. He had nothing to say.

Arthrena, however, continued to speak.

'Your answer was not relevant to my question. What is the one thing you want?'

Maya shook her head as if trying to clear it of mental fog and then stopped as she noticed something about Arthrena.

'You're not taking any notes. Why is that if our answers are so important?'

'I am in constant contact with the Council of Three. What is the one thing that you want?'

Maya stared at the small woman. There was no sign of friendliness, of concern for them in her demeanour. But she had to assume they were not in danger until it became evident they were. Then, if that time came, she would act, and act fast.

'We want to reach the surface of this planet Earth. We believe there are people there who can help us with certain problems.'

'And what are those problems?'

'That is none of your business. Are you willing to help us get to the surface?'

'We may be. But there is much we wish to show you of Subterra first. And then we will decide what to do with you.'

Two

Arthrena left shortly after delivering that unnerving comment. Karn looked at Maya, hoping for some reassurance, but she seemed lost in her thoughts and did not notice his pleading expression.

Two matons arrived after Arthrena's departure and announced that they would escort Maya and Karn to their sleeping quarters. After the shelter of their waiting room, Subterra's heat hit Karn like a punch in the belly as he emerged like a cicada bursting out of the cool soil. The World had been hot, of course, but nothing like this. He glanced at Maya, but, as he had expected, she was totally unaffected.

'Don't you find it hot?' he finally asked, strangely annoyed by her composure.

'I am aware of the heat,' she replied, 'but only as a measurement. It doesn't interfere with my workings.'

On the occasions she used words like those, Karn was unpleasantly reminded that despite all the grace and litheness of her form and movements, he was dealing with a mechanism, not a real person composed of skin and tendons and warm, red blood. It was a very unnerving thought, and he resented being reminded of those facts. Far easier to believe she was simply what she appeared to be: a lissom, well-sculptured young woman. Because if she was not, what was the difference between her and the matons that marched with them; one in front and one behind?

Unaware of the discomfiture her simple reply had caused Karn, Maya was on high alert, scanning her surroundings as they walked further into the town. Her initial thoughts had proved correct: this was a culture of a high order, much, much more advanced than Karn's. Like the World, it must be descended from an initial Burrower colony, but one that had somehow retained at least part of its science.

Or was that to underestimate Subterra: had it in fact built upon the knowledge that had allowed the initial colonists to escape the terror of the Destroyer? She frowned; it would have been ridiculously effortless to deal with the World had its inhabitants proved hostile, but Subterra might be a genuine danger. Glancing around, she could see that the buildings they were passing were well constructed, being made from various metals and dressed stone. The windows were made of fine glass.

And there were other signs of an advanced society: in the furnace-hot air, she could detect unusual compounds like sulfur dioxide, carbon monoxide, minute traces of sulfuric acid and hydrogen, and other non-equilibrium chemicals. Adding it all together produced a single conclusion: this was not a subsistence economy such as the World—it was industrial.

They stopped in front of a structure separate from the rows of neat buildings they had seen up until then. It was single-story but possessed large windows on either side of the door. Compared to the cell they had just quitted, it looked positively domestic.

The maton behind them spoke.

'This will be your dwelling until the Council of Three decides to call you. There are no Sleep-Periods in Subterra. We do not believe in periods without work. But I have been informed that you are probably in need of a period of unconsciousness.'

(Neither he nor Maya noticed her familiarity with the phrase "Sleep-Period.")

'If that means "sleep",' Karn muttered, 'then they've got something right.'

The leading maton opened the door and then both stood aside as Karn and Maya entered. The pair heard the door shut behind them and found themselves alone.

Their new accommodation was refreshingly cool, and a very gentle breeze told Maya it was air-conditioned. There was a table and two chairs. A separate room held their sleeping arrangements.

Karn wasted no time looking around and headed for one of the beds in the other room. Flinging himself upon it, he wallowed in the softness of the mattress, rolling gently from side to side with a beatific grin illuminating a face which, up until that moment, had been set in grim lines.

'This is wonderful!' he said, his voice muffled due to him being face-down on the mattress, 'These people must be friendly!'

Maya said nothing. Thinking perhaps she had been a little too blasé about the possibility of their being watched, she slowly stretched herself out on the other bed. Her feet hung over one end. Nothing must be done to arouse suspicion about her true nature; she might need the element of surprise at some point. She was powerful; vastly more so than a biological being of her size, but she was far from invulnerable. She set her apparent breathing rhythm to a slow regular pulse and put most of her other systems on standby. Her eyes closed; to an observer it would have appeared she was sleeping.

But even on standby, she was monitoring the immediate environment. She could even detect any activity just outside the walls.

Nothing.

She powered down a few more systems and, as much as it was possible for her to be, she was sleep.

***

After the pre-set interval, which she had judged to be a believable sleep-period, her eyelids lifted and she slowly swung her legs off the bed. Karn was snoring loudly a few metres away. She entered the main room of the building, and there, on the table, were another two plates and a tray of food. She looked down at the food, noticing the usual fruits and strips of fungus-protein, but there were two other items she did not recognise. They were rectangular objects of a dark red-brown colour. She held one close to her face and scanned it.

189

Meat.

Now that was unexpected. She knew from Karn's description of the World that there was no meat consumption because there were no animals. It was possible the inhabitants of the second settlement had resorted to cannibalism before they succumbed, but that was a horrible event, only to be done *in extremis*. Meat was foreign to the People.

And yet, here it was apparently a standard part of the diet.

Metal. Worked stone. Things called "matons" which were actually simple humanoid robots. Sulfur dioxide.

And now meat.

She noticed Karn had soundlessly awakened and had joined her, and she watched him as he sat and began eagerly attacking the fungus. She smiled as he slowed considerably when he had consumed that and had moved on to the fruit. Finally, he came to the meat, which he stared at with great suspicion. He prodded one of the pieces with a questing finger, apparently to see if it moved.

'What's this?' he said, the doubt dripping from his words.

Maya explained.

Karn was horrified.

'What slices taken off things like the rats? That's awful. I'm not eating it!'

Nor did he. The meat was still there when the door opened without warning, and Arthrena walked in. As usual, her face was completely emotionless. She could have been staring at a wall.

As she approached, Maya once again noticed the faint sheen of something very thin and transparent covering her torso. Without touching it, it was impossible to make any estimate of its nature.

If Arthrena noticed the direction of Maya's gaze, she did not comment. Instead she pointed to the tray and said, 'Why have you wasted food?'

Before Karn could say something uncomplimentary, Maya quickly said, 'I'm afraid meat-eating is not practiced by our people.'

190

'Why? It contains substances essential for health not found in mycoprotein.'

Maya spread her hands to show bafflement.

'It's the way we are. We are a very primitive people.'

'Apparently. The Council of Three will not be pleased by this waste.'

'Then I can only apologise. When will we meet the Council, so I can apologise in person?'

'Soon enough. I have been instructed to show you more of our city, so you will understand that we of Subterra are very far from being a primitive people.'

Maya smiled to show her appreciation, an expression of gratitude lost on Arthrena.

But her thought was *Very good. The sooner I know all there is to know about these people, the sooner I can determine if they can help us get to the surface.*

The heat was waiting for them as they exited their dwelling. Maya glanced at Karn: perhaps he was getting used to it. She was running calculations through her head as she walked out: *The elevator had taken them downwards. What was its speed? How long had they been moving? Subterra was nearer the Earth's mantle and was therefore hotter because of the reduced distance to the core. But how much closer? Where were they?*

It was no good: she had been too concerned with escaping the fearsome second predator to have collected any data. A lightning-fast search of her memory banks revealed nothing— except the unwelcome recollection of slavering horror.

And then her attention was dragged back to the present. Arthrena was standing in front of what was obviously a wheeled vehicle. Another example of Subterra's sophistication.

Karn looked up at Maya.

'What is this?'

'Remember the machines you saw in the tunnels, the broken ones? Well, this is a smaller version of those. And presumably, a working one.'

'You are to get on,' Arthrena said curtly.

191

Maya studied the vehicle before obeying. It was four-wheeled and open to the sweltering air. There was a seat at the back, wide for her and Karn, and a single seat in front of them for the driver, who controlled the vehicle by a standard system of pedals and steering wheel.

'This is a remarkable vehicle,' Maya said, hoping to ingratiate herself and Karn with their unemotional guide.

'It is a standard product of Subterran engineering,' was the only reply.

The vehicle moved off, smoothly and quietly.

Electrically-driven, Maya thought. She decided to ask a question before they got too far into the journey.

'I would like to ask something: You seem not to have expected us, so why did you send me that message?'

'What message?'

' "We are here. We search." '

'We sent no such message. Or any other message. You came to us. We did not invite you.'

Maya leaned back on the seat. She was shaken. It had seemed obvious that Subterra had sent the message; they had an advanced technology and, although she had not known what the carrier wave had been, it surely had been these people who had sent it.

Except it hadn't.

She relapsed into silence, her thoughts churning as they tried to reach some believable conclusion. Arthrena was silent also, leaving Karn to look around without anyone to explain what he was looking at. But it was not long before he saw things which needed no explanation: People. Or at least humans who were of the same general type as himself. Their hair colouring differed, indicating they had come from separate settlements, but they were all his own kind of human, and would not have looked too out of place in the World. They just wore shorts—or nothing at all—such was the heat. But looking at them as they drove slowly and silently past gave Karn an almost unendurable sense of loss. Memories of Grath, The Supreme Leader, Thylassa, Yarl, came bursting unbidden into his mind, and for a moment he felt his eyes become moist as images of the World swept before his inner vision. Perhaps he could end his journey here, and wave goodbye to Maya and her obsession with the surface.

The open-topped vehicle was so low he could have reached out and touched them as they passed but he contented himself with waving and saying 'Hello!'

They did not respond. It was as if they did not see Karn. They stepped out of the vehicle's path, but that was the only sign they made of awareness of others. Their faces were totally without expression, and they moved as far as possible in straight lines, taking avoiding action if a collision was likely, but otherwise not interacting with their fellows at all. For a few moments he watched them going about their business; going into large buildings; coming out of large buildings; moving in straight lines and right-angled turns. As Karn became aware that it was not just isolated individuals displaying this behaviour but the entire population, the weirdness, the *wrongness*, of the situation became evident and he felt his earlier joy at seeing other humans evaporate, leaving a cold, concerned mixture of emotions at his core. Once again, things were not right. He looked at Maya to see if she had come to the same conclusions, but she was staring with an expressionless face at the distant roof of Subterra. For an unpleasant moment, he thought she was having another seizure, but she became aware of his stare and, looking at him, said, 'What? What is it?'

Karn pointed at the passing pedestrians.

'Them. These people. Do they look normal to you?'

She stared at the people for a short while, and then said, 'They seem very abstracted.'

'If that means you agree they're behaving strangely, I agree.'

Maya still had not stopped wrestling with the conundrum of the message, and simply said, 'Well, I've seen worse. I think unfriendly natives are the least of our problems.'

They drew up alongside a long, smoke-stained building and Arthrena looked over her shoulder and said, 'I have been told that the Council of Three would like you to see something of our engineering achievements. Follow me.'

Maya had already noticed the amount of noise coming from the structure; the clanging, the banging, the clattering, which suggested metal-working.

And so it proved.

Inside the structure was a vision of Hell. In one stupendous enclosure, great cupolas were pouring yellow-white, viscous streams of molten metal into moulds. On wires above them, vessels were moving from one part of the room to another, where yet more liquid metal was disgorged. Karn looked nervously at one vessel as it passed directly over him, thinking of the horrific death it contained.

The noise was almost literally ear-shattering and Maya had to step her receptors down several levels to be comfortable. Unfortunately, Karn had no such abilities, and he had clapped his hands over his ears even before they had entered.

And the heat! The interior of the building made the outside seem almost arctic.

And yet the workers, males and females, and all of the same type as Karn, looked unaffected as they moved the vats of bubbling metal around, or swung red-hot girders onto stacks of older ones, ones which had cooled to a dull, sullen crimson.

Maya looked at Arthrena. She also seemed unaffected, although the odd lustrous coating which appeared to cover her torso seemed to be shimmering more obviously. She indicated it was time to leave.

As they sat back onto the vehicle seats, she said, 'We mine ore from many sources, all of them outside Subterra proper as we have advanced drilling devices. As you can see we can then fabricate the metal into any structures we choose. This vehicle or the outer casings for the matons.'

'Why do you call them "matons"?' Maya said. She was getting extremely tired of mysteries.

'Short for "automaton." The term "robot" has too many misleading and foolish connotations for the liking of the Council of Three.'

'And elsewhere in Subterra you have factories which turn the metal into more finely machined components? And you also have places which produce semiconductors for the matons?'

'Obviously. The Council of Three has given me no orders about those establishments. Do you wish to see them?'

'No. There is only one thing which I wish, and that is you help us get to the surface. It is very kind of you to show us the wonders of your civilisation. It is truly remarkable all you have achieved down here, but we don't wish to outstay our welcome.'

'There is no danger of that,' Arthrena said, and somehow her lack of intonation made the statement slightly ominous, 'but The Council of Three wishes you to see another example of our abilities.'

Karn groaned audibly. Ever since he had failed to get a response from the inhabitants, the sense of unease had been growing. Getting out of Subterra was becoming more and more urgent with each statement from Arthrena.

'Very well,' Maya said, replying to Arthrena, 'but we would like to meet your Council, thank them for their hospitality, and be on our way.'

'You will meet the Council of Three shortly. They are somewhat disappointed that you wish to cut your tour short, but there are other things they intend to show you.'

She drove off down the narrow streets, the inhabitants moving out of her way without looking at her.

As they drove along, Maya saw a structure that looked significantly different from the others. It was a long, rectangular prism made of what looked like a gleaming ceramic, and it was blindingly white in the harsh Subterran light. Oddly, there was no-one around it, or, in fact, anywhere near it. Maya was instantly reminded of a hospital.

'What is that building?'

'That is of no concern of yours.'

195

Odd. Arthrena had always been anxious before to impress upon them the superiority of Subterran civilisation.

Maya decided to probe.

'I would like to see inside that building.'

'No.'

'Why not?'

'The Council of Three does not wish it. It is…' There was a notable pause, as if Arthrena were awaiting instructions. She resumed speaking. 'It contains many holy artefacts of our culture, which strangers must not see.'

Maya considered that answer: this was the first time there had been any suggestion the Subterrans had a religion; until that moment the culture had seemed resolutely secular.

'I promise I will treat the holy objects with respect.'

'No. The Council of Three forbids it.'

Maya noted that this was a topic the Council obviously found very sensitive, but she had a strong feeling the reason could not be religious. This was not the moment to press the matter but, perhaps, there might be time later to do some exploring on her own.

Perhaps.

They approached another large, industrial-looking building. Karn began to squirm on the seat, looking more and more uncomfortable.

'What is it?'

'I can smell them,' he said, his face contorting, 'rats!'

Maya tested the air. There were compounds in it indicating the closeness of some form of animal, but not necessarily rats.

'It's alright,' she said, forgetting herself and patting him on the head, 'I don't think we're dealing with rats.'

Nor were they. Arthrena ushered them inside. It was dimly lit, and full of cages whose walls were made from tightly-meshed wire. There was a continuous chattering coming from inside the cages and Maya approached the nearest; Karn hung back, casting the occasional glance at the open doorway.

The cage was full of small mammals, which formed a living carpet on the floor of the cage. They rushed into a corner as Maya approached and congregated into a squirming, furry mass, glaring up at her and showing yellow teeth.

'Rodents,' Maya said and looked at Arthrena. 'This is where your meat comes from?'

'From these, and others,' she replied, and pointed further into the dim interior, 'Come and see.'

Karn remained near the doorway, but Arthrena ignored him, seemingly only interested in Maya. Each cage contained a grunting, chattering, squeaking mass of furry animals; each cage holding a different type. Some were as small as mice; others as large as pigs. But they all had one thing in common.

'They're all rodents,' Maya said, 'you've been breeding different types from a single ancestral, rodent stock.'

'Not breeding,' Arthrena said, 'this is Subterra with which you are dealing. We have genetically engineered them from a single common rodent stock. Unfortunately, that stock is all our ancestors had to work on but, as you can see, we have done well.'

Maya stood motionless as she absorbed the implications of that statement. She had not expected the phrase *genetic engineering* to enter the conversation. Every time she had thought she had the measure of Subterra, there had been another revelation to show she had underestimated them. They had engineering, technology; they could manufacture simple humanoid robots; and now it was revealed they had genetic manipulation capabilities. And all this, at some unknown depth in the Earth's crust, so far down that they could feel the heat from the semi-molten mantle. For the first time, she wondered if, should they prove hostile, she had come up against something she couldn't handle. It was an unnerving thought: she had been tolerant of Karn's innocent simplicity; maybe even been condescending to him. Maybe she had taken her superiority as an absolute. Maybe she had become complacent.

She felt lower, deeper strata of her mind click into awareness. Instantly, she could detect the faint traces of hydrogen and sulfur compounds coming from the industrial area; she could smell the male and female hormones given off by the food-animals; their sweat, their urine, their faeces. Distant objects came into sharper focus and her hearing encompassed frequencies above and below what she had been conscious of until that moment of alertness.

And what of Arthrena? She turned her enhanced senses on the woman.

All seemed normal. She could tell that Arthrena was in a better physical condition that Karn had been when she had first met him.

She looked deeper, penetrating the outer layers of flesh.

Ah, there it was! A small ovoid capsule, just below the surface of the back of her neck. Obviously a radio communicator of some kind. That was how she had been able to tell them what the Council of Three had been thinking, what they wanted.

But was there more? She stared at Arthrena's chest. What was that shimmering, glistening, coating that covered most of her torso? She studied it in infrared, visible, and near ultraviolet, but it remained mysterious. It was something she had not encountered before but, knowing Subterra as she now did and knowing their powers, it would not be there for decoration.

But Arthrena was aware she was being studied. And was there a slight expression of emotion, perhaps amusement, in her face at last?

'I see you are eager for knowledge, Maya,' the woman said, but Maya had the distinct impression that she was being used simply as a receiving and transmitting device, and that someone else was actually doing the speaking. 'You will know everything about us shortly.'

Karn decided he had stood near the doorway for long enough and joined them.

'Can we go now? I don't like the smell of these animals.'

For almost the first time, Arthrena acknowledged his existence.

'Yes, of course. It will soon be time to meet the Council of Three.'

Three

'You know it is imperative for us to get to the surface,' Maya said.

'Yes. I believe you have told me that a number of times.'

'Do you know about the surface?'

'Yes, we know a great deal about it. We have been there many times.'

'Then you have a way of getting there!' Maya said, her excitement rising.

'That goes without saying. I was going to take you directly to your residence, but as it appears to be a matter of great importance to you, I will take you to one of the transfer stations.'

'That would be very helpful,' Maya said, casting a glance of triumph at Karn, who looked less than impressed.

'Very well. It is not far.'

Arthrena changed direction and headed for one of the colossal grey walls of Subterra. Maya soon espied a squat building hard up against the corrugated grey stone of one of the tremendous cavern's walls. They dismounted and Maya had to restrain herself from pushing past Arthrena. The surface seemed so near now she could see it in her imagination. Perhaps its denizens would be sufficiently advanced that her consciousness could be transferred to a biological home.

To be a real woman again! To love and be loved! The feelings, the sensations, the ecstasies that only a creature of flesh, of blood, of bone, could ever know!

And pain? Yes, she would gladly accept some pain as the price of such a homecoming!

A transparent door comprising the outer part of an airlock opened automatically as they approached and she stood before a platform on which was displayed a caterpillar-tracked machine very similar to the ones she and Karn had seen in the tunnels. But this one looked newly constructed and completely functional. The transparent hood over the internal seating was unbroken, unblemished, and scintillations from the strip lights glinted on its smooth surface.

She turned from admiring the machine to Arthrena. For a mad moment, she felt like kissing the woman.

'It is functional?'

'Completely.'

'But how does it reach the surface? I see no ramp that the vehicle could ascend. Does the tube it sits beneath go all the way?'

'It is obvious that you are very excited,' Arthrena replied dispassionately, 'so let me disentangle those questions. The shaft does reach all the way. From time to time crustal movements close it, but our matons are quite capable of restoring it, especially when they are aided by the people you have seen in the city, who are selected to do the finer work. The final stage is a ramp to the surface which the vehicle ascends under its own power after it has quitted the ascent platform.'

'So how does the transporter ascend in the first place?'

'The platform it sits on has rocket motors at the four corners. The conduit is then evacuated to a high vacuum before they are ignited. The vehicle is fully sealed under standard Subterran atmospheric pressure.'

Maya could see an airlock on the side of the machine so that particular statement at least had to be true.

'Can I take a closer look? I assume this conduit is not evacuated at present.'

Arthrena remained still and silent and Maya now knew she was seeking and receiving guidance. After two minutes she said, 'Yes. You may have a very brief look.'

The inner glass-like door slid aside, and Arthrena and Maya walked up to the transport vehicle. A bored Karn waited outside.

'Can I get inside?'

'No.'

No, that would be giving me too much information, Maya thought, *but I am not as helpless as you think.*

She turned back to the transporter and, unbeknownst to Arthrena, ramped up her senses to the absolute peak of their sensitivities. It was not a state she could remain in for long, such was the tremendous drain on her power pack, but with her vision of a longed-for life on the surface driving her on, she flung the sum total of her sensory powers at the machine. Eagerly, she gulped down huge blocks of data about the vehicle's operating procedures and abilities. So great was the influx that she swayed a little and just managed to stabilise herself before Arthrena could grasp her.

Maya did not want the other woman to touch her: too much might be revealed about her true nature by a skilful touch.

'You are all right?' the other said.

'Yes. It is just the heat. I am not used to it.'

'You will soon acclimatise,' Arthrena said, not entirely reassuringly. 'But now we must go. This visit was not part of the planned itinerary, and I must now return you to your lodgings while the Council of Three decides when to call you.'

Maya stood looking at Arthrena, apparently not doing anything, but in reality stepping down her sensory abilities from the screamingly high level at which they had been operating. As her senses dropped from level to level, she saw Arthrena change from a collection of bone and tissue and pulsing blood to a fabric of sheeted muscles and fascia to finally the normal surface of the woman.

Even so, the nature of the shining coating over her torso eluded Maya.

Presumably unaware of how deeply she had been probed, Arthrena said, 'I hope you have recovered from your problem with the heat. You have been behaving very strangely during these last few minutes. Are you sure you do not need medical attention?'

Maya shook her head. 'It has passed. I feel completely normal now.'

'I am glad to hear it. Fortunately, it is not far to your lodgings.'

Shortly afterwards, Arthrena's vehicle glided to a halt outside their new home. Arthrena's last words to them were 'It will not be long now before the Council of Three calls you,' and with that, she was off.

Inside, Maya threw herself on the couch, her mind whirling as she strove to organise the mass of data she had harvested into a coherent whole. Karn slumped into a chair and threw Maya an annoyed glare.

'Why did you make that journey even longer than it had to be? I hated every minute of it—dreadful, noisy factories, horrible animals, and then staring at that machine for what seemed like a whole Wake-Period!'

'I'll explain it all later,' Maya said, no longer trusting that they were not being overheard, 'I'm sorry you were bored.'

Karn fell into a sullen silence while Maya continued organising her thoughts.

She eventually had marshalled her findings about the transporter into a coherent whole and was reasonably certain she could operate it if she needed to—and got the chance.

But what of Subterra—was its true nature and purpose any clearer?

Arthrena had been cold and distant—but that didn't make her an enemy.

But there were still occurrences which did not fit into a reassuring whole.

Take the incidents in the tunnel. The rats had not attacked until after the light had been switched off. And it *had* been switched off: the way it had been restored after the attack was proof of it. So who were the watchers and, given that there were watchers, how could their intentions have possibly been benign? And the hideous thing that had chased and nearly caught them— was that connected to Subterra?

And, in another conundrum, if Subterra had not sent the *We are here* message, who had? Could those unknown entities have been the ones who had gloated over the battle in the tunnel, leaving Subterra as the innocent party?

She glanced at Karn. He was asleep.

There was one crucial datum she needed to decide whether the Subterrans were friend or foe.

That white building. Her straining senses had told her it was an important piece of the puzzle, and Arthrena's steely determination not to let her learn anything about it only made that more certain.

Something told her that if she could get inside, she would have the solution to the Subterran enigma.

But if Subterra were hostile, the danger was great.

There was no night in the gigantic cavern; not even a dimming of its harsh light.

For a long time—by her standards—she sat and thought.

But in the end, she could see only one course of action.

If she entered the building and was seen to do so, there would be only two outcomes.

Subterra benign: a mere embarrassment, an understandable error by a stranger in a strange land, which would be soon forgiven and forgotten.

Subterra hostile: the mask would have fallen, and she would be ready to wage war on the Council of Three. Subterra was an advanced society but had it ever encountered a being like her before—the apotheosis of the finality of late twenty-fourth century science? A science that had dared to defy the might of the Destroyer?

She stood and left the building.

Leaving Karn to dream pleasant dreams of fungus gently bubbling under a softly glowing Sun.

***

The streets were crowded and more than once Maya thought she was about to collide with one of the many pedestrians, who all seemed totally unaware of her. But at the last moment, they always swerved to avoid her, never making eye contact. Never once did she find herself looking into the eyes of another; never once did anyone turn their heads to follow her movements after she had passed them.

She would have known if they had.

Nor did she see any vehicles: everyone was on foot. And although they did not look at her, she looked at them. She could only use the simplest tools of her armoury after the draining experience of using the full panoply of her senses at their maximum resolution whilst examining the transport vehicle. And as everyone she passed was bare chested, she soon realised that all of them carried the glistening layer on their bodies; the glistening coating which steadfastly refused to reveal its identity.

She had been too exhausted to attempt to interpret Arthrena's unusual covering when they had stood together in the transfer station, and now she would be unable to reach those heights again for some time. The drain on her finite energy would be too great, and also she would have to remain motionless while doing the scan—and she did not want to spend one second more than she had to away from the dwelling house.

Were they aware that she had left the building?

Almost certainly. Maya now realised she had consistently underestimated the Subterrans. Surveillance would be a simple task for such people. But the same conclusions would follow whether or not they were watching her. If friendly—no action would be necessary; if not—she would act. And what of this throng of Karn-like people, walking silently in their straight-line paths—were they part of the Subterran elite? If so, why did they seem so placid, almost machine-like?

She put them from her thoughts because now the enormous structure was in sight, its porcelain-like surface shining brilliantly in the cavern lighting.

The entrance was on the other side of the structure, and she walked around it as swiftly as possible until she saw the large portal. There were heavy, sturdy doors open and flanking the entrance and she could see some way into the interior, but nothing was visible.

Speed was imperative; it was futile to try to creep unobserved into the entrance. Get in, see if her intuition had been correct, get out.

And then decide what to do.

There was one more vehicle-less road between her and the doorway, and she crossed it quickly, not bothering to look left or right. There was a maton either side of the door.

'Halt!' one said. 'You do not have permission to enter.'

Boldness be my friend, Arm me audacity! She thought.

'The Council of Three have given me permission.'

A pause while they opened a communication channel.

'We have no record of such an authorisation.'

'Nevertheless, I have such an authorisation. Do you wish to anger the Council of Three and risk disconnection?'

The redness of their eyes dulled somewhat as they diverted power to consider the possibility. Apparently, outright disobedience was a totally foreign concept to them. They did not move.

And Maya was inside.

The air had a clinical, antiseptic tang to it, reinforcing the feeling she was inside a hospital of some kind.

The interior was dim and, by Subterran standards, cool.

She moved further along the shadowy corridor.

It opened out into a tremendous hall with walls covered in a framework that held transparent coffin-shaped boxes, large enough to hold someone of Karn's stature. There were identical boxes on the floor, with narrow walkways between them. A translucent tube emanated from each box and joined with three others to produce a single larger tube. And each larger tube connected with an opaque box. The pattern was repeated throughout the entire hall: four thin tubes from four containers making a large tube that disappeared inside a box, and the thin tubes appeared to be made of a red substance that looked almost black in the hall's faint light. Or perhaps they were transparent...

The entire room was silent apart from a faint rhythmic pulse, like a giant's heartbeat heard through intervening layers of muffling insulation.

She approached the nearest floor-level container; there was a dark, motionless shape within it. Stepping up her visual resolution, she could now see there was a dark object within every box, like a grub inside a flower bud. She stood over the nearest container and looked down at the contents.

It was a naked woman of Karn's physical type, and a tube emanating from her arm was part of the same tube which left the casket.

She recoiled, and, spinning around, realised that each container held a human being who was donating blood.

Donating? Or being harvested?

The shock was so great she almost fell onto the container. Thoughts roared in her head; terrible thoughts of fear and horror.

Subterra could not be the welcoming haven she had hoped for! Something dreadful was happening here, something beyond her experience, beyond her belief!

Get out, get out, get out! Her subconscious screamed.

It was then she felt a metal appendage close upon each arm and clamp tight. There was a maton behind her.

And then there was a maton in front of her.

'The Council of Three has not given permission for you to be here. You have broken the rules of your stay. The Council of Three is very angry with you.'

'Is that right?' she snarled. She diverted her energies into her arms and felt the hydraulics of those arms stiffen against the vice-like hold of the maton. The other approached. She kicked it where the belly would have been in a human being. It rocked and swayed but did not fall.

Then it too was holding her, this time by the legs.

The hydraulics in her limbs screamed as they fought against the pincers holding her; screeched and shuddered as they fought the tenacious grasp of the matons—but to no avail.

207

She switched off the extra power she had poured into them. Her limbs were in danger of rupturing, and she now knew for certain there would be no repairs for them in Subterra.

'I won't fight you anymore,' she said, 'there is no need to continue to hold me.'

No need, she thought, *where can I run to? And what about Karn?*

'We will continue to hold you,' the maton behind her said, 'the Council of Three has ordered us to bring you before it immediately and has told us we will be disconnected if you escape. So we will walk with you to meet the Council, each of us holding an arm. Should you make any attempt to escape, we will each pull an arm off.'

And now we will see exactly what Subterra is, she thought, *the mask is off. But what lies beneath?*

Four

The matons did indeed walk with Maya in the manner they had promised, holding her arms out horizontally with just the right amount of tension in their grip to remind her there was great power waiting to rip them off.

But they did not walk any great distance. There was an open-topped vehicle waiting at the first crossroads, with a third maton in the driving seat. They pushed her onto the back seat, with the original matons taking up stations on either side, still holding her arms, with that slight vibration in their own limbs to warn her they could explode into dismembering action at a moment's notice.

Maya did nothing but stared grimly ahead. Her power reserves were still low after the great expenditure of energy at the transfer station. But she could feel her stores slowly replenishing under the fierce decay of the superheavy radionuclides that gave her movement, volition, thought. She would gradually become stronger, but at the moment, she was no match for a single maton—let alone three.

The vehicle slipped silently through the streets, surrounded by crowds which, although dense, were unnaturally quiet as the individuals comprising those crowds were their usual eerily silent selves, moving in straight lines or making right-angled turns. Maya suddenly felt her disdain for them swept away by a wave of pity: these people had only one destiny, and that was to fill the hall in the white building with their inert bodies as their blood was drained away. Maya knew that when she met the Council of Three, she would hate its members with an abiding hatred. She would bring war down upon them even if it meant she could never stand on the surface, under the cold blue sky of the outer world!

She soon realised she was no longer in the part of the town she knew. Her surroundings were basically the same: to either side, the mighty ridged and furrowed walls of the Subterran cavern slowly rose to create the roof at an immense height above the rapidly moving vehicle. But the buildings were gradually thinning out like a crop mistakenly intruding onto barren soil. Then they seemed to have crossed a line and there were no more buildings on either side of them, only diminishing shapes behind. The final building of the main part of the city appeared to be another industrial establishment, given the copious black smoke pouring from its chimneys. And in the near distance she could see a massive pile, a castellated, turreted, buttressed monstrosity of a dark green stone. It looked like an attempt to copy a medieval European castle by an unskilled architect who had only briefly seen a picture of one.

'The lair of the Council of Three, I presume,' she said. She expected no reply and she was correct in that assumption.

The Emerald City, she thought, *all I have to do is click my heels together, and I'll be home—wherever that is.*

The vehicle drew up soundlessly in front of a massive door, flanked by dark green Doric columns, and with a line of broad steps leading up to it. Beyond the doorway was darkness. Cold darkness.

'You will leave the vehicle and come with us,' the maton driver said, without turning its head.

She said nothing: there was nothing to say. Standing before the steps, she held her arms out and immediately felt the firm metal grip of the original two mechanisms on them.

'Don't you think you could trust me now, boys?' she said.

No response. They tugged forcibly and she was forced to ascend the steps. To her surprise, the air inside the building was distinctly cool, not simply relative to the furnace heat of the Subterran exterior but actually cool, even by the standards of the recording room.

Her captors frogmarched her down a long corridor which opened out into a spacious, colonnaded room. A balcony ran three-quarters of the way around the room, although there was no one on it as they dragged her into the room. There were no chairs or any other item of furniture in the room, but on the side opposite her was a set of two doors, which reached from the floor halfway to the ceiling. The matons halted and released her, moving some metres to the opposite sides of the room as they did so. She was left alone and staring at the two doors. For some minutes, nothing happened, and then she heard faint sounds coming from behind the doors, as if something was approaching from that side.

The doors opened, and three matons came out, one from the left hand door, the others from the right-hand door. They were larger than the ones she had seen up to that point, over two metres tall and correspondingly bulky.

But they were not the primary focus of Maya's attention.

Each of the new type maton was carrying a metal plate with upturned edges, like a large tray on which the evening meal could have been balanced. But there was no meal on those trays.

Instead, each metal plate held what seemed to be a miniature human being, but a hideously wrinkled, wizened human being with skin that was simultaneously leathery in texture but a pallid, off-white in hue, like skin that had been under a bandage for a long time. Each person—if that's what they were—was clothed in a one-piece tunic just covering the torso, leaving the limbs and face uncovered. The legs, which were crossed, were almost fleshless sticks that did not look capable of supporting the body. Each tunic was a different colour, but those colours were only faint pastels that hovered on the edge of becoming monochrome: bilious yellow on the left, sombre red in the centre, and necrotic green on the right.

And the faces! Each was built from rolls and jowls and wattles of that deeply lined, leathery skin, which mysteriously managed to convey the look of desiccation and oleaginous grease at the same time. And yet, the eyes looked young and vivid, and Maya knew she was the centre of attention of those rapacious eyes.

The middle creature spoke, but the voice did not match its moribund appearance, being strong, firm and giving the immediate impression of one who was used to command.

'Welcome, Maya! We comprise the Council of Three. Welcome to our Citadel. I am Thran, the Chief Councillor, and on my left, I have Deputy Councillor Tharn, and on my right, Deputy Councillor Ranth.'

'Is it your custom to bear names which are anagrams of each other?' Maya enquired, still not quite certain what these eldritch creatures were.

'It is,' Thran replied, 'We have many traditions in Subterra, not least our famed hospitality to our guests.'

'That's good to hear.'

Ranth spoke next and Maya was startled to hear the calm, melodious voice of a young woman emanate from the withered lump of flesh on the tray.

'But perhaps our famed hospitality does not extend to you, Maya. Is it not true you entered Subterra unbidden?'

'We were fleeing from a terrible danger. Our entry into your nation was unplanned, but necessary. We do not wish to burden you with our presence; all we ask is for guidance and, if possible, help in reaching the surface of this planet.'

'And what was this danger?' Tharn asked in a warm dark-brown baritone.

'A dangerous carnivore.'

Thran's face developed a new wrinkle, almost a gash, and it took Maya a second or two to realise he was smiling.

'What—a carnivore like this?' He made a motion to one of the original matons. It crossed to one side of the room and pressed a switch on the wall.

'Was it like this, by any chance?'

Maya turned to watch as the wall slid back, revealing a cavity beyond.

And in that cavity was—the foul thing that had chased them before their escape to Subterra.

With sick horror, Maya saw again the drool dropping from clashing mandibles, serried row after serried row of steak-knife teeth, claws and talons and pincers in an impossible riot of killing devices. It was a thing that should not be—that *could* not be!

Yet there it was.

Maya stared at it in sick horror.

'This is one of our creations—Eater,' Thran said didactically.

'What, "eta", the Greek letter?' Maya said, striving to remain in charge of her emotions, striving to control the urge to run, and keep on running until she had fled beyond the bounds of Subterra.

'No, his name is the noun relating to the action of eating. And his name, though extremely short, perfectly encapsulates his chief function. To *eat.*'

Eater had seen the occupants of the central part of the room and crashed onto the transparent barrier which separated it from the occupants. Thwarted in its attempt to get at them, it reared up against the partition, displaying a segmented underbelly pulsing like an obscene heart.

Maya gladly turned her attention from the terrible eating-machine, such a short distance away, and faced the Councillors again.

'So it was you who controlled the light in the tunnel. You who sent the rats against us. You who watched Yarl being devoured. You who sent a thing like Eater against us.'

'Of course. We had watched you for some time as you wandered helplessly in the tunnel. You intrigued us greatly. Your two troglodyte pets were of no value to us, but you... you are different.'

Maya felt a tremor of fear. She had relied on her true nature remaining unknown, so she would have the element of surprise in any attack, but if they already knew...

'In what way?' she said, in a dull monotone.

'We know all about you, Maya,' Thran continued, 'we had our suspicions when we saw how easily you dealt with the rats,

213

so we manoeuvred you into coming here by introducing you to one of Eater's brothers in the tunnel. And then, did you not wonder why we took you on a completely unnecessary tour of our main city? That vehicle was packed with recording instruments which analysed you from your silicon skin down to your titanium bones. We know exactly what you are.'

She said nothing.

'Don't you realise how ridiculously easy it is to determine your nature? You can't hide from the Council of Three. For instance, you give off an aura of soft X-rays from your power source. I wonder if you told Karn that when he was hugging you for his comfort.'

Maya tried desperately to retain the initiative in this conversation.

'You said you created Eater. What did you mean?'

Tharn and Ranth turned simultaneously to Thran as he smiled again.

'Trying to delay the inevitable while you try to think of a way to escape? I applaud you, Maya, but knowing full well you cannot escape, I will continue my discussions as I really do enjoy talking about our achievements.

'We are genetic engineers. We create living machines to aid us in our enterprises. We developed the rats in an early "proof of concept" experiment. But they were not a particularly impressive creation, so we let them roam free in the tunnels. It is not unusual for things like Karn to wander into them, so they are happy enough, and if no foolish explorer is available, they eat each other. However, the species of which Eater is such a fine specimen is a far nobler development, a true testament of our abilities, as an animal with his mixture of characteristics from different phenotypes, different phyla even, could not evolve naturally. We keep him, and his brethren, for special occasions.'

'He will not enjoy eating me,' Maya said, in a show of defiance that was not entirely genuine.

'Perfectly true. But he is more than capable of biting off your limbs, leaving you as a helpless torso. Think on that if you have any stupid ideas about defying us.'

'Seeing as I cannot be a meal for your animal, why do you want to hold on to me? Why not let me carry on to the surface?'

Thran leaned so far forward that for an instant, he looked like he was going to topple off his plate.

'Because we want the secrets of your construction. You are vastly different from anything else we have encountered. You told Arthrena where you come from, but the stupid bag of skin did not understand. We had trouble converting the time period you gave her into our own system, but eventually we succeeded. We now understand that you are from the extremely distant time when the planet Jupiter nearly destroyed Earth. You are the product of a transcendent science which has been lost in all the years that have passed since the extinction event.' He rocked back and looked at each of his companions, and then back at Maya. 'So much has been lost! So much we could have used! We Subterrans are a great people, but for many terrible millennia we struggled to survive in the turmoil that followed the close passage; millennia in which we could have built on the knowledge of our ancestors. Instead, we were forced to fight for existence against flame and earthquake, crawl like worms in the earth! It is a testament to our strength that we succeeded in hanging on to some of the science of the last days. It took thousands of years, but eventually we came to understand and then master our new environment, down here near the base of the crust. And slowly, so very slowly, we built on the scraps of knowledge that we had managed to bring down with us when we escaped from the Destroyer. We build matons; we manipulate living matter and sculpt it into new forms more pleasing to us. But it is not enough.'

'I cannot help you,' Maya said, 'Only one man knew the details of how to create a being such as I. And he is now part of the dust of the earth you dig in. But even if I could help you, I wouldn't. If you won't help me reach the surface, the least you can do is release me. And Karn,' she added, after a moment's thought.

All three smiled, terrible vulpine smiles in lined, jowly faces; faces that in a vastly earlier age would have reminded the observer of Halloween masks.

'You fail to see the obvious, Maya. You are clearly not as intelligent as you think. We don't want you to sit down with us and go through technical drawings and plans, painstakingly recreating the science of your day, minute step after minute, laborious step. We are going to examine you, electronic neuron by electronic neuron. We are going to take your brain slowly apart and place every one of your AI processors on our laboratory benches and stimulate them in various ways, measuring the input, recording the output. Your chassis, your body, is of some interest to us as it appears to be extremely efficiently constructed, but understanding your mentality is vastly more important. Somehow an entire human consciousness has been copied into an electronic matrix. Your scientist must have been a truly great man. Compared to you, our matons are no more than inert lumps of metallic ore.

'But we must have the secret of your mental construction. And we will have it.'

If Maya's mouth had been capable of becoming dry, it would have done so. So she had no physical difficulty in speaking, but it was still a great effort to speak.

'And when you have the secret of my consciousness, what will you do with it? Improve your matons?'

'Yes, that is one very small thing we will do with our new knowledge. I'm afraid there has been no progress in their development in the thousands of years since the passage. With improved brains, they will become a great army which we will use to more easily conquer the other societies scattered throughout the crust. But that is only a minor side-effect, a bonus, if you will.'

'And the main benefit?'

Thran leaned forward again, and his eyes seemed to be gleaming, as if lit from within by a hungry fire.

'You entered the Harvesting Building without our permission. What did you see?'

'I saw blood being taken from what appeared to be comatose human beings.'

'And what would be the purpose of us doing that?'

'I have no idea.'

Thran's smile became broader. Stumps of yellow teeth which had once been fangs became visible between the greasy lips.

'That is the problem with a physics-based education; your understanding is so narrow. For example, are you aware that in the twentieth century of the Common Era in a long-gone place called Berkley, research was begun into the rejuvenating effects of young blood plasma on the aged?'

'No.'

'It was an effect first demonstrated in mice, but it was soon found to apply to humans as well. The blood from teenaged subjects was found to improve heart and liver function and even to initiate neurogenesis. And we are living proof of young-blood therapy. We conquer other settlements and harvest their younger members. We use their plasma to keep ourselves alive. For instance, take me—can you determine my age?'

'No.'

'I am over three hundred years old.'

'You look it,' said Maya, knowing it no longer mattered if she angered the Councillors or not. 'But can plasma injections affect other causes of ageing: the degeneration of the mitochondria, mutations in DNA?'

'Of course not!' Thran snapped, presumably annoyed by Maya's comment on his appearance, 'but with the ability to upload consciousness and then download it into a biological frame, we could live forever, moving from body to body, not caring what excesses we put those bodies through, what years of wild abandonment, as we would know there would always be another body we could utilise once we had worn the current one out in an endless explosion of pleasure!'

Maya was silent. The scenario Thran had outlined was not totally unlike her own dream of returning to a biological container. It had simply not occurred to her that if it could be done once, it could be done an infinite number of times.

'Well,' Thran continued, 'are you not pleased? Your dissolution and study will mean we will no longer need to drain blood from those poor unfortunates. Instead, we will have a much superior system of attaining immortality. And it all be thanks to you, you wonderful person.'

Maya remained silent. It seemed there was nothing she could say; nothing she could do to alter the dreadful fate that was hurtling towards her. Her strength had grown measurably since the visit to the transfer station but, even if it were at its peak level, she doubted she could overcome six matons simultaneously.

Thran curtailed his speech and looked over Maya's shoulder. 'Ah, here's our other guest!'

Yet another maton entered the room, carrying a sack in which something was wriggling and twisting. The maton undid the fastening of the sack and threw its contents onto the floor.

It was Karn—as she had known it would be.

He rolled onto his hands and looked around. He saw Maya and relief flooded his face.

'Maya, thank the gods! Where am I?' He stood, and then recoiled as he saw the Councillors for the first time. 'What— what are these things?'

'Your new rulers,' Thran said. 'It is no good looking at Maya. She can't help herself, let alone you.' He looked Karn up and down, like a farmer appraising a new breed-animal. 'Yes, we'll keep you in the foundry for a while. You're unusually well built for your type. Then to the Harvesting Building, of course. You should be able to supply us for quite a while, I think.'

Karn looked around desperately, and then went rigid with fear as he saw Eater's belly hungrily pressed up against the

218

transparent wall. His legs buckled, and he collapsed in front of Maya.

Her gaze flicked rapidly from maton to Councillor, from Councillor to maton, in a dizzying sequence. She checked her power levels. If she could capture one of the Councillors, she might be able to bargain her way out. The maton which had brought Karn in had something in his hands—she knew not what. Maya's mind whirled into a vortex of indecision. What to do? What could be done?

In a mad turmoil of conflicting emotions, she snarled, 'I will make war upon you, you foul half-dead things. I'll make you completely dead!'

They laughed, the dry crackle of dead leaves stirring in a sudden gust.

'None war upon the masters of Subterra. We could break up this world in our wrath.'

She determined the distance between her and the Councillors. She calculated the leap she would need to make, the power that would be required, the arc she would describe as she leapt up at them.

'I'll...' she began as she tensed for the leap.

The newest maton raised the object it had been carrying and pointed it at her. There was a transient electrical discharge. Maya writhed madly like an animal receiving an electric shock and then collapsed with a heavy crash upon the floor, silent and motionless.

'Electromagnetic pulse,' Thran said to Ranth, 'works every time.' He turned away from his fellow Councillor and looked down at the motionless form of Maya. 'I'm sorry dear, what were you saying?'

Six

Maya stood on the rubble of the fallen building and looked up at the night sky. It was a splendid sight: Jupiter was at opposition in its spiralling path towards the Sun and blazed near the zenith. It was a disc about one third the apparent diameter of the full moon, but was already just as bright. A keen eye could now distinguish the brown and cream cloud bands on the disc, and the Galileans too were well displayed, three on one side, and one on the other. It was a magnificent display.

Except it meant death.

Not just death to a few; to the old; to the sick.

Everyone. The entire population of planet Earth. Colossal Jupiter had been torn from its orbit and was now sweeping inwards, towards the Sun. Its eventual fate was unknown: some thought it would be swallowed by the Sun; others that it would take up an orbit sunward of Mercury; others that Earth would join its existing major satellites and become a new moon of the rogue planet.

But whatever happened, there would be death. Billions of individual deaths but one global catastrophe; a cataclysm such as had never before afflicted humanity. Already the giant planet was tugging, pulling, at the orbits of the inner worlds, stretching them out like feeble strands of cotton.

Maya shivered: it was a clear night and a cold one. She hugged her little wooden doll, still clad in a few scraps of torn fabric, and made her way back to the settlement. She didn't want to look at Jupiter anymore.

She picked her way through the fallen timbers and piles of bricks to the community centre. Her mother, Isabella, looked up from feeding the baby as she came in.

'Maya Moreno, where have you been!' she said in what was meant to be an angry voice, but Maya knew she was more concerned than angry. 'I need you to look after Alejandro for a while.'

'I haven't been away long, mother,' Maya said, 'just looking at the stars.'

'Looking at the stars!' her mother said, in exasperated tones, 'there're chores to do around here and you go off looking at the stars!'

'I wasn't away long, mother,' Maya said, 'I can't stand being in here all the time; it's so noisy, so dirty!'

'You should thank the Good Lord you have a roof over your head,' Isabella said, 'that's a lot more than many people have!' She pulled her blouse over full breasts and thrust Alejandro into her other child's arms. 'Here, do something useful. He's been fed; see if you can wind him otherwise he'll sick it up again.'

Maya looked into Alejandro's brown eyes as he lay cradled in her arms and wiped some breast milk away that had been drooling onto his little tunic. Then she looked up at her mother, her eyes holding an accusatory gaze.

'Are you going to see that man again?'

Isabella stopped in mid-turn and returned to stare at her daughter.

'What's it got to do with you? Who's the mother around here?'

'He hit you last time,' Maya observed, 'I can see the bruises from here.'

'Raoul is a good man,' Isabella said, but with a hint of hesitation between the words, 'he has a lot of responsibility running this place and looking after us all. So don't you bad mouth him, my girl.'

Unwisely, Maya did not take the hint.

'You know he's seeing two other women, don't you?'

'He's good to me; I get extra food for you and Alejandro.'

'But what do you have to do for it? You know the other women hate you, don't you?'

That was too much. Isabella leaned down and gave Maya a stinging slap across the face. Maya flinched but did not cry out, but Alejandro had picked up on the bad feeling and began to whimper. Maya hugged him to calm him, heedless of the stinging red mark spreading across her face. But Isabella had not finished. She reached down and snatched the little doll from Maya's lap.

'You are a wicked little girl, talking about your mother like that! You'll never see your little Maria again!'

And with that, Isabella strode off into the main hall, shouldering other people aside in her anger. In the distance, just as she was about to disappear into the throng of people, Maya saw her bend down and give the doll to a small girl of about Maya's age. The girl was too far away to hear anything, but Maya could lipread her effusive thanks.

Maya sighed and hugged Alejandro even tighter. She kissed his little forehead and as she did, she wondered if one day she would have a little boy of her own to hug. Her face grew stern. If she did, the father would not be like the volatile Raoul; he would be a kind, considerate man, and they would be happy forever.

She raised Alejandro up against her shoulder and rubbed his back vigorously. The baby rewarded her with an enormous belch, coupled with a little jet of partially-digested milk. Maya smiled. He would sleep now.

As Alejandro did indeed slip into a contented slumber, she looked around at the crowded hall. It was much like any other night, full to overflowing with poorly dressed, poorly washed people: men, women, and crowds of children. All looked underfed and, even from this distance, gave off an air of exhaustion, of desperation.

Maya knew what had brought them to this state. She had learned to read at very early age and had shown an understanding far beyond her years. Her mother had found her precociousness somehow disturbing, as Maya often talked about things that other girls her age did not—like stars, planets, even whether the lightsail craft launched nearly a century ago had any chance of escaping the doom of stars. Maya could even describe how the catastrophe had occurred. In her naïveté, she had occasionally uttered the hated name of the hated woman who had caused the disaster—brought the black hole into the system and ruined

222

everything. That woman's name had become an obscenity, a term of abuse to be used only in moments of the deepest, most animalistic rage. It had taken many slaps before Maya had accepted that it was a word not to be used in polite company.

As Alejandro slumbered, she looked upon her fellows with great sadness. She saw them all with her tired eyes: some trying to sleep wrapped in thin blankets, some stirring tepid cornmeal mush in chipped bowls, some trying to forget their problems with flagons of cheap beer. Even though it was midnight, there was a continual roar of voices filling every corner of the hall; there were fights breaking out; there were couples fondling each other. Those who wanted to sleep had long since learned to shut the noise off in their minds.

She wondered how long it would be before her mother returned and whether she would have any fresh bruises. Isabella insisted that Raoul loved her, even against the glaringly obvious evidence that he did not. But she brought extra food back; that part was true, and her children were glad of it.

Was there a way out? Maya wondered. She loved Alejandro and her mother, despite the frequent slaps, but she wanted more from life. She wanted peers she could talk to, without seeing incomprehension or indifference slowly spreading across their faces.

There were stories that the Westranian Government had agents in the field, looking for children who could be taken and given a higher education. Maya didn't want to leave her family, but neither did she want to stay forever in this noisome, riotous existence along with all these people who had no hope. Some of the men were employed on rebuilding projects, but with the earthquakes becoming ever more frequent it was a line of business that could not last much longer. Everyone else depended on welfare payments from the Government.

And how much longer would there even be a Westranian Government? Every year the climate became more disturbed, the ground shook more, the waves in the Gulf of Mexico became higher, the forest fires started earlier in the year, so that soon there would be no forest to burn. No one lived near the sea anymore, even in those places where the coast had not slipped under the rising water.

But soon, there would be nowhere left for increasingly desperate humanity to find refuge.

Nowhere.

And with that, she finally did begin to cry.

Fortunately, Alejandro slept through it.

***

We have reached the earliest stratum of memory that we can decode. Is there anything to be gained from this level?

No. This section appears to be merely memories of a very early stage of her family life. The system of encoding is still not apparent. We should move on.

Understood.

***

Maya was nervous.

'Mother,' she said, 'I'll like you to meet Andrew.'

She stood aside, allowing Isabella to see the slight, young man who until that instant had been hidden behind Maya. Isabella looked him up and down. She was not impressed.

'Pleased to meet you, I'm sure,' she said, extending a hand, 'what can we do for you here?'

'Could we sit down, Mrs Moreno?' he said, 'there's quite a lot to talk over.'

Isabella turned to look into the kitchen.

'Alejandro!' she yelled, 'get your ass off the chair and go out and play!'

'Aww, mom,' the child said, 'it's too hot out there!'

'Git!' his mother hissed, but there was love in her eyes. The dark-eyed, dark-haired boy slid past Isabella and Maya, casting a quizzical glance at Andrew as he went by.

'Come into the kitchen, Andrew,' Isabella said, 'it's cooler. Not by much, but we need every bit of shade these days.'

'Thanks, Mrs Moreno,' he said and, sitting down, cast a quick glance around. 'Nice place you have here.'

'It's a lot better since they put the roof back on,' she replied. 'Raoul's boys were a big help.' She threw an acerbic stare at Maya. 'Unlike some people I could mention.'

'Mother,' Maya said, ignoring the unvoiced accusation, 'Andrew has something important to tell you.'

Isabella stared at the young man, who wilted somewhat under her stare.

'Well?'

'Mrs Moreno,' Andrew began, 'as you know we are all living in difficult times.'

Isabella's stare became stonier.

'Yeah, I guess so. Is that what you learned in one of those fancy colleges?'

'How did you know I was a college boy?'

'Please.' She waved a hand at him and then pushed a greying lock of hair out of one eye. 'Just because I live in a shack that's held together by spiders' webs, don't think I'm a fool. You don't look or talk like any of the men around here. Any one of them would have you for breakfast.'

'Mother!'

Isabella winced.

'Sorry about that. It's not easy trying to hold this family together, especially with one child who won't get her hands dirty.'

'I'm not a child, mother.'

'Please.' Andrew broke into the conversation, and both women looked at him, both slightly surprised. 'Could I explain why I'm here?'

Isabella shrugged.

'Sure. I can't hang around here all day. There're lots of chores to do.' She leaned back in her chair and gave a stage laugh.

'Hey! What am I saying? There're always chores to do around here!'

'Mrs Moreno,' Andrew said, 'I am here as a representative of the Westranian Government…'

She laughed.

'What! Are those blood-suckers still around? I thought they'd all flown off to Alaska or some other goddamn place where it's nice and cool!'

Andrew's lips thinned.

'Mrs Moreno, as Jacksonville is now underwater the Government is at present in residence in the far north of Westrania, but, as always, they are working hard to try and give us all a better quality of life.'

She shrugged.

'Pardon me. When they stopped sending us welfare checks I took it they'd lost interest in us poor folks. Too busy sipping champagne up there with the polar bears.'

'There aren't any polar bears anymore, Mrs Moreno. They all died out when the ice melted. And your Government is trying to find ways to stop us going the same way.'

'Like what?'

Maya stiffened with sudden tension. This was it.

'Mrs Moreno, these are desperate times. Everyone can see what is happening just by looking at the sky. In only a few years we will be at our closest to Jupiter, and I assure you what we have suffered up until now will be just a fleabite compared to what will be happening then.'

'Thanks. You've really made my day.'

'It's no good pretending otherwise, Mrs Moreno. We will pass through the inner magnetosphere and the surface will be sterilised.'

Isabella looked at Maya.

'Magnetosphere?'

'It's a dangerous place, mother. Very hot.'

Isabella put her hands behind her head and leaned back, fixing Andrew in an unbreakable stare.

'OK. So why exactly are you here?'

Maya could see Andrew was also feeling nervous.

'Mrs Moreno, the Government is selecting young people who show promise of high intellectual potential to put into a task force who will be doing their damdnest to find a way to get the maximum number of people to survive.'

'You talk as if most people ain't gonna make it.'

'I'm afraid that's certain. It will be made public soon so I don't think I'm giving anything away when I tell you the Government will soon be distributing medication; medication which will allow people to slip away painlessly.'

The kitchen was furnace-hot but it suddenly felt bitterly cold; cold as the temperatures which still lingered around the South Pole.

'Things that bad?'

'Yes. Which is why we need as many intelligent young people as we can. Time is short, terribly short.'

Isabella shook her head.

'No, that's not gonna happen to Alejandro and me. We'll be OK. I'll damn well make sure of it!' She looked again at Andrew. 'And you're here—because...'

'Because Maya is one of those intelligent young people. Our agents have been watching her for a long time.'

Isabella glanced suspiciously at Maya.

'And how can this girl help you? There's nothing around here. Everything's been knocked flat. There's nothing here, except sand and bits of smashed-up cars!'

Andrew looked helplessly between the two women: the strong, selfless mother and the young woman who had nothing to offer but her intelligence and youth.

'That's right, Mrs Moreno. I'm afraid we'd have to take Maya away for an accelerated system of learning, cramming as much knowledge into her as is biologically possible.'

Isabella leaned toward Andrew, and her face was now twisted in anger.

'Never mind your fancy words. You ain't taking her away from me. Who's gonna look after me? I've got more things wrong with me that you could start to count. Who's gonna help me bring up little Alejandro? Tell me that, you dickless cocksucker!'

Andrew said nothing. He looked down at the rickety table, hammered inexpertly together from broken shards of timber. Isabella turned her fury on Maya.

'And you, Little Miss Perfect, tell this City Boy you're not going anyplace. Tell him you're staying here to help your mother!'

Maya knew the moment had come.

'I'm going with Andrew, mother.'

Isabella became completely motionless, her face frozen into a strange mixture of anger and disbelief. Then she stood and, very deliberately, slapped Maya across the face with all her strength. Maya toppled backwards off the chair. But she did not cry out.

Isabella stood over her. She spoke in a cold, controlled hiss.

'Get out, bitch. Get out now. Don't let me see you around here ever again. I'll tell Alejandro you're dead. And you know what, bitch, you are dead.' Her voice rose to a scream. 'Dead!'

Andrew helped Maya to her feet and, together, they went out into the blazing sunlight of the last days of the planet Earth, a planet on which a sentence of death had been irrevocably passed.

***

Still too far from the period of interest. This is taking too long. Move on.

***

Maya looked up from the monitor as Giorgio entered the lab. She took a few seconds to admire his slim body, his curly black hair, his general demeanour which, even across the

228

intervening space, transmitted the impression of someone who hadn't a care in the world.

Half of her hoped he hadn't noticed her looking; half of her hoped he had.

She smiled inwardly as he came up to her and slipped an arm around her waist. Women of an earlier age would have objected to such familiarity, but now they had other things on their minds.

Like the end of the world.

'How's it looking?' he said, momentarily tightening his grasp and then removing the offending arm.

She smiled as she looked at him. Smiling was not something that happened much these days, but Giorgio somehow managed to conjure at least one out of her whenever he showed up.

'Not too good,' she said, admiring him under half closed lashes, 'the calculated absorbed radiation levels will be even higher than we feared. At least five Sieverts.'

He whistled.

'Nasty. But it's still a level that could be shielded against.'

She hated to contradict him, but this was important.

'In theory. But at the same time there will be all manner of physical events happening continuously: seismic shocks, tsunamis, super-hurricanes. It's difficult to see how any surface structure could withstand all those happenings simultaneously.'

'We can rule out tsunamis,' he said, all traces of levity, of light-heartedness having evaporated, 'survival bases in the deep interior of any of the major continents will be safe from those.'

She tried to ignite light-heartedness within her own mind, but even with Giorgio so close, she could not.

'That's true. But you know as well as I do, that tsunamis are not the main threat. The combination of major earthquakes and ionising hard radiation will be the real sterilisers.'

He nodded—reluctantly.

'Yes, perhaps shelters can be constructed in cratons—you know, areas of the Earth's surface which are particularly stable, less prone to seismic events. And you know, I, and quite a few others, think our future lies underground, and when I say "underground" I mean *deep* underground. And some people are talking about space-arks to be stationed out beyond Jupiter. I'd like to think that could be done, but it'll be a hell of a project; it'll make building the pyramids look like playing with sand-castles!'

Maya wanted to be carefree, light-hearted; she wanted to laugh and flirt with Giorgio, maybe a kiss or two: but she could not. Instead, she found herself looking earnestly at him and saying: 'Giorgio, be honest—what do you think our chances are?'

'What—the human race?'

'Yes, in a way, but I really mean you and me: individuals, ordinary people caught up in a terrible slaughter that was none of their fault.' She dropped all pretence of gaiety. 'Giorgio, I'm young. I want to laugh at silly little things, I want to wake up in the morning and not worry about what's going to happen. I want to have fun, I want to put on make-up and nice clothes and go out dancing, I want to date boys.' (Giorgio grinned broadly at that.) 'Is that too much to ask?—it never used to be!'

Suddenly she was crying, and Giorgio moved closer and gently allowed her to rest her head on his shoulder. He was conscious of the softness of her desirable body but he made no move. He just let her cry.

'Giorgio, Giorgio,' Maya whispered, 'why were we born in this terrible time? What did we do to deserve it? I'm so damn young, why should I die? I don't want to die!'

Giorgio struggled to say something that was genuine comfort, something not trite, something not a fortune-cookie platitude, but it was not easy.

'Maybe it won't be so bad,' he finally whispered into her short, black hair, 'maybe we'll go quickly. Without too much pain. There'll be the pills at the end.'

She pulled away; her face reddened from the tears.

'I don't want to go at all! I want to live! I'd do anything to carry on living. Life, for God's sake, when did that become too much to ask!'

He stood watching her, helplessly.

She sat on a stool and looked up at him, brushing a fugitive tear from her cheek.

'I've been doing a lot of reading recently. Religious stuff to see if they had any answers. I picked up a long poem called "Paradise Lost." In it, a character says something that really affected me. He says, "For who would lose though full of pain this intellectual being, these thoughts that wander through eternity?".'

He shook his head.

'I don't get it.'

She smiled thinly.

'He's saying that even if he's in pain, he wants to carry on living. Life is more important than pain.'

Giorgio turned and looked at the computer screen and saw the calculations that Maya had been working on. He could read them as well as she, and he understood only too well the dread message spelled out by the numbers and Greek symbols. He read the Warrant of Execution for the human race.

'I guess it depends on the degree of pain, doesn't it? I've seen people who begged for death. There'll probably be a lot more of them soon.'

Suddenly she leapt off the stool and wrapped her arms around him.

'Giorgio, Giorgio, make love with me, please! I don't want to die in some radioactive firestorm not having known love. All I want is to love and be loved!'

He slowly, gently, pulled her arms from around him and looked deep into her dark eyes.

'No, not here, not now. Maybe somewhere else, another time. We'll open a bottle or two and just see what happens.'

She smiled.

'I'd like that.'

He turned to go, stopped, and then turned back.

'Oh, I nearly forgot. There's a man here, interviewing all the physics students. He especially wants to meet you.'

'Oh, I wonder why? I didn't think I was that important. What's his name, have I heard of him?'

'A big wheel in cybernetics, apparently. A man by the name of DeGroot, Cornelius DeGroot.'

***

There was an upsurge in electrical activity when that name appeared. I believe DeGroot might be the key to our understanding.

Yes, she must have discussed the principles with him. A woman of her intelligence would have wanted to know the fine details of the procedure. Let us move to the next period. I am eager to begin the disassembling of the brain.

***

They were all there in the room, all of them: Cornelius DeGroot, Maya Moreno, Veronica McQuade, Alain Duquesne, Bernard Hilbert, Shiro Takemoto.

DeGroot was not happy.

'McQuade,' she said, fixing the woman with a sabre-sharp stare, 'are you seriously telling me that after all this time, you still have no progress to report on the time crystal?'

McQuade faced him squarely.

'Professor, you are a great man in your own field, so please give me a little respect when we're dealing with mine. But contrary to your obvious opinion, I am neither a simpleton, nor a potcheen-guzzling country bumpkin. And I assure you, I do not have learning difficulties!'

DeGroot stared at her for a few moments, and then his face softened.

'I'm sorry, Veronica. I shouldn't have snapped at you like that. I'm under a great deal of pressure.'

But McQuade was not satisfied.

'*You're* under a great deal of pressure! What do you think the rest of us are doing—painting our nails! The time crystal is a quantum artefact and you know how easily disrupted they are!'

'Yes, yes, but if it doesn't work properly, we might not wake up at the right time. We might overshoot by centuries.'

'I know that as well as you.' And with that, McQuade turned her back and returned to the great cylinder which held the precious time crystal.

The others hung around, awaiting their turn to suffer under the lash of DeGroot's tongue. But he seemed chastened by his encounter with McQuade and returned to studying his computer screen.

After a while, Maya felt brave enough to approach him. She was not sure whether she was trembling or whether it was the floor shuddering under yet another quake.

'Professor,' she began, feeling her timidity striving to overcome resolution.

He did not turn from the screen.

'Yes?'

'Are we doing the right thing? I mean, it's so beyond any human experience. I...'

Now he did turn, and the face he presented to Maya was a weary one, the face of a man forced to consider options which hitherto no member of the human race had been forced to contemplate.

'I know what you're going to say. Is copying the consciousness of a human being to a machine brain the right thing to do. You've known about that procedure from the beginning. Why are you questioning it now?'

'Because then it was just a theory, just a collection of simulations. You showed everyone a rabbit and a dog that had had their minds transferred, but the digital copies couldn't speak. They couldn't tell us whether or not they were suffering.'

'So you want humans to have their minds copied and uploaded and report back, as long as it's not you, is that it?'

Maya looked at the floor.

'No, no, it's not that. But dying, that's the part I can't face.'

'The copying process is classical, not quantum. It cannot accept two versions of the same object—in this case, a mind—

233

in existence simultaneously. But it's not really dying: in three hundred years, you'll awake, and it will be as if everything that happened to you was only a few seconds ago, even though three centuries will have passed.'

'But we will awake as a machine, a robot.'

'No!' DeGroot was angry. 'Not a robot! For the thousandth time, when your new body is printed, it will look exactly as you did at the instant of copying: every freckle, every hair in your armpit. It will be you! And more importantly, it will be you for a thousand years, such is the durability of your new body. And what a body! Enormous strength! The ability to recall libraries of data in an instant! Powers the fantasy writers have only dreamed about—but they'll be real. And yours.'

'But not flesh. Professor, I am a woman. I want to be nothing more than a woman. I want to have children. I want to love and be loved.'

DeGroot was silent for a while, then: 'I am beyond the lusts of the flesh—they mean nothing to me now, if they ever did. But I understand that, as a young female, you still have those needs. But don't despair, Maya. I am sure that as science advances, it will eventually be possible to return your mind to a biological container. It might take nine hundred years for science to reach a sufficiently high level—but what will such a short time be to the new Maya?—immune from infection, immune from cancer, possessed of powers far beyond what primitive organic chemicals could ever generate. You know, Maya, that many philosophers see biological beings as only a stepping stone to the achievement of true intellect. Incredible machine-minds that could behold the emptiness between the stars and conquer it; unlike those pathetic fools in their primitive lightsail ships!'

She said nothing, desperately trying to find a flaw in DeGroot's certainty. But he had not finished his lecture.

'And what is the alternative? Do we stay here on the surface and wait to be fried in the heat and radiation as we pass through the inner magnetosphere? To scrabble in the dirt like those deluded Burrowers, trying to maintain human dignity in some

234

hell-hole in the ground? We can leap-frog all that and awake in a time when the catastrophe is behind us.'

Maya finally nodded her agreement.

'Yes, thank you, Professor. I want to live, more than anything I want to live. I've always known you were right, but as it gets nearer, I, I...'

He patted her hand in a fatherly fashion.

'I understand, Maya. It is a terrible burden to be young in a time of so much death. The loss of friends, of family.'

She tried to smile but failed. She hadn't heard from her mother or her brother in ten years. Her messages had come back to her, undelivered. She did not know if they were refusing contact with her or whether one of the now-frequent natural disasters had carried them off.

And now she never would know.

But DeGroot was not to be spared further interrogation.

As Maya went back to her work, Takemoto replaced her, and he too was worried.

'I heard what you were saying to Moreno, Professor, and I agree with your plan for preserving our mentalities, but there is one thing which worries me.'

DeGroot raised a weary eyebrow.

'Yes?'

'Your plan is predicated on your belief that Earth will be deflected into a stable orbit, roughly where Mars used to be. I must tell you, Professor, not everybody agrees with you.'

'I am aware of that, but I put my trust in eternal mathematics—not mortal men. And I am in constant communication with my brother on Space Ark One and he assures me everything is fine with them. They are ready and eager to begin the task of reconstruction, of rebuilding our world. The radiation of the surface is induced, not inherent. It will die away quickly once we're out of the magnetosphere.'

'But you are a cyberneticist, Professor, not an astrophysicist. I...'

DeGroot had suffered enough. He leapt to his feet, and his voice roared in the room.

'I am utterly tired, completely sick of you people trying to undermine me! If it's not McQuade botching her job, or Moreno whining about not having children, it's some other intellectual pygmy thinking they've seen something I've missed. I am one of the greatest mathematicians of my time, I could have given Baldwin a run for her money! So now you have two choices: one: you stay with me and we work as a team, or, two: you get the hell out and take your chances on the surface!'

No one spoke.

He crossed to the televiewer screen and a picture appeared on its hitherto inert surface.

It showed a ruined city with mighty high-rise buildings laid in splintered ruin. Great fires were burning, and a black cloud hung over the city like a tremendous shroud, a shroud flecked with crimson flame and blue-white thermal lightning.

And on the horizon, dimly visible underneath the cloud was a great glowing hemisphere; a hemisphere crossed with churning cloud belts like paint poured into water.

Jupiter: The Destroyer—now only twelve months away from its closest passage to the stricken Earth, an Earth so minuscule, so utterly insignificant, it could have fallen into one of those swirling cloud masses and not be noticed.

And so they bowed to DeGroot's will and his plan continued to its ordained conclusion.

They died and, in the instant of their passing, their minds were copied and safely uploaded.

And far above the machines that were faithfully storing those minds, literal Hell was visited upon the surface. There was fire and storm and tsunami and earthquake. The entire planet thrashed and squirmed like a whipped dog.

And the Destroyer passed.

***

This is the crucial point. We can work on the neurons from here.

236

Seven

Karn did not know how long he had been unconscious: it could not have been long because when he came to, Maya was still lying motionless on the floor next to him. And Eater was still pressed up against the transparent wall, its belly pulsating, its mandibles snapping and drooling. As he stood, he saw again the Council of Three, squatting on their trays. They smiled lustfully as they saw they had caught his attention.

Thran it was who spoke first, as was protocol.

'Ah, the troglodyte has recovered from his shock at seeing his mistress disabled. Or maybe it was the understandable terror at seeing Eater pressing against the wall, so eager to make his acquaintance.'

Karn stared at the Council, motionless and speechless, as they introduced themselves. He finally regained the power of speech when they had finished.

'What have you done with Maya?

Thran turned to Tharn.

'Listen to the creature. See how familiar he is with his superior, using her name instead of saying "mistress." We will have to watch this one—looks like he has some fight in him!'

Tharn laughed.

'If he has, he's a lot different from all the other trogs we have collected!'

Ranth also gave a yellow grin, but said nothing, instead running her gaze up and down Karn's body, seeing a torso that now was only just contained in his tight-fitting garment. Finally, she said, 'He's a better physical specimen than all the others. Do you think I could have him for a while?'

'No, Ranth. We don't have time for your usual diversions. There wouldn't be enough of him left to work in the foundry if I gave him to you, even for a short while.'

She shrugged.

'I suppose not.'

Karn walked nearer to them, until he was not far from being beneath their holding plates.

'I asked you what have you done with Maya?'

Thran grinned again, much as a wolf might have done had it the necessary muscles.

'She is not dead, my little one. I don't know if she told you this, but she isn't the same as you, not a creature of flesh and blood, but a very sophisticated mechanism.'

'She did.'

'And, as such, she was vulnerable to a pulse of energy which disrupted her circuits.' He paused. 'I don't know why I'm telling you this, as you almost certainly don't understand a word of it. You're just a simple animal after all.'

They laughed.

'What are you going to do to her?' Karn said, staring up at them with hatred growing steadily in his features.

'We are going to probe her mind with a preliminary, non-destructive procedure. And when we have determined the most interesting parts of her brain, we will take her apart.'

'You are monsters.'

Thran laughed, looked at his companions, and then back at Karn.

'Yes, I suppose we are from your point of view. But your point of view means less than nothing to us, unfortunately. Anyway, enough of this foolish talk. You can accompany us while we ready your mistress for examination.'

Karn suddenly felt strong metal arms encircle him, and he was lifted from the floor. The matons holding the Council of Three also moved, a section of wall slid open, and all of them went through. Karn caught a last horrible glimpse of Eater before the partition closed behind them.

Soon, he was in a long antiseptic-looking room, illuminated by harsh strip lights tuned to the normal Subterran spectrum.

The maton carrying Maya lowered her gently onto a slab of some gleaming white material. There was a bank of softly glowing instruments to one side. Karn watched with growing unease as two matons placed terminals on either side of Maya's head and then, their work completed, they stood back. The Councillors approached on their maton carriers and spent some time looking down at their supine captive. The matons gently dropped Karn to the floor.

'Is she awake?' he asked.

'Oh yes, she is fully conscious. She has lost control of her limbs and so is completely helpless, and I believe she is unable to hear or see anything we do to her as we have disconnected her sensory apparatus. However, even if she could see, she won't know what we are going to do to you, my amusing little friend, because the procedure will be performed in another room.'

Karn said nothing. His palms were moist, his heart was racing, his throat dry. He knew there was nothing he could say which would make the slightest difference to his fate or Maya's. He felt a terrible sense of pity along with the terror; pity that Maya would never stand on the surface and see her dreams realised.

'There will be nothing to see for quite some time,' Thran said, 'the machines have to calibrate themselves against her mental architecture and then slowly infiltrate themselves. In the worst case, it could be several days before we get any results.'

'Leader,' Tharn said gently, 'let's not forget we still have to deal with Karn, and then we can get on with our proper work.'

'Thank you, Tharn. I was getting carried away with the thoughts of all the riches we shall gather from this young lady's brain. Yes, we must attend to Karn and then get back to work.' He spoke to the matons. 'Take us to the Biocentre.'

A maton scooped Karn up, and they resumed their journey, leaving Maya motionless on the slab, the mysterious instruments of the Council humming contentedly as they began their investigations.

It was a long walk to the Biocentre, and Karn noted a change in the quality of the air. It changed from being an antiseptic, machine-dominated atmosphere with that very faint tang of ozone that characterises such places, to one in which there was a completely different undertone. A suggestion of living things, of animals.

Finally, they entered another large room, one in which there were open vats, with wisps and curlicues of vapour rising from them, and cages in which strange creatures prowled hungrily back and forth.

They came to a halt near one of the open vats. The shape instantly reminded Karn of the fungus containers, although the smell was completely different.

'You are a stranger in Subterra, and also a supremely unintelligent stranger,' Thran said, resuming his lecture, 'so you do not realise that our true strength lies in our abilities to mould and develop biological material. We are sculptors of flesh, designers of tissue, artists in bone and blood. Our goal is immortality, to live forever in the flesh. The young blood of your fellow-unfortunates is a big help, but we are nearing the end of its power to keep us alive. That is why we are studying your mistress. The ability to upload an entire mind and then download it at some future time into an organic body—that would be the power of a god! We could spend one millennium as a digital mind, solving all the mysteries of the cosmos, and then another as a living, breathing being: adventuring, fucking, torturing to our heart's content. What endless possibilities there would be!'

'You're evil,' Karn simply said, 'you don't deserve one second of life, let alone a forever.'

Thran raised a bony finger and wagged it slowly at Karn.

'You don't know your Nietzsche, little trog, do you? A great man from many, many millennia ago, but by some wondrous chance a few of his writings survived. You see, you speak the morality of the slave, the eternal resentment of those who crawl at the bottom of the hierarchy, holding the others up with their tears and blood. But how would those slaves revenge themselves on their superiors if they could reach the heights; how quickly they would shed their morality and begin their own reigns of terror.'

'I've never heard of Nietzsche,' Karn replied, 'but I know that Maya said that all she wanted was to love and be loved. I prefer the sound of those words.'

'Ah, but you've never been tested, have you little trog? Never given the opportunity to torment and torture, without possibility of retribution. But, unfortunately for you, you never will be given that opportunity. Your story ends here. I must say, without meaning to cause offence, yours is a supremely uninspiring story; we have known of your miserable wormhole for over a millennium but you are so degenerate it was beneath our dignity to conquer you.'

Thran motioned to one of the matons that carried no burden. It moved to the nearby vat and put its grasping appendages in. It pulled out a dripping, glistening, mass of pulsating membrane. The transparent slime writhed in the metallic grip.

'This is one of our creations, a descendant of the group *Myxogastria*, once known as slime-molds. We have modified it in many ways, not least in that it can now infiltrate the mammalian nervous system. We will place it on your chest. It will feed upon you, but do not be alarmed, its nutritional needs are minimal and you will not suffer greatly. But what it will do is rob you of all independent thought, of all volition, so that all of your so-called mentality is totally subsumed into our needs and wants. We will then put you to work in one of our mines or factories; we have a great need of metal, especially when we build our armies of new matons. The work is very demanding, so we will soon spare you further suffering and take you to the Harvesting Building where we will use you to supply us with the fresh proteins and trace elements which only fresh young blood plasma can supply. You need not be alarmed at the prospect; it is entirely painless.'

Karn felt his legs begin to buckle and he fought to stay upright. The blood roared in his head. He looked around, but there was no escape. A maton extended a scalpel-like projection from its hand and sliced a thin line down Karn's tunic. Another peeled the tunic away leaving him naked, defenceless, afraid.

The first maton approached with the writhing thing held out in front of it. Suddenly other arms of metal clasped his own and bent them back, leaving his bare chest unprotected.

The transparent slime flowed fluidly from the maton's appendages onto his skin.

And suddenly nothing mattered anymore.

***

Karn loved his job. It felt like he had always been doing it, and he certainly intended to carry on doing it as long as he was able. He no longer felt the temperature of the furnaces, even though they added to the terrible heat that was inherent in life in Subterra. Even without the slime-mold on his chest, he would have glistened as if he had been dipped in oil. He was still completely naked, clothing being completely redundant in the terrible heat.

He loved to watch the molten steel as it poured from the cupolas into the waiting troughs and slowly cooled from yellow-white, through orange, through red, until it reached the solid, strong grey of the finished metal; a metal that was still dangerously hot, of course.

Then the finished ingots would be taken to other parts of the foundry to be hammered and twisted, bathed in vats of potent chemicals, drilled and machined, eventually to become parts of vehicles, transporters, walls and, of course, the ever-watchful matons.

There was usually a maton near to him, and it would occasionally warn him not to get too close to the fused metal.

'Why not?' he had asked in the beginning, 'I can stand the heat.'

'Questions are not permitted,' the maton had replied, 'do not get within three metres of the vat.'

Once Karn had disobeyed, so great was his love for the potent liquids, and had received an electric shock from a watchful maton.

He had not approached within three metres again.

Karn slept in the factory in a simple cot, like the rest of his fellow workers. He rarely spoke to his co-workers, as they even more rarely spoke to him. There was only the work; always the work. There was no night in Subterra and so the work never ended, shift succeeding shift, in a permanent cycle.

He was happy and wanted no more from life. And he knew that eventually when the work had become too much for him, he would receive his reward by being transferred to the Harvesting Building, where he would help his beloved Council of Three to continue their existence by giving them the gift of his precious blood. What better consummation could be wished for!

And so he toiled happily. He did not know how long he had been working in the factory; time meant little in the land of eternal day, eternal work. But sometimes as he lay in his cot, hearing the thunderous crashes of the metal being moved or worked on, he would sometimes see pictures of a very different world flash momentarily through his mind, a world where darkness followed light and was in turn followed by light. It seemed to be a very slow-paced existence compared with the real world. He saw someone, he knew not who, standing on a platform, stirring a greyish substance with a long pole. Very little seemed to happen in these visions, compared with the never-ending activity of reality, and he soon became bored with them.

But less frequently, he saw another vision. In this one, there was a woman—but a woman unlike any other he had ever known. She was tall, raven-haired, strong and resourceful. Sometimes the delicious fantasy came to him that she was *his* woman, one he could do with as he liked, punish as he liked.

And yet the concept of "punishment" didn't seem to fit too well with this particular woman.

The visions seemed to be happening more frequently, especially the ones which contained the tall, black-haired woman. It was as if some tremendously important memory was trying to rise up to some surface, like a great bubble of superheated gas ascending through layers of molten steel.

He slept, oblivious to the tumultuous clangour around him.

***

Tharn was worried, and he felt distinctly nervous bringing yet more bad news to his unforgiving superior.

'We are not making adequate progress, Leader,' he finally managed to say.

Thran looked like an irascible vulture as he sat on his resting couch, a black cloak covering part of his head and beaked nose, his small eyes somewhat rheumy. He had obviously just awakened, which meant his mood would be even worse than usual.

'Explain.'

'As you know, we reached the part where the subjects were copied into digital form and uploaded.'

'I do know, so get to the point.'

'We have not been able to deduce the mechanism of transfer. It's as if...'

Thran raised a thin, white eyebrow.

'As if?'

'As if she's fighting us on the mental level, resisting our attempts to get past that event.'

To Tharn's relief, his superior did not explode with anger, but simply leaned back slightly, letting his sleep-cloak fall away.

'Intriguing,' he said, 'we have no experience of dealing with such a mind as hers, of course, so it is beginning to look as if we have underestimated the task. We cannot begin the dissection until we have more data, otherwise we risk damaging the neurons and making the entire brain unusable.' He looked sharply at his subordinate. 'Increase the electrical potential by ten millivolts.'

'Yes, Leader!'

From time to time, Karn ran his fingers over his chest. He did not like the feel of the slime-mold intervening between the flesh of his fingers and the flesh of his chest. It was not particularly painful when the mold fed; merely a sharp pang once in a while. It was not an issue. Soon, he didn't notice its feeding times at all.

From time to time, he made an attempt to talk to his fellow workers, in the few periods between the back-breaking work and near-catatonic sleep. Usually, he was met with blank stares, or even worse, no recognition that he was even there, let alone having spoken. But occasionally someone did speak to him. He found out from the two people with whom he established contact that they had been living in worlds not too dissimilar to the World. But their idylls had been destroyed when one day part of one of the walls suddenly started rumbling just before collapsing to reveal a huge void. And out of that void had come weird metal men who then captured the youngest of their people, both males and females. These metal men cared nothing for the ancient, sacred ceremonies, of how the women had to be punished at set times or the fabric of the Universe might come crashing down. No, they herded their captives into strange machines which could move under their own volition. And after a long time they had been brought into the endless day of Subterra.

And there, their stories merged with Karn's. They too had received the gift of the slime-molds and immediately learned to love their work.

As did Karn.

But one day, not that long after his arrival, something strange happened. He was attending to a system of rollers down which the cooling ingots sped. They were fresh from the presses and blazing hot, hot enough to burn flesh even at a distance.

Karn had noticed that one of the rollers was vibrating rather than spinning with a smooth, fluid motion. He moved cautiously closer to examine the offending roller when his slime-mold decided to take a larger meal than was normal. The sharp pain made him cry out and, losing concentration for an instant, he tripped and fell much closer to the blazing metal than the matons permitted.

For a terrible, mind-destroying, moment, he felt the true power of the heat held captive in the metal, of how it wished to escape to burn and char his watery flesh. He screamed and flung himself backwards to escape the fleshhooks of pain. He crashed onto his back, his world consisting of nothing but terrible heat.

Slowly, he raised himself, looking desperately around to avoid punishment from a watching maton. By some miracle, there was not one near. He staggered away from the spinning rollers and glanced down at his chest to see if he had been burned.

There was a red patch under the mold, but it was already fading.

But there was something else. A portion of mold had been charred, no doubt shielding the skin beneath, and the substance next to the char was white and brittle. Experimentally he pulled at the charred portion and an entire section lifted away slightly, revealing the reddened skin.

And as it pulled away, a very strange thing happened.

From nowhere, a name swam into his mind.

And that name was *Maya*.

Eight

Tharn looked down at Maya as he sat on a tray held motionless by his personal, steadfast maton. He could still remember the pleasures of being with a woman, sinking into the warm flesh, watching her whimper as he roughly took his own pleasure and then discarded her.

Maya, though merely a mechanism, looked exactly as she had at the instant of her digitalisation. And at that moment, as the great planet Jupiter had filled the entire sky of the tortured surface of planet Earth, she had been a desirable female. Tharn felt desiccated glands attempt to stir into stuttering life, but the task was beyond their paper-thin tissues. Still, he enjoyed looking at her, wonderful memories stirring, even if the glands could not. Her features were fine and symmetrical, her body slim but pleasantly curved at the same time. Her jet-black hair was too short for Tharn's tastes, but that would be a trivial problem.

At least, it would have been if Maya were flesh and blood instead of silicon and metal.

Tharn forced his wandering thought back to the readout on the pad held before his eyes by another maton. He felt a pang of concern as he read the numbers. He had increased the potential as ordered by his Leader, but it had had no effect. Her mind was like a sphere of the finest marble; no tool could get a purchase on it but simply slid off. He knew, even if Thran apparently didn't, that increasing the potential again might start to burn the neurons out, rendering the whole operation futile.

But the prize was so great—it could not be allowed to slip through their fingers!

To have the power to digitise their minds and make them incorruptible while the Subterran computers worked on the problem of reloading those minds into young, strong bodies!

The idea was so wondrous, so delicious, that Tharn shuddered with actual delight and the promise of delight to come.

247

'Take me nearer to the subject,' he commanded his maton.

The maton lowered him onto the seat in front of the bank of instruments which were controlling and recording the procedures being employed in understanding Maya's brain; techniques which varied between all-out onslaught and sly insinuation. Neither had worked very well.

'Very well, my pretty one,' Tharn mused, 'let's try this one.'

His gnarled and knobbly fingers moved stiffly over the controls and slowly, the electrical waveform twisted and turned on the screen.

***

Darkness.

Nothing but darkness. Not a single photon was being detected.

They have blocked my sensory inputs, she thought, *I can't see anything, hear anything, feel anything. But I know they're out there. They're probably sitting next to me right now, looking at me, wondering how long it will be before they can find a way in.*

She had been forced to watch scenes from her past; some of which she had not wanted to remember. If she could have wept, she would have done so when, once again, she saw her mother throw her out. That was the last time she had seen either her or her brother. She did not know what had happened to them, but it would have been unusual if it had not been bad.

She saw herself whisked away on that fateful night, bundled into a helicopter and flown away into the continental heartland of the dying Westranian Republic, far away from the raging seas, and its tropical storms which nearly always matured into megahurricanes.

The base had been situated as carefully as possible, away from faults, from known seismic areas, from ancient lava tubes which might be reactivated at any moment, far from monstrous waves that touched the sky as they swept landward. And there she had been force-fed with as much of the physical science of the twenty-fourth century as the human brain could absorb.

How miserable that time had been! No parties, no burgeoning young love, no kisses after class, only an endless torrent of formulae, of laws, of principles. And behind all the formulae, the laws, the principles, the rules of inference, stood the austere figure of Cornelius DeGroot, harsh, unbending, impatient with failure, contemptuous of any inability to see how conclusion followed from premises. She hated him then: his pinched, lined face, his thin grey hair, his total absence of humour, of lightness of spirit. He could follow innumerable lines of complex reasoning through the labyrinths of higher mathematics, but fail to understand a simple joke. His other students hated him too, especially Veronica McQuade, who alone seemed to have the courage to stand up to him and remind him he was not the only one who could follow an argument to its conclusion.

But in the end they all bowed to him, because over them, like the deadly sweep of the pendulum, loomed the ever-growing majesty of the King of Planets, sweeping ever closer to the Sun, utterly unconcerned with any specks of matter which might lie in its path, or those insignificant particles which, cursed with self-awareness, might beg and plead to be spared.

She turned her mind, trapped in its solipsistic prison, away from the past and considered her present state: sightless, hearing-less, touch-less, utterly alone in a world of endless night.

But no—perhaps she was not completely alone. From time to time, she felt another presence, but one that brought no comfort, no speech, no rescue, just an insidious probing, an invisible tendril malevolently worming its way in.

She knew exactly what was happening: the members of the Council were trying to open her mind so they could drag its powers into the harsh light of their understanding and use them in plans too hideous to contemplate.

So far she had been able to resist, to deflect, to absorb.

But for how long, trapped in the darkness, could she continue to resist?

***

The days passed, unnoticed, uncounted. Karn had no conception of the term "day"; he knew only the Wake-Period and the Sleep-Period. They had always been exactly the same length each time they had come into the World, and so he had always known when it was time to stop his monotonous stirring of the fungus soup and be back in his hut in time to see the Sun slowly dim. But in Subterra there was not the slightest variation in the light's colour or intensity: it was always the same: harsh with a slightly bluish tinge, so very unlike the comforting yellow light of the Sun of the World.

He had become very good at his tasks, and his muscles, which had already swelled since his arrival at the recording room, grew harder and more prominent. Even some of his hitherto silent fellow-workers were impressed with his dedication to his work. But, of course, it was impossible to build any sort of friendship with them because, no sooner had he established some kind of rapport with one of them, he or she would disappear. And when he asked, the answer was always the same—They had been taken to the Harvesting Building to gladly give up their plasma for the greater glory of the Council of Three!

But something had changed in Karn; ever since the time that unknown word had burst into his consciousness he had wondered about what it meant.

Maya—what did the word mean?

And then one "day", after his shift was complete and welcome sleep was soaking into his body, he had an epiphany. The woman he had seen in his dreams, the tall, dark-haired woman—she was Maya!

His head spun as understanding exploded within it. Maya— he had known her! They had faced terrible danger, side by side, and triumphed.

Where was she now? Why could he not remember more?

All thoughts of sleep banished, he lay back in his cot and closed his eyes. He sent his mind back and back, searching for any scrap of information that might be the key to unlock his memories. But as he went further and further and further into the misty past, unseen forces tugged at his mental probe and pulled it out of his intended course. Sadly, he abandoned the attempt.

But he opened his eyes and stared at his invisible enemy, eye to eye with malevolent mystery.

'So,' he said finally, 'you do not want me to remember—but I will!'

***

'I am displeased,' Thran said, in a hissing voice that would have reminded his listeners of venomous reptiles—if there had been such in Subterra.

Tharn and Ranth said nothing, and with downcast eyes, sat limply on their metal plates.

'I gave you both a simple task—open up this machine's mind to analytical study. Seven time-periods have passed, and you have not gone beyond conjuring up pretty pictures of her family life. It was amusing to watch her mother abandoning her the first time, but the pleasure dulls after the third viewing. Tharn!' The named individual jerked upright at the sound of his name. 'You were the lead investigator–explain your failure!'

Tharn, unhappily and unwillingly, met his superior's caustic gaze.

'Leader, we are inexperienced with this kind of mentality. We are used to the matons and their low-level mental states. This is many orders of magnitude above them—many orders.'

'I want to hear about your next set of procedures—not whimpering excuses. This is a priceless gift that has fallen into our hands, an unexpected bounty that could transform the fortunes of Subterra and make us supreme beyond any possible

251

challenge. There are many more settlements scattered throughout the crust, inhabited only by pathetic troglodytes. We thought it would take a huge amount of time to subdue them all, but with this thing's abilities in our hands, it would be a matter of moments. And have you forgotten the ultimate prize: the ability to switch between digital and physical states at the merest whim; to live forever, watching the Sun itself bloat into a red giant and die while we, with unlimited time, spread throughout the galaxy? Who knows what species we would encounter out there among the stars, mediocre subhuman cultures we could plague and torment at our leisure.' His voice rose to an eldritch shriek. 'And there lies the vehicle which contains all those treasures and you tell me you cannot extract them!'

His audience returned to staring at the floor. But Thran was not finished.

'Tharn!' Once again that unfortunate's head jerked upright. 'You were the lead investigator and you I will punish first" he directed his next words to the maton holding Tharn's resting plate. 'Maton! Place Councillor Tharn on the floor!'

Tharn said nothing, but Ranth whispered, 'No, Leader, please no!'

The maton, having received its orders, obeyed them instantly. It lowered itself until Tharn's plate was a few centimetres from the floor and then with the end of one appendage pushed the Councillor unceremoniously onto the floor.

'Place his resting plate there,' Thran said, pointing to a spot about four metres from where, like a pile of soiled rags, Tharn lay sprawled on the floor. 'Your punishment,' Thran continued, mainly unemotionally, but perhaps with a touch of the exasperation that a lecturer might feel towards a failing student, 'will be to reach your resting plate within seven short time-periods. If you reach it within that time, I will forgive you; if you do not, a maton will withdraw a certain amount of your blood and give it to me. You will survive, of course, but you will not be exactly yourself for quite a while.' Thran's hard face became even harder. 'Now!'

Under Ranth's horrified gaze, Tharn began to drag himself along the floor towards his plate. His stick-like legs gave little thrust, and the floor was extremely smooth, giving his hands almost no purchase. To an observer familiar with such life-forms, he would have resembled a very large beetle that had lost the use of some of its legs and was desperately trying to escape an approaching predator. Thran intoned the passing short time-periods as Tharn painfully, with deep, rasping breaths, pulled himself, agonisingly slowly, towards his goal.

And on the announcement of the last short time-period, a claw-like hand just touched the rim of his plate.

'Well done,' Thran said, 'I was sure I was going to receive an extra injection of plasma, but you cheated me at the last moment.' He spoke to the waiting maton. 'Pick him up and bring him before me.'

Staring at his chastened subordinate, Thran said, 'You escaped serious punishment this time, Tharn, but next time the task will be much harder, and the punishment will be to let Eater play with you for a while. Not kill you, of course, I need subordinates, but you would find the experience, shall we say— unpleasant. Now back to business. Are you listening to this, Ranth!'

'Yes, Leader.'

Thran lifted himself as much as he could, although it made a negligible difference to his perceived height, and scolded, 'I want results. You have four more time-periods of study, and then I want the dissection to begin. Of course, I will want every artificial neuron connected to an input-output device almost immediately after that procedure.'

Tharn did not raise his head, and said, in a voice which was almost a whisper, 'Leader, your command runs the risk of destroying the brain, losing everything we have hope for. I...'

'Silence!' Thran thundered, 'I want no more weak whimpering. You will do what I said.' Then he looked sharply at

253

Ranth. 'This was the day for Tharn's punishment. The next time it shall be your day.'

And with that, he urged his maton to take him away, leaving his shaken subordinates staring at each other in dismay.

***

Karn had two periods of sleep with nothing memorable occurring, but on the third period he saw her again: tall, slim, sure of her ability, sure of her strength. He longed to reach out and touch her, yearned to hear her speak, longed to hear her explain what to do, what this mad world was all about. But she did not speak, did not seem to see him, and stood staring into the far distance, a stiff breeze hardly troubling her short, flawlessly black hair.

He could not shake off the feeling that she was the image of an actual person and that their lives had been intertwined at some point. The image had moved him so deeply, his work was not up to the required standard on the next shift. The nearby maton detected the decline in his output and gave him a warning to improve, or he would receive an electrical shock the next time. Karn said nothing; it was impossible to have a conversation with a maton as their speech consisted entirely of orders or threats.

He knew his time in the foundry was approaching its end. Soon, he would receive the reward for his hard work and transfer to the Harvesting Building, where the rest of his time would be spent helping the Councillors to receive the gift of long life they so richly deserved.

And yet, he was troubled—a deep stratum of his being told him there was something amiss with that selfless promise; the terms in the equation did not balance.

Something was not right. And the woman of his dreams—a woman he now knew to be named Maya—would tell him what was wrong with the situation, what menace his understanding had missed.

But how to contact her?

How?

He stood back slightly as a cupola poured a stream of molten iron into a series of troughs. He watched the smooth curve of the molten metal as it poured over the scarred lip of the cupola, a miniature waterfall of blazing yellow-white death. Even from where he stood, he could feel a great wind of burning air rushing out from the cascade of hellish liquid. Karn felt its probing fingers of pain gently pulling the sheet of mold that covered his chest, playfully tugging, licking, twisting the gleaming sheen of the thing that clung so hungrily to him, testing its own fiery hunger against the insidious hunger of the mold.

And as he stood there, watching the cascade of incandescence so very near to him, another memory stirred in the muddy depths of his memory. He remembered how when he had been too close to the fire the mold had reacted badly and how for a brief instant his mind had cleared and the memory of Maya became sharper; he recalled how that mysterious memory had crystallised out of the turgid currents of a befuddled brain.

And then a great calm descended, and he knew what he had to do, what he *must* do if he wanted to speak to Maya, to seek her guidance.

And so he walked towards the cascade of agonising death. Each step brought an increase in the heat; at first it was tolerable, just the playful beginning of agony, merely a hot breath from the depths of a furnace. But each step increased the heat, sent pain higher and higher and higher in the scale of unendurable pain, maddening pain. Pain which destroyed the mind and left the sufferer as an insane animal.

Karn stood in the centre of a hurricane of heat and lifted his arms so the hungry scalpels of heat could cut into him. But it was not just him they cut into.

He looked down at his chest and saw the mold twitching, twisting, then curling away from his reddening flesh, saw it go first milkily opaque, and then browning, blackening, charring and finally whirling away in the dragon-breath of the iron.

He screamed as his unprotected chest felt the full blast of the heat and, overtaken by a primal urge to survive at all costs, he flung himself away from its murderous fangs. He rolled on the dusty ground, clutching his chest and let out a high-pitched scream. As he turned and twisted in the dust, he saw his chest, red-raw like a piece of hammered meat.

But through the red mist of agony came knowledge.

He knew where he was.

And more importantly, he knew who he was.

He saw the soft light of the World, he saw Grath; he saw Yarl.

He saw the recording room and the facsimile of DeGroot.

He saw the rats.

And, like a shaft of sunlight cutting through a deck of grey clouds, he saw Maya.

He saw her writhe on the floor after the electromagnetic pulse and then stretched out like an experimental animal in the Council of Three's laboratory.

He staggered to his feet and felt his chest. Looking down at his hand, he saw blood on it, fresh, bright red blood. He had been badly burned, that was certain.

But there was no time to waste—he had to get to Maya!

A shadow fell, and he realised that the watching maton was almost upon him.

He rolled away from it and crashed into a stack of steel rods. Acting upon instinct, he pulled a rod from the stack and thrust it between the legs of the advancing maton. It toppled in front of him and his new musculature drove the pole into the thing's head, punching through the metal in a dancing shower of blue sparks. He leapt to his feet and ran out of the foundry into the harsh light of Subterra. Now he must find Maya before he collapsed.

He looked around, desperately trying to determine his location relative to the laboratories of the Council.

Through the red mist of pain, he saw its grim ramparts rearing up beyond the bounds of the city.

And so he ran, feeling the hot air of the prison world wash over him, air which felt cool and refreshing after his incarceration.

He passed matons, which, having no orders, ignored him.

He pushed his way through a silent crowd, interrupting their straight-line walking, their right-angled turns. Then the city ended and he began to run across a blasted, cinder strewn wasteland to the forbidding lair of the Council of Three.

He entered the laboratory building, walked down corridors between its many dread and dreadful rooms. To his great relief there seemed to be no-one around, human or maton. Suspicion furrowed his brow: the place was unnaturally quiet. He had the feeling he was being allowed free reign as a source of amusement to the watching Councillors who had already shown they regarded him with contempt.

We shall see, he thought with grim determination.

He found a drinking fountain and gratefully splashed luke-warm water over the agony of his burnt chest.

He saw the lab where the slime-mold had been attached to him, and hurriedly avoided it.

He began to despair. Surely they would soon notice an intruder running through their building? Surely a metal hand would soon grasp his shoulder?

And then with an electric shock of recognition, he realised where he was.

Almost at the room where Maya was a captive in an electronic prison!

Soon he was inside it—and there she was, stretched motionless on a bench, two terminals fixed to her head. As despair claimed him, he spun around, hoping against expectation there would be someone to help.

He was alone.

Karn rushed to the bench and stared down at her.

His head swam, and for a few moments he almost forgot his pain.

She was as beautiful as his vision—no, more so!

It looked just as if she was in a deep, restful sleep. No emotion disturbed the serenity of her face.

Karn studied the situation. She was not in any way restrained; there were no chains, no manacles, no bonds of any kind. There were only the terminals on her head. It must be them, and them alone, had put her into this trance, had cast this spell.

He grasped the terminals and attempted to pull them off her head.

They did not move.

Muttering swearwords he had almost forgotten he knew, he grasped them again, and threw all his strength into tearing them from Maya's head.

The old Karn could not have even begun the task, but now his strengthened biceps bulged, and veins stood out in his forehead in blue cords as he threw all his strength into removing the leech-like terminals. His tortured chest muscles screamed.

He pulled the terminals off her head, bringing a few fragments of her skin polymer with them.

And Maya's eyes opened.

Nine

There was only darkness. There could only be darkness.

Maya knew her struggle to be over. She could no longer face being the only consciousness in an empty, black, starless cosmos. Madness was now near. No mind can endure the absolute absence of any stimulus for very long. No longer was she even aware of the presence of the probing fingers of the Council of Three insinuating further and deeper into her decaying mind. This was the end of it all. For this, she had deserted her mother and brother; for a reward of ebon emptiness had she begged DeGroot to preserve her life, to save her from the Destroyer.

All for nothing. She had joined all the myriad others whose lives had been snuffed out by the world-shaking cataclysm unleashed by Baldwin; all the innocents who had been given up to the fire.

And then it ended. On the instant, it ended.

Her mind reeled under a sudden cascade of every sensory input that her systems were capable of delivering. Sight, sound, touch, smell—all of them came thundering into her in a massive flux that momentarily overwhelmed her ability to process them.

Then she regained control and looked around. For a moment, all she could see was the ceiling of the laboratory in which she had been imprisoned, until she remembered she could move her head. And more than that—she could move off the couch on which she had been lying for an unknown time.

She did and saw Karn staring at her. She was shocked to see his chest was red-raw and dotted with white blisters.

Karn—she knew it was Karn.

'What happened to you?' she said, 'you've got second-degree burns!'

'It's a long story,' was all he said.

She examined his chest.

'You've got to get those burns covered up,' she muttered, 'got to keep infection out!'

Then she remembered she was in Subterra, a place not known for its concern for the sufferings of others. No-one would be coming to help, only to mar and maim.

There were alcoves further along in the lab, and they were closed off by plastic sheets. She ripped one from its fastenings and tore it into strips. One she wrapped around Karn, tying it with a tight bow below his shoulder blades.

'That'll have to do for now,' she said, 'how did you get here?'

'I just walked in.'

Her brow furrowed. Suspicion. Doubt.

'Just walked in? Then they must know by now there's an intruder among them. They'll be on their way. They've just been playing a sick game with you.'

Karn's face showed the terrible strain he was under.

'What can we do? They'll hit you with that gun-thing they have. What can we do!'

She nodded, but her expression was grim, conveying a quality as of granite, except the mineral would have been softer.

'Exactly. Listen, we haven't much time—they'll send a maton with the pulse generator first, with them following behind to gloat. I'm not going back into that darkness—I'll kill myself first! The only hope we have is to capture Thran and use him as a bargaining chip. Do you know which one is Thran?'

He didn't, so after describing him, she said, 'Whichever one of us is nearer will have to do it. It might not be me.'

'Why?' Karn said, his eyes widening with alarm.

But she was already in another part of the lab, and was bending a sheet of metal into a kind of helmet shape. Then she pulled a thick strip of fabric from the couch and wrapped it on the inside and around the bottom edge.

'Because I'll be blind,' she called to him. 'I'll be wearing this Faraday Cage. I can't have any eye slits in it to allow the pulse in.'

Karn had no idea what a Faraday Cage was, but it seemed to him there was a major flaw in Maya's plan.

'What about the rest of you? That won't be covered.'

Maya halted moulding her helmet, and said, 'The pulse isn't intended to fry my circuits. It's to knock me out. As long as I protect my brain processors, I'll be able to keep my limbs moving.' She fell silent, cocking her head slightly as she listened to some sounds beyond Karn's perception. 'Here they come! Just tell me where the matons are and I'll do the rest!'

With those words, she moved into the alcove nearest the door and pulled the plastic sheet across, waiting like a wolf-spider in its burrow

With a hammering heart, Karn awaited the revenge of the Council of Three.

It was not long coming. The door crashed open and a maton strode in, carrying the same device that Karn had seen send Maya to the floor.

'It's right in front of you now!' Karn yelled. Immediately Maya flew out of the alcove, wearing her makeshift Faraday Cage. She smashed into the maton, sending it spinning across the room but not before her whirling hands had found the pulse generator and snatched it from the mechanism's grip. Another instant later, her mighty arms had twisted it into an unrecognisable metal pretzel and flung it to the floor.

But there was another maton—also carrying a pulse generator. And before Karn could utter a syllable, it had raised it and, as it had been programmed to do, fired directly at Maya's head. A horrified Karn saw Maya stagger drunkenly and crash against a wall, but then, mercifully, she righted herself.

But did not know where the second maton was.

'To your left!' he shouted. He remembered the units Maya used. 'A metre away! The gun is at your shoulder height!'

Maya's right arm flashed out, fingers found the second pulse generator, tore it from the maton, and in seconds it had joined its mangled fellow on the floor.

'Any more?' came her muffled shout.

'No!'

She removed her Faraday helmet but placed it within reach.

The two disarmed matons stood before her, searching within their programming for an algorithm to deal with this unexpected development.

Perhaps they would have found such an algorithm; perhaps not. But that remained forever unknown, for with the sound of rending metal, both their heads joined the twisted pulse generators on the floor. Then, devoid of processing power, their bodies crashed beside the decapitated heads almost immediately.

But three more matons then entered the lab. However, they were not carrying pulse generators. Instead, like restaurant staff bringing in a meal fit only for ogres, they were carrying the trays which bore the withered and repulsive forms of the three Councillors.

'Shut the door, Karn!' came Maya's thunderous command, and he obeyed instantly, leaving the Council of Three inside the lab, with the mangled remains of their mechanical vanguard in front of them.

Tharn and Ranth looked around blankly, but Thran had already recovered his composure.

'Brava, Maya, brava. You are indeed a force to be reckoned with. But I must point out there are more than two pulse generators, and a great deal more than five matons, in Subterra. You cannot possibly evade the paralyzing pulse forever. Sooner or later, you will be back on the couch with your extracted brain in pieces by your side.'

Maya stepped out so she was directly before them.

'Not necessarily, Councillor. As you know, I am powered by radionuclides from the far reaches of the periodic table. Normally, they give a steady and stable flow to keep my mentality ticking and allow me to move around, with the deadly results you see before you. But under the right circumstances, they can be coaxed to liberate all their energy at once. If I were to order that detonation, the fireball would be an awesome thing to behold. I don't know the exact dimensions of Subterra, but I am prepared to guess that the explosion in the confined space of this cavern would annihilate a significant portion of it.'

'That is a somewhat unusual ability for any being to possess,' Tharn said, 'why should we believe you possess it?'

'It kind of goes with the territory of having a nuclear reactor instead of a heart; there's always the risk of a big bang going off, even though DeGroot never thought it would come to that. And you see, I had a lot of time to think about things during the time you cut off my sensory apparatus, and during those lonely days, I remembered that I have a self-destruct facility and the commands necessary to activate it. And knocking me unconscious again would not save you as it is a purely mental command. The only way to save yourselves would be to destroy my brain—something I believe would end your foul dream of eternal tyranny. And another thing, during the long rest you gave me, my power cells have carried on charging themselves. I am now at a full half of maximum efficiency. And if you think that's not very much, it means I can move faster than your matons and knock the living fuck out of them. So what do you think of that?'

Thran bowed his head in Maya's direction.

'Brava again, Maya. I have obviously made the unforgivable error of underestimating my enemy. But I don't think my situation is quite as hopeless as you are bravely trying to pretend. You see, I've studied your past; I have lived your memories. You are the person you are because you have a child's fear of death. When it came to the supreme moment, you chose DeGroot's procedure as a way of escaping it. If there is a solution which does not involve self-immolation, I know you will take it.'

'I have already told you what that solution is: help us get to the surface, and I will end my war against you.' (*For the time being,* she thought.) ' And I swear I will not harm you even if I should be in a position to do so. Even though I hate and despise you, I will not harm you if you help me get to the surface, I promise.'

Thran made reply but Maya turned away abruptly, uninterested in his words.

For into her head had come a message: *We are here. We search. We are here.*

Her mind tried to reply, to send her own message: *I am here. Who are you? I am here!*

Silence.

Nothing.

Dispirited, defeated, she turned back to her repulsive opponent.

'I'm sorry—I missed that. What did you say?'

Thran smiled, the smile of a snake eyeing a mouse.

'What's the matter, Maya—your vaunted clockwork systems failing you?'

'Get on with it.'

'I was offering you a boon, a hand of friendship.'

'Go on.'

'I suggest a truce while we consider our positions and work out an amicable solution, acceptable to both parties. Now, I can see that your pet is suffering. I believe he got too near to hot metal in one of our foundries. We can help him; if we are anything, we are master biologists. We can give him salves and creams which will speed up the healing and dull the pain I am sure the poor creature is under.'

'Then do it.'

'We would have to take him to the Biocentre.'

She laughed.

'Thran, that is simply not worthy of you! You take him there and either kill him or slap another slime-mold on him. Not going to happen! You can bring the medication here, you know you can.'

Thran raised his arms in a classic posture of defeat.

'You win, Maya.' He looked at his two subordinates. 'I will send these two useless piles of flesh to bring the medication. Is that acceptable? Then we discuss a solution that is acceptable to the two of us. I fear you have sadly gotten the wrong impression of us; we are not monsters. You can have no conception of the struggles we have had to make merely to survive down here. If you knew our history, you would know of the epic heroism our ancestors displayed when they succeeded in escaping the

Destroyer by burrowing into the crust. You would not judge us so harshly then. Is it any wonder we are a somewhat callous people?—Adversity has made us that. Do not judge us if you have not suffered what we have suffered.'

Maya was silent. Could Thran be right? She had no detailed knowledge of what the Subterrans had gone through, how they must have had to struggle in an environment never meant for humans.

Karn stared at her, sensing her mental turmoil. He was astounded; how could she even consider accepting Thran's words! She must be confused, he thought: imprisonment in dark emptiness immediately followed by a desperate struggle for survival had left her bewildered, unsure. There was danger here. He yelled, 'Maya! Don't listen to him! It's all a trick!'

She ignored him. Instead, she said to Thran, 'I have had enough of fighting. Heal Karn and we'll talk. You promise you know a way to the surface?'

'Of course. The transport vehicle you saw can take you there. We have been there many times.'

Maya's head drooped and, although she had no need for oxygen, she sighed.

'I don't want any more of this endless violence. I'm so tired of it. All creatures should work together for their common good, isn't that obvious? Send the other two to get Karn's treatments.'

Thran nodded to his silent subordinates. They stared at Karn and, reluctantly, he stood away from the door. They and their matons disappeared into the corridor beyond.

Thran continued his discussion with Maya.

'I am delighted we are finally dealing with this issue as adults. You have suffered. We of Subterra have suffered. Let's put an end to it. Come with me to the room next door; the other two Councillors will meet us there as soon as they have the medication for your helpless little friend.'

Maya nodded.

'Gladly.'

The other room was much larger and entirely empty. On entering, Maya looked around for any signs of deceit but saw none. Just an empty room. A bare blank wall faced her. They waited. In one hand, Maya held onto her makeshift Faraday Cage.

'How is it that you in Subterra have science, technology, when the other Burrower colonies do not?' she asked.

'It was all an incredibly long time ago. We had actually lost count of how many centuries had passed since the catastrophe. It was only when we read your mind that we learned just how long ago it was. Our records are scanty but as far as we understand it we were the last colony to be established under the leadership of a far-seeing man whose full name is lost. There is only one reference to him and it is incomplete and corrupt. We just have the first letter of his forename, which was "G". That's all we have. But he understood we needed to hang onto humanity's scientific knowledge if we were not to be reduced to mere animality—as appears to have been the fate of the other colonies. So he ensured that libraries stored on imperishable materials were carried down by the colonists. And they were not in digital form as he knew that without functioning machines able to interpret the symbols, the knowledge would be beyond recovery.'

Maya considered Thran's words. Beginning with "G"—could it be possible that the charismatic leader had been?...

She thrust the thought away. It was impossible to be certain and she had more immediate issues to consider.

Thran turned slightly on his plate as the door opened behind him. The other two Councillors came in, borne by their faithful matons. Ranth was holding a small metal device.

Maya stared at the approaching Councillors in growing puzzlement. Ranth handed the device to Thran.

'Where is the medication?' Maya began, looking from Councillor to Councillor, as doubt began to claim her.

Thran smiled.

'Shhhh, my pretty one. We have medication, but it is for you, not the little trog.'

He made a series of quick, deft movements on the surface of the device.

Maya heard the grating sound of moving machinery behind her and spun around.

The bare wall behind her was sliding back.

It opened fully.

And Eater came through.

Ten

The horrific creature came towards them, leaving a trail of bubbling slobber on the floor behind it.

'You betrayed me!' Maya yelled, 'I told you I'd kill myself rather than go back in the darkness!'

'You did,' Thran said gently, 'but you won't. We have seen your memories, remember. You are pathetically afraid of death, of dissolution. But if you yield to us, we will spare Karn. We will not send him to the Harvesting Building. Instead, he will live out his days in comfort, with plenty of food, plenty of females. It will be a good life and the credit for his happiness will be yours. Would you really take that away from him, just for a few unimportant items of knowledge which you possess? Isn't that rather selfish?'

Maya backed away from the advancing horror.

'And my reward?'

'Once we have obtained the knowledge we require, we will put you back together. We will rebuild your brain and re-insert it into your admirable body. As you are only a mechanism, there isn't much else we can offer you. You have no need of food, and, presumably, no need of males. But you will lead a calm, reflective life. There are our libraries which you can study. I am sure you will find them interesting. Eater is now going to bite off your limbs so you cannot do any more fighting or throw things around in that annoying habit you have. But your brain will be undamaged, and you will still be able to consider our offer.'

Karn stared in unspeakable terror as the thing continued its relentless progress into the room. His mind swirled in a whirlpool of despair as he watched Maya retreat in front of it. His legs almost gave way but he forced himself to stay upright, aware that Tharn and Ranth were watching him with the lust for violence in their eyes. Ignoring them, he threw a glance at Thran, who was eagerly watching the beginning of the gladiatorial conflict. *Our only hope is to capture Thran*, she had said. But how?

The maton was holding him above any leap that Karn could make. Despairingly, he returned to looking at the unfolding battle before him.

Maya knew there was no more point in attempting to escape. Eater was almost upon her and now, finally resigned to the fight, she rapidly scanned the creature. It was obvious nothing remotely like it could have evolved naturally: it was a construction, a deliberate melange of all the characteristics humans find repulsive. It displayed features of the reptile, the arachnid, the mantidae, the chilopoda, all skilfully combined into one horrific but highly efficient package.

Compound eyes stared back at her, mandibles chomped, pincers snapped, a red toothed tongue flicked in and out of dripping jaws. The thing appeared to have more than one orifice for the purpose of eating.

Maya stood motionless as Eater approached, the sound of its clashing appendages and mandibles drowning out Karn's desperate cries. Now fully accepting of the need for conflict, she used all her sensory equipment to search its hideous body for weak spots.

There were none.

This was not an enlarged version of a natural predator, as the rats had been; this was a killing machine designed by a sadistic, but fiercely able, intelligence.

It was upon her.

She darted to one side and, as it flashed past, she delivered a fierce punch to its armoured flank.

Her fist rebounded, leaving no mark.

Eater had overrun her but, despite its size, it turned easily and leapt at her. Attempting to dodge, she slipped in its drool, but unable to stop in time it passed over her, giving her a close-up view of its pulsating abdomen. She could see that small wriggling parasites were hanging from it. Shakily, she got to her feet as Eater came to a halt and turned back to her. For a few seconds, both combatants were motionless, staring at each other.

She scanned it again. Was there any weakness at all, anything she had missed?

There was not, and Eater launched itself at her again in a thunderbolt of power. Two wickedly curved mandibles caught her and began to close on her waist to cut her in two. Before they made contact with her skin, she grasped them and struggled to check their inward motion. They shook beneath her hands as Eater redoubled its efforts to close the gap.

The power of the thing was incredible for a biological organism!

But using them as pivots, Maya swung her legs up and, with servos whining at full power, drove her boots into Eater's dripping face. It shook its terrifying visage back and forth as she kicked again and again, and the power of the mandibles dipped slightly.

It was enough. She dropped out of their deadly embrace and rolled away from the attacker. She leapt to her feet, and with every watt at her command, she struck again at the mathematically exact spot she had struck before. Again her fist rebounded, but this time Eater staggered away.

Once again they circled each other. Eater was now noticeably more cautious in its combat style. No doubt, it had never encountered a prey-item that had lasted so long, or, indeed, fought back. But it showed no sign of abandoning its onslaught. Karn glanced at the Councillors. They had long ago forgotten all about him, and, with rapt hungry faces, were leaning so far forward they seemed in imminent danger of tumbling off their carrying-plates. Karn watched Thran, hoping he would do exactly that—but he did not.

Eater hurtled forward again. A spiny appendage reached for Maya but instead of grasping her, knocked her off her feet and sent her crashing into a wall. She ended up on her side, facing the wall as Eater rushed upon her to finish the job. She rolled over in time to see two razor-tipped limbs descending upon her. She grasped one, dodged the other, and threw her own power into amplifying Eater's charge so it too crashed into the wall. As it did so, there was a wet ripping noise and the appendage tore off its heaving flank, leaving Maya holding the thing while viscous green slime slowly dripped from the torn end. In disgust she threw it away, not noticing that she had nearly hit Karn with it.

Maya backed away. Checking her power levels, she realised the fight was draining her reserves at an alarming rate. All Eater had to do was keep up its attacks and victory would inevitably come to it.

She backed into the centre of the room, keeping low, scanning the creature to be aware of when it was about to attack.

It attacked. Once again, she spun away at the last moment. Once again, as it passed, she struck the mathematically exact point she had struck twice before, once again with every watt her arm could deliver. And this time she punched through the steel-hard carapace, and green fluid jetted out. She did not hear the gasp of astonishment from the Councillors, or Karn's ragged cheer. For an instant, her fist was stuck inside Eater's innards, and she was dragged a few metres before she was able to extricate herself. She backed away as Eater skidded to a halt on a floor now wet and slippery with both its drool and its vital fluid.

But Maya soon realised that the wound was not a fatal one and, once again, Eater had no intention of giving up the battle, let alone yielding. It leapt again, and this time Maya was not as swift as she had been and was tossed into the air, describing a graceful somersault before crashing heavily to the floor. For a few dizzy seconds, the impact jarred her optical processors and all she could see was a series of rapidly moving, multicoloured zig-zags. When her vision cleared, it was to see Eater's chomping jaws centimetres away and then, gripped in the mandibles, she was lifted off the floor to hang dangling, looking down into the hateful compound eyes of her terrible foe. She knew then she had lost.

The mandibles began their ineluctable closure as she impotently beat her fists upon them.

271

Karn stared in sickening horror at the dreadful scene, seeing his friend and protector about to be cut in two. All his muscles tensed as he prepared to rush onto the floor to distract the terrible carnivore, but as he did, his foot encountered something lying in front of him.

It was Eater's detached appendage.

He never knew how he was able to decide what to do and then do it so swiftly, but he did.

He lifted the heavy appendage and swung it in an arc that terminated on Thran's bony shoulder. Thran and the controlling device tumbled off the plate into Karn's waiting grasp. Karn rammed work-hardened digits into the Councillor's neck.

'Call the thing off! Now!'

Thran said nothing, his eyes flicking back and forth.

'Don't try to call a maton!' Karn snarled. He lifted Thran off the floor: he seemed to weigh nothing at all and Karn backed rapidly away from the other, astounded, Councillors. 'I can kill you in an instant, Thran; you're just a pile of rags and puke! Make that thing drop her now! If Maya dies, your death will be as slow as I can make it. Now!'

Thran nodded dumbly. His fingers flew over the keys of his device under Karn's steely gaze, a gaze which was ready for the next act of treachery.

There was none.

To Maya's utter amazement, Eater gently lowered her to the floor and moved away. The wall opened and the bleeding monstrosity disappeared behind it. Befuddled by what had happened, she gratefully turned away from the closing wall to see Karn holding Thran in a headlock. She smiled as she approached.

'You've done it again, Karn. I'm beginning to think it was a good idea bringing you along, after all.'

He grinned good-naturedly.

'All part of the service, Maya.' He looked down at the silent pile of rags that was Thran. 'What are we going to do with this thing?'

Maya did not answer. Instead, she gazed upon the other two Councillors, sitting silently on their transport plates.

Do they need Thran? She thought, *or will they merely take his place and the show goes on? Time for a test.*

'Pass Thran to me, Karn,' she said, not taking her eyes off the remaining Councillors, 'I'm going to kill him.'

Karn held the now-squirming Thran out to her.

Immediately the hitherto motionless Councillors exploded into a flurry of agitated energy.

'No, no!' 'Don't kill him!'

'You can keep him,' she said to Karn, indicating she no longer wanted the Leader of the Councillors, 'I don't want him—just yet.' She addressed the others. 'A few questions: Why do you need this worthless mass of flesh? Why shouldn't I kill him?'

'He has the codes, only the Leader has the codes,' Ranth said, 'without them the Biocentre would cease to function, the Harvesting Building would fall silent.'

Maya nodded. That was vitally important—it meant that as long as Thran lived, she and Karn were safe. But if anything should befall him and the codes were lost: it would be she and Karn against the whole of Subterra.

As if to emphasise the point, there was a noise outside the door and a group of men burst in.

And they *were* men. They were taller than Karn, though still some distance below Maya, and possessed of trim, healthy physiques. A few even had the beginnings of beards. And they carried weapons that looked like rifles.

'And who are these, pray?' Maya murmured, addressing Thran.

'These are members of the Elite Guards,' Thran replied, 'did you think the Council of Three ran Subterra all by ourselves? These are the population from which the next Councillors will be drawn, and after a series of rigorous selections by combat, the winners are elected Councillors, and receive the gift of the plasma from the slave-people.'

'Karn,' Maya whispered urgently, 'pass me Thran—now!'

273

As the Guards approached, she lifted Thran high above her head and waved him at them.

'Put those guns down or Thran dies. And the codes die with him. No more Councillors, no more lovely plasma. Is that what you want?'

'We can shoot you before you have time to harm our Leader,' the Chief Guard said, keeping his rifle trained on Maya, 'we have very swift and sure reflexes. It comes with being a Guard.'

But Thran was alarmed.

'Larz, put the rifle down. This woman is not what she appears. She has superhuman abilities. She survived a struggle with an Eater.'

There was a murmur of awed surprise from the Guards. Slowly, reluctantly, they lowered their weapons. All except Larz, that is.

'Good, we've established the pecking order,' Maya said, a little puzzled as to what part of her mind that phrase had come from. 'I won't kill Thran, and so you keep your promise of long, miserable, worthless lives.'

There was another susurration from the Guards but this time it was of anger. Maya ignored it and continued, 'I want medication for my friend. He has been badly burned and his treatment is now urgent.'

'We are not nurses,' Larz sneered.

'Karn, look after Thran for a moment, will you?'

That having been done, she crossed to Larz in a blur of speed and tore the weapon from him. Holding it before his astounded face, she bent the barrel into a perfect "U" shape and threw it at his feet.

'Get the medication,' she said, with a sweet smile, 'Now!' She looked around at the thunderstruck men. 'That means all of you. Get out!'

After they had gone, she returned to the Councillors and Karn. She didn't want them to know, but the battle with Eater had severely depleted her energy reserves. Those reserves would recover but not instantly. And what of her radionuclide power source itself? It had sat unused for one hundred and seventy-five thousand years. What portion of its half-life was that? It was not inexhaustible or self-renewing.

But an idea came to her.

'What is the source of the power here in Subterra?' she demanded of Thran, 'you seem to have enough of it to waste, what with leaving the lights on permanently.'

'Geothermal,' the Leader said, 'it is not far to the mantle, and even the core, from Subterra.'

A secret known only to her and Karn was that she had a power input socket hidden in her hair, designed for emergency top-ups. None, of course, had been available until they had reached Subterra.

'I will need access to one of your power stations,' she rapped, 'and an engineer who can modify electrical contacts.' She picked up the motionless blob that was Thran and glared at the remaining Councillors. 'You can go now. And don't forget that I have extremely sophisticated sensory apparatus; I will know if you are plotting against me.'

The matons took their weird burdens out of the room. And one maton had no burden at all.

She, Karn and Thran were alone.

'You cannot control my men forever, you know,' Thran observed from where he lay on the floor, 'eventually either one of the Councillors will devise a plan to obtain the codes, or one of the Guards that you so foolishly humiliated will rebel.'

'Where are the codes kept?' Maya asked, in as disinterested a tone as she could manage.

'I will tell you, as you cannot get them. They are in my brain, written at the molecular level so they cannot be forgotten. At the time of transition to a new chief of the Council, the Leader is put in mental rapport with the chosen replacement and the codes are transferred. However, it is theoretically possible they could be extracted from a dead brain, so your threat to kill me is ultimately futile. One of them will eventually reach that conclusion and you, and the primitive creature that hangs around you, will be finished.'

'I don't want to kill you,' Maya said, 'I don't believe in unnecessary killing.' Her face hardened. 'But there is such a thing as necessary killing, and killing in a manner which would reduce both your brain and its codes to ash. I doubt if your science can get much information out of a pile of grey dust.'

Both Karn and Thran stiffened slightly at those words. She saw their reaction and smiled tolerantly.

'No, I won't do that to you, Thran—yet. But there is something which should not exist on this planet, something unnatural and foul. Eater. I am going to kill Eater. With my bare hands.'

Eleven

Maya felt the electrical strength flooding into her, felt it reach to her extremities, reinvigorate her brain, pour into her musculature in a torrent of potent energy.

It was enough. She put a hand to her head and disconnected the terminal, and lowered the flap covering the input socket. She patted her hair back into its usual trim bob and rose from the couch.

'Thank you,' she said to the wary technician who had jury-rigged the recharging system. He was of the same superior body-type as a Guardsman, but somewhat less physically imposing.

She looked around the power station, seeing massive machines, power cables as thick as her thigh snaking from and between colossal turbines, heat-exchangers. There was a warm, welcoming *thrum* of mighty engines running smoothly, an almost imperceptible vibration in the floor, the familiar sting of triatomic oxygen in the air. It was strangely comforting after the biological horrors of Subterra. Through a mighty window next to where she stood, she could see into a great sub-cavern of this underground empire. It was here that liquid water was pumped far underground and where superheated steam rose from the mantle and produced the superabundant energy which powered Subterra.

She was now carrying all the energy her superb frame could hold. Not an extra ampere could be introduced. If this was not enough to defeat Eater—then nothing could.

Karn was worried. There was a sack at his feet. Occasionally the fabric would ripple or bulge, showing that it contained some living thing. And that living thing was, of course, Thran.

'Maya,' Karn was saying, 'you're not thinking sensibly. Why risk your body in another mad fight with Eater? You're risking everything we've gained, and for what, some ridiculous feeling of power, of pride? I thought only men acted so stupidly.'

She did not answer. Swinging the sack over his shoulder, he planted himself before her. The Subterran treatments had worked well, and for the first time in his life he felt strong, resolute. And the fact that he was now fully clothed again somehow gave him more confidence when confronting his imperious companion.

'There's only one thing we should be doing and that's shutting down the Harvesting Building.'

She shook her head.

'No, we can't do that.'

'What?' Karn's face passed through bewilderment to fury. 'What! Not shut it down! There are people in there; people like me, being drained of their life, their blood!'

'Maybe I should have said *not yet*. Think about it, Karn. If we shut it down, we've lost our hold over the elite here. They'd have nothing to lose from attacking us then. I can't fight them all.'

Karn was not convinced.

'So when do we shut it down?'

'I'll tell you when. Now, leave it at that, and follow me.'

'To where?'

'To have a quiet word with Eater.'

***

Maya was in discussion with Thran. She held his control pad in her hands and was studying it. And she was *really* studying it, using sensory abilities of which Thran had no conception. Using those abilities she had quickly learned that Thran was only telling her part of the story. But then she expected nothing less from him. Many of the supposedly-hidden commands were used to control any part of the population thinking of revolt by a system of electrical shocks, and she had no interest in those.

She and the others were in the vast room in which she had battled with Eater. Apart from her and Thran the only other occupants were Karn and Larz. Thran had insisted on the chief of the Elite Guard being present during his interrogations by

Maya, and she, foreseeing no danger from one man, had agreed. However, she had insisted on him being unarmed and staying a minimum distance away. As she glanced up from the study of Thran's control device, she was surprised to see Karn in an intense conversation with the Chief of the Guards. The topic of conversation would have surprised her more.

'We ordinary Subterrans are not to be blamed for the excesses of the Council,' Larz was saying to an attentive Karn. 'You must understand that the Council has the power of life and death over all the people.'

'So why haven't you rebelled? You told me there are hundreds of the common people and only three Councillors. Even in the World, we would not have accepted such tyranny.'

Larz shook his head.

'The matons. I don't believe you had matons in the World, did you? There are far more matons than Guardsmen. It would be a one-sided battle.'

Karn thought about that and couldn't find fault with the argument. But Larz hadn't finished.

'You're not entirely happy with Maya, are you?'

Karn was torn. He didn't want to say anything that could be used against his friend and protector.

'What makes you think that?'

'We Guardsmen are not without resources. I don't think I'm telling you anything you hadn't already guessed when I say we've been eavesdropping on some of your conversations. It's our job, after all. We knew nothing about you when you arrived uninvited; perhaps you intended harm to Subterra. We had to know.'

Karn thought about that. It seemed reasonable.

'Go on.'

Larz tried to get closer to Karn, but the latter warned him off. Larz retreated with a gentle smile.

'We know you think she's got her priorities wrong. This forthcoming fight with Eater—what's that about? If she was really on your side, she'd be trying to rescue the people in the

Harvesting Building, wouldn't she? I mean, they're the same race of people as you. That doesn't sound very caring to me.'

Karn said nothing but his lips compressed into a thin line. He was spared the problem of replying when he saw Maya stand up and away from Thran, who, as usual these days, was sitting in a huddle on the floor. It seemed she had reached a decision. She came over to them.

'Karn, pick up Thran and get to the back of the room. Larz, I want you out of here completely. I know you'll be watching with your spy equipment, so don't worry. You won't miss a thing.'

'You're going through with this ridiculous fight, are you?' Karn said.

Maya saw Larz was still there and pointed first to him and then the open doorway. He left.

'What's he been saying to you?' she demanded.

'Nothing that I haven't been thinking about myself. I think you might be having a few mental problems again.'

Maya was momentarily speechless. Then: 'What did you say? How dare you!'

But Karn was not to be silenced.

'This fight: what's it for? If you win, so what? If you lose, I'm left alone in this gods-forsaken place, and Thran gets to sit back on his little plate like nothing ever happened. Can't you see it's not worth it? Why aren't you helping the poor souls in the Harvesting Building?'

Maya straightened her back so she was no longer looking down at him.

'I've told you. Thran is the only hold we have on these people. Once he's no longer valuable to them, we're finished. If I destroy the Harvesting Building all those people who wanted centuries of life will rise up, their hopes gone. This fight with Eater is to give them something to think about, it will cow them so they think twice about taking me on.'

'And then?—assuming Eater doesn't tear you to pieces, like he very nearly did last time. Someone had to rescue you, I believe.'

'I just need a few more pieces of information from Thran and we can be on our way. To the surface.'

Now Karn was angry.

'The surface! The surface! That's all I ever hear from you! I'm sick of the word! I know exactly why you want to go there—because you think there'll be scientists up there who can put your mind back into a bag of flesh. Make you a real woman. So you won't be a mock-up of the real Maya, a walking puppet that looks like a long-dead person!'

Now Maya's face twisted.

'I am the real Maya! I told you that! My mind is Maya's—I am Maya!'

'So you're not going to help those people?'

'Not yet! I can't conquer Subterra by myself. But when I've met the surface people, we'll come back down with a proper army and put an end to this sick society.'

'That's not good enough. They're my people in there, being sucked dry!'

Maya turned away, picked up the silent Thran and dumped him at Karn's feet.

'Then you rescue them! Think of all the wonderful things you can teach them—like how to stir fungus.'

A terrible silence fell. Karn and Maya turned away from each other as the ghost of a smile played on Thran's withered lips.

Then Maya turned back.

'I told you to get to the back of the room. There'll be a guest arriving in a moment you won't want to get too close to.'

With a glaring silence, Karn picked up the shrivelled Councillor and retreated to the far end of the room, as far as it was possible to go and not be in the corridor.

Maya shouted after them.

'I want you to watch this, Thran. I want you to know who you're dealing with!'

And with that, her slim fingers danced over the control pad, which she then sent sliding across the floor to Karn. She turned to face the far wall. It slid back. And Eater emerged.

There was a crusted green patch on its hide where she punched through earlier. And it walked more awkwardly as it was now missing an appendage.

But it did not look to be wary of its small opponent and strode confidently towards her, its pincers held high, its mandibles chattering, its jaws clattering. Strands of drool dripped slowly from the jaws, forming long, glistening trails behind it like the tracks of giant slugs.

Maya was ready. She lifted her fists, confident in the abundance of power surging in her body.

And then she went stiff and silent.

After a few seconds, she muttered, over and over again, 'Semi-major axis. Transfer of momentum. Path could become parabolic, I…'

Karn knew the signs; knew she was having another seizure. His muscles went rigid as he started forward, only to bring himself to a quivering halt.

He was helpless.

As was Maya.

'Your mistress has a peculiar fighting style,' Thran observed dryly.

And then Eater was on her. Once again, she was lifted high above the ferocious jaws; once again she was thrown up like a rag doll, describing graceful somersaults as she tumbled through the air. One of Eater's appendages caught her as she neared the floor and, as if it were playing some Hellish ball-game, batted her away, sending her crashing into a wall.

'A most peculiar style,' Thran said, his leathery throat attempting to issue a chuckle.

Maya rolled onto her hands and knees as Eater approached. Pincers closed on her sides, and she was lifted up, to dangle high above eagerly chomping mandibles. Karn was too far away to discern facial features but, if he had been close enough, he would have seen the vacant look vanish from her face. She knew again who she was, where she was.

The pincers began to lower her into slavering jaws. But again, she used them as a pivot and brought her boots up under the lower jaw in a savage kick. Then she pushed the pincers apart and landed, cat-like, on the floor. Eater turned to follow, to wound, to tear, but the space a sickled-claw swept through no longer contained her. Instead, she stood aside, letting the creature pass. Once again, a fist shot out and struck the armoured hide. Once again, Eater shuddered under the blow but, once again, it turned to wreak bloody revenge.

It swung a scimitar-tipped appendage which she ducked under. She delivered another pile-driving blow on the exact spot. Eater trembled under the impact but whirled another appendage in a vicious arc, sending her spinning away.

She crashed onto her back and the great head of the raging carnivore lowered to feed.

Her boots crashed up into that head and the entire animal was knocked upwards, balanced only on its hind legs. She rushed forward, placed her hands between the wriggling parasites hanging from Eater's loathsome abdomen and forced the writhing monster against the wall.

Now it would feel the full force of her blows, would have to accept the total energy contained in the thundering fists of its implacable opponent. An appendage struck out at her.

She tore it off.

With the precision of a master geometer, each blow landed in exactly the same spot, with a tolerance of micrometres. Blow and after massive blow smashed into the shuddering abdomen, blows that could have shattered rock into a haze of dust.

And then the entire monstrosity burst open in an explosion of green slime, and she had to jump to one side to escape Eater's dying fall. Gobbets and strings of slime flew across the room, befouling the floor and walls.

And her.

Calmy triumphant in her victory, she walked to her astounded audience.

She smiled.

'I think I need a shower,' she said.

***

'I'm sorry for what I said to you,' Maya said, smiling an uncertain smile, 'you know nothing about science or technology, but that was no fault of yours. I was unfair and I'm sorry.'

'I'm sorry too,' Karn said. Maya had locked Thran in a small room to give Karn a rest from guarding him, and he and Maya were alone. 'I can't free those people. I don't know how to remove the mold. You do, but you have your reasons for not doing it. I have to trust you when you say after you meet the surface people, we'll return to Subterra and finish this job. But why are we still here? The longer we take, the more those poor people are suffering. You've got Thran; you got your revenge on Eater—for whatever that was worth. So surely we should get out of here before Ranth or Yarz comes up with a plan to finish us off?'

Maya looked across at him.

'Come as close as you can, Karn. I know Yarz has spy equipment that could pick up what I'm saying. I'm sending out a frequency I think interferes with it, but I can't be certain. By the way, Thran mentioned I neglected to tell you I send out a small amount of X-rays, but it's a lot less than you'd get at the dentist, even when you're right next to me.'

Karn didn't know the meaning of "X-rays" or, for that matter, "Dentist" and so he obeyed at once and sat so close to Maya that they were almost touching. Karn realised he hadn't been this close to Maya before without being in some kind of potentially fatal peril. He took the opportunity to examine her. Even at this distance, her skin looked like real flesh. There were two small light-coloured patches on the side of her head where

284

he had wrenched the terminals off, and her knuckles were looking slightly ragged after the conflict with Eater.

But that was all. She looked exactly like a woman—a distinctly attractive woman.

An odd thought struck him—did she feel like a woman?

He became conscious of a strange feeling pulsing through his veins, and for some seconds he failed to recognise it.

And then he realised what it was—the closeness to Maya was making him aroused.

However, the skimpiness of Subterran costume failed to hide that state from Maya, and she smiled, very gently.

'I'm afraid not, Karn. I look like an adult human female from the outside and I have the necessary openings, so penetrative sex would not be impossible. But I'm afraid DeGroot was not interested in the necessary neural pathways and did not include them. So—to coin a phrase—the pleasure would be all yours.'

Karn added blushing to his list of recently remembered states, a colouration which was also impossible to hide, given the usual near-white state of his complexion.

'I'm sorry, Maya! I, I didn't…I mean…'

She gave his arm a gentle pat.

'Forget it. I'll take it as a compliment. Now, where were we? Ah yes, why are we still here?' Karn moved slightly away and looked at the ceiling; a very cool-coloured, completely unarousing ceiling. 'Karn, we both want the same thing—the destruction of Subterra. But there's so much I don't know. How many more towns like this are there? Are the towns autonomous, like they were in the World, with each having their own Council of Three? What weapons do they have? Are there any more Eaters?—an army of them would be something I'd rather not think about. The one I killed wasn't the same one as we saw in the tunnel, so if there can be two, there can be hundreds. Before I return with the surface people to destroy this perverted culture, we must know all of that. And when I do, an entire regiment of Eaters won't stop me!'

Karn ventured to look at Maya again.

'There's one problem. How do you know these surface people are advanced enough to be able to help you? You've put a lot of faith in people you haven't met. Maybe they're just primitives.' He hesitated, 'Primitives, like I was.'

'Don't you think I've thought of that? If DeGroot is right, they would have to have retained a technological culture to be able to survive on a much changed Earth. The Space Arks are the key—they would have been the flower-heads that re-seeded the ravaged planet. They would have kept the flame of science alight.'

'And how do you know this wonderful DeGroot *was* right?'

'He was the last eminent scientist of pre-Catastrophe Earth. I am the living proof of that. The late-lamented, supposedly indestructible, Eater is the non-living proof.'

'But he wasn't one of my gods, he was just a man. Maybe there was something he overlooked.'

'Then I'll find out when I stand on the surface again. I'm long overdue.' She smiled. 'One hundred and seventy-five thousand years overdue!'

Karn was calm again now; the effort of ratiocination had been like a splash of cold water.

'But couldn't we free just one person, even if it would be only a test for what you could do when you come back? And Larz says the people hate the Council, so they would welcome them being deposed.'

Maya stood and walked to the other side of the room. Then, turning, 'Not that again! Haven't you realised that no-one in Subterra has said a single true word since we got here?'

Karn examined his hands and then looked back at Maya.

'I agree Larz could be lying; trying to drive a wedge between us. But we could still release one Subterran from that disgusting mold to see what they are really like. Then we might get to the truth.'

Maya was silent for a few moments, and then she said, 'You're right again, Karn. We don't really know what an ordinary

Subterran is like without the mold controlling their brains. Perhaps they're all very nice people who look after their aged parents instead of euthanising them. One thing we can do is destroy the mold cultures in the Biocentre. Then there'll be no point in the Council capturing any more victims if they can't reduce them to living matons. And I'll take the mold off one individual.'

She turned to open the door to Thran's prison for another round of interrogation, but Karn was suddenly beside her.

'Maya, I want to apologise again for what happened back there.'

'I said forget it.'

An odd look came into his face, a kind of pleading.

'It's just I've never met anyone like you before, whether you're made of flesh, or metal, wood or stone. You're a real woman and I care for you more than I ever felt possible.'

But her face was devoid of emotion, as if it were part of a sculpture of an aloof goddess, far above earthly concerns.

'No, Karn. You can't care about me. I've already told you that.'

***

They had assembled in the Biocentre: Maya, Karn and Arthrena. Arthrena was lying on a couch under a large circular object composed of crystalline facets that glinted prismatically. As usual in the Subterran climate, she was naked from the navel up.

'What are you going to do to her?' Karn whispered.

'No need to whisper, Karn. She has obeyed the instruction I gave her to lie there. If I were to say no more to her, she would lie there until she died of starvation. As to what I'm going to do to her: it's very simple. A series of short blasts of UV-B, around three hundred nanometres. They won't penetrate the dermis; in fact the mold should prevent most of it even penetrating the epidermis.'

Karn gave Maya a long stare and then finally said, 'Thank you, Maya. That's very clear.'

Maya smiled at Karn, having not noticed his irony, and turned to Arthrena.

'Now, Arthrena. You may feel a warm sensation in your chest but there should be no pain. Do you understand?'

Arthrena did not turn her head and her gaze remained fixed on the lamp, which was now slowly descending towards her.

'Yes, master.'

Maya turned to Karn.

'Stand back; the UV won't affect me, but it could wreak havoc on pale skin like yours.'

Karn backed away after that ominous comment, and stood some distance away as Maya activated the lamp. Karn had expected some dramatic visible effects: a great purple ray blasting down, or some kaleidoscopic dance of dazzling colours. But there was nothing.

There was however an image of Arthrena's torso on the televiewer screen, and as he watched, he saw the shimmering mold begin to curl up at the edges, lifting up from Arthrena's flesh. He became more and more excited as he saw those edges begin to crisp and brown. And then suddenly, the entire sheet turned black and broke into whirling pieces.

Unable to contain his excitement, he forgot Maya's warning and rushed over to the supine woman. Fortunately, Maya had turned off the flood of invisible energy, its work complete. Karn stood over Arthrena as the UV lamp pulled away, watching to see if there were any signs of animation, of self-awareness in the hitherto robotic woman. She was deathly still, her eyes firmly shut, and, for a moment, he thought Maya had miscalculated and had killed her. Then her eyes opened, slowly, haltingly, as if fighting some adhesive substance that had been holding them together. Karn's face filled her field of vision.

For some seconds she seemed stunned by the incredulity of what she was seeing and her blank expression was replaced by one of growing alarm. And then, like a sunbeam bursting through a bank of cloud, the apprehension disappeared, and she smiled. She lifted her arms and put her arms around his neck, pulling him close.

'Mawn, you have returned! Why have you stayed away so long, my love?'

Karn gently disentangled himself and pulled away.

'Arthrena, how do you feel? We have taken away the thing which was enslaving you. You're safe now, so how do you feel?'

She did not answer at first but looked around at the Biocentre. She swung her feet off the couch and, unsteadily, got to her feet. Karn held an arm to keep her from falling. She continued to look around.

'What is this strange place?' Her gaze swept over the vats of chemicals, the cages containing eldritch creatures, and then found Maya. She started visibly.

'What—what is that? Is it a woman? She is so tall!'

Karn patted her shoulder.

'Yes, it is a woman and a friend. Her name is Maya.'

Maya started to walk over to introduce herself but Arthrena looked away, apparently having lost both her fear and her interest in her surroundings.

Except for one thing.

She grasped Karn's neck and pulled his lips down upon hers. As they broke away, she whispered breathily, 'Mawn, my love. You have returned to me!'

Twelve

'Don't walk away, Mawn!' Arthrena called, 'come away from that strange woman! Don't you love me anymore?'

'We have a problem,' Karn said, glancing over his shoulder to see what Arthrena was doing, 'she thinks I'm her lover.'

Maya took a look at Arthrena, who was standing with arms akimbo and glaring ocular poison at her.

'It looks like we have. It seems to be an example of imprinting—like new-born ducklings were said to, fixing on the first thing they see as their mother.'

'I don't mind being her mother,' Karn observed, 'but I'm not ready to be her lover.'

'Although it has its amusing aspects,' Maya said, 'it could well be a serious problem. It could put the whole liberation of Subterra in jeopardy.'

'How so?'

'I assumed removing the mold would simply make them wake up, as if they were coming out of an anaesthetic, but Arthrena seems to have regressed to the state just before she was captured in a Subterran raid. That would make readjustment a lot more difficult. It might make it impossible.' Maya came to a decision. 'Look, Karn, it's no good me talking to her; she seems to regard me as some kind of love-rival. You've got to become friends with her and see if you can gently guide her into reality. Find out about her past before she was captured and slowly, very slowly help her to accept where and when she is.'

'Does that mean I don't have to watch Thran anymore?'

'Yes. For the time being at least.'

'Then I accept the deal. That pile of filth makes me feel ill.'

He went over to Arthrena who smiled broadly, and then cast a gloating look of triumph at Maya. Maya watched them go with a half-smile playing on her lips. Could it be that Karn's hitherto barren love-life was about to take an unexpected turn? But the half-smile soon degenerated into tightly closed lips. The thought of Giorgio came rushing into her mind in a vision so strong, so real, she could almost believe he was standing in front of her. She felt she could reach out and run her fingers through his curly black hair, draw a finger gently down his cheeks to his lips.

But Giorgio was dead, had been dead for almost a geological age. His dust now formed part of the soil of the surface.

Her head bowed slowly.

She felt that tears should be flowing—but she was incapable of producing them.

***

Thran spoke softly, quietly. He was reasonably confident that he could not be overheard, but he was a man who took no unnecessary chances. No-one who had clawed his way to the summit of power could have had that weakness.

'Yes, I can understand you,' Larz was saying, 'but are you sure this line is secure?'

'Of course! It's on a tight beam to the hub, and from there to you it's by shielded cable. Even if she knew about this system, I doubt she could tap into it. Let this be a lesson to you, Larz: take nothing for granted; make as few assumptions as possible; always check your responses for overconfidence. Maya never wondered how I knew so much about what was happening; for instance, how I knew she had not told her pet about her X-ray aura. It never occurred to her she might not be the only one who had been neurologically enhanced. She never looked for an implant, despite being merely a mechanism herself.'

Larz sounded humble, penitential, grateful. Of course, no-one else could have heard Larz being humble and penitential as his words were being transferred directly into Thran's brain via the implant. It was not strictly necessary for Thran to speak during these conversations as his implant registered and transmitted his thoughts, but he had found speaking made it easier to construct those thoughts.

'Yes, thank you, Leader, for sharing a secret that only the other Councillors knew.'

'Yes,' Thran said, impatience already rising to the top of his mind, 'so now you know about my transmitter implant. Just below the surface, so it looks like another one of my warts. A moment's study from Maya would have revealed it, as she had with Arthrena, but she was so sure of her superiority. But enough of this small talk. You are sure she does not know the full numbers of the Elite Guard?'

'I am. She has not visited us since our first encounter. Instead, the spies report she is spending nearly all of her time in the Biocentre. Apparently, her little troglodyte creature has persuaded her to remove the mold parasite from at least a few subjects.'

Thran smiled to himself in the empty room.

'That will endear her to the mass of the people of Subterra! Losing their hope for a long, easy life will win her no friends, no allies. Fortunately, the slaves' freedom from control will only be extremely temporary. So make sure all the common people get to hear of her stupidity.'

'My men are already doing it, Leader.'

'Well done. I think, Larz, I will consider putting you on the selection programme for possible promotion to the Council.'

'Leader! I, I don't know what…'

'Calm down, Larz,' Thran said, 'you will start ejaculating if you get any more excited. We must hurry; that machine-abomination could come in at any moment. I want you to contact our other cities and assemble a force of matons to add to the numbers of the Guards. And listen carefully, gather together as many pulse-generators as you can obtain.'

'Pulse-generators, Leader? I am not sure if I…'

'Shut up, you fool! You don't need to know what they are, the matons do and that's all that matters. I've already sent an instruction to them that they are to use as many as they can carry against that unnatural thing that calls itself a woman! No makeshift defence will save her the next time, and if Tharn and

292

Ranth want to keep their organs inside their bodies, they'll start dissecting her immediately!'

'I understand, Leader. I'm afraid it will take a little time to contact the other cities and bring the—uhh—pulse-generators here.'

'Then, if you really want to be put on the selection programme, you'd better start acting rather than talking, otherwise, I might put you on another waiting list; for a procedure that transfers plasma from your veins to mine.'

'I will start immediately!'

'Good.'

Thran cut the connection without further comment and rocked back on his heels. And only just in time, because the door to the small room opened and Maya came in. She was carrying something but put it behind her so Thran could not make out what it was.

'Talking to yourself, Thran?'

He adopted a downcast expression.

'Yes. It is very lonely in here, Maya. I am a man who is used to constant activity, weighing alternatives, making split-second decisions that affect the whole of Subterra. This enforced idleness is completely foreign to me. I think it's driving me mad.'

Maya folded her arms as she stared down at him.

'I doubt that, Thran, as you are already mad.'

He stared at the floor.

'You are very cruel, Maya.'

'I think not. I'm sure you are fully aware of what cruelty actually is, and it's something you revel in. You've only ever been on the giving end, of course.'

'You know nothing about me. Or Subterra. What have you actually done except hide from death inside a metal box, like a whimpering little girl?'

Maya fought down an urge to strike Thran. The man was a master at finding weaknesses, of inflaming a nerve with a mental scalpel. It was part of what had made him the unchallenged ruler of his world. It was beneath her to react, and to allow him to get through her defences would be an admission of defeat. He would welcome a blow. And so she did not respond to his question. Instead: 'I want nothing more than to get out of this living Hell you have created. I want to stand on the surface and breathe clean air, free from the stink of you and your cronies.'

Thran looked thoughtful.

'Is that what you want? I suppose you've heard the old saying, "You can't always get what you want"?'

Under Thran's gloating gaze, Maya's right arm rose slightly, but she forced it back down.

'Enough of this.' She revealed what she had dropped. It was a sack.

'You know,' she continued, 'DeGroot once told me of an old legend of his culture. Of a being called Krampus who would put naughty children in a sack and carry them off. You are a very naughty boy, I'm Krampus, and you're going in the sack.'

Thran knew it was impossible to resist her titanium arms, and so he did not struggle as she pushed him into the dark interior of the sack.

'If there were more people around than Karn and me, I could leave you under guard, but as it is, I have to take you everywhere.'

'And where are we going?' came the muffled question.

'Not far. Just the Biocentre.'

***

Karn gently removed Arthrena's arm from around his neck.

'You know you don't have to hold onto me every minute, don't you?' he said.

Arthrena pouted.

'Why? Don't you like it? I thought you enjoyed being close to me.'

Karn had the feeling he was being slowly boxed into a corner.

'Yes, of course, I like it, but occasionally I want to move around a little more freely.'

'Oh, so you want to be free, do you? So you can go off with that Maya woman, I suppose!'

'No, no, I...'

Karn found himself silently praising the gods as Maya came around the corner, carrying a large sack over a shoulder. He could see there was something in it, as from time to time there was a movement within.

But Karn had already known what it was. He had seen this before, many times.

'Maya,' he said, 'glad you're back. Is Thran behaving himself?'

'As much as he's capable.' Maya dropped the sack to the floor, none too gently. She looked around at the Biocentre. 'Are we ready to begin?'

'Yes. I can hardly wait.'

He heard Arthrena hiss something that sounded like, *I bet you can't!* But ignored it.

Maya studied the Biocentre. This was the visit she had promised Karn, and she stood motionless for a few moments, recalling that she had been unconscious under the pitiless stare of the Council of Three while Karn had stood here alone, and had been made a host to one of the mold-parasites.

There were many tanks in the spacious room, some open to the air with a faint haze of vapour hanging above them; others were sealed but with transparent panels on their sides, revealing their contents. The Biocentre was a babel of different animal noises; grunts, squeaks, hisses, growls, and many more only Maya could hear as they bellowed through the infra- or ultra-sonic.

And the smells were uniformly rank; a vile concoction of many different animalistic stinks, blended together into one foul miasma that clung to them with invisible fingers. But unlike Karn and Arthrena, she could switch off her olfactory module — which she promptly did.

295

Maya handed the sack to an unwilling Karn and Arthrena and approached one of the sealed tanks. She peered through the dark transparent panel.

And nearly recoiled.

There were things in there in a dark red liquid that looked thicker than water; twisting, coiling things with black, rubbery hides. She watched them forming curling patterns around each other, and then one came snaking towards the panel and planted its ventral portion against it. She stared at the underside of its head and saw a horrific disk of concentric circles of teeth, getting smaller and smaller as they approached a pulsing red orifice she assumed to be the mouth.

She moved on.

There was a bank of cages against one wall; some large enough only to hold a domestic cat, others large enough to imprison a gorilla. Each one contained an animal of some description, although Maya encountered some that were beyond any description.

There were things looking like giant wood-lice, except they had human-like eyes atop restlessly quivering tendrils; others were simply blobs of a red gelatinous material which, as she passed, suddenly spouted thin tendrils which reached hungrily toward her. One contained what was surely an immature specimen of Eater's species. Others held small skittering things which eagerly pressed themselves up against the transparent covering as she looked in at them, their eyes glowing with the green of poison; and there were many other things, things which have no simple descriptions in the usual languages of humanity.

Finally, she reached a small cage that contained an animal about the shape and size of a small dog. It looked at her with big, liquid eyes and a small pink tongue lolled out of one side of its mouth. It rubbed a head covered in soft, orange-brown hair against the mesh of its cage and made a faint mewling noise.

She had never had a dog as a child as her mother had said they could not afford to feed it. And yet, she had always wanted one and had played with those of her neighbours in those brief periods when she wasn't working. She remembered one that had always been excited to see her and had licked her face madly whenever they met. Suddenly, she felt the need to reclaim part of her childhood. She began to peel away the wire mesh from the front of the cage. She thought she heard Arthrena shout something, but her mind was focused on the cuddlesome little animal. She pulled the mesh completely away and gently removed the small creature. She cradled it in her arms and gazed into the soft brown eyes.

It was then she felt something on her arm and, looking down, saw a quivering pink tube was protruding out of the creature's belly, swiftly joined by a second and then a third. They stabbed and sucked at her arms but could not break through the resistant polymer. All the while, the animal continued to gaze up at her with an expression adorable enough to melt the flintiest heart.

She stamped it flat into a red ruin.

She returned to her companions. Karn was looking at her with concern, Arthrena with contempt.

'I've learned my lesson,' Maya said, 'I now realise in Subterra everything wants to kill you. I should have known.'

'Yes, you should have,' Karn said, 'so let's do what we came to do and get out.'

'Not quite so quickly. I have to check every tank and vat to ensure that nothing can get out when we disconnect their intakes. They must all die where they are and not go crawling around looking for a meal.'

With the others in tow, Maya did a complete tour of the Biocentre, checking everything about the containers and the horrors inside. She used the full panoply of her senses, safe in the knowledge that her power packs could now be recharged. On several occasions, she found possible escape routes and sealed them off. One by one, she disconnected the power supplies which kept them warm, or closed the pipes that supplied oxygen or methane. One by one, she watched them die.

Finally, she came to the rank of open vats from which faint streamers of vapour were gently ascending. Instantly, she recognised the mold-parasite. Neither Karn nor Arthrena would go anywhere near them.

And so it was, that with great pleasure, she killed every one of the squirming things.

And the Biocentre fell silent.

***

Having shut down the dread Biocentre, Maya knew she had to get out of Subterra before it rose in revolt against her. But there were still a few things she had to learn before she returned in triumph at the head of an avenging army from the surface. She still did not know the full extent of Subterra and what weapons it could muster against her forces.

And so she suppressed yet again the fierce desire to leave this world of horrors into which she had been flung; a desire which was always with her. She did not sleep, could not sleep, but if she had been able to, she knew she would have dreamed of only one thing: the surface. It seemed so close that she sometimes felt her arms lift to grasp it. She saw herself walking on its cold steppes, watching the shrunken sun rise above the mists. And there she would find the descendants of the brave men and women who had kept watch from the Space Arks, watching century after century as their tormented homeworld slowly healed; oh, so slowly!

And that meant yet another interview with Thran.

She had dumped him in a room along with some dry food and water and a receptacle for his wastes, which she had been left with the task of emptying.

She watched Karn and Arthrena as the latter giggled as she ran her fingers through his hair. Occasionally, Arthrena would glance at Maya as if to say, *I have someone, you do not!*

Maya never responded, simply glad to see that Karn had finally found some company, maybe even some happiness, with someone who was definitely a woman, and not an all-powerful simulacrum.

All-powerful! She gave a wry snort at her own words. If she had been really all-powerful, she'd have torn Subterra to shreds there and then. But as she watched the pair go off by themselves, not once glancing back at her, an ancient quote came to her about another woman who had been alone, without hope of companionship: *I am half-sick of shadows.* But she was instantly ashamed of her weakness. Perhaps the surface science had truly become advanced enough to restore her to what she had been. She would gladly give up the abilities which had defeated Eater for that resolution! To feel the softness of lips resting against hers as she eagerly responded!

None of this was in Karn's mind as he walked with Arthrena to the room she had chosen as hers. In vain, he protested that he had to keep watch on the remaining Councillors. He knew that wasn't strictly true as Maya had locked Thran's subordinates in another room in the complex with a single maton to attend to their needs, as they were helpless once removed from their transfer plates. *Only for a short while!* He told himself, *and then I'll get back to them.* He found Arthrena's puppy-like devotion to him somewhat unnerving.

He sat in her room. It looked like every other room he had been in; Arthrena had been unable to add any feminine touches to it, as the necessary materials were not easily found in Subterra.

In earlier meetings, he had asked her about her life before Maya had removed the parasite. Of her time under parasitic control, she could remember virtually nothing, just that she had moved around from place to place and given instructions to various people. But what those instructions had contained she could not remember and, more to the point, did not *want* to remember.

But of her time before she had been abducted, she had a few more memories: she had lived in a world not too dissimilar to Karn's, except it had not been quite so primitive. Algae had been as least as important in their diet as yeast had been in Karn's.

Neither had there been any weakening of their suns. But those were the only differences.

But she could not be shaken in her belief that Karn was in fact her betrothed lover, Mawn, and refused to call him anything else. And she kept asking about Maya.

'Why were you with that strange woman, Mawn?' she kept asking. 'Had you forgotten about me?'

Not wanting to hurt her, Karn would reply along the lines of, 'Of course not. How could I forget you?'

This was another of those times and she smiled warmly on receiving the assurance. The room had basic cooking facilities, and she had made some simple flatbreads which they ate together. They were almost completely without flavour but Karn's taste buds had long ago atrophied and so he made no complaint.

'You do understand we are going to leave Subterra, don't you?' he asked, wiping a fugitive crumb from his lips.

'I will go anywhere with you, Mawn,' she said. 'Surely you believe me?'

'It will be very different, Arthrena. Very cold, so Maya says.'

'Maya!' she said, 'can't we ever have a conversation without that woman being mentioned!'

'Maya's been very good to us, Arthrena. She took the parasite off you. She's saved my life several times.'

'And you've saved hers!' she snapped, 'so let's stop talking about her or I'll get angry!'

An awkward silence fell, finally broken when Arthrena indicated a low couch on the other side of the room.

'Let's just lie down for a while, Mawn, and just hold each other. We've had enough troubles in our lives, haven't we?'

'I've got to get back, I...'

She jumped to her feet.

'So you don't love me! I've wasted all my time with you!'

Karn was flustered.

'No, no, it's not that. We're not safe yet, Arthrena. We won't be safe until we're out of Subterra. There'll be time to rest then, I promise.'

But she was not to be pacified.

'Come and lie with me now, or I will hate you!'

He followed her to the couch. It was wide enough for both of them to lie side by side. He lay there, motionless, conscious of her regular breathing.

And then her breath seemed to become shallower, quicker. He felt her hands move slowly over his body, exploring, caressing.

'Mawn,' she whispered, 'I want you. Take me now!'

His thoughts whirled.

He had not been with a woman since the last time with Thylassa, when the Sun had begun to fail. He still felt the anger and humiliation when he had found her with Yarl, not very long afterwards. Surely he had been without release for long enough?

Of course he had!

Hurriedly, they both removed their thin clothes, and Karn began to respond, kissing Arthrena with increasing vigour.

'Yes, Mawn, yes!' she said in a voice that came from deep in her throat, 'Yes!'

He rolled on top of her, exulting in his masculine power, triumphant in his mastery.

And then, for no reason he could find, the smiling image of Maya came into his mind, and his incipient demands died.

He leapt off and, turning, shouted, 'I don't want you. I want Maya!'

***

'You're still here, I see, Maya,' Thran observed, 'you must be starting to like our little paradise.'

'Not a word I would use,' Maya said, 'but when I have the last item of information, my friends and I will say *au revoir* to you.'

Thran raised a sparse white eyebrow.

'*Au revoir?* You mean we'll be meeting again?'

'Most definitely. I can't allow a culture like yours to continue.'

'And by what right are you the judge and jury of what cultures survive and which are destroyed?'

'You clearly didn't ask yourselves that when you conquered the other Burrower settlements and placed their inhabitants under the worst kind of slavery imaginable. I will destroy you.'

Thran shrugged.

'I'm tiring very rapidly of your delusions of grandeur. Hurry up and ask your last questions so I can get rid of you.'

'Don't you want to know what I've been doing? Wouldn't you be interested in the fact that I've destroyed your Biocentre?'

Thran knew about that, but he feigned shock.

'The Biocentre? What will we do now?'

'Nothing. I assume that was the only one?'

'Yes, of course. Subterra isn't big enough for more than one. It served our entire nation.'

He thought to himself, *It will take a while to restock it from the other sites, but we will succeed.*

'The people will need time to readjust,' was all he said.

'They will be given time. I do not plan genocide.'

'That's reassuring. But surely you already know all you need to know?'

'Not quite. I want to see maps; I want to know the extent of Subterra to make sure I've got the measure of you bastards.'

'I will ignore your needlessly unpleasant language. You will find the maps and much else in the Library. You may remember I offered you access to it.'

'Under rather strict conditions, as I recall.'

Thran shrugged again.

'We all have restraints within which we must operate.'

'One thing I don't understand. Why are there so many slave people wandering around this city? What do they do?'

Thran's features jerked into his equivalent of a smile.

'They don't do anything. They are spares. The requirements we place upon them in return for feeding and sheltering them are quite onerous. There is—ahh—a high turnover. Not everyone makes it out of our manufactories. The people in the city don't mind walking around aimlessly; they're not really conscious. So why care about them? I don't understand.'

'The Universe doesn't concern itself with innocent suffering: I do.'

Thran shrugged.

'I can't help your problems.'

She stared at him emotionlessly.

'Exactly the response I expected. I don't suppose I will get any more out of you, so I will now go to the Library and get the remaining information I need about this sick society. Fortunately, I am a very quick reader. And then we will be on our way.'

'Not that I want you to leave us, of course, as I have found conversing with you most stimulating, but are you sure you know how to utilise our surface craft?'

'I am. I can't explain to you how I gained such knowledge without any help from the Council—but rest assured, I can operate the craft.'

Again the smile that was not a smile.

'That is reassuring. I wouldn't want anything to happen to you or your extremely amusing companions.'

Maya stared at him for a few moments. An unpleasant thought was crawling in the basement of her mind, one that was trying to warn her of danger. There was something fundamental she had forgotten, some ridiculously obvious thing about Thran that she should have checked.

What was it?

She could not remember.

After Maya had left, Thran contacted Larz again.

'Is everything ready?'

A silent message entered his brain.

'Yes, Leader. Everything you ordered to be done has been done.'

'Good. Standby for one more command, and then you will rise up and rid us of this dreadful nuisance who has caused us so much trouble.'

The conversation over, Thran remained in deep thought for a while. A sinewy hand reached for his pitcher of water.

Soon, he thought, *Soon!*

Thirteen

Maya stood in the Library of Subterra, which was held in another part of the sprawling Citadel of the Council of Three. Before her was a great monitor screen on which glowing characters were rolling swiftly from bottom to top.

The characters were foreign to her, but she had known they were probably from either the Latin or the Cyrillic alphabet, with a smaller probability of being from Hanzi. Based on a few obvious correlates, she was able to deduce the meaning of the majority of the remainder. Coupled with her knowledge of the Subterran dialect, she was able to read the documents in a reasonably short time.

And what she had found was troubling.

Contrary to what Thran had said, Subterra was much larger than the environs of this city. In fact, there were several more cities on either side at a distance which could only be hundreds of kilometres, with villages interspersed in the gaps between them. This was a problem: the greater the dimensions of Subterra, the greater the difficulty there would be in bringing it to heel.

Much greater.

She called up another map and found she had to zoom out several times to see the full extent of the great cavern in which the cities resided. So large was the cavern that it must need artificial support to prevent it imploding from the pressure of the encircling rocks.

She had found several histories of the Subterran culture, but all of them had been written from a vainglorious perspective, accepting that it was manifest destiny to subdue the other peoples. And none of the histories went anywhere near to the beginning of the subterranean settlement: there was Subterra; there had always been Subterra; there always would be Subterra.

She switched off the display. A cold sickness was beginning to spread through her. Thran and Larz had both lied; that was no surprise, but she was beginning to understand the enormity of what had been done to her, of how she had been guilty of a reckless naiveté, a naiveté that had now put all their lives in danger. Conscious of her physical superiority, she had forgotten that others might be her master in guile and subterfuge.

No longer could she be sure that her destruction of the Biocentre had been a mortal blow; undoubtedly these other cities would have them too. And, more importantly, the population of Subterra was not to be measured in hundreds—but thousands. Thousands which at that very moment were being marshalled against her!

And then the message which had been crawling in the roots of her mind came thundering into her consciousness from deep below: *Get Out! Get Out Now!*

She switched off the monitor and was about to turn off all the other displays when she realised she was wasting time; every second might be vital. There was only one thing to do, and that was to collect Karn and Arthrena and get to the surface!

For the first time since the initial battle with Eater, she felt genuine fear. They might already have sealed off the shaft to the surface and put guards around the transporter itself.

Fool! Fool! Her mind shrieked.

She shot out of the Library; her heightened senses scanning in all directions for encircling foes. Subterra, which she had hitherto regarded with a kind of lazy contempt, now seemed a deadly trap. Every doorway could hold an enemy; around every corner could be an ambush.

She burst into the room in which she had last seen Karn and Arthrena.

Not there.

Where the hell were they!

She went from room to room in gathering desperation, flinging open doors, scanning the interiors, moving on.

Where were they?

Then she remembered Arthrena had chosen one room as her own personal dwelling-space.

She burst into that room like a thunderbolt to find Karn and Arthrena in a state of undress, but sitting in total silence with their backs to each other.

'Get dressed! We're leaving!'

Arthrena glared at her.

'Don't people knock doors where you come from?'

Maya ignored her and, addressing Karn, yelled, 'We've been betrayed! Where's Thran?'

'He's locked in the room next door,' Karn said, obviously puzzled and disturbed by Maya's agitated state, 'what's wrong? He's still in there; there's no way out.'

'Everything he's said has been a lie,' Maya said, 'Everything!'

And then, standing in front of her baffled and increasingly frightened companions, another horrible thought struck her. How deep had Thran's deception of her actually gone? Was his composure merely the sign of someone who had reluctantly accepted a temporary defeat, or was it the self-assuredness of a General who had known all along exactly what was happening?

Could it be that all this time he had been in contact with his forces, planning his reconquest and a terrible revenge?

'Come with me!' she said, and, not bothering to unlock the door, smashed it open and burst into Thran's prison room.

He looked up mildly and said, in an eerie echo of Arthrena's complaint, 'Don't you believe in knocking? That's our property you're wantonly destroying.'

For an answer, she leaned down and picked him up with one hand, holding him so their eyes were on a level.

'You lied to me, you miserable little shit! You've been lying to me all the time!'

'I don't know what you're talking about,' he said, 'and I must point out your grip on me is quite painful.' He looked at Maya's increasingly nervous companions. 'Dear me, I think your Mistress has gone mad. I would leave her here, if I were you.'

Arthrena and Karn looked at each other but did not move.

Maya shook Thran so violently that he became a blur for a few seconds.

'You're coming with us, Thran! You are our little shield. As long as we have you, they won't try anything too violent. You've still got those codes in that rat-brain of yours, haven't you!'

Thran's expression changed; no longer was he a cowering penitent; he seemed to grow in her grasp; become straighter, stronger, masterful. His voice, which hitherto had been quiet and respectful, became strong and masterful once again. And, once again, he was the all-powerful ruler of his realm.

'Give it up, Maya. You can only bring suffering upon your friends, who will surely die in the forthcoming unpleasantness. My offer to you was magnanimous, though you chose to throw it back into my face. I promised to put you back together again after we have sucked the knowledge from you, but that promise was not open-ended. So give up now and it still stands; continue with this ruinous defiance, and, after we have finished with you, we will turn you into a collection of kitchen implements. Parts of you will make very attractive colanders.'

Ignoring his warnings, Maya continued to hold him with one hand as she began to search for his carrying sack. She found it, turned him upside down, and thrust him into it.

'Get dressed, now! And let's go,' she said to the bemused man and woman.

'Go? Go where?' Arthrena said.

'To the surface. Where else?'

'I'm not going there!' she said, reaching for Karn.

'Where Maya goes, I go,' Karn said.

Arthrena thought about it for a second and, reaching for her clothes, said, 'Let's go!'

Maya tossed the sack over a shoulder, and, after a hectic dash through dimly-lit corridors, they burst out of the Citadel's great portal; through which she and Karn had entered at the beginning of their time in Subterra, so blissfully unaware of what was waiting for them within.

The bluish light of the enemy land beat down upon them; unchanged, unchangeable. They ran across the narrow, withered strip of land separating the Citadel from the city. It seemed deserted: but that was ominous, for none of them had ever seen it without its hordes of robotically moving slaves. It had an eerie feel to it, as if they had been transported to a city of mausoleums; a city of the dead. Silence pressed down upon them, carrying a warning of peril.

'Where are we going?' Arthrena called from behind Maya.

'To the transporter station,' Maya said, 'you took us there, remember?'

'No.'

They ran on through the empty streets, but as they did, Maya began to hear faint, low sounds, sounds the others could not hear—the noise of numerous people on the move.

They had acted not a second too soon.

But to her relief, the transfer station came into view, looking like a random collection of small boxes against the stupendous might of the cavern walls. For a brief instant, Maya felt something approaching respect for the Subterrans and how they had carved a kingdom out of the living rock.

But that feeling did not last long as another example of their efficiency made itself manifest. As they came closer to their longed-for escape, a mass of matons and men emerged from the streets on either side of them. And somehow, even in the depths of his sack, Thran knew they were there.

'You now have only a few seconds to accept my offer, Maya, a few seconds to avoid the shame and guilt of having led these innocent dupes to their deaths. A few seconds to avoid being stripped down to your components and, after we have destroyed your brain, turned into base implements fit only for the hands of peasants. Let me down, and the offer stands. Continue to attempt to abduct me, and your childish adventure ends here as you watch your companions choke on their blood. Decide!'

All three of the fugitives came to a halt next to a Subterran road vehicle as they watched the two hostile groups merge together into one threatening mass of men and matons. Larz stood in the vanguard, his pistol aimed squarely at Maya. Smiling, confident, he detached himself from the throng and took a few steps towards them, keeping his weapon trained on Maya.

'In the name of all Subterra, I command you to release our Leader and deliver yourselves into our hands. If you obey now, I promise you will be treated leniently. But refuse, and the consequences will be very different.'

Maya rapidly scanned the opposing group. Most of the Guardsmen were carrying rifles, although a few of them, like Larz, had only pistols. She knew nothing about firearms, never having fired one in her life. There had been none in the recording room—why should there have been?: they were going to emerge among friends. DeGroot, an academic unused to violence, had not given the possible need for defence a moment's thought.

She finished her scan and reached her grim conclusion. Unlike Karn and Arthrena, she could not be killed by a single shot, but a volley would punch enough holes in her to drain her hydraulic fluid, leaving her immobile.

And the matons: most of them were unarmed, but three were holding what could only be mobile pulse-generators. At lightning speed, she ran through all possible actions coupled with their probable outcomes. But part way through her planning, she felt a wave of unreality begin to sweep over her, a kind of detachment from the real world in a way that reminded her of how she used to feel just before sleep, in the dead days when she could sleep.

She went rigid and said tonelessly, 'A parabola is the set of all points $M(A,B)$ in a plane in a way that the distance from M to a definite point F, known as the focus, is equivalent to the distance from M to a definite line, known as the directrix.'

Karn groaned and fell slightly against Arthrena, who looked helplessly back and forth between him and Maya.

'We are waiting,' said Larz, 'but not for much longer.'

Somewhere in the submerged depths of Maya's mind, her true self fought against the seizure, fought to ascend back up through clinging blackness, back to horrible reality.

She succeeded and, bursting back into consciousness, looked around again. Larz was beckoning to the matons holding the pulse-generators, urging them to move to the front of the crowd.

She completed her analysis of possible actions and probable outcomes. There was only one possible way out of this trap.

'Get ready to hold what I give you,' she whispered to Karn, who was standing open-mouthed with the glad realisation that she had recovered so quickly, 'I am about to move very fast.'

And she did.

She flung Thran's sack at Arthrena, who, although dazed by the speed of what was happening, managed to catch it. But before Arthrena's hands had fully grasped the sack, Maya was in lightning-fast motion. She ripped a sheet of metal off the side of the vehicle next to them and thrust it into Karn's waiting hands. He lurched as he took its full weight, but did not drop it.

'Shield me from the pulses!' she commanded, and, even as she spoke, she had lifted what remained of the vehicle like a toy and sent it spinning into the crowd of men and matons.

Their reflexes, even the electronic ones, were not as fast as hers and the central swath of her would-be captors went down like bowling pins before the deadly impact of the tumbling machine.

'Run!' she yelled.

They ran.

Karn saw a maton raise the single remaining pulse-generator and interposed the metal sheet between it and Maya. The invisible pulse struck the sheet, its energy generating whirling eddy currents in the metal, heating it to painful levels, sending electric shocks up his arms. Some of the energy lapped around the sides, and Maya stumbled as it washed over her.

Stumbled but did not fall.

They leapt over the bloody remnants of the Guards, the crushed remains of matons. They came to where the mangled vehicle had come to rest, and she picked it up to use as a fearsome javelin a second time and sent it spinning through the air to take out the maton with the pulse-generator.

But Larz had managed to leap out of the path of her improvised missile, and he shouted, 'Shoot them, you fools, they are taking our Leader! Shoot them!'

Immediately the low-powered rifles began to bark. Suddenly, Karn felt as if a red hot iron had been thrust against his arm, and saw it now bore the red and bleeding track of a glancing shot. He dropped the metal sheet, unable to carry it anymore.

They were close to the transfer station now.

Still the rifles barked, and he heard the whine as bullets passed near. Several hit the building ahead of them, and he saw stone dust burst out in little puffs, blowing away to reveal small craters.

He turned to relieve Arthrena of the burden of carrying Thran, who was kicking and wriggling wildly in his tight prison. As she passed it to him, he saw her jerk and a shocked expression fill her face, swiftly replaced by blankness.

She fell forward heavily onto her face, revealing a growing red stain on her back.

He stopped his mad run, and kneeled beside her, heedlessly dropping the sack. He rolled her over to stare into the face of a dying woman. She lifted a hand to him and whispered, 'Karn', and then fell back, motionless. He stared down at her for a few seconds, and then a mad rage gripped him. Leaping to his feet, he was about to charge at the Guardsmen with murder in his mind when a strong hand grasped his shoulder, restraining him.

'No,' she said, above the noise of the guns, 'not now.'

She looked down to see Thran half out of his sack and attempting to crawl away. In one fluid motion, she stopped his escape, and, with one arm, held him above her head, waving him back and forth so he could be clearly seen by the approaching Guardsmen.

'I have your leader,' she shouted, 'I have Thran! I have promised not to harm him, and I won't, but I am taking him to face justice for the crimes he has committed against all the other Burrower nations!'

The mass of Guardsmen came to a halt, but Larz marched on until he was only a few metres away.

'Give him back,' he said, 'you have encroached on the sovereignty of our nation and abducted our Leader.' He levelled his pistol at where Maya's heart would have been. 'Give him back.'

Maya smiled.

'It won't work, Larz. One shot won't do me much damage, and before you fire another, you'll be in several pieces. I know you're not interested in Thran's health and happiness, so don't try to fool me. You only want the codes that are in this fucking turd-brain. You want to be Chief Councillor and punish and torment to your rotten heart's content. You know, perhaps when Thran has received his sentence, I'll release the codes to a reformed, democratic Subterra. Perhaps not. But I have him. You have killed one of my friends, and you want to kill a few more. But you're no match for me. Let us go and Thran will live. Try to take him, and he and you will both die. Whoever finally becomes Chief Councillor won't be you, I regret to inform you.'

Larz remained still and silent, his features working through various expressions as he strove to decide what to do. Then he lowered his pistol.

'Do I have your word you will not harm our Leader?'

'You do. There has been enough killing.'

He looked around, desperately trying to avoid saying what he had to say, but it could not be avoided. He turned to face the remnants of his troupe.

'Lower your weapons! Matons stand down! I am allowing them to go; they have promised not to harm our Leader!'

There was a sullen buzz of noise from some of the surviving Guards. Apparently, not all agreed with Larz. He turned back to Karn and Maya, who was now holding an enraged-looking Thran close to her chest.

'You pathetic coward,' Thran spat at him, 'I will make sure you share a cell with an Eater when I get back!'

Larz managed to avoid Thran's scornful look and said quietly, 'You'd better go now. The men are not happy, and I don't think they will obey me for much longer.'

Maya nodded and said, 'Thank you.'

Leaving Arthrena where she lay, they turned to the entrance to the transfer station. It was locked, but not wanting to waste any more time, Maya simply tore the outer door off. The inner door was not locked and so they were soon inside the station.

Displays of her strength were not required with the transporter machine itself, which was sitting somehow expectantly on its platform. It was locked by a code, but one which Maya had already obtained on her first visit.

'You will regret going to the surface, Maya,' Thran said, as she tucked him under an arm, 'You will regret it greatly.'

'Don't you ever get tired of making threats, Thran?' she said, 'don't you ever feel the need to talk about the weather or your grandchildren?'

He fell silent. And a second later she stuffed him back into the sack.

She turned to Karn.

'Are you ready?'

He smiled weakly.

'I suppose I am. I'm finally going to get to see this wonderful, marvellous, incredible surface you've been talking constantly about. It's just...'

He looked behind him. Several Guardsmen were now outside the inner door, making threatening gestures.

'Arthrena. I wasn't very kind to her.'

Maya touched his head, having forgotten Karn's aversion to that type of familiarity.

'I understand. She deserved better. But then we all do.' She glanced outside. 'We must go. I think Larz has lost control of his men.'

As Karn entered the transporter, he noticed the double door construction of its portal. He was now able to understand what was its function and a thought danced fleetingly over the surface of his mind: *It looks like an airlock. Why would the vehicle need an airlock? We won't be getting out once we're in the shaft.*

And then the thought was gone.

Maya sat in the control seat, with Karn and Thran behind her.

'I think you can let him out of the bag now, Karn. He's not going anywhere. Except to face the music.'

'Are you sure you know how to operate this thing?' Karn said, the anxiety in his voice unmistakable. He looked at his arm; it was still bleeding, but not as badly. 'I don't want to get stuck like we did last time.'

'I think Thran might have been kicking and screaming if this thing was unsafe. Correct Thran?'

'Correct.'

'Then we will delay no longer.'

She felt volcanic excitement begin to build within her.

At last! After all the false starts, all the dangers, all the close encounters with death, she was finally on her way!

Her finger jabbed one of the many buttons on the control panel. In a heartbeat, the shaft was emptied of air.

The rockets fired into flaming power and the platform carrying the transporter first shook itself and then began to rise through the unresisting vacuum.

Rising more and more swiftly to the expectant surface.

REVELATION AND RESOLUTION

One

Karn could only see the back of Maya's head, but he could see from her rigid posture just how excited she was.

He glanced out of the window not blocked by Thran, but there was nothing to see. Their speed was so great that all details of the shaft through which they were hurtling were smeared into a smooth, grey blur. And so tremendous was that speed their unwilling guest had been compressed into his seat, so he appeared to be just a small bundle of rags.

The roar of the rockets was deafening.

'How long before we reach the surface?' he asked the bundle, but there was no reply. He shrugged: he was not sure he could have heard even Thran's powerful voice over the thunder of the rockets in any case.

Then he felt an odd sensation in his arm. The wound was now crusted with red-black dry blood and still hurt badly but that was not the sensation which had caught his attention. Instead, he looked closely at the skin and saw it was covered in little bumps, many with a whitish hair sticking out of them.

'What?' he said, lifting his eyes from this new mystery. And then he shivered. This was a new sensation; never had he encountered this extremely unpleasant feeling before.

'It appears to be getting colder,' Thran said in an unconcerned tone.

Karn looked around the interior of the transporter to see if some coolant vapour was jetting out.

There was none.

'What is…' he began and stopped. There was a loud CLICK! from behind him, and a welcome blast of warm air suddenly washed over him in a breaking wave.

'It appears the heating systems have activated,' Thran said, in a voice as unconcerned as a voice could possibly be.

'*Heating* systems?' Karn repeated: that was crazy! How could there possibly be a need to *produce* heat? He called to Maya, 'What's happening?'

There was an unexpected pause before he heard her voice, and it had a peculiar, strained quality to it.

'I'm not sure.'

And then she fell silent as the platform continued its thunderous meteoric ascent.

Karn was troubled: this didn't feel like the joyous, triumphant journey he'd been expecting. Once again, he looked out of the window away from Thran. The speed seemed to have slowed somewhat; he could just make out differently coloured patches on the shaft wall before they were swept away downwards. And a short time later, he noticed the wall was displaying a glistening appearance under the glow cast by the vehicle's interior lights. With a start, he realised that the wall was wet with a thin film of moisture. Also, there was a thin faint whining noise coming from outside the vehicle, like a wind attempting to slither through a crack in a window. Thran had been watching him, and as Karn turned away from the window he found himself facing a leering smile from the Councillor.

'What are you grinning about?'

'Nothing. It's just slightly amusing watching your inadequate mentality wrestling to comprehend what should be patently obvious.'

Karn knew there was some aspect of the situation he had not grasped. Had they declared victory too soon? What had they overlooked? He heard Maya mutter something that sounded like 'Air is getting into the shaft', but he did not know whether or not that was significant.

He then realised the platform had changed its speed again, without him noticing just how severe had been the deceleration. Soon it was stationary, hovering on vastly reduced power. He leapt up in alarm: this wasn't the surface! Was this what Thran had been gloating over, that they would be trapped in this dark tunnel until death claimed them?

But then two metal arms extended silently from either side of the shaft and slotted into waiting hollows in the platform. The rockets died completely, and a great silence fell: a silence that seemed to be overlaying some terrible secret.

'What's happening, Maya?' he called, but she did not answer, her attention seemingly fixed on the displays in the control panel. Then there was a grinding vibration detectable through the floor and a section of the wall in front of the transporter slid away, revealing a well-lit chamber. Automatically, the vehicle's motors whirred into life, and it rumbled out of the shaft and through the expectant orifice.

Behind them, unobserved, unnoticed, the platform began to descend back into the sweltering heat of Subterra. The wall closed behind them and, in the gloom, Karn could see a massive door blocking their way. Again, he panicked before he understood they were simply in another airlock. The shaft had been airless but presumably their destination was not. And just as his concern began to fade, the door opened with a deep-throated rumble. He realised that he was hearing external sound because his surroundings were now filled with a life-giving atmosphere.

The vehicle rolled smoothly into a tunnel lit by panels set at regular intervals in the wall; panels glowing with that slight bluish tinge which was now so familiar to Karn. Then it began to slope upward with a gradient of about thirty degrees.

We're still going up, thought Karn; *whatever happens we won't be stuck in that gods-forsaken shaft!*

He realised Thran was stirring beside him, now that the acceleration was no longer pressing him into the seat.

'Are you ready to take me back yet?' he asked.

'Take you back? Why would we do that?'

Thran's face was transformed by what was undeniably a leer, a transformation which made his unpleasant expression even more so.

318

'You'll see—as you have so lamentably failed to anticipate what is about to happen.'

Karn ignored him and moved to the front of the transporter, sitting next to Maya so he could see if they were any nearer their destination. Her hands were resting on the controls, but it was clear the machine was driving itself.

'How much longer?' he asked.

'I don't know,' Maya said in a curiously flat, lifeless tone, 'we'll have to wait and see.'

'Maya, is anything wrong?' he said, expecting to be told there wasn't, but to his slightly alarmed surprise, she said, 'I don't know yet.'

He sat back down. His scalp prickled as a gnawing concern began to crawl over him.

Why was Thran so confident that things were going his way?

And then ahead a light began to show itself, a luminescence that spanned the entire width of the tunnel; a pure white radiance.

They emerged from the tunnel into a large area in which stood several transporters of a very similar design to theirs. The area was under a huge, superbly transparent dome, beyond which the sky was finally displayed in all its glory.

Its cold, black, star-shot glory. Hard, unblinking dimensionless points of silver scattered randomly into a curving cliff of ebony.

Karn looked up at that sky in awestruck wonder.

'It's beautiful!' he gasped. 'It's like the World was after the Sun went out; but what are all those little points of light? Is this what you meant by "night", Maya?'

Maya did not reply. She sat as if turned into a statue, gazing at the same sky that had enthralled Karn—but she did not look enthralled.

Eventually, her hands began to move over the controls, and, on one of the monitors, a series of letters and numbers appeared.

She stared at them, the power of a reeling mind commanding them to display some other readings.

But they remained as they were, resolutely telling her the terrible facts she did not wish to know.

But slowly, agonisingly, she realised she had always known it, but had not allowed herself to accept that bitter truth.

And then that crucial conversation came back to her, the conversation she had held with the refugees from the World, not long after they had met, which all along had held an insidious reality hidden in its seemingly innocent words:

'You say the World is slowly getting colder,' she had said to them both, although Yarl had been staring at a monitor screen.

'Yes, at least that's what the old men said.' Karn had looked puzzled. 'But this place is much colder than the World.'

Maya did not respond to his comment but said, mainly to herself, 'Getting colder; that implies a steep thermal gradient.'

'Thermal gradient?' Karn had asked (Yarl had still been looking at pretty pictures of the Lost Earth).

Maya had ruffled his hair as if she were talking to a child. Karn disliked the implication, but he enjoyed the closeness.

'Yes, it's very simple. It means that somewhere, somewhere in contact with the World, there is a place which is colder, very much colder.'

'How could that be? This place is much too cold for us. There couldn't be anything colder.'

"There couldn't be anything colder."

The irony embedded in those words had, all the time, been showing the futility of her hopes, had always contained the complete refutation of her dreams.

One of the readings on the screen before her was that of the outside temperature:

Minus two hundred and twenty-three degrees Celsius.

Before Karn's horrified eyes, she suddenly leaned forward and began to beat her head against the control panel.

'DeGroot, DeGroot!' she screamed, 'what have you done to me! What have you done!'

Karn's hitherto dormant fear erupted into his mind like a lightning strike. For a moment, the interior of the transporter swam before his eyes. To see Maya, the supremely confident, effortlessly able master of every situation, reduced to this howling wreck was too much. He didn't understand what was wrong, but he knew it was something very, very bad; worse than anything they had ever encountered before.

'What is it?' he finally managed to say, 'what's happened?'

She turned in the chair and, to his horror, he saw her face was now a mixture of rage and despair.

'Can't you see, you stupid little idiot,' she rasped, 'can't you see with your own moronic eyes!'

He cowered before her fury but forced himself to ask again.

'I see a dark sky; why is that so bad?'

She checked another reading and then pressed the control which opened the transporter's airlock. A short set of steps extruded from the machine's flank.

'Come.'

Heedless of what Thran might do, they left the vehicle and approached the edge of the dome.

'Look outside.'

He looked. He saw a black sky dotted with steady, dimensionless points of light, some dim, some bright. One, near the horizon, was extremely bright and beautiful. Karn did not look at it long enough to notice it was slowly moving, slowly rising higher.

It was the land which held his attention, held him motionless and mesmerised, as if he were a mouse and it a viper.

Under the light cast by the dome, he saw a featureless surface, glinting in a pastel blue-white colour. There were no trees, no buildings, no flowers, no insects buzzing through the air. There was only the soft blue-white substance, which gave the impression that it was a vast coverlet that had been thrown over the underlying ground, completely hiding it.

There were mounds and drifts and hillocks of the substance, but there was nothing else. Nothing at all. It went on and on, stretching far beyond the great circle of light cast by the dome.

'Do you know what that covering is?' she said, standing by Karn, but not looking at him.

321

'No.'

'It's air, Karn, solidified air. Above the surface is only a vacuum, a horrible, empty vacuum. And look at this.' She pointed at the ground near the exterior base of the building in which they were standing. He saw a small rivulet of a pale blue liquid trickling away from them and disappearing into the soft mounds of the solid material.

'That,' said Maya, 'is what you breathe. Oxygen. But it's liquid oxygen, melted from the frozen air by the heat of this building, but not getting very far before it solidifies again.'

'But what has happened? This isn't the surface you talked about.'

Her head fell against her chest. She wanted to cry but could not. After some time, during which Karn could only stare at her in helpless terror, she lifted her head.

'Let's go back into the transporter.'

They listlessly returned to the silent vehicle. Her feet suddenly felt incredibly heavy.

They found Thran sitting exactly where they had left him.

'You knew,' she said, staring at him accusingly.

He gave another of his smiles, which was far from being the smile of anything remotely human.

'Of course, I knew. Tharn knew. Ranth knew. Every thinking being in Subterra knows. Perhaps you're not very good at thinking, Maya.'

'But you said nothing.'

'You would not have believed me. You would have thought it was another one of my tricks, designed to keep you in Subterra so we could take you apart. Is that not the case?'

'Yes. I would not have believed you.'

'And now,' said Thran, 'now you realise you have no hope, you will return me to Subterra. Because I feel your disappointment, your pain, your terrible, terrible loss, I will prove I am no monster by reinstating my offer of clemency. Yield to us and we will reassemble you after we have learned what we want to know.'

'And Karn?'

'He is of absolutely no interest to us. We have thousands like him. You can keep him, if he can provide you with some kind of solace. Sex perhaps; you must miss it. Although with him, it wouldn't be far removed from bestiality.'

Maya drew back a killing fist, but Thran raised a finger and wagged it at her.

'Now, now. You promised not to harm me.'

She lowered the fist.

'But what has happened?' Karn asked again, 'I don't understand why the surface isn't what you expected.'

'What I *wanted*,' Maya corrected, 'I now realise I've been fooling myself all along. I still have some human weaknesses, it seems.'

She found a seat where she could look directly at Karn.

'I told you about Baldwin and how she accidentally sent the giant planet Jupiter towards Earth.'

'Yes,' said Karn, and wondered what kind of woman could wield the power to destroy a solar system.

'DeGroot convinced us all he had calculated that the close passage would toss the planet Earth outwards, so it would take up a stable orbit near to where the planet Mars had been. Of course, the climate would be vastly different, but humanity would be able to re-establish itself after the heat and radiation had died down. We trusted him because he was a man of truly brilliant genius; after all, this body I'm in is all his work. But I now realise, like many scientists before him, he was overconfident and strayed outside the field he was expert in, into one in which he was just an interested amateur.

'Jupiter did indeed fling Earth out of its orbit. But it did not simply move it into a nearby orbit. It flung Earth completely out of the Solar system. We are drifting in interstellar space and have been for a hundred and seventy-five thousand years. The Space Arks must have all failed once there was no world to colonise. This planet is dead. We are alone. The terrible cold is spreading inward towards the core. That's why the World had those

323

earthquakes as the rock shattered as it cooled and shrank. All the equipment the Burrowers created is failing as it wears out.' She looked away from Karn. 'As I am worn out.'

Karn fell back away from Maya. He now understood enough to realise Maya's words entailed a choice of one of two bitter alternatives: death on the frozen surface of Earth or a living death in Subterra.

And then Maya went rigid, and all animation was washed from her face: even the dreadful emotion of despair. She began to intone what to Karn was meaningless nonsense.

'The various forms of planetary trajectories can be understood from a study of conic sections. Two of the curves are closed, but the parabola and hyperbola are open. They...'

She stopped at the beginning of the sentence and shook herself. She stared at Karn.

'Another seizure?' he asked, hoping he didn't already know the answer.

'Yes.'

She put her head in her hands.

'All I have done, all my struggles, all the people I have helped—and this is my reward!'

She looked at Thran, but now there was no scorn in her eyes, no contemptuous defiance. Instead there was the beginning of submission, of deference.

'What does it matter, what does anything matter now? Vanity, vanity, all is vanity. I'll take you back.'

He shook his head.

'No need, my dear. I have been in contact with the new Head of the Elite Guards, and they are already preparing the platform to come and collect us and will be here very shortly. I will do my best to keep my promise to you, but apparently this new man is very harsh and unbending. You see, you have rather humiliated our people with your escapades, and he is a great believer in the manifest destiny of Subterra to rule all. So I may have a little difficulty in persuading him to accept my overflowing kindness.'

324

'You're the supreme ruler of Subterra!' Karn roared.

Thran spread his hands apologetically.

'I'm only human.'

Maya's grimace was the terrible rictus of a madwoman.

'Yes, I'll come with you. Take me apart and throw the pieces away! Nothing matters anymore! Not a fucking thing!'

It was then that a message came into her mind. It was the same as before, but now much stronger, much clearer.

We are here. We search. We are here.

Two

Maya's expression changed at once from despair to alert excitement. She did not know how distant was the source of the enigmatic message, but the fact it was so much stronger must have meant it was nearby!

She re-ran the message through her memory, trying to find if there was any hidden information in it but, lacking triangulation, all she had was the direction.

But that was infinitely more than she had possessed a few minutes earlier. And then she stopped herself: *one message.* Was she, once again, placing too much faith in others? What if the originators of the signal were another hostile group?

She decided. Having nothing to lose, she would try to find the originators of the message. But she had one last thing to try. On every previous occasion, her attempt to reply had failed—but now she was so much closer…

Maya cleared her mind of every extraneous thought and concentrated on one thing, and one thing only: Communicate. Unfortunately, the message had come through on a very narrow band, one which was not easy for her to generate.

But she gathered her waning strength together and sent her signal, arrowing across the desolate wastes of the frigid Earth: *I hear you! I am here! Where are you?*

The seconds flew past.

Nothing.

And then: *We hear you! We are not far!*

There followed a distance and direction.

Hope flared brightly within her. The units the unknown people had given were definitely based on old Terrestrial measurements, not the very different Subterran ones. Whoever the signallers were—they were not of Thran's people.

'Let's be on our way!' she said, extending her arms to the control panel.

But then her limbs began to tremble uncontrollably. Her head clicked back and forth like a metronome.

'What's the matter?' Karn gasped.

With difficulty, she steadied her head and said, 'The degeneration. It's reaching my motor functions. Karn, you'll have to drive.'

'Me? I've never controlled a machine in my life. I'd never even seen one until recently!'

'Then it's about time you learned. Come and sit with me.'

He obeyed, and gradually, slowly, her trembling stopped.

'The degeneration spasms will come back before long,' she said, seeing the pleading hope in his eyes, 'it's irreversible. But driving this thing—it's not too difficult. It's basically autonomous, but you have the power to override it if necessary. Here, let me show you.'

Karn's forehead corrugated until it resembled a freshly ploughed field on old Earth as she explained what the controls did and how to operate them. Several times, he had to ask her to stop and go back over something, but eventually he nodded and said, 'I think I've got it.'

She smiled.

'We've wasted enough time. Let's go!'

They had changed places, so she now sat beside him on the front seat. Thran was left to his own devices behind them. Karn tentatively manipulated a few controls, and, with a violent jerk, the transporter moved forward again, heading for what was clearly another airlock.

'It should open,' she muttered, 'it should open.'

It did. Both the inner and outer doors opened smoothly and silently after the evacuation of the frigid air of the dome, and then the vehicle was out on the blue-white wilderness of the silent Earth. Brilliant headlights snapped on automatically, sending the snowy land into coruscant relief.

Immediately, the heating system whined into its highest power as it felt the intrusive fingers of near absolute zero begin their attempt to infiltrate the interior. Despite its efforts, the cabin temperature began to plunge steadily. Karn, still dressed only in his Subterran costume and having virtually no experience of temperatures below the comfortable, began to shiver violently.

'Hold on, old friend,' Maya said, 'you can handle it.'

Karn felt a warm glow spread through him as he digested her words.

Old friend! Those were the first words of endearment from her he had ever heard! For such words he would fight Eater itself!

The transporter rumbled onwards, cresting dunes and hillocks of the powdery oxygen and nitrogen, throwing up short-lived parabolas of the frozen atmosphere as they crossed flatter areas.

They had been cruising for some time in the direction from which the message had come when Thran suddenly stirred himself behind them and spoke, in a voice which was trying to be unmoved but which had excitement bubbling below it.

'It might interest you to know that the transporter carrying the Elite Guardsmen has just reached the surface.'

Karn glanced at Maya at those words, but her profile remained impassive.

'Just concentrate on your driving,' she said quietly.

Many more ominous minutes passed.

The landscape remained essentially unchanged, featureless plains and low rolling hills of frozen gases, set against a starry, ebony sky.

And now directly above them, and thus unseen, a particularly bright star was approaching the zenith.

Then Karn caught a movement right on the edge of his peripheral vision.

It was another transporter, presumably the one crewed by the Guardsmen who had remained loyal to Thran.

'Looks like the game is up,' they heard him murmur behind them.

'They're travelling faster than us,' Karn said, 'they've obviously got a better driver than me. They're going to come alongside at any moment.'

Maya made no comment. Instead, she leaned forward and placed her head and hands against the control panel. Karn glanced at her, fearing another seizure, but she seemed to be completely alert. Her fingers made odd dancing movements over some controls she had not explained to him.

He glanced out of the canopy. The other vehicle was much closer and now obviously on an intercept course. He could see some Guardsmen in the front of the machine.

Beside him, unknown to either of the passengers, Maya had interfaced with the vehicle's sensor array. She threw the last dregs of her strength into enhancing its range and resolving abilities, looking for a way of escape.

Then she straightened and pointed ahead of them.

'Go around the flat area there.'

He took his eyes off the controls to stare at her.

'What! That'll waste time we don't have! They'll just cut across it!'

'Do it.'

And her voice was imperious.

Used to not understanding Maya's motives, Karn obeyed, as he normally did. The transporter lurched to the right and began to plough through oxygen snowdrifts, sending up huge curtains of bluish powder.

But, just as Karn had predicted, the other vehicle began to cut straight across the small plain, on a trajectory that would intercept him in a matter of minutes.

'This is it, I'm afraid,' came a dry, contemptuous voice behind them. 'I'll soon be warming these frozen toes back in beautiful Subterra. And I can hardly wait to drain some vegetables through what remains of you, Maya.'

'Karn, stop,' Maya said, 'you can look at them now.'

Karn complied, and a comparative silence fell, broken only by the rhythmic idling of the transporter's motors. He watched

329

the other vehicle come barrelling towards them across a level region of ice.

And then, suddenly, abruptly, unexpectedly, it lurched over, the tracks on one side lifting clear off the surface. Karn saw a sudden crazy spiderweb of cracks race in all directions away from the stricken transporter. It tilted further, and some of the cracks became fissures. The machine, now nearly on its side, began to slip away into an ever-widening rent.

There was a brief fountain of pale-blue liquid.

And the transporter was gone.

'What?' Karn said, unable fully to believe in his salvation, 'What happened?'

'I was able to detect there was a hotspot right there. It was just warm enough to keep the oxygen as a liquid, and it was covered by a thin cap of carbon dioxide ice. Their momentum carried them onto it, and by the time they realised what was happening, it was too late. They were so far across they didn't have time to turn back before the weak ice collapsed.'

'I was going to thank the gods, but I think I'll thank you instead, Maya.'

She smiled, but then her head began to tremble in an ever-increasing rhythm.

She fought it stationary again.

An angry voice came from behind them.

'They were good, brave men! My loyal, faithful people! You'll pay for this. The two of you. No more talk of clemency!'

She ignored him.

'We must press on. My deterioration is rapidly getting worse.'

Karn put the vehicle into motion again, carefully skirting the hidden lake.

They drove on through the gelid landscape; alone in a frozen world, one as dead as a long-bleached skull; driving over the frigid corpse of a murdered planet.

Maya muttered incomprehensible statements about orbital trajectories, her eyes blank and focused on nothing.

Karn heard Thran chuckle, and he strove to keep both sounds from his mind.

On they went.

Maya came out of her latest seizure and looked around, disappointment plainly written on her features.

'Where are they?' he heard her say, 'where are they?'

Then, unknown to Karn or Thran, she heard them again.

You are very close. Soon we will meet. Soon.

The transporter climbed slowly up the flank of a ridge of solidified air.

It crested the ridge.

And there they were.

Three

Three pairs of eyes stared down at the mysterious set of structures at the foot of the ridge, but only one pair had any comprehension of what it was seeing.

Maya saw a group of low buildings arranged around a much larger one. All were of the same basic shape: a semi-circular prism. In the near distance rose an almost perfectly conical hill, clothed in the purest white.

But some objects a substantial distance from the group of buildings were what really interested her. Each one was a cylindrical object with short, stubby wings. From her memory of transportation from one hundred and seventy-five thousand years earlier, she knew what they were: shuttle craft for reaching low Earth-orbit. But it could not have been manufactured on Earth by some as yet unknown Terrestrial civilisation because, as the planet no longer had an atmosphere, any kind of wings would have been redundant.

And, of more interest to Karn, were apparently human figures in the areas between the buildings, shrunk by distance and motionless. Maya was sure that if they could have been seen close-up, all would have their attention fixed upon the caterpillar-tracked vehicle slowly descending the slope towards them under Karn's nervous guidance.

'What is all this?' he said to Maya, alternating his eyes between the slope and the controls as the vehicle tried to slide sideways.

'Hope,' she said, 'hope.'

Thran had said nothing, but she knew he was also staring at the unexpected sight.

The transporter came off the slope and began to move jerkily towards the buildings.

'Careful, Karn,' Maya said, 'we don't want to get off to a bad start by running any of these people over.'

But there was no danger of that, as the inhabitants of this little group of buildings moved far apart as the massive vehicle rolled past.

'Head for the big building,' Maya told her driver, 'that must be where we'll find the answers.'

Karn obeyed and, to his own surprise, succeeded in bringing the transporter to a sedate halt just outside what appeared to be the building's entrance.

'Now what?' he said, mainly to himself.

Some of the inhabitants of this hamlet started to cluster around the new arrivals.

Maya looked carefully at them. They were covered by bulky protection suits which hid their features but it was obvious they were of the standard humanoid structure: two legs, two arms, a head. They pointed at the great doors which comprised the entrance to the main building.

'Why should we go in?' Karn said, 'we don't know what we're getting into here.'

'Karn,' she remonstrated gently, 'we just left Subterra, a hell-hole ruled over by that revolting thing behind us. Is it likely these people will be any worse?'

Karn shot the object of her scorn a quick glance. Thran stared mutely back.

'No, I guess not,' Karn finally said, and put the vehicle in motion again.

The doors parted silently in the vacuum, and, once again, they were inside a huge airlock. As air rushed in they saw hoar frost magically appear on the freezing metal of the vehicle as the moisture in the air froze out. The transporter rocked gently under the influx of an atmosphere.

Ahead of them were two indicator lights, one of which was shining a bright red. Then it blanked out, and the one next to it became green.

'Seems like we've arrived,' Maya said.

'But where?' Thran said, 'don't relax too much, Maya, you might be over-estimating your womanly charms.'

'We'll ask these guys,' Maya said, pointing to the group of figures which had surrounded the transporter as soon as standard air pressure had been established. 'Karn, please pick up Thran and we'll go and meet our new hosts.'

Karn pulled a wry face, but leaned over the seat and picked up the diminutive Councillor. Maya pressed a control and, with a soft soughing noise, the two doors of the vehicle's airlock opened in turn, disgorging a short set of steps after they had fully opened. They descended.

One of the mysterious figures approached, still clad in its exterior suit. It said something in an echoing, amplified voice. Maya shook her head.

'Sorry, I'll need a few more points of reference before we can communicate.'

The figure seemed to understand and pointed to a door in the side of the building's airlock. They went through it and, to Karn's (and no doubt Thran's) satisfaction, a wave of pleasantly warm air washed over them. Karn began to shiver as his tightly coiled tension started to work its way out, and he realised for the first time just how cold the cabin had gotten. The leading figure pointed to a couch against the wall, and Karn eagerly sat down, parking his repulsive burden by his side. Maya remained standing, watching the rest of the figures file in from the airlock.

She began to say, 'I think you must...' but stopped as the unknown people started to remove their bulky vacuum suits.

The leader took off its helmet, and Maya found herself looking at a smooth, gleaming head of what was obviously an artificial being. Its androgynous, unlined, unblemished features gave it something of the look of a pre-Catastrophe shop-mannequin. But unlike the mannequin, the face was mobile and the eyes sparkled with something which could only be understood as intelligence.

'You're a robot!' Maya finally said.

The being cocked its head slightly as if re-running her words in its mind. Then it looked at Maya and said, slowly, haltingly, as if it were learning her language in real time, 'Yes, we is ro-bot.' It looked her up and down. 'But so you.'

'I am not!' said Maya, 'but let's not argue. I'm speaking Twenty-fourth century English. Do you know it?'

'Twenny-for sentree Ingliz,' the robot said, seemingly feeling the words with its tongue, and then, an instant later, 'Yes, of course, Twenty-fourth century English. A most expressive language. Such wonderful literature, of which so little survives. And your friends, do they also speak the same language?'

'They do not,' Maya said, and went on to explain what tongues Karn and Thran spoke.

The robot gave a reasonably convincing smile.

'That will not be a problem. It is a simple matter to make morphisms between the various modes of speech.'

Karn touched Maya's arm.

'Maya, are—are these things matons?'

'In a way, Karn. But there's almost as much a difference between these robots and the matons, as there is between you and the matons.'

Karn did not look too pleased at that comparison but said nothing.

The robot smiled again.

'You may call me Thrix. I am sure you must be hungry and thirsty after your trip. I will also get you more appropriate clothing.' It stopped and looked at Thran. 'That might take a little while longer in your case, sir.'

'Don't bother with that for me, Thrix,' Maya said, 'I have much more urgent things to do. I want to see whoever's in charge here. I have some urgent things to discuss with them. Very urgent.'

'The Co-ordinator knows you're here and will be here soon. He is a most busy man, you must understand. But don't be alarmed. We are very pleased to see you.'

Maya's expression became almost pleading.

'Please tell me you are the ones who sent the message.'

Thrix smiled again, and now they were used to his slightly unusual appearance, the smile seemed to have become more natural.

'You mean *We are here. We search. We are here?*'

'Yes, yes!'

'Yes, of course that was us. We *are* here and we *have been* searching. In fact, we have been searching for quite some time.'

'Searching for what?'

'Why you, of course. What else? Now you must eat and drink. Perhaps shower. We have all the facilities you could possibly want on EB-1.'

'EB-1?'

'Earth Base 1. Now, for your own health and well-being, no more questions until you have done as I have recommended.'

Maya looked unhappy but complied; like the other two.

***

The robots had noticed Karn's wound and placed his arm in a cylindrical object which had opened and closed like a clam. Karn had complained he felt an unpleasant tingling but stopped complaining after they removed the device to reveal healthy, undamaged flesh.

Then they had a meal; that is Karn and Thran had a meal. Neither of the men had much experience of the profusion of tastes, flavours, and odours that food outside their exceedingly restricted native cuisines could provide. Karn, whose diet had been even more restricted than Thran's, found it overwhelming, and confined himself to the more basic, blander dishes, while Thran roamed far and wide over the delights provided. Early on, his inexperience with the richness of the new food caused his overloaded stomach to regurgitate a significant proportion of what he had consumed, but he soon recovered, and resumed attacking the rich and varied fare so generously provided, as if his last hours had come.

Maya stood and watched them, counting down the remaining hours of her sanity with increasing impatience. And then she heard a voice behind her.

'Maya, may I speak with you?'

She turned and found herself looking directly eye to eye with a man. After so much time spent looking down at people considerably shorter than she, it was a somewhat startling experience.

The man was almost a caricature of the ideal male: broad-shouldered, narrow-waisted, possessed of large, powerful hands, wavy chestnut hair and a pair of piercing blue eyes. His voice was a rich, mellow baritone; the type sometimes referred to as "dark brown." The same colour as his skin, in fact.

'I'm sorry to startle you, Maya. I should not have come up behind you like this. I apologise, but I understand you are anxious to see me.'

Maya found herself strangely flustered.

'That's alright, and you are?'

'Co-ordinator Omar Akeem. I'm in charge of EB-1. You have a problem which you wish to discuss, I believe.'

'A problem? Yes, you could call it that, though from my point of view it's more an "existential crisis".'

'That sounds unpleasantly serious. I think your friends will be occupied for quite some time with the wonders of our cuisine, so we may safely leave them. Please come with me to my office.'

But as he turned to lead the way, she gently touched his shoulder.

'Co-ordinator Akeem, are you a...'

He smiled.

'A robot? No, I am entirely human. I'm surprised your enhanced senses did not reveal that to you, Maya.'

'They would have done, but I am forced to conserve every watt at the moment.'

Another smile; the regular teeth showing like ivory against skin the colour of polished mahogany.

'That is one problem you needn't worry about, Maya. We have an abundance of energy here.'

She didn't bother to ask how he had known about her enhanced senses: she had been through that routine with Thran. He pointed down a corridor and turned away.

But she couldn't just stand around in a restaurant as if she were on some kind of all-inclusive vacation. This time she clutched his shoulder, more forcibly than she had intended, and he turned back to face her.

'You have seen the creature called Thran.' She stabbed a finger in the direction of the Subterran, who was busily demonstrating that his appetite did not match his stature. 'He is the very dangerous leader of a degenerate culture called Subterra. I insist that he be separated from Karn and me and incarcerated!'

Again the flawless smile.

'Maya, I'm afraid I am the only one who insists on anything in EB-1. I have only just met the three of you and my overriding emotion at the moment is joy and relief that Earth still has inhabitants. I will not be incarcerating anyone unless I am convinced that it is in everyone's best interests to do. I must say that Thran does not look like much of a threat to any of us. And I am surprised you can use a word like "creature" about a fellow human-being.'

Maya felt frustration and anger rising.

'It's not his appearance, man! It's what he represents, the power he holds. He is...'

But Akeem was holding up a hand, and his smile was gone.

'Maya, I understand that you have been under a great deal of strain and you are worried about your future, but I will do nothing but make the three of you comfortable until I am given undeniable reasons as to why I should act otherwise. Is that clear?'

She nodded reluctantly, being careful not to look at Thran, who she was certain would be smiling wickedly if he had been able to follow the conversation.

338

It was not long before Maya was sitting on the other side of a desk made from what looked very much like genuine wood, staring in increasing wonder at the Co-ordinator.

'So who exactly are you?' she finally said, 'This isn't the surface I was expecting, so I don't see how you can be the surface people I was expecting. And why have you been looking for me? What do you want?'

He waved a hand.

'One thing at a time, Maya. You have already said time is short. I will tell you and your friends all about us soon enough —but first your problem?'

A wonderful swell of relief surged through her, cooling her, calming her. She felt the tension drain out of her circuits. She looked into his blue eyes, which, unlike the bitter ices beyond the walls of EB-1, conveyed no feelings of coldness, and which seemed to be drawing her *into* them, *through* them.

But finally she spoke.

'I am a mechanical-digital construct, the result of the work of Cornelius DeGroot at the time of the close passage with Jupiter.'

He leaned back in his softly upholstered chair and steepled his fingers.

'Yes, DeGroot. We have very little information on him as he was of no interest to the crew of the *Spes Nostra*. All we know about him is he had some exceptionally complex plan to survive the doom of stars.'

'Yes,' she continued, becoming increasingly excited by the thrill of talking to someone who could match her in his understanding, 'I am part of that plan! My consciousness was copied at the instant of my death and uploaded digitally, to be downloaded again into an electronic body some three centuries after the passage.'

'And that did not happen, I assume.'

'No, something went wrong with the time crystal, which was supposed to stabilise the process. Instead of three centuries, I awoke to find over one hundred and seventy-five thousand years have passed.'

'A long time, even by our standards.'

'Far too long. The digital copy had become corrupted in all that time and was unstable. To put it bluntly—I am losing my mind. And the loss is accelerating.'

Akeem looked genuinely concerned.

'That is most disturbing. We must see what we can do.'

***

She lay at rest with terminals on her scalp. Initially, she had been very reluctant to allow it, with the memories of the Council's probing of her brain still raw in her mind.

But for some reason, she trusted Akeem and made no objection when the time came for the examination to begin.

And he was there, looking down at her, the warm mahogany of his features enhanced by a comforting smile. She and he were alone in a room filled with softly glowing, softly murmuring machines performing functions whose purposes were completely beyond her.

She reluctantly closed her eyes, and once again the tapestry of her life was unrolled before her.

She saw Isabella and Alejandro in the dying settlement on a dying world; once again she lay down, knowing that in a few moments, her body would be no more and her consciousness copied.

Again, she battled the rats and Eater.

She tried to shut out the images; so much strife, so much sadness.

She had seen enough of it. She was sick of these unpleasant memories perpetually being dredged up from the sludge of the past.

And then it was over and Akeem was helping her get to her feet.

'I could see our examination was painful for you,' he said, 'I accidentally saw some of the images but decided not to intrude any further into your memories. You have suffered much.'

'Haven't we all,' was her swift reply, 'when do I get the results?'

'I'm not entirely sure. We have never met your like before: a human mind being maintained by a mechanism. DeGroot was obviously a very great man for his time.'

'Not great enough,' she replied curtly, 'otherwise the suffering you saw would not have happened.'

'No doubt you're right. But they say misery loves company and you have had plenty of company down the millennia.'

She said no more for a while: perhaps the past should be left untouched for the sake of the present.

As long as there was a future.

And so she forced a smile and, turning to him, said, 'Now, you know who I am—who the Hell are you?'

***

Akeem had given another winning smile but had said no more in response to Maya than, 'I will speak to all three of you at the same time so you all understand us at the same time.'

And so they were all together in a spacious room, sitting in comfortable chairs with a drink at their elbows. Thran and Karn were wearing earpieces that translated Akeem's words into their dialects; he, on the other hand, needed no such aid in reverse, having already learned their speech. He stood in front of them.

'No more speculations. I understand you want to know exactly where you are, exactly who we are and exactly what is happening.

'First of all, me. I am Omar Akeem, at present Co-ordinator of EB-1. But my main job is Captain of the great starship *Adekola*. This starship, in fact.'

He pointed off to his right and a wall of the room transmuted into a large viewscreen. At first nothing was visible

341

but blackness, dotted with stars. And then slowly, a lustrous metal prow came into view from the side of the image, morphing into a gleaming cylinder, studded and dotted with instruments and sensor arrays, designed for purposes Maya could only guess at. The dimensions of the cylinder seemed endless, as if it were of infinite length, but eventually the stern appeared, terminating in colossal exhaust-stained nozzles, somehow proclaiming the power they could release; power which was at that moment locked in slumber. Maya, and only she of the original trio, realised she was looking at a truly immense vessel, a stupendous, magnificent, craft that could dare to cross the horrific gulfs between the stars.

'It's incredible,' she breathed, 'how big is it?'

'Over nine kilometres in length, but much of its volume is taken up by the reaction mass and the mesonic reactor. It is now orbiting Earth, of course.'

She noticed both Thran and Karn were looking at her for guidance as to what they were seeing, but she ignored them. She had no time to waste.

'And where are you from?'

'The planet Gaia.'

'There is no such planet in the Solar system.'

'True, but we are not from the Solar system. We are from the system of Alpha Centauri A.'

She felt a stab of alarm.

'What—you are extra-Terrestrials?'

'Technically, yes, but we are of human descent. We are the distant children of the first colonists to reach the Centauri system.'

'Colonists? But there wasn't time after the Catastrophe!'

'Our ancestors left before the Catastrophe. You have heard of the lightsail craft launched from the Venusian Cloud Cities?'

'Yes, but DeGroot said they had all failed.'

'Another example of his less than God-like status, I'm glad to say.'

Akeem looked around.

'I'm afraid I will have to sit down. This is taking longer than I expected.' He collected a chair from another part of the room, and then sat facing them. He seemed momentarily lost for words as he looked at his unusual audience.

'Lightsail craft?' Maya prompted.

'Yes, the lightsail vessels; initially powered by gigantic laser complexes in orbit around Venus. Unfortunately, there was only time to construct and launch five such vessels: the *Spes Nostra*, the *Nea Avgi*, the *Zhen He*, the *Resurgam* and the *Magellan*. The *Nea Avgi* was destroyed before it could clear the Solar system. The *Magellan* reached Alpha Centauri but was unable to decelerate and passed straight through the system, back into interstellar space. Its fate is unknown.'

'And the others? They made it?'

'Yes, but only the *Spes Nostra* arrived with its full complement. The other two were in a very bad state.'

'So was there something different about the *Spes Nostra*?'

'By a strange chance, the initial crew contained a young woman who had been mentally enhanced. She was able to make major improvements to the life support systems, which, unfortunately, the other two did not have. As the crossing took centuries, even small failures in the systems and planning became life-threatening.' Akeem's face altered; it became suffused with an almost religious awe. 'The story of the struggle to establish the Centauri colony with so few settlers is an epic story which could fill libraries. There is nothing else like it all of human history! Several times over the course of centuries, the fragile human presence was nearly extinguished.

'But finally, they became secure, and, after millennia fighting simply to survive, they could begin: first taming their hostile environment, and then moulding it into a garden.

'And here I am.'

Karn was silent, unable fully to comprehend any significant fraction of what he had heard, but Thran snapped, 'And why are you here? What were you looking for?'

Akeem looked slowly between all three.

'We are here to rescue what remains of humankind. We were sent from Gaia to look for the shattered remnants of our people and bring them home.'

'Home?' Thran asked.

'Yes, home to Gaia. We have been on Gaia almost as long as humanity was on Earth before the Catastrophe. It is as much home as Earth ever was.'

'But to make such a tremendous journey,' Maya interjected, 'I assume you are still limited by lightspeed?'

'Regrettably so. I'm afraid anything else will only ever be a fantasy. Of course, we can reach much greater speeds than the old lightsail craft. I think they were driven by desperation almost as much as by the Terawatt lasers. Also, we have rediscovered the Baldwin technique for generating Einstein-Rosen bridges, but, in order to prevent another cataclysm, they are only generated between established colonies—of which there are now several among the nearer Sunlike stars. And given average lifespans—barring accidents—of about a millennium, plus advanced hibernation techniques, the stars are no longer that far apart.'

Karn felt Thran stiffen and saw him lean towards Akeem, a hard glitter seemingly shining in his eyes.

'You said average lifespans of a thousand years?'

'Yes,' Akeem said, 'we have improved the original biological basis of humanity. We have remodelled our proteins so they are more robust; we have enhanced our nucleic acids with artificial bases so they do not degenerate anywhere near as swiftly. Nanobots patrol our bodies, removing plaques, revivifying neurons, hunting and killing rogue cells. There are a thousand other developments that give us our modern lifespans, but I won't bore you with them.'

'But these enhancements? We could have them?' Thran said, grasping his chair so firmly his knuckles had turned white.

'Some of them. You can certainly have the nanoscale robots.'

Thran sat back, a great smile adding even more wrinkles to his face.

'There are other improvements to humanity,' Akeem continued, 'for instance, we can choose what gender we can be during our long lives. Sometimes we are male, sometimes female, sometimes neither. I, to take a simple example, have been female three times and a mother twice.'

Karn looked at the ceiling. He didn't want to hear any of this; Thran was lost in his thoughts.

'I can see I'm boring you now,' Akeem said, good-naturedly. 'I will leave it at that. You will see it all when you get to Gaia.'

'Gaia!' Maya said, suddenly alert.

'Yes, of course. Our mission here is to find all the survivors and evacuate Earth. We are like a mother hen gathering in her helpless chicks. Given your brief lifespans, we will put you into suspended animation for the long journey to Alpha; there should be enough room on the *Adekola*. You must understand, having come so close to extinction, we see our purpose as seeding life throughout this empty galaxy.'

Karn looked alarmed.

'But what about our way of life? Our rules, our rituals?'

'I doubt if many of those will survive life on Gaia. Even if you hang onto them, I doubt your children will.'

But Thran was already planning: *There is one culture you won't find and alter.*

Later the same day, when alone in his room, he sent an urgent message to the Council, down through the frozen atmosphere, down through the rock strata.

There is great danger. You must begin the plan for the evacuation of Subterra, and prepare for a period during which you will run on minimum energy to avoid detection. But you may well have to fight. Be ready.

He said a great deal more; even revealing where an earlier version of the scared Codes could be found.

Then confident that all that could be done, had been done, he sat back.

345

I may never see Subterra again, but these Gaians seem to be soft; unused to subterfuge and violence. Maybe they can be manipulated.

Four

'This is an unusual request,' Akeem said, 'we wouldn't normally undertake any kind of procedure without further study of you personally, and your culture.'

'I appreciate that,' Thran said, 'but it will aid your great enterprise.'

'How so?'

'Let me make sure I understand your plans: now you know Earth is still inhabited, you intend to bring down vast resources from your orbiting vehicle and seek out all the subterranean cultures.'

'Yes. We have many instruments which will reveal exactly where the pockets of population are. We appreciate it is an enormous volume, in between the layers that are too cold and those that are too hot, but our robots and automatic instruments will make short work of it. No more than thirty years I estimate.'

'Yes, thirty or so years is no time at all for beings of your duration, of course; however, I doubt I shall be around then.'

'Around? Oh, you mean still alive. I'm afraid you're probably correct. Our bioscan of you was very strange. It shows you are basically an unmodified human and yet you appear to be about three hundred years old. Those two characteristics don't usually go together. But it does appear that you are nearing the end of a strangely long lifespan.'

'I don't doubt your estimate, but that is precisely the issue I wish to discuss with you. I have a proposition for you which will make your task easier and perhaps prevent violence.'

Akeem leaned forward, suddenly very interested.

'That is very good to hear. Please explain.'

Thran strove to stop a satisfied smile reaching his lips and succeeded.

'I hope you will not be taken in by any drivel that mad woman-machine may be gibbering. My culture—Subterra—is a strongly traditional one. It has a very strictly defined set of mores and permitted behaviours. One thing it demands is that its leaders be not only wise and humane, but very long-lived. I come from a special caste, which by selective breeding has a lifespan much greater than the common population. We are venerated as literal gods by our people. However, just before I was kidnapped by Maya and her slave...'

Akeem put out a hand to stop him.

'Kidnapped? Slave?'

'Oh, you hadn't realised that? I'm sorry, I thought it was obvious. You are aware Maya is dangerously insane, I suppose?'

'Well, not insane,' Akeem said, frowning over Thran's words, 'but she is undergoing a period of great mental instability.'

'Well, it's very generous of you to put it in those terms, but I have been on the receiving end of her "instability." In one of her wildest periods, the two of them snatched me from Subterra and placed a commoner on the throne.'

'Why would they do that?'

'Are you asking me to explain madness, Co-ordinator? Suffice it to say that is what they did. And in so doing they brought great suffering upon Subterra. I'm afraid to say that was their intention, all along.'

'I'm sorry to hear about your people's turmoil. But how will injecting you with nanobots help your people?'

'You intend to do that in any case, do you not?'

'Yes, but only when you are safely on Gaia after a period of dreamless stasis, and we have rescued all your people. All their, and your, suffering will be over at last.'

'Which will be too late; there will have been an orgy of violence and innocent deaths in my absence. Only my presence, for many more centuries, can help return peace and order after the chaos that Maya and her creature have visited upon us.'

Akeem drummed his fingers on his desk.

'I don't know. It would be most irregular.'

The Gaians had given Thran a robotic framework to aid his mobility and he could now move around by himself. He now used it to rise from his stool, and turn his back on Akeem.

'I understand, Co-ordinator. It appears I have overestimated your people. I thought they had moved beyond petty bureaucracy, rules and regulations, and were concerned only with the alleviation of suffering. I assumed drying a child's tears would mean more to you than completing the correct form. I am sorry to have wasted your valuable time, but I am even more sorry to think of the terrible barbarism which we Subterrans are now fated to suffer.'

Akeem rose hurriedly.

'No, stop, Thran, stop! I hadn't realised things were so bad among your people. Of course, you can have the nanobot infusion. I will arrange for it to be performed as soon as possible!'

Thran stopped his movement towards the door and turned back to Akeem.

'Co-ordinator, you are exactly the man I thought you were.'

***

The injection of the medical nanobots followed shortly after Thran's interview with the Co-ordinator.

In actuality, he felt exactly the same after the shot, but in his mind he convinced himself he felt stronger, clearer. The robot that administered the injection had told him he should start to feel the benefit after a few weeks, and from that time onwards would start to regain more and more physical strength, even if he would never recover his full height.

It was enough. He was looking forward immensely to feeling certain endocrine glands reactivating.

Communication with Subterra was also going reasonably well.

It was prolonged because of the tenuousness of the link, now it was being attenuated by the intervening ice and rock. Many times entire sentences had to be repeated. But he learned the evacuation was going to plan. The population would be distributed between many hidden uninhabited caverns, where they would arm themselves with every weapon known to Subterra and await the return of their rejuvenated leader.

In the fullness of time, he would lead a robot squad down from EB-1, supposedly on a noble quest to rescue the poor Subterrans, but they would find those same Subterrans not so lacking in resources as expected. By a series of subtle questions, he had learned for certain what he had expected from the beginning: the Gaian robots were incapable of violence.

But his matons assuredly were so capable and, despite being an inferior technology, his mechanical servants would prevail in any war of the robots. A broken fingernail or two would surely be enough to compel these would-be saviours to scurry back to their homeworld!

It was incredible that Maya's assuredly hopeless quest had resulted in making the Subterran way of life invincible! Surely there was some Cosmic Purpose at work here!

***

Maya stared at the Co-ordinator.

'You're sure,' she said.

'I'm sorry, Maya. We have tried every way we can think of to stabilise you, but we cannot. You see, DeGroot's rather clumsy technology was never rediscovered during all the thousands of years of the Centauri colony because we had no need for it. We had developed purely biological methods of prolonging life and our robots were never less than our obedient, trustworthy servants. Whether they are actually conscious is a philosophical problem we have never solved.'

'Along with not solving my problem,' she said.

Bitterly.

Akeem's head lowered slowly, so he was no longer looking directly at her.

'No. We haven't solved your problem either. I am so sorry.'

350

She turned her eyes away from his, apparently to stare at the ceiling.

'So for you, a paradise world. Robot servants for your every whim. The ability to visit the stars as easily as people used to visit their neighbours. A thousand years of glowing health, one minute fertilising a woman, another, giving birth.

'And for me: this body designed by DeGroot will last just as long, but instead of what you have, I am gifted with a thousand years of insanity, a millennium of madness.'

'I am sorry, Maya. With all our knowledge, all our science, we did not know beings like you existed, could exist. Given the crudity of your construction, we cannot halt your mental deterioration.'

'How long?'

He spread his hands.

'We are not experts in this field, Maya; I've told you that. You probably know the answer better than we do.'

She continued to look at the ceiling.

'I would say permanent dissolution is imminent. Days.'

'I think you're probably right.'

She sighed.

'So all that *We are Here, We Seek* business was for nothing. I'm no better off now than when I woke up in the recording room. I expected to go out to help people on a world no more hostile to life than Scandinavia had been; and, perhaps, one day to be a woman again. All I wanted was to love and be loved.'

Once again, she felt like tears should be flowing, but once again, she couldn't.

'What a wonderful body!' she said, 'I can punch holes in rock but I can't even fucking cry!'

Akeem was no longer looking at her. Instead, he seemed to be finding the surface of his desk fascinating.

'I know nothing I can say can take away your pain, Maya. You have been treated very badly by this uncaring Universe we inhabit. But if it had not been for you and your determination to find us, we might easily have abandoned our mission here. We

351

were far from certain we would find life here, which is why the majority of our people are still on the *Adekola*.'

She continued staring at the ceiling but nodded slowly.

'That's something.'

'Thanks to you,' he continued, 'we can help Thran return to Subterra and save his people.'

Immediately, she dropped her gaze and stared uncomprehendingly at Akeem.

'What did you say!'

Five

How easy it had been to secret the knife away in the folds of his clothing! Thran thought as he ran a gnarled finger along one side of it, admiring the serrations on its business edge.

He almost began to wish it had been more of a challenge, now that the Gaians had been revealed to be little better than gullible children. He no longer needed to dream of revenge against Maya either; he had learned from his ever-helpful domestic robots that her new hosts had been unable to help her. Thran also knew she'd had two more seizures since he'd last seen her and could not be long for this world, or any other. No, Maya was now to be mocked, not feared.

So that just left Karn.

Ah yes—Karn. The primitive savage who'd had the effrontery to knock him to the floor just as Eater had been on the point of despatching Maya. He could still feel the thrill of watching those massive jaws closing on the helpless machine-woman; a thrill interrupted when he found himself lying bruised beneath his maton attendant. Yes, that was an affront which could not, *would* not, be forgiven.

Would the Gaians believe his story about acting in self-defence against a crazed Karn? Why wouldn't they? Lying and dissembling were joyously absent from their society. No, they were so busy wrapped up in their self-congratulatory maternal culture of tolerance and co-operation they were easy meat. They were sheep who had forgotten there were wolves roaming the pastures and thus did not recognise one when it was amongst them.

He looked around the room which had been assigned to him in EB-1, seeing its comfortable bed, dining table, washbasin, shower, easy chairs, small stool, and a large televiewer screen. He had activated it a few time before realising it only showed extremely boring documentaries about the scenic splendours of Gaia. If he saw another majestic waterfall, he would scream. But how strange to think it was here, in this cosy domestic setting, that Karn would breathe his last!

He placed the knife under a cloth on the table, having wiped with it an antiseptic tissue. He would make sure Karn's fingerprints were on it before calling for help. A pair of gloves sat innocently nearby.

Now to collect Karn.

It was amazing to be able to stand almost perfectly upright after fifty years of squatting! The first time had been almost orgasmic as he watched his legs straighten underneath him before he took his first tottering steps from chair to chair. Now every day they were noticeably stronger than the day before. The domestic robots had assured him he would not need his Gaian exoskeleton much longer. However, that time was not yet so it was fortunate the Co-ordinator had put him and Karn in nearby rooms, so he would not have to put too much strain on his burgeoning walking abilities.

Leaving his door ajar, he walked the short distance to Karn's room without much difficulty. Now for the fun part!

He banged on the door, yelling, 'Karn! Karn! Quickly!'

The door opened, and a hostile-looking Karn's head appeared around the side.

'What do you want?' he demanded.

'It's Maya,' he said, trying to sound desperate, an emotion he knew very little about, 'she came to my room and now she's collapsed! She's calling for you!'

Karn's expression changed instantly and he burst out of his room. Thran was amused to see he was now wearing an open-necked shirt and long trousers; presumably the most clothing he had ever worn in his life, but then his amusement died as Karn rushed ahead of him. If he got there too quickly he would see the room was empty and come back out!

'Karn, wait!' he called, 'Maya said I must tell you something.'

The other stopped and waited for him to catch up.

'What?'

'You have to press on a certain part of her neck a number of times. It will help control the seizure.'

Karn looked sceptical, but allowed Thran to join him.

'I've never heard her say that before.'

Thran said nothing. Nearly there.

They went in together, and the door locked itself behind them.

Karn looked anxiously around, his eyes, searching, searching...

'She's not here,' he said.

Thran came up behind him.

'No, but this is,' he whispered, as he lifted the knife.

It was the reflection in the televiewer screen which saved Karn. He saw an arm, terminating in a deadly knife, rise behind him and begin a killing strike.

He dodged as the knife came down, and it passed through empty air. In his sudden panic, he tripped and staggered, but managed to strike Thran's arm as he fell, sending the knife spinning away.

But Thran was not so easily thwarted. As Karn tried to rise, Thran's newfound strength brought the stool down onto his head. Karn went limp.

Thran slipped on the gloves and retrieved the knife, giving it another cleansing wipe. He would make sure Karn was holding it when he was found.

He stood over Karn, who was groaning and beginning to stir.

'Oh no, you don't!' Thran breathed, and the killing arm went up again.

But in the instant between two of his heartbeats, his door was sent spinning into the room as Maya kicked it off its hinges. She and the Co-ordinator walked in through the empty doorframe. But it was Maya leading the way.

'All the proof you need, I believe,' she said calmly.

Akeem stood motionless, staring at Thran and the knife.

'I would never have believed it,' he said, after a long pause, 'violence against another human being. But why?'

Thran gave it one last try.

'He attacked me!' he said. 'He burst in and tried to kill me with this knife! I only just managed to get it off him!'

'I might have believed you,' Akeem said, 'if Maya hadn't convinced me to install a camera in your room. We were watching it all just outside. Even then, I couldn't believe what I was seeing, and we almost were too late. For that mistake, I apologise to you,' he added, addressing Karn, who was now upright, but holding his head in obvious pain.

'You could have warned me,' Karn said, looking at Maya.

'Yes, I'm sorry.' She grimaced. 'I'm not thinking too clearly at the moment.'

Two robots came in behind them and wound transparent tape around Thran, rendering him immobile. They stacked him in a corner where he could do nothing but observe the scene playing out in his room.

Maya crossed to Karn and kneeled before him, so their faces were on a level. She placed her hands on his shoulders, and her face was illuminated by a smile that was soft and loving.

'You are a good man, Karn. You are proof that despite all the terrible suffering, all the endless disasters the human race has endured, there is still goodness and decency left in us. I say "us" because I know I am still a woman; this shell is just that—a shell. I am still the little girl who played with my doll and cuddled Alejandro, still the young woman who so desperately wanted Giorgio to kiss her. All the fighting, the struggling—I never wanted that, never wanted to be a hero. I never wanted to be able to smash rock with my fists: I just wanted to love and be loved. That was all.

'I am so very happy to have known you.'

A terrible fear began to invade Karn's features.

'Wait. Stop. It sounds like you're saying goodbye!'

She stood before him. The Co-ordinator was silent.

'I am. I am trapped in this shell, Karn, I've tried my best, but I can't get out. Neither can I die for a very, very long time. But I can't accept a thousand years of insanity. Once I was a young woman, and I tried to evade death, but it is not so easily tricked. I see that now. I should have had a proper death and not grabbed hold of DeGroot's promises, like a drowning woman clutching a piece of wood.'

She turned and looked scornfully down at Thran.

'And in the end, Akeem believed me, not you, when I told him about the horrors of Subterra. Fortunately, the Gaians could see into my memories, so it was not my word against yours. And now they will bring down from the starship their men, their women, their robots, their machines, power you cannot even begin to understand, and they will rescue all the wretches trapped in their dying worlds. And they will eventually find Subterra, and—now they know they won't be welcome—they will be ready for you, prepared for conflict. Yours may not be the last tyranny of the human race, but it will be the last one this sad planet will ever see.'

Thran's face transformed into that of a crazed gargoyle; one overflowing with esurient hatred.

'We will fight to the end with an implacable fury that these pitiful children have never seen. We will trap them in a maze of tunnels. We will launch an army of Eaters upon them. We will overrun them with hordes of warrior-matons, followed by legions of patriots eager to shed their blood in the defence of their homeland. So rot in Hell, Maya!' he shouted.

'I've already been to Hell, Thran, and I did not rot. Hell is Subterra.'

She looked back at Karn and there was a softness in her eyes, one it would have seemed impossible for mechanical constructs to carry.

'So now it's time for me to go. Do you want to see me off?'

Now the tears were rolling down Karn's face.

'Yes, yes! Is there nothing I can say to stop you!'

'No, not now. All I ask is that you do not forget me.'

357

They walked to the airlock; the robots carrying Thran, whom they gently positioned on the floor, facing the rest of them. Maya turned to the Co-ordinator.

'As I told Thran once, one benefit of being powered by an atomic reactor is that I can release all the energy at once in a satisfying conflagration. There's a hill about ten kilometres away, and I'll get behind it. The explosion will only be in the kilotonne range, so EB-1 will be safe.'

Akeem nodded.

'That agrees with my calculation.'

'Good. At my top speed, I can be there in minutes. Best to hold onto something when I go.'

Akeem nodded again but did not speak.

She turned to Karn, one last time.

'Goodbye, my friend.' She smiled again, 'I'll give Yarl your best wishes!'

Maya entered the airlock.

Karn watched carefully which buttons she pressed. He noted the position of the manual controls in the lock chamber itself.

The door closed. The Co-ordinator sat down and looked at the floor.

There was a whirring noise, and a red light flashed.

Thran stared at Karn, triumphantly trying to catch his eye, but Karn made sure that did not happen.

The minutes passed.

Then there was a terrible blue-white flash in the direction of the conical hill they had seen when they arrived. There was no sound in the vacuum above the ground, but the floor bucked and heaved, and transmitted a thunderous growl as frozen gas and soil and rock volatilised, all equally impotent beneath the nuclear blast.

Maya was gone.

'The weird machine-thing is dead,' Thran said, with a leering grin, 'Oh, such a tragedy! Will these eyes never be dry!'

Karn did not speak.

Instead, he crossed rapidly to Thran, scooped him up and carried him to the airlock.

Thran realised what was planned.

'Wait!' he cried, 'you promised not to harm me!'

'Maya promised,' Karn said, 'I never did.'

He pressed a few buttons, and as soon as the inner door opened, Karn tossed the Councillor inside. He had already noted that the manual controls were too high for Thran to reach.

'Wait!' Thran called, 'I...'

The inner door closed, cutting off whatever it was he was trying to say.

There was a whirring noise, and a red light flashed.

Akeem approached Karn, who was leaning against the airlock door, drawing in air in great ragged gasps.

'That was the wrong thing to do,' Akeem said, 'I was already making arrangements for him to stand trial on Gaia.'

'Then I've saved you one more form to complete.'

Karn's legs suddenly gave way, and he slowly slid down the inner airlock door to end up in a huddle. He looked up at Akeem.

'So what now?'

Akeem gave a conciliatory smile.

'I won't pursue charges against you for murder, if that's what you're wondering. These are dangerous times, not what we were expecting at all. We thought it would be just a rescue mission; we did not expect all this passion, this strife.' He helped Karn to his feet but had to hold him, as the smaller man was trembling.

'But I can offer you this: we can put you into stasis while we begin our real mission here. Then when you awake, you will be a citizen of Gaia, and all this will be ancient history. And your nanobots will make you healthier than you have ever been.'

'No,' Karn said, 'I'm going back down. I want to lead the conquest of Subterra, whichever holes its human vermin are trying to hide in. I want to see all those slave-people released from the Harvesting Buildings. My people. My blood.'

Akeem shook his head.

359

'Karn, now we understand the Subterrans will be actively trying to evade us, or even preparing to fight us, we realise it will be a much longer and more difficult mission. And if there can be one hostile group, there can be others. The subterranean world is vast. I know Thran thought we are too soft to be a threat, but he did not read our history. We know very well what this Universe is capable of. As for you, your nanobots will keep you in the best condition you can possibly be in, at every stage of your life, but they can't give you a stronger protein base; they can't stabilise your nucleic acids. Karn, this campaign will be a blink of an eye for us, but it is unlikely you will see the end of it. We will win without you, so why not read about it in the comfort of your new Gaian home, and then forget all about this poor, murdered, cemetery planet?'

'No,' he said, 'I have unfinished business. Maya almost brought them to their knees, but she could not complete the job. But I will do that in her memory.'

Akeem nodded.

'She obviously meant a lot to you. It is good to have a friend.'

Karn looked directly at Akeem, and the latter, for all his knowledge and ability, all his awesome responsibilities, felt himself quail slightly under the power of that fervent gaze.

'No, it was more than that. I loved her.'

Other books by Martyn Rhys Vaughan published by Cambria:

Quantum Exile: ISBN 978-1-9161619-6-2
The Cave Of Shadows: ISBN 978-1-9161619-9-3
Hideous Night: ISBN 978-1-8380752-2-4
Doom of Stars: ISBN 978-1-8382805-6-7
Devouring Darkness: ISBN 978-1-8384289-5-2

Follow *Martyn Vaughan's Science Fiction Work* on Facebook.

I'm also on Instagram, Pinterest and Goodreads.

www.ingramcontent.com/pod-product-compliance
Lightning Source LLC
Chambersburg PA
CBHW050029030726
47506CB00001B/192